ACID

CONNECTIoNS

PART 3

A Novel By:

Deanne
T.
Smith

This is a work of **FICTION**. Names, characters, businesses, places, events and incidents are either the products of the author's imagination or used in a fictitious manner. Any resemblance to actual persons, living or dead, or actual events is purely coincidental.

Deanne T. Smith
FB, IG, Twitter- Deanne T Smith
deannetsmith@gmail.com

Cover Designed By: Devon Guillery
Editors: Val Pugh-Love & Charlee Redman

Dedication

Acid Connections 3 is dedicated to my sons,
Dylan and Ehsan.
You are my heart, soul and universe.
You've made me the amazing woman
that I've grown to be. Thank you for always being
my motivation. I love you boys with all my heart
and am blessed to be your mom!

Acknowledgements

I want to thank GOD above all for making this dream become my reality. GOD is so super awesome!

To my **FRIENDS** and **FAMILY**. I APPRECIATE you. Thank you for always being in my corner. I THANKED everyone in books one and two, so this time I'm going to keep it super simple.

Nana, I always tell you, you are the realest on my team! You're cut from a special kind of cloth! I love you. You're the tiniest woman but always going to be my BIG DOE.

Mommy, thanks for being my right hand. You're always the voice of reason. When the world seems to be crashing, I can always count on you to lift it up and make it alright. Love you!

Sisters, I love you ladies. You are all different in your unique personalities, but I love you ALL the same! Yawl hold a special place in my heart that you'll never understand.

Sister friends, you ladies are my MVPs! I love you and appreciate you for always loving me for ME! Yawl might be the only ones who do! (insider)

Chanae, we've built a special kind of friendship. I love you so much. All I can tell you is NO one can replace you and you ARE stuck with me forever.

Uncle Chris, I love you more than words. You truly are my favorite guy in the world!

Dummy Brain, I love you! Thank you for believing in me from day one, supporting me, and never letting me down!

To my **READERS, ACID CONNECTIONS 3 IS FOR YOU**!!! You patiently waited, and I believe I more than delivered! I would like to express my sincere gratitude to those of you who have stayed on this ride with me with ACID CONNECTIONS. Thank you for your continuous support, and for believing in me. Yawl breathe life into me, and you are why I keep going. If it wasn't for your continuous support, my writing would just be a hobby so I can't thank you enough! I hope you enjoy and are ready for what's in store!

CHAPTER 1

The intensive care unit doctor watched everyone's faces quickly become sobs, cries, and screams. He'd made a terrible mistake.

"Geesh by golly me... I'm so sorry," the naturally red, pie-faced doctor with blond, balding hair said. "I made an ever-blasted mistake," Dr. Ganuby stated. "I've been here for thirty-eight hours. I was on my way out when all the shooting victims came in. I stayed to help. So please forgive me for getting my names crossed. Miss Del Gada isn't deceased. She has some ways to go, but we were able to stabilize her. Her hipbone was shattered from one bullet. The second bullet grazed her arm, and fortunately for her the third bullet went straight through her side and out her back. It just missed her spine by an inch. The bullet in her hip has been removed, and she is actually heading up to surgery as we speak. She's one lucky lady, though. I'll tell you that."

Everyone breathed a long sigh of relief and wiped their tears. A few seconds prior, they believed Tavares had passed away. Dolonda wanted to punch the doctor in the face, but instead gave him a look of death while yelling, "If you can't get patients' names correct, it's time for you GO! I thought my daughter was dead."

"I do apologize," the sincere doctor said.

"It was an honest mistake. We're just glad she's still here," Holton cut Dolonda off just as she was about to go off even more.

Then, he silently thanked God for sparing Tavares's life. He wasn't ready to say goodbye to his newly discovered daughter just yet. They had too many years to make up for. Tavares's friends hugged one another, knowing that burying their best friend would have changed them forever. Abdora was emotionless because he didn't know what he would do if he had indeed lost Tavares and become a single father. Hearing that the love of his life was alive softened his almost frozen heart.

The doctor's tone of voice changed as he began to speak again.

"The young man, Damien Stasher, is indeed in a medically-induced coma."

Doll screamed and hollered, "Oh, my God! No, doctor, no! Doctor, please! Not my baby. Please tell me that he's gonna make it."

"Ma'am, at this point, we really don't know. It's hard for us to determine if the coma is temporary or permanent. He could wake up tomorrow, next month, or next year. The caliber of the gun, the impact, and the angle of the entry and exit wound makes his recovery a fifty-fifty chance. The bullet caused hemorrhaging on the brain. We are trying our best to keep the bleeding from coming back and the swelling in the brain from recurring. My team is doing their best, but right now it's really out of our hands and in the hands of the man people call God."

Damien's mother began to sob. She couldn't breathe and began to gasp for air. Holton grabbed Doll, as she looked like her legs were about to give out. Her oxygen level drastically plummeted, and her heart rate declined at the same time.

"Code blue! Code blue!" the doctor yelled.

A team of nurses came running and rushed Doll to a room in the back of the emergency room. They put an oxygen mask on her and gave her a sedative via IV. The lobby of New England Medical Center was at maximum capacity. You would have thought government cheese or Section 8 vouchers were being dispersed the way people were holding up the white walls of the hallway, lying in the uncomfortable rock hard brown chairs, and standing any place there was room. Some were waiting to go see their loved ones, while others were waiting to see if their loved ones were going to survive, or worst-case scenario, if they'd be planning funeral arrangements.

Holton's stomach started growling like a bear. Dolonda slowly turned her head when she heard the rumbling in her first love's belly.

"You better take care of that. I know we haven't eaten, but you sound like you haven't eaten in a month of damn Sundays."

"I know. I'm starving. The last time I ate was when I had dinner with Tavares early yesterday evening."

Dolonda hadn't eaten since the previous night either, but food was the last thing on her mind since they entered the hospital.

"I'm not hungry, but I do need to put something in my stomach," Dolonda said, rubbing her empty mid-section.

"You got it," Holton said before leaning in and kissing his daughter's mother on the forehead. "I have to go make some phone calls. I'll order food while I'm out there."

While Holton was gone, Dolonda used the time to get to know her daughter's friends. They spoke very highly of Tavares. They informed Dolonda of her daughter's accomplishments and didn't leave out the kind of loving, loyal, go-getter that her daughter had flourished into during her absence.

"I'm glad my daughter has good friends like y'all in her life."

"Well, some of us," mumbled Randee.

Leslie gave her a look and said, *"Don't start."*

"What does that mean?" questioned Dolonda with a puzzled look.

"There are two more of us. Mona-Lisa was shot, too... Well, grazed. She's getting doctored up, but there's a missing amigo. She and Tavares are on the outs because of some bullshit she did with Damien," Randee said.

"And, just what did she do?" Dolonda asked, highly curious.

Leslie was giving her friend the eye to close her big mouth, but Randee paid her no attention.

"She was messing with Damien."

"What?" Dolonda said, shocked. "And she was Tavares's friend?"

"Yep, and they haven't spoken since before Tavares had the boys."

"Well, ain't that a slimy bitch," Tavares's mom said. She was hurt for her daughter that a friend could betray her in such a way.

"Well, that hussy better not show up here acting all concerned, I know that," Dolonda said with her Dominican accent jumping out, while snapping her neck and rolling her eyes.

"Oh, you can believe if she does show up, she'll ask about Tavares. But, nine times out of ten, she'll really be here checking for Damien," Randee confessed sadly.

"Excuse me?" Dolonda said, in shock. "That trifling bitch better not dare. She will learn today that Tavares don't get her gangster from her Papi but from her Goddamn mama!"

"Hmmm, I know that's right," Leslie said, knowing that her best friend's mama meant what she'd said. Leslie hoped and prayed her friend didn't come to the hospital and make Tavares's mother get out of character.

***

Big-T was knocked out but heard his partner in crime's special ringtone.

"What's up, Montiago?" Big-T asked in his natural deep voice that was groggy from just opening his eyes.

"I need you to get up. We got big business. I need a meeting with the twelve apostles. Actually, make that eleven of the apostles because one is lying in a coma. Last night, there was a shooting. Damien and my daughter got shot."

"What the fuck!?" Big-T screamed. "Why are you just now calling me?" he questioned, popping up out of the bed.

"It's been a long, hectic night and morning. But, I need to get with them. So, do what you do. Set up a meeting at our Month of March spot, and tell them to come in character as to not draw any attention."

Every month Holton met with his local heavy hitters in the game some place different. He picked the Month of March spot for the emergency meeting so he could be close to the hospital.

"The police will be on me once they connect the dots that one of the shooting victims is my daughter. They'll be expecting me to make moves and retaliate, so we want to cover all bases."

"I'm on it, Montiago," Big-T said, calling Holton by his last name as he'd been doing since they were kids.

Big-T was Holton's childhood best friend, second in command of Holton's multi-million-dollar drug operation, and head of operations for Holton's construction company. He was one of the few people Holton trusted with his life.

"How's your daughter?"

"She's gonna make it, but the doctor said a bullet just missed her spine."

"Damn, God bless her."

"That's the same thing I said. But listen, make that happen ASAP, and I'll see you there at four sharp."

Holton ended his call and rang his mother.

"Hey me baby," his mother answered.

"Mommy, I need you to come to the hospital and sit with your granddaughter. Me and her mother need to run out for a while. There's a whole bunch of people here for her, but it would ease my heart a little more if you would come sit while we're gone."

"Say no more. I get dressed, and I be on my way," Holton's mother said in her sweet, thick Trinidadian accent.

"Thanks, mommy. I love you."

"I love you more."

Holton heard his stomach talking again.

"We're at New England Medical Center in the lobby. But, by the time you get here, Tavares should be out of surgery and in her room. Would you like me to send Big-T to come get you?"

"Fah what? Me not cripple. I can drive me damn car."

Holton laughed because his mother hated to be offered help with anything.

"See you in a bit."

Holton ended the conversation and placed his last call.

"Maine's Wings and Things, can I take your order?" the owner answered.

"Yeah, you old fool, let me get one of everything on the menu."

"The only old fool on this phone is you. What's up, my G?"

"I need a large order."

"Holton, you would call on a Sunday when the Patriots are playing. You know I got a million orders. But, what you need?"

"I need five hundred wings. Give me a variety of the Roxbury Raised Ranch, South End Sweet Chili, Dorchester Death, Mattapan Honey Mustard, Blue Hill BBQ, Dudley Dry Rub, Codman Square Curry, and the Basic Bitty Plain. I also need twenty pizzas. Do all twenty the crazy crack five cheese. Fifty large orders of French fries and onion rings. And, because you're old, don't forget the plates, forks, and napkins."

"Goddamnnnnnn," Maine said, writing everything down. "Who in the fuck are you feeding, dawg?"

"I'm at the hospital and feeding everyone in the lobby," laughed Holton because he knew he forced it.

"Dawg, you gonna have to let me finish what we have and get my whole staff on this."

"Will do, and I'll send you a hefty tip for you to trick at the strip club," Holton laughed, referencing the fact that his friend frequented strip clubs often.

"Man, fuck you. I don't trick. I like watching the art of a woman working a pole," laughed Maine, because he knew he was full of shit. "What the fuck you doing at the hospital? You getting your shot for the chlamydia again?" Joked Maine.

"Nigga, I ain't never had none of them diseases you get from your strippers," Holton fired back. "My daughter is here."

"DAUGHTER!" screamed Maine. "I know that old ass dick ain't still making babies. You gotta be shooting blanks by now."

"Bullshit, just ask your sister. She knows I ain't shooting no blanks," chuckled Holton.

He and Maine always joked about each other's sisters because coming up they were off-limits to each other.

"Nah seriously, I found out a few months back I have a twenty-two-year-old daughter."

"Get the fuck outta here."

"No bullshit. It blew my mind. Her mother was the love of my life, but as life had it, I married Lilly. It's a long story, but we'll chop it up."

"That's some wild shit, but I hope she's going to be okay."

"She is, but pray for her anyways. And, what's my damage for the food?"

"Just send me what you want. You know how we do."

"Good looking, Maine. And, I'll be through there to catch up as soon as everything settles."

"No doubt, just give me like two hours on the food."

"Goddamn, my ribs are touching my back."

"Shut up and go get a muffin or something, you cupcake ass nigga," laughed Maine.

***

Carmen was trying to distract herself by doing some work. Being a boss bitch, the one thing she hated more than anything in the world was being ignored, and that was exactly how she felt at the moment. She'd called and texted Holton too many times for her liking to not get any response. So, instead of snapping, she was comfortably tucked away in her home office trying to focus.

Looking at the pictures in front of her, she asked out loud, "Who do I hate more?" Carmen couldn't decide if her hate ran deeper for Abdora Santacosa or Tavares Del Gada.

"I hate both of you, and I'm going to enjoy every moment of taking you down when the day comes. I don't care if you end up doing time or six feet under, but know that I'm coming for y'all," she said to the pictures as if they could actually hear her.

She had unsuccessfully tried to trick Tavares into thinking she had evidence that implicated Abdora for the murder of a young lady said to be last seen at his club. She went so far as to tell her she was seen there, but Tavares didn't bat an eye. Carmen had hoped Tavares would give her what she needed to make a case, but to her surprise, she didn't break under pressure like most women did. So, she was screwed because in reality she didn't have an ounce of proof. There were a million things that Abdora could be charged with, but due to his precision, diligence, and intelligence, there was never enough proof to take Abdora Santacosa down. This time was no different.

However, if it was the last thing Carmen did, she was going to successfully take the Street Kingpin down. Granted, he allegedly killed, kidnapped, extorted, conspired, bribed, paid local and state agencies, sold drugs, and ran a criminal enterprise, but really Carmen didn't give a damn about any of that. Hell, she made her biggest income as a player in the criminal underworld. Still, Abdora's illegal activities gave her the means she needed to make him crumble for her own personal reasons.

Holton's soon-to-be ex-girlfriend had been calling him since the day prior. At first, she was just calling and texting, but with him not answering or responding, she started blowing him up. When that failed, she began flooding him with text messages. Holton looked at her thirteen missed calls and eight text messages of worry about him and debated if he should call Carmen back or not. He wanted to call her to ease her mind, but with all that he currently had on his plate, he didn't know if it was a good time.

Holton knew that sooner than later he was gonna have to inform his mistress of the last decade that it was over. They'd had a good run, great times, and lots of memories. However, in his heart, he wanted to be with Dolonda, spend his life with her, and make up for all the missed time. Although he'd led Carmen and himself to believe that one day he would leave his wife and be with her, he never factored in or imagined the possibility that his true love would end up back in his life. He had a lot of love for Carmen, but nothing could compare to the love he had for Dolonda. Hurting Carmen was the last thing he wanted to do, seeing that she had been his ride or die, partner in crime, friend, and insatiable lover for so long, but he wanted to do right by Dolonda. He knew that when he did call Carmen he would have to close the chapter of their dealings, so he was hesitating with good reason.

Not only had he been having relations with Carmen for well over ten years, she was also a big part of his business. Holton didn't want to believe that ending things with Carmen romantically would affect their business relationship, but he knew better. Women were emotional creatures by nature, so the moment Carmen's heart was broken he knew it would affect her ability to continue getting money with him. She played such a crucial role in his drug organization, and he didn't know how it could operate without her onboard. Carmen imported all his cocaine straight from the Dominican Republic. She had lawyers, judges, police, border patrol, and city and state officials on the payroll, which made his organization run without any problems. Holton didn't know how he was gonna work this out, but until he did, he decided that it was best to not call Carmen back. Instead he sent a text: "Hey babe. Sorry I haven't been able to call you, but I had a serious family emergency. Things are real hectic right now, but I'll call you when things are settled."

Carmen was in a deep trance staring at the seemingly happy couple she despised when her phone chimed. Recognizing the special alert, she quickly dropped the pictures and snatched her phone off the far right side of her cherry oak desk. Reading the message, she blushed and felt relieved to finally hear from Holton. She'd been worried sick about him. It was unlike him to not respond to her messages and not return her calls or reach out to her for more than twenty-four hours. She replied with a simple, "Okay. I love you."

Although Holton was married, Carmen never felt like she was in a relationship with a married man. It was like she had a normal relationship, except her boyfriend shared his house with a wife he tolerated, took care of, and couldn't leave. Holton was there on her birthdays and holidays, and they were always taking trips. He called her daily, sent flowers, and showered her with attention. Furthermore, he never made her feel insecure about his wife.

Yes, Carmen was worried about Holton's well-being when he wasn't answering his phone or responding to her texts. She was also a little worried that he was occupied playing husband to his wife. It just wasn't like Holton to not speak to her or return her calls. For the first time, she'd been feeling insecure. She didn't know if it was because this was the first time he'd ignored her, though the reality was that her man had a wife and she only knew what he told her, or the fact that Holton had seemed a bit detached and distant the last month or so. But, after reading his text, she told herself that she was just overreacting and needed to see her man.

With all his calls wrapped up, Holton exited the icy Boston air of twenty-three degrees and hurried back into the warm lobby that was filled with even more people than before he'd left. Holton noticed that Damien's family had arrived. He made his way over to Doll's mother, Dancy, and gave her a tight hug. They expressed condolences to each other.

"Holton, I don't know what I'll do if my grandson doesn't make it. My Doll will never be the same if she loses her son."

"I know. So we can't think like that, Miss Dancy. We gotta be strong, pray, and give it to God."

"You got that right, because my God is a good God. I know he'll see my grandson through this."

Their conversation was interrupted by a ruckus from the crowd as the police entered the lobby. Most of the people there disliked the police and didn't care to associate with them. The officers were making their rounds asking questions, but unfortunately everyone there was sticking to their street code—they didn't see who was shooting.

"Listen up!" the large polar bear-sized, pale faced, plain-clothes detective yelled. He was frustrated that he and his men weren't getting anywhere. "We want to catch the people who did this, but we can't do that if no one is willing to talk. I find it hard to believe that out of the seventy-five to one hundred people in this room, not one person saw anything. This no-snitching thing isn't going to get anyone justice. Moreover, we do not want people going out committing acts of retribution, so please help us help you."

Not a single person in the room responded with words. Some sucked their teeth while others rolled their eyes, and some never even looked up.

"Okay, have it your way," Detective Burke said and snapped his fingers, signaling to his men that they were leaving.

One of the three black detectives locked eyes with Holton. He was fixated on Holton and Holton was giving him the ice grill right back. The two had been good friends in their teens, but when Andre Brown decided that he was going to be a police officer and play for the other side, their friendship ended. Holton had no love for the cops except to keep them on his payroll. Andre thought he was gonna save the world and despised people who didn't make an honest living. So, he and Holton hated each other for over two decades. Andre made a mental note to inquire who Holton was at the hospital to see. Holton knew that with that bitch ass Uncle Tom-wannabe Andre seeing him, he would for sure have to move in silence. Still, he wasn't worried because they both knew that he had Andre's superiors on his payroll.

While the hospital was filled with grieving people, Lilly was two miles north about to do what she knew how to do best when grieving—get high. She was devastated enough that Holton was Tavares's father, but how he treated her in front of everyone—especially Dolonda—sent her straight to

Orchard Park Projects, to the crack house on Hamden Street.

Lilly hated to get high in crack houses, but she didn't know where else to go at the crack of dawn to get a hit fast. She hated crack houses because they were a mirror without looking at glass. She dressed better than the people she sat amongst, lived better than the people she smoked with, and didn't have any worries after she walked out of the door. However, the crack house was a sad reminder that she was a crack addict just like them, no matter how much she hated to admit it. With heartbreak and devastation consuming her, her pride was out and she was going to sit with the people she detested to get high with.

Upon entering the duplex-level townhome, she saw an ugly, unfamiliar crater-faced, husky man parked in the living room. He was serving everyone as Lilly approached him.

"I have a thousand dollars. Please don't try to short me because I have my own scale."

He looked Lilly up and down, trying to figure out what the well-dressed, diamond-blinged woman before him was doing in the trap house before the sun was up.

"You ain't no cop, right?"

"No. I'm here to get high just like everyone else. So, do you have enough to sell me, or should I take my money elsewhere?"

"Listen, lady, I gotta ask because I don't know you," the twin of a gorilla stated. "And, if you look around, ain't no one in here spending what you asking for."

"Well, I'm here with the same monkey on my back. So, can you help me or not?"

"Stay right there."

Bubba got up his three-hundred-pound self and slowly climbed the stairs to find the owner of the house. She was probably some place sucking a dick for a hit or threating to throw people out if they didn't share with her. When he got to the second floor and opened one of the bedroom doors, sure enough Stacey was doing what he imagined.

"Listen, you old funky motherfucker! This is my house, and if you think you just gonna sit in here and get high all fucking morning and not give me shit, you got me fucked up. So, either give me a tiny piece or get the fuck out!" Stacey said in her already too high, burly-man voice to the elderly toothless man who just wanted to get high without Stacey begging for once.

"Yo, Stacey, let me holler at you," Bubba said.

"Here I come, Bubbs," Stacey said, getting off the air mattress in slow motion.

Before making it into the hallway, she lowered her shirt like Bubba was interested in her saggy titties. He'd fucked her a few times on a drunk night or two, but sober, he wouldn't touch her with a ten-foot pole.

"Hey, what's up, Bubbs? You gonna let me suck your dick for a twenty rock?"

"Nah, you done sucked enough dick for crack tonight. You ain't touching my shit. I might fuck around and catch gonorrhea just from all the dick and cum you done swallowed with your nasty ass."

"Come on, Bubbs. I'll suck it good and lick your ass."

"You're one nasty ass bitch, Stacey. You ain't getting shit from me without no money. I came up here to ask you what's up with the Spanish lady. She dressed kinda fancy, blinged out, and asking for a grand worth of shit."

"Oh yeah?" Stacey said, her eyes getting big knowing exactly who it was. "That's Lilly. She's cool. Comes through every blue moon, always spends big money when she comes. And, if she runs out of money, she's good for whatever she cops. She gets up when she's done spending. She'll get your money, pay, and be out until her next visit. I don't know where she comes from or why she got so much money, but she always spends big."

"That's what I'm talking about," Bubba said, breathing extra heavy between each word. "Go clean yourself up, take a shower, and wash your funky pussy that I can smell just standing here."

Bubba made his way to his stash to get Lilly's drugs and then made his way back downstairs. Lilly was patiently waiting for him to come back, but silently wishing he would hurry up. He passed her the drugs, and she put ten crisp hundred dollar bills in his hand. Then, she turned her back and went to find a place to get high in peace. Most of the people were passed out. Those that were awake were sharing the little bit of drugs they had. Lilly wasn't trying to share her shit, so she went to the tiny half-sized bathroom. She looked around at the filth. It looked like it hadn't been cleaned in months and smelt like nothing but lingering crack.

"It will do," she said while locking the door.

She pulled out her glass pipe, lighter, and crack rocks. She placed them on the bathroom sink, took her pecan-colored cashmere coat off, and was ready to beam it up to Scotty. Before she could begin to get high, she was interrupted by a light tap on the door. "Someone is in here!" she snapped.

"Lilly, it's me, Stacey. Let me in."

"No."

"What do you mean no? It's my fucking house! Let me in."

Lilly cracked the door and passed two nice-sized fifty rocks to Stacey.

"Here, I've paid you. Now, leave me alone."

Lilly didn't wait for a response. She shut the door, locked it, and got ready to smoke 'til she couldn't smoke anymore. With each long hit that she inhaled, she felt further and further away from reality. When she felt herself coming down and reality trying to creep into her mind, she loaded another rock. Lilly wasn't ready to accept that Holton knew she got high and that he was finally leaving her. And, he wasn't just leaving her—he was going to be with Dolonda. Every time the thoughts ran through her mind, she rushed to load her crack pipe.

Hours passed, and she was still locked in the closet-sized bathroom. She'd gotten high, passed out, woke up, and went back to getting high. Between her bouts of getting high, she kept checking her cell phone and wasn't surprised that Holton hadn't called. However, it just depressed her more and more. If Lilly had it her way, she would be in the crack house for the next few days until she was ready to face the sad reality that her marriage was over, and she would have to find a way to support herself and her outrageous habit.

***

Jazz was sitting in a small, old-smelling, outdated room at the Ramada Motel in Room 126. She'd listened to all the feet passing her door over the last twenty-four hours. Yet, no one stopped and knocked. Her eyes kept gazing at the stone-age clock radio on the poorly crafted cheap wood nightstand. Time had long passed since she was due for company. Periodically, she picked her phone up. She hadn't received the call she'd been waiting for all morning. In fact, no one had called her except for Nadine, the neighborhood news reporter. Jazz hadn't answered because she was in a funk and not in the mood for her gossiping neighbor. She was feeling like a real idiot because she'd paid for a hotel room only to end up being in it all alone.

For the second day in a row, Damien had stood her up. He was supposed to come the night before and called two hours after she checked into say he couldn't make it. He'd forgotten that he had plans that he couldn't cancel. He promised to come early the next morning, no later than 8:30 a.m., for them to go to breakfast and talk. However, it was noon and one hour until check-out. He hadn't even called, and she couldn't believe he'd played her.

She thought that she'd finally gotten him to come around after the awful blow out argument they had. Last time they spoke, Jazz asked him where they stood and where they were going because she loved him and was pregnant with his child. He flatly responded, "I wasn't fucking you to wife you, to fall in love, and damn sure not to have my baby. Get rid of it ASAP. You knew what it was from day one, so don't try to switch shit up in the ninth inning." After crying and telling him he wasn't shit but a no-good, selfish motherfucker who didn't care about anyone but himself, she slammed the phone down. Jazz was brokenhearted because she truly thought he was gonna wife her, but instead, he cut her off after her meltdown.

Dame hadn't taken her calls or responded to her texts in over two weeks. Earlier in the week she texted him, saying she needed to talk to him about something important. To Jazz's surprise Dame responded: "Okay." He really didn't care what she wanted to talk about. He just wanted her to suck his dick the way that only she could. She texted him back "The Ramada Saturday night" and prepared for her talk. She hoped he had a change of heart on their status after their talk. Only, he'd cancelled and still hadn't shown up like he promised he would. Jazz wanted to cry. Instead, she got up to get dressed so she could check out of the room she'd wasted her money on. She was stepping in the shower when her phone started ringing. She ran to it with a glimmer of hope that it was Dame calling. She damn near tripped over her feet only to be disappointed. It was Nadine calling again.

"I'll call her back after I get out the shower," she said to herself with teary eyes.

***

Meanwhile, Holton's mother, Vadaleen, was dressed to kill in indigo blue jeans, tall chocolate brown riding boots, a plain white long-sleeved shirt, and her brown authentic fur vest. She entered her living room and found her husband sitting in his favorite beat-up recliner chair that he refused to get rid of. He saw his wife looking like a million bucks as always without a sparkling natural silver hair out of place.

"Where you going, Black Girl?" That was his nickname for his wife of over forty years.

"To the hospital, White Boy."

"For what? What's wrong?"

"Nothing is wrong."

"Well then, who in the damn hell is in the hospital?" asked the love of Vadaleen's life.

Your granddaughter."

"Who—Kayla or Abby?"

"Neither."

"Woman, what in the sand hell are you talking about? We only have two granddaughters."

"Well..." Vadaleen said and paused. "Holton found out he has a grown daughter. She's been shot, and he asked me to come to the hospital."

Harvey Sr. sat up and quickly gave his full attention to his wife.

"Holton has a grown daughter? What? When did he find out about her? Why didn't he call and tell us about this?"

"My love, I can't answer any of those questions. But, upon my return, I hope to have all those answers."

"Do you want me to come with you? Let me get some slacks and a shirt."

"No. You watch your football. If I need you, I'll call you."

"Wow, we have a grown granddaughter," Harvey said in a state of shock.

His grandchildren were his heart, so he couldn't fathom that he had one that he'd missed out on knowing.

"Are you sure you don't want me to drive you?"

"You sound like your damn son. I don't need anyone to drive me anywhere. I don't have that fancy car outside for no reason," Vadaleen said, referring to her S550 Benz that was a gift from her children for her sixty-fifth birthday.

"Well, Black Girl, please call me and keep me informed."

"Will do," Vadaleen said before she kissed her husband and made her way to Boston.

***

Jazz checked out of the motel and climbed into her Jeep Cherokee. She was still in the parking lot when Nadine called once again. *She must have some real serious juicy gossip*, Jazz thought to herself, picking her phone up off the seat.

"What up, Nadine?"

"Bitchhhh... Why haven't you been answering your phone? I been blowing you up," said the around-the-way gossiper with her voice racing.

"I was kind of tied up. Damn, what's up? You must got some spicy shit to drop on me the way you been calling my ass."

"Where've you been that you don't know what went down?" Nadine asked, confused by Jazz's composure. "Yo, you must haven't heard because you sound real damn calm if you did. Shit went down last night at the Roxy. And, I do mean downnnn. It was a shoot-out, and mad people got shot. Most had non-life-threatening injuries, but some are in critical condition. So far, two people have died."

"Get the fuck outta here," Jazz said in utter shock at the information.

She was clueless from being locked up in that room hoping Damien would come. Jazz hadn't spoken to anyone or even been on social media since she checked in to the hotel.

"Bishhh, your peoples got shot up, too!" Nadine yelled. "That's why the fuck I been blowing you up. I wanted to make sure you was good."

"Nadine, slow down. What the fuck are you talking about?"

"Yo, your girl Tavares got shot. The shootings have been all over the news, and it's all over World Playground."

"Get the fuck outta here! Oh, my God, that's crazy. I hope she's gonna be okay," Jazz said half-sincerely.

She loved her friend, but she was mad that Tavares wasn't messing with her for fucking with her ex. She didn't even want him, and Jazz actually loved him.

"Honey, that's not the half. It was her and her Boo, Damien."

Nadine couldn't resist throwing a low blow at Jazz. Everyone was aware Jazz was shamelessly fucking her old best friend's ex. However, Nadine the News Reporter knew firsthand from seeing Dame picking up and dropping Jazz off all the time. Nadine wasn't a saint, but she thought Jazz was real grimy for how she did her Tavares.

Jazz wasn't ready for what she'd just heard. The phone fell from her ear, bounced on the passenger seat off her lavender overnight bag, and hit the floor. She swerved from shock and realized she'd heard right. Tavares and Damien had been shot at the club the night before. She could hear Nadine still talking, but she couldn't reach for the phone. Her heart had dropped, and she was shaking.

She finally managed to scream, "Hold on! Shut up and hold on, Nadine."

Jazz pulled her truck over on Freeport Street, threw it in park, and retrieved the phone.

"Nadine, you've got to be fucking kidding me. I was waiting on Dame, and he never showed. I thought he was on some bullshit, and now you're telling me he got shot. OMG, this isn't happening to him again. I just hope he isn't one of the people that got hurt bad. Do you know where he got shot or how bad it is?"

Nadine instantly picked up that Jazz had more concern for the nigga she was jumping off with than for her best friend of many years. She was repulsed and didn't hesitate to tell Jazz about herself.

"Jazz, you're a fucking piece of work. A real live piece of fucking work!" Nadine said with utter disgust in her voice. "That girl was your best friend, your ace boon coon, and partner in crime since we were kids, and you didn't ask one Goddamn question about her. Gonna give me that ole fake ass concern, but the moment you hear Damien got shot too, you damn near have a heart attack. I get it—her old nigga is now your new nigga by default. But damn... Don't be such a bottom feeder ass bitch that you're more worried about dick than someone who was once your friend."

Jazz knew that she'd done exactly what Nadine had called her out on, but she wasn't going to admit it. Instead, she got defensive.

"What the fuck you want me to say? I said, 'I hope she's going to be okay.' Her being my friend is the past. So no, I'm not as worried about her as I am my man."

"Your who?" screeched Nadine at the bullshit that Jazz had just let come out of her mouth. She wanted to bellow over in laughter and let Jazz know how stupid she sounded, but she suppressed her laughter. Yes, Jazz was fucking Damien, but he sure hadn't wifed her. If he had, she would have known by now, because there wasn't much that went down in Roxbury that she didn't know about.

"Honey, that nigga is the pipe layer who's laying pipe to a few of you bitches. So, don't claim him until he puts the pipe away and claims you. And, it's sad you give a fuck more about a dog ass nigga than a solid bitch."

"You know what, Nadine... fuck you. I don't have time for this. I need to find out where my MAN is," Jazz said, hanging up on Nadine's truth-telling face.

***

As time passed, the hospital had become even more packed—if that was at all possible. There wasn't a place to stand, sit, or hold up a wall. It was beyond max capacity. Nana Dancy and her family were sitting congregated around Doll. They'd been comforting her since her return. A young lady who looked like she'd been crying based on her red puffy eyes interrupted them.

"Hi. I'm Talesha, Damien's girlfriend. We were together when he got shot."

There was silence as everyone looked at this delusional lady that they'd never met.

"Is that right?" Nana Dancy asked with pure sarcasm.

"Yes, ma'am."

"Girl, what makes you think Damien is your boyfriend?" Damien's grandmother asked, cutting her deep with her lack of kindness.

The young lady was embarrassed by the response from the woman whom Damien always spoke so highly of.

"Ma'am, Damien is my boyfriend. He and I have been together since he and Tavares broke up."

"Humph, I'm sure y'all have. But, honey, just because you give a man your cookies a few nights a week, doesn't make him your boyfriend."

"Nana!" Hershey shouted, trying to stop her grandmother from making the girl feel any worse.

"Don't Nana me. Listen, honey. I know my grandson. You may have been sleeping with him, going out with him, and spending time with him, but he isn't your boyfriend. If he were, we would know you. Now, go on and find a place and take a seat like everyone else."

The now distraught woman didn't know what else to say. She simply dropped her head in shame and turned to walk away with tears running down her face.

"Nana, did you have to be so cruel?" Hershey questioned her grandmother with a look of disbelief on her face.

"Girl, please. We're here as a family waiting on the fate of my grandson. I don't want to hear no bullshit about someone being his Goddamn girlfriend. The only real girlfriend he's ever had is lying in a hospital bed, too. That damn girl can tell her story to someone who gives a damn. I'm sure another three or four women somewhere in here think the same foolish shit. Do you see them making fools of themselves coming over here trying to be a part of our family unit?"

"Ma, but you didn't have to be so mean," Doll interjected.

"Oh well," Nana Dancy said with the least bit of regret.

CHAPTER 2

Bella had been calling her fiancé, Mason, and her homegirl Tavares since 10:00 a.m. She was fuming mad that neither of them were answering their phones.

"Where the fuck are they!?" she cursed, throwing her phone to the foot of the bed.

Between calling and texting Tavares and Mason, she cussed them out while watching the commercials of *Law and Order* reruns. Beyond her boiling point, Bella decided to peel herself from underneath the goose down comforter. She rolled out of her circular bed that she'd been lying in all morning. After taking a long, steaming hot shower, she was still as infuriated as when she got in the shower. Standing under the heating lamp, she dried off her tall, slender frame, tossed on some black and white boy shorts and a white wife-beater, and decided to go cook some cheese eggs, grits, and fried haddock. While she cooked breakfast, she was as hot as the grease she was frying her fish in. She cussed her fiancé and friend out some more.

"I can't believe neither one of these motherfuckers ain't answering their phones. I don't know who I'm gonna stab first," she said out of rage. "Bella, woosah," she said as began taking deep breaths.

That was supposed to be a technique to help her not go from zero to a hundred. As she was inhaling and exhaling deeply, her phone rang. She snatched it off the black granite countertop quicker than a flash of lightning. Mad that it wasn't one of the two people she was looking for, she answered with a snappy "Hello!"

The twenty-four-seven bubbly voice on the other end said, "Hey! Happy Sunday."

Then, the third person on the phone chimed in, "We called to see if you could stop sucking

Maniac's dick long enough to come out for Sunday Funday."

"Listen here. Mason better hope he has a dick attached to his body when I catch him, and ain't nothing happy about this Sunday," Bella responded to her two best friends, Cali Cakes and Rocky.

Cakes's first name was Cali, but everyone said them together as one name. She was Bella's first cousin. Since they came out of the womb, being only three months apart, they'd been best friends their whole lives. Physically, they were polar opposites, but they were twins in every other way. Cakes was a sweet chocolate cutie. She was average height, thick in all the right places, and had a personality that shined bright like a diamond. Bella was an amazon savage with a pancake rump and DD breasts. Besides differences in their physical features, they were alike in every way from their attitudes, their style, their dislikes, and their hobbies to their loyalty. When you messed with one, people automatically knew it smoke with both of them.

Rocky was their childhood friend from their block on Seventh Street. Her name was more than fitting for her. She'd been whooping ass since the sand box. Her real name was Rocky Ali Brown, and she was the daughter of a semi-professional boxer who named her after his two favorite boxers—Rocky and Ali. Being the only girl of four children, her father and brothers had been teaching her boxing moves since before she could walk. Rocky was a beast with her fists. Standing at only five-foot-five, she'd beat up the biggest of bitches and a few boys in her days.

Rocky and Bella had been childhood enemies since elementary school. They were both too tough for their own good, so they were always bumping heads. Cakes never had beef with Rocky. She always said they didn't get along because they both had such strong personalities. Bella was walking home from school their seventh-grade year and saw some girls jumping Rocky. She jumped in, and together they put a hurting on the five girls trying to jump Rocky. From that day, they'd been friends. They always got into arguments that ended with "Fuck you. No, fuck *you*." Cali Cakes just laughed and called them both stupid. No sooner than the arguments ended, their bi-polar asses were speaking like nothing ever happened.

Cali Cakes, Bella, and Rocky were three the hard way. When Tavares came along, at first, Rocky and Cali didn't want to meet Bella's "new" friend that she spoke so highly of. They never let outsiders in their circle, and she wasn't an exception—no matter how highly Bella spoke of her. However, they gave in and had lunch with Tavares and instantly opened up to her. She was very fitting to their circle. Rocky was throwing Tavares mad shade on their lunch date. Tavares was letting her live, trying to be nice until she had enough. She finally said, "Bitch, kill the shade. Ain't nobody trying to take Bella's overly crazy ass from you." Rocky busted out laughing and said, "I like you." She thought because Tavares was so pretty she was gonna let Rocky punk her. However, checking her like one of her day one friends would, Tavares had won her over. Now, Tavares was a part of their circle like she'd come up with them.

"Why you having such a bad day?" Cali asked.

"Girl, don't even get me fucking started," Bella yelled.

"Well, bitch, you better start some place," Rocky said, snickering at her crazy friend.

"First, Mason didn't come home, and then Tavares missed our 9:15 a.m. conference call with the event planner for the wedding."

"Skirrrrrt, back that shit up!" Rocky yelled.

"What do you mean, Maniac didn't come home?"

"You heard exactly what I said. I been blowing that nigga up since I woke up and realized he wasn't in the bed with me. I know he went down Patterson to handle some shit. Usually, if he ain't coming home he'll call and say why, where he is, or something. I ain't heard from that nigga since he was on the highway last night. And, I swear to God if he isn't lying in the hospital or a jail cell, I'm sure gonna put him in a hospital bed for trying me. Just because he didn't call, I think he's laid up some place. Just for making me think it, I'mma stab his ass."

Cali tried to calm Bella down by being optimistic. She was always level-headed and positive.

"Stop thinking the worst. Maybe something happened, and he couldn't call. Don't just jump to conclusions. That man knows you deserve a coo-coo check and loves you too hard for you to assume he's laid up."

"Cali, fuck that shit. You always find a way to look at some shit in a positive light. That nigga calls me any other time. So, like I said, he better be in a cell or a hospital bed. If he's not, he's gonna wish he was. There's some shit that I'm willing to tolerate because I know how the game goes, but there's just some shit that I'm NOT tolerating. He has a better chance of seeing Jesus and Allah doing a cameo in Kanyeezie's next video before he thinks I'll tolerate his ass cheating and not coming home. We done been there and did that. Now we're getting married, so he got me all the way fucked up."

Cali and Rocky both overpowered the phone with laughter.

"Bitch, you stuuuuuuupid," said Rocky.

"Not a cameo with Jesus and Allah. I told you she deserves a coo-coo check," Cali repeated.

"Girl, I'm not playing. Unless Jesus and Allah are busting rhymes in videos, he better try again."

"And, what the hell happened with Tavares?" Cakes questioned.

"I have no fucking idea. I been calling her ass since ten this morning. She ain't answering and her phone is going straight to voicemail. Have either of y'all spoke to her?"

"Nah." "Nope," Bella's right and left hand answered.

"Last I spoke to her was last night when we were all on the four way," said Cakes.

"Yeah, that was right before she went to dinner with her father," Rocky said, thinking back to when they'd spoken.

"Well, I know one thing. She missed our conference call, and she's the one who has all these bright ideas for this wedding. Shit, I was fine with a destination wedding. It would have been simple and easy, but I let her ass convince me to get married here. So, I don't understand how the day we have this big ass conference call her ass is MIA."

"Knowing her and Abdora's freak asses, they're just somewhere laid up and she forgot," Cali Cakes threw out.

They all knew that their friend and Dora were good for blocking the world out when they couldn't get out from between the sheets.

"Did you call Dora?" asked Rocky.

"I did, but his phone is going to the voicemail, too. I got something for her and that fiancé of mine."

"Well since you're over there on a hundred, you might as well get dressed and go to the City with us," Cali said, hoping her cousin agreed to meet them. "We're probably gonna hit Manhattan for dinner, and then go uptown to Harlem to hang for some daytime drinks."

"How you doing that, super housewife?" Bella asked, being sarcastic. "Where's Javan?"

"He's out playing daddy daycare with his damn son. I told him I wasn't cooking, so he better make it happen. I played his part and my part as step-mama for the last year when he was sitting in county jail. So, my super wife, awesome stepmom ass isn't cooking today. I'm having Sunday Funday with my crew. So, get your ass up and come and meet me and Rocky."

"Right, you ain't doing shit else but over there mad as hell. Get dressed, bitch, and don't take all day," Rocky said to their friend who had zero sense of time.

"I just might take y'all up on the offer, Frick and Frack. I have a hair appointment in an hour. As long as Bree gets me out in good time, I'll come meet y'all."

The ladies shot the shit for a few more moments before agreeing to check-in a few hours later and said their goodbyes.

***

It was early afternoon before Mason awakened from a long night of rock-star partying in Patterson, New Jersey. He wasn't supposed to go out, let alone get wasted and wake up with a woman on each side of him.

"What the fuck?"

He cursed himself for his reckless behavior of not making it home and never calling Bella to tell her he was staying down in Patterson. He knew he was fucked as fucked got when he did make it home. Bella understood the life he lived; she just commanded he respected her in the process. Not calling her to say he wasn't coming home was blatant disrespect that he knew she was going through the roof about. She took a lot of shit, but being a no-call no-show was one thing that she played zero games with.

"Fuck, fuck, fuck!" he cursed out loud as he looked at each naked body lying on the left and the right of him.

He started replaying the night back as much as the headache that was beating in the front of his head would allow. After handling the Murder Mafia business with his comrades, he was supposed to head home. Somehow, he ended up at The Mansion, a hood club that was beyond popping every Saturday night. He told his homies he had to drive back, so he was having two drinks with them and hitting the highway. After the second shot, he locked eyes with his old sidepiece, Jamie. The moment they locked eyes, Mason should've bounced knowing the night would cause him to wake up how he did—not at home with his fiancée.

Mason had met Jamie some years back when he and Bella had been fighting a lot over dumb shit. She was a Phoenix, Arizona native who'd only been living in Newark a few months when they crossed paths. Mason couldn't get over how simply and naturally pretty she was. At only five feet tall with a thin frame and a sexy short haircut, her beauty was just flawless to the natural eye. He was in King's, Dora's club, when her beauty knocked him off his feet. Mason sent her a drink. To extend her thanks for the drink, she sent him back two drinks. A conversation sparked between them, and Mason became intrigued with her.

She was a square to heart and didn't know anything about the streets. All her life, she'd been a bookworm. She ended up in Newark after she watched the Mexican Cartel kill both her parents for trying to short them on their money. They spared her life, having watched her grow up from years of doing business with her parents. Alexandro knew Jamie was a gifted child born to shady parents. He didn't have the heart to kill her even though she appeared from the back room after they'd tied her parents up, tortured them, and shot them execution style. After the cartel paid to bury her parents, Alexandro gave her a half-million dollars, told her to find a family member to take her in, never open her mouth, and she could live the rest of her life. Jamie called her distant paternal grandmother, hopped on a plane, and did just that.

By the time her conversation ended with Mason, he found her to be a breath of fresh air. She liked simple things like jogging, reading books, and watching the stars. She even wanted to be a chemical engineer. Jamie was just the complete opposite of him, his life, and the girlfriend he was always fighting with. Having exchanged numbers, they were off and running from there. He was lying to Bella and spending every moment he could with Jamie when he wasn't handling his business. After six months of sharing their worlds with each other, Jamie became Mason's drug of choice. He wanted to be with her every chance he got. He didn't mind boring museums that he otherwise wouldn't visit if it wasn't for her. He came to love long walks and talking about everything from politics to their dreams. He turned her on to rap music and strip clubs. The volcanic attraction was mutual.

A friend of Bella's spotted Mason out to dinner with Jamie and carried the information back to her. Bella didn't say a word. Instead, she started her own private investigation. She started checking his phone and calling him more often to check his whereabouts. One night, she followed him when was supposed to be going to meet the fellas. Mason pulled up on South Orange Avenue and to Bella's heartbreak, a beautiful girl about her age came bouncing out the door, smiling from ear to ear. She instantly cried as she watched his face light up as the girl got in the car and gave him a kiss. Before Mason could pull off, she cut his car off and hopped out with a tire iron. Bella commenced beating the shit out of Mason's old-school car that he'd invested twenty thousand dollars into fixing up. She was screaming, "You no good, cheating motherfucker!" the whole time as she beat the car, crying in unison.

Jamie looked shocked and frightened and Mason knew that this wasn't going to end well. Struck with so much shock, Mason threw his car in reverse and took off. Bella jumped in her car and a high-speed chase took place. He was running red lights and taking sharp turns with Jamie on his side yelling, "Who is that, and what's going on?" Mason was so focused on trying to lose Bella in order to save both theirs lives that he couldn't pay Jamie any attention at that moment. After ten minutes of hitting side streets and making quick turns, he finally lost Bella— or so he thought. However, she'd activated the location services on his phone, so she knew exactly where he was.

He was at a red light breathing a sigh of relief when the next thing he knew, Jamie's door went flying open. Bella snatched her out and beat Jamie so badly that she literally almost killed her. When Mason finally got her off Jamie, she beat him with the tire iron. People in traffic just watched. No one dared to help the couple getting the shit beat out of them. After Bella was done, she jumped in her car and took off. Jamie lay half-conscious in the street with Mason holding her. Bella was crushed—not because she caught him cheating, but because of the twinkle in his eye when the girl got in the car. She knew he really cared about the woman.

After beating both of their asses, Bella thought she was off scot-free. She was at home crying and bleaching all Mason's clothes when there was a knock at the door.

"Hello!" Bella screamed.

"It's Newark Police. Ma'am, please open the door."

The onlookers didn't help, but one had called the police and given them a description of the attacker and her license plate. The police ran a trace and were at Bella and Mason's house to arrest her. She opened the door with a tear-stained face and politely asked, "How can I help you?"

"Bella Patterson, we have a warrant for your arrest for assault and battery with a dangerous weapon and attempted murder."

With no regrets, she placed her hands in front of her to be cuffed. The officer read her rights to her and hauled her off to jail. Jamie had suffered broken bones and a concussion. She told the police it was a crazy lady who chased her and her boyfriend down but she didn't know her name or anything about her. Mason had broken ribs, but when asked who did it to him, he said he didn't know. He couldn't throw Bella under the bus even though she'd tried to kill him and his mistress. Instead, he called Dora and told him what happened. He then gave Dora the code to his safe and told him to go to his house and get money to bail Bella out.

When Jamie learned that Mason had lied to the police, she was shattered and couldn't believe he would let the woman who'd done this get away with it. This was where the division in their worlds came in. In his world, you didn't snitch on people—and for damn sure not people you loved. In her world, when you committed a crime, there were consequences. Even after explaining to her all about his longtime relationship with Bella and how he'd been cheating with her, she still didn't get it.

"Mason, she tried to kill us. How can you not cooperate with the police?"

"Jamie, that's not how things work where I'm from. I can't do that to her."

"You can't do that to her?!" Jamie yelled, lying in the hospital bed still in pain. "What about me and what she did to me?"

Mason just hung his head down because he'd caused this, and there was nothing he could do to make this non-street girl understand how things worked when you were from the streets. Dora bailed Bella out for ten thousand dollars. She was so broken that she didn't have the heart to look her brother in the face. Dora wanted to talk, but he let Bella look out the window and cry instead. It was a long road of fighting the case with Jamie as a cooperative victim. Nevertheless, with a high-price attorney, Bella made out with a clean record. She got probation and had to do mandatory anger management classes. It wasn't easy, but she and Mason fixed what he'd broken and came out stronger and more in love than ever.

From that day forward, no matter how bad he tried to simply apologize, Jamie wouldn't have a thing to do with him. So many times, he called and she wouldn't answer. He sent flowers out of guilt, and she refused them. Jamie had fallen for Mason, and he broke her heart. After the whole ordeal with Bella, she'd picked up, taken the money she'd stashed away, and moved down to Patterson. She finished college and became an engineer. Only on rare occasions when he was down her way and she happened to be out and about, they would cross paths. It was over a year before she would even look his way, and another year before she would speak to him. They never got physical until the night before. Mason loved Bella. However, as he looked at Jamie sleeping, he truly believed that if they'd carried on much longer all those years ago, he probably would have left Bella for her. She was that much of a beautiful soul inside and out, which was how he ended up in bed with her and her girlfriend after they'd drunk Remy all night.

Mason climbed out of bed because he knew he had moves to make and music to face with his fiancée. Looking around the room, it was appeared that things got wild from the clothes that were everywhere, the big bottle of Remy he purchased at an after-hour spot, and the two women who were ass naked and knocked out. Finding his True Religion jeans, he pulled his phone out and noticed it was dead. He placed it on the charger and quietly made his way to the shower to wash the sinful night and scent of the women off him. After showering, he was dressed in no time and ready to get back to his regularly scheduled program. Before leaving the room that was paid for, he dropped a couple hundred on the nightstand and was out the door. He checked his messages and missed calls. To no surprise, Bella had called a million times and sent a dozen text messages cussing him out and threatening him. He was shocked, though, that Dora hadn't called him once. That was weird, seeing that they checked trap and spoke every morning.

Bella finally made it to the Beauty Bar and couldn't have been any more aggravated when she walked in and saw the face sitting in Bree's chair getting rollers put in her hair. Rolling her eyes long and hard at the woman being serviced, Bella hugged her hairstylist and made her way to the back to get washed. When she finally made it back to the dryer room, she sat under the only empty dryer. It was opposite the woman who, even though she hadn't done anything to her, she just didn't care for. It was Bella's opinion that she was just too thirsty to be a boss's wife, and that rubbed her wrong. So, even when she was dealing with Dora, she never showed the girl any love nor did she ever invite her into the circle.

Bella had dozed off under the dryer when her phone woke her up.

"What's up?" she answered.

"Hey, heffa?" Cali said, super cheery as always.

"What's the word?" Rocky asked. "You hooking up with us, or you going to catch a homicide on Maniac?" she joked.

"Yeah, I'm coming to meet y'all. I'm under the dryer now. All Bree has to do is bump what little bit of hair I have."

"Have you heard from Tavares?" Rocky asked, worried about her girl who was missing in action.

"No, I haven't heard from Abdora's gorgeous girlfriend," Bella said loudly enough for the woman to hear and make her body stiffen.

"What the hell is that all about?" Cali questioned, confused at the way Bella had answered.

"Yeah, I know they're just so in love and have them beautiful twins now. I don't think it'll be much longer either 'til Dora puts a ring on it."

The woman was steaming and pretending not to be listening, though she was sucking up every word and cringing on the inside.

"Bitch, what the fuck are you talking about?" Rocky yelled.

"Oh, nothing," laughed Bella. "I just have an onlooker down my throat, so I figured I might as well let her in on the conversation, too," Bella answered while looking the woman across from her straight in the eye. "I just know I would hate to beat the fuck out of a bitch today."

Cali busted out rolling.

"You're so damn crazy. Leave whoever that is alone."

Rocky wasn't so nice and added fuel to the fire. "Slap that trick! Slap that hoe," she sang before laughing.

"No, seriously though… You haven't heard from her?" Cali said, getting more than a little worried.

"Nah, I haven't. Why don't you call Dora?" Rocky suggested.

"I tried him, but his phone was going to voicemail. As a matter of fact, let me try him again because that was right before I left the house."

Bella added Dora to the three-way call, and his phone rang this time.

"What up, Bella?" he asked, not sounding like himself. Everyone noticed that he sounded odd. Bella just went straight in.

"Where the fuck is your girlfriend? I'm gonna kill her fucking ass. We had a conference call appointment with my wedding planner, and that heffa hasn't answered my calls or texts all damn day."

Before Dora could respond he heard, "Hey Dora," "Hi Dora." Recognizing the voices, he knew all three stooges were on the phone.

"Y'all be quiet. I'm not done yet. And, where's my fiancé? He's on my hit list, too, for the same shit. So, whichever one you speak to first, tell them I'm gunning for them."

Dora took a deep breath. "Bella, can you please shut the fuck up for a second?" His voice was low and fragile. "Tavares is lying a hospital bed. She got shot last night."

Not expecting what they heard, they all gasped and screamed in unison.

"OMG no," Cali said, her eyes filling with tears.

"She's gonna make it, but if the bullet would have hit her a hairline over, we could have been planning her funeral."

"What the fuck!?" yelled Rocky.

"I'm just glad that she's gonna make it, because I would've hated to bring that bitch back from the dead and kill her again for dying on us," Rocky said, trying to lighten the conversation.

"Yo, I'm at the hair salon, but I'm heading home to pack a bag and hitting the highway. Fuck, fuck, fuck," Bella said, remembering tomorrow was a big day at work. "I have a huge meeting at work tomorrow, but fuck that shit. They're gonna have to reschedule it or fill me in."

"Sis, you don't have to come. Go to work. She's gonna be here for a little while."

"Excuse me, bro? I don't have to, but that's what the fuck I'm doing. What's up, Cali and Rocky? Y'all riding out with me?"

"You already know," Rocky said. "I'm throwing some shit in the bag now. I'll park my car at your house. Cali, what you doing?" asked Rocky.

"I'm gonna call Javan and tell him I'm out. Rocky, come get me before you head to Bella's."

Abdora loved these women that he'd known his whole life. They had a love for their new friend that was so real and genuine that you couldn't do anything but respect it.

The nosey Jade was under the dryer, still ear hustling. She didn't know what had happened, but it sounded like something bad happened to Dora's girlfriend who she despised. Seeing that Bella wasn't crying, she knew that the girl who'd taken her man hadn't died like she wished on her so many days. It was all because of Tavares that Dora dropped her like a bad habit. She so badly thought he was gonna wife her and make a life with her. Just when she was so close, he gave her the boot. Whatever happened to his girlfriend, she hoped it was awful and she didn't have any regrets about her ill thoughts.

"Dora, have you spoken to Mason?"

Dora had to choose his words closely because he indeed hadn't spoken to Maniac since he was headed down to Patterson. If Bella was asking about him, that meant he didn't make it home.

"I spoke to him when he was down in Patterson, but my phone has been dead since last night. So, I don't know if things got handled. If not, he had to stay down there. But, the moment I speak to him, I'll have him get with you."

Maniac was gonna live a long time because he was beeping on Dora's other line. He didn't divulge that info, though.

He just said, "Let me know when y'all are heading this way. My phone is blowing up from being dead so long. I gotta take this call, so y'all get with me."

Dora clicked over and didn't even say hello. Instead he said, "Nigga, where the fuck you at? I was just on the other line with Bella Mafia, and she got an APB out on you, nigga."

"Man, listen," Maniac answered. He had to take a deep breath. "I fucked around and went out last night after I handled our business. I bumped into Jamie. Next thing I know, I woke up in the tellie with her and another chick. The night got wild on the Remy, my nigga."

"Niggggga, you done lost your mafucking mind," Dora said, laughing for the first time in over twenty-four hours. "Don't fuck around and let Bella catch you slipping and for sure not with Jamie. You thought she went ham last time. Nigga, this time she's for sure gonna put you six feet under. So, don't say I didn't warn you."

Dora was crying in laughter thinking about the last incident.

"Dora, you ain't gotta tell me. That's why I hopped up, saw Bella's crazy ass messages, showered, dropped some dough on the nightstand, and took flight," Maniac said, falling out laughing. "I love the fuck out of Bella and she ain't gonna kill me before I get a chance to marry her ass. Yo, what the fuck did Bella say? Did you tell her you ain't heard from me?"

"Nah, my nigga. I played it neutral. I told her that if you didn't get shit handled, you had to stay down in Patterson."

"Good looking, my nigga. Her messages had a nigga scared to go home," Maniac only half joked. "I woke up like fuck, my bitch is gonna kill me."

"Well, you might be Gucci, my nigga. Tavares got shot, and I need you to get to Boston ASAP. She's gonna be good, but I need my right-hand niggaz out here. Bryce, Middeon, and Hawk are out here with me, so you get here."

"WHAT!?" yelled Maniac. "Nigga, why the fuck we just have a whole conversation, and you just informing me of this?"

"Because I had to warn you before you walk in your house and Bella stabbed your ass. You know she's certifiably crazy," Dora said factually about his sister from another mister. Still, he loved for who she was. "So, check trap, homie," Dora said with a solution to Maniac's problem. "You took the homegirl Nicole's car down there, right?"

"Yeah."

"So, take that shit to the airport and hop on the next thing smoking to Boston. Bella and the crew are driving down. You'll beat them here. When you get here, call wifey and tell her you were handling business 'til mad late. When you got the word from Middeon about 3:00 a.m., you went straight to the airport to fly out there. But, by the time you got to the airport, your phone was dead. However, now you're here settled, you got a charger, and you're sorry that you weren't able to call. In the meantime, I'll get you a room. We about to put in that work," Dora said, knowing that someone was going to pay with their life for shooting his girl.

"That'll for sure work, my nigga. I'm hitting the airport now. While I'm in motion, I'm gonna hit Nicole and tell her to have one of the niggaz from the hood bring her to pick her car up. I'll see you shortly."

Maniac hung up and was in shock that Dora's wifey was in the hospital shot. He was sorry to hear that shit, but it had saved his ass at the current moment. He made his phone calls while he burned rubber on the highway. He arrived at Newark Liberty Airport in no time.

By the time Jazz made it home, she was still a hysterical mess after hearing about Damien. Trying to regain her composure with weak legs and a tear-stained face, she made her way into the house. When she made it to her room, her phone started to beep with the low battery indicator.

"Fuck!" she yelled. "My damn charger is in the car."

Tossing her cell phone on the bed, she grabbed the cordless phone off the dresser and began calling around to see which hospital Damien and Tavares were in. She called her friends first, but all their phones were going straight to voicemail. Next, she started calling all the hospitals. She called Boston Medical Center, Beth Israel, and Brigham & Women's Hospital. All were dead ends. She decided to give Tufts Medical Center a try.

"Thank you for calling Tufts. How may I direct your call?" the operator answered.

"I'm trying to locate my sister and brother-in-law," Jazz said, thinking it sounded a lot better than "I'm looking for my ex-best friend and her ex whom I've been fucking."

"What are their names?" the proper-speaking Caucasian male answered.

After giving their names, Jazz waited hoping her search was over. A flag in the computer system went off that no information was to be given out. Once he read that they were admitted as shooting victims, he knew why the flag popped up.

He responded, "I'm sorry, ma'am. I can't give any information on these patients."

Jazz hung up because he didn't say they weren't there like the other hospitals. She didn't know why, but she hung up and dialed Damien's phone number. She was hoping he would answer and say she'd heard wrong and he was alive and well.

"Hello," a weak, low female voice answered.

"Oh, I'm sorry. I dialed the wrong number," Jazz said and hung up without a second thought. *Damn, I'm moving so fast I dialed the wrong number,* she thought to herself and slowly dialed Damien's number again.

Seeing the same name up calling back, Talesha answered with a slight attitude.

"Hello?"

It hit Jazz that she had indeed called the right number, and a chick had Damien's phone.

"Who is this?" Jazz snapped.

"Excuse me?" the woman responded with her voice no longer low. "You're calling my man's phone, so I need to be asking you that question."

Jazz immediately became infuriated that a woman had the audacity to not only be answering Damien's phone, but to be calling him her man.

"Listen, bitch, I don't know who the fuck you are. But, you sure ain't his fucking girlfriend."

"I don't know who the fuck you are since your name pops up as The Guzzler," Talesha said, stinging Jazz below the belt. "However, I don't have time to go back and forth with you. My man's in a coma and arguing with his side bitches is the last thing I'm about to do."

Talesha was getting angrier by the moment as Damien's phone kept ringing with a million bitches calling.

"Bitch, what? You think you're special because you got his phone? Well, newsflash, honey-booboo, you ain't. And, I hope you're talking that side bitch shit when I get there."

Jazz slammed the phone down, grabbed her keys, and was in her car two minutes later.

"Who the fuck was that?" Taya, Talesha's cousin, asked.

"Another groupie bitch."

Taya didn't want to be the bearer of bad news at a time like this, but she had to speak.

"Honey, for this to be your man, he sure got a lot of groupies. Are you sure he's been on the up and up as you think?"

Talesha hated to admit it, but it seemed like he hadn't from all the calls he'd gotten since she'd charged his phone.

"Cousin, I don't want to lie to you or myself. I don't know what he's been doing when we aren't together. I don't even know if he has indeed been fucking all these chicks. But, the last conversation we had, he told me we were together."

Taya didn't give a fuck what bullshit he'd fed her cousin. Damien was still fucking a gang of bitches and the proof was in the pudding. There were way too many emotional, sobbing, angry women questioning Talesha every time she answered his phone for him to have been on the up and up about their relationship.

***

The waiting room was still overcrowded with families and friends waiting patiently for the fate of their loved ones—whether it was for them to come out of surgery, be moved to their rooms, or worse. Everyone from Damien's family was congregated together trying to keep Doll's spirits up. Tavares's friends were chatting with her parents and Dora not too far from them. With so many people in the waiting area, they hadn't been paying attention to the coming and goings of the people around them. Jazz entered the over-capacity dwelling and couldn't believe that so many people were crammed in one place. She was scanning the room trying to determine who should she approach—Damien's family or her friends, who were sitting with Holton and an unfamiliar woman.

Before Jazz could determine which group was the lesser of two evils, she spotted her homegirl tucked away in a corner and made her way over there.

"Waddup, Taya?"

"Ain't shit, bitch. Here with my cousin."

The women, who had seen each other in passing but didn't know each other personally, said cordial hellos.

"Her man was one of the people that got shot last night."

"Damn, I'm sorry to hear that," Jazz said. "I hope he's going to be okay. I'm here for the same reason. I just got wind that my dude got shot and ain't doing well. I had no idea he was even here. I was waiting on him all night, and he never made it. Then, my neighbor called me and told me what jumped off at the club. So, I flew here."

Taya was trying to play it cool because she knew that her cousin and Jazz were there for the same man. She knew, like everyone else in the hood, that Jazz had been creeping with Dame ever since he and Tavares had split up. She just hoped that it ended since Dame claimed to be in a relationship with her cousin. But her gut told her differently. The hood was small and to date, the news still flying around was that Jazz and Tavares weren't friends and that Jazz was happily fucking her ex-best friend's longtime boyfriend. Taya wasn't in the mood for the bullshit with her cousin and Jazz. Especially when it was evident that Dame was the dog and just playing everyone.

Talesha wasn't paying her cousin and her friend she was talking to any mind. She was in her own world thinking about Damien and constantly sending people to voicemail as they blew up his phone. She was getting more and more irritated with her man's phone.

Not even realizing, she released her frustration out loud, and blurted, "These bitches are getting on my nerves blowing Damien's phone up!"

Taya's heart dropped at the same time Jazz's mouth did.

"What the fuck did you just say?" Jazz snapped.

"Chill, Jazz," Taya said, trying to defuse what she knew was about to become an ugly situation.

"Chill my fucking ass. Did your cousin just say she's tired of bitches blowing Damien's phone up?"

"That's exactly what the fuck I just said!" Talesha snapped back.

"Oh, so you're the one answering Dame's phone like you're motherfucking special and shit. Newsflash! Damien isn't your fucking man."

Taya hopped up out of the seat that was warming her butt.

"This ain't the time or the place. Y'all need to chill the fuck out."

Talesha was already aggravated. So, if this bitch wanted to rumble, then that's what they were going to do.

"Listen bitch. I don't know who the fuck you are or what night you be sucking my man's dick, but Damien is definitely my motherfucking man."

"Bitch, you better get your motherfucking mind right. Damien is far from your man. If he was, he wouldn't be fucking me and whoever else a few times a week," Jazz chuckled.

Her last comment was so loud now she had the attention of the people congregated around them.

"Oh God," Dolonda said, hearing the word exchange. "I knew it wouldn't be long before some drama stirred up in here over some two-timing no-good ass nigga."

Hearing the argument with the familiar voice and looking through the crowd, Randee and Leslie gave each other the eye. Catching them, Dolonda asked, "What's wrong? Y'all know them?"

Their argument rang throughout the waiting room. "Fuck you, bitch!"

"Bitch, come outside, and I'll bust your fucking ass!" Everyone was looking at Jazz and Talesha just waiting for a punch to be thrown.

"Miss Dolonda, that's our friend Jazz we were telling you about."

Dolonda grabbed her chest and said, "This bitch got a lot of fucking nerve."

As Dolonda went to get up out of the chair, Holton politely sat her back down by tightly grabbing her arm. "Mind your fucking business. That shit ain't got nothing to do with our daughter."

Nana Dancy heard, "Damien, Damien, Damien" and it hit her that they were yelling like fools over her grandson. She hopped up like a bat out of hell.

Hershey yelled, "Oh, God, here Nana goes! Someone get her."

Doll wasn't moving, entertaining, or saving either one of the two delusional women from her mother. Neither was anyone else in Damien's family. The two women making fools of themselves arguing over a man who wasn't either of theirs were about to learn today.

"You two dumb bitches. Who the fuck raised you monkey ass bitches? Dumb bitch one and dumb bitch two, he ain't your man or your man. And, dumb bitch one, give me my grandson's phone."

Dancy snatched the phone as Talesha halfway extended it to her.

"Who the fuck stands in a hospital arguing over a man who isn't even breathing? No one but dumb bitches. I don't give a fuck who sucked his dick better, who he fucked better, or who he fucked more! Neither one of you dumb bitches is his girlfriend. If you dumb bitches were raised right or had some self-esteem, you would know he was playing both of you dumb bitches."

Nana Dancy called them so many dumb bitches that the whole waiting room and the hallway now knew they were nothing but dumb bitches. She was about to go for a second round of her dumb bitch session, but the new doctor caring for Tavares interrupted her.

"Hi, I'm looking for the family of Tavares Del Gada."

Hearing her granddaughter's name, she didn't get started. "Listen here, you dumb bitches. You've embarrassed yourselves, my grandson, and my family. When I get back, both of you dumb bitches better be gone."

Dancy left both the dumb bitches dumbfounded at how badly she'd dogged them out. They felt so low that they both just gathered their things and made a quick exit.

CHAPTER 3

The doctor escorted Tavares's tribe to a private room.

"Hi, I'm Dr. Berksbee. I've taken over for Dr. Ganuby. I'll be Tavares's attending physician," the fairly young green-eyed, blonde-haired doctor stated. "I have some good news and some not so good news."

"So what's the good news?" Dora asked, getting annoyed with all the chitter chatter. The doctor needed to cut the chase and get to it.

"Miss Del Gada is going to have a full recovery. The not so good news is that she lost a lot of blood during surgery. I do mean a lot. She's still unconscious, so I need to know who can consent to a blood transfusion."

"Me," Doll said before the new generation Doogie Howser had finished his sentence. "I'm Tavares's next of kin."

Three of the five people the doctor was speaking to turned their heads in disbelief at what Doll had just said.

"Bull fucking shit you're my daughter's next of kin. I'm her mother, and her father's right fucking here. You don't have any say-so in her medical treatment."

"Oh, now you're done smoking crack, and you want to be the mother of the year? In case you forgot while you were on more than a ten-year crack binge, I've been the only mother your daughter has had."

"Doll, I don't give a fuck if I smoked crack for twenty years. I'm back, so fuck you. And, seriously, I don't fuck with you like that. So, I would tread lightly."

While the argument was taking place between the women, Dhara and Me-Ma were at the front desk.

"Hi, my name is Dhara, and I'm looking for my daughter-in-law Tavares Del Gada. She was brought in as a shooting victim. I don't see my son or her parents in the lobby. Has she been moved to a room?"

The pretty silver-haired polite older nurse said, "No sugar. The doctor has the family down the hall talking to them. Go down this hallway and knock on the fourth door on the right."

Down the hall, Doll snarled, "Of course you don't fuck with me. You've always been a part of the side bitch team. Side bitches of a feather flock together. I've always been a main bitch, which is why Holton never brought you around me. Lilly always been my girl, not you."

Dolonda cracked up laughing. "Who the fuck was a side bitch? Because neither Dhara nor me were side bitches. You and Lilly were fighting to hold on to men that didn't even want y'all."

Abdora's neck snapped, and he turned his attention to Dolonda. Holton wanted to grab Dolonda's no-filter-having ass. The doctor was questioning how he got stuck with such chaos having just started his shift. Then the door swung open.

"Did I just hear my name?"

"Yeah, I was letting the cat out the bag that Miss I'm-better-than-thou was indeed Dorian's side bitch and not you."

Dhara was all confused. She'd known way back when that Dorian had dealings with a woman in Boston, but she had no idea it was Doll, Damien's mother. This was a woman she'd been around a million times since Dora and Tavares had been together—the lady she sat and talked with a million times. This was unreal at the moment.

"So, you was the bitch fucking my man all those years, huh?" Doll asked, letting old hurting feelings of over twenty-five years resurface.

"Honey, I don't know what the fuck is going on, but you got me twisted." Dhara looked Doll straight in the face. "If I were you, I'd watch my words. Dorian was my man, my husband, and the father of my sons. If anyone was a side bitch, it was you."

"Well, Dhara… Newsflash. We share the same fucking baby's daddy. Dorian is both my boys' father as well."

Dhara lunged and Dora grabbed her. Dora couldn't take another minute of this stupid ass bickering over his dead father.

"What the fuck!?" he yelled. "Would you both shut the fuck up? Just shut the fuck up, nowww!"

His voice was as cold as Antarctica. It was so loud that he knew for sure the whole lobby had heard him.

"Doctor, I'm sorry for this ignorant bullshit. I'm Tavares's healthcare proxy. Call Beth Israel, and they'll fax it over. Give her the blood transfusion now."

The doctor agreed and was out the door so fast that he damn near tripped over his own feet. As soon as he closed the door, the two women wasted no time.

"I don't give a fuck that Dorian married you. He was my man, and you and Dolonda weren't nothing but trollops running around with two kept men."

"Kept men my motherfucking ass," Dolonda said. "Holton never wanted that bitch Lilly. And, if Dorian was yours, he wouldn't have married the trollop. Sucks to be a bitter bitch," laughed Dolonda. "And Lilly… She used that keep a nigga baby to make Holton stay. But, look where he is now."

"Fuck you, Dolonda! And, Dhara, you ain't nothing but a side bitch who ruined my family."

"You better watch your mouth about my daughter," Me-Ma said, ready to set it at sixty-five.

"Well, your daughter shouldn't have been fucking my daughter's man," Dancy chimed in.

Dora and Holton's heads were spinning with the mother and daughter tag team that was about to jump off. Holton looked at Dolonda with evil eyes because she'd started all this. His face let her know she was going to catch it when they were alone. For now, he didn't want to hear this bullshit another minute.

"Would you two shut the fuck up? Dorian loved you, Doll. And, Dorian was in love with you, Dhara, which is why he married you. I was hoping this day never came that y'all learned that Damien, Dora, Mid, and Rollo were brothers. I knew it would, but I hoped it wouldn't. It is what it is, so shut the fuck up and move on."

No one saw what was coming next.

"That bitch ass nigga ain't me and Mid's brother."

Dolonda gasped. Dhara and Me-Ma weren't shocked. Doll went postal.

"Watch your motherfucking mouth about my son. That's my fucking son, and he's fighting for his life."

Dora still didn't care.

"Doll, no disrespect to you, but your son is a bitch ass nigga. Even if he did come from my pop's sperm, he ain't my brother and he ain't cut from the same cloth as my mother's sons. All the fuck shit he did to Tavares since I met her, he can't be no brother of mine. Me and my brother ain't fuck niggas. I don't care if he's fighting for his life. He ain't me and Mid's brother."

Nana Dancy lunged for Dora's face to claw it off.

"You cold son of a bitch."

Me-Ma grabbed her from behind and put her in a chokehold. The daughters jumped to their defenses, leaving Dora and Holton to defuse the old lady and senior citizen catfight. Meanwhile, the door swung open.

"What in de hell gone on in here? You two old heffas fighting in a hospital," Vadaleen said, walking in on the tail end of what appeared to be a fight between two women her age. "Holy damn hell. Darlene, your old ass still fighting?" Holton's mother asked her friend she hadn't seen in ages.

Dhara and Darlene were in one corner and Doll and Dancy were in the other. Each mother and daughter was a duo looking like they were still ready to rumble. Vadaleen cleared the smoke in the room by reminding everyone that this wasn't the time or place. She reminded them that her granddaughter and Damien were lying in hospital beds and everyone needed to focus on what was important. By the time everyone departed, Dancy and Darlene were calling each other a million bitches. Doll and Dhara were acting like it would be on and popping the next time they'd come face to face outside the hospital. Dora gave Holton dap.

"I'mma go check in with the doctors and get with you as soon as I get my gangster granny and murder mommy settled at Tavares's house."

Holton had to laugh because that was exactly what they'd been acting like. It was just Holton, Dolonda, and Darlene left at the hospital.

"I can't believe them damn ass crazy people fighting in de hospital."

"Mommy, please stop acting like you won't give someone the hands. Because if I can recall, you beat the cashier up at the grocery store not too long ago for trying to short-change you."

"Shut up and mind your damn business. You trying to make a sweet old lady look bad in front of your lady. Speaking of which... Dolonda, although we have to meet under such unfortunate circumstances, it's a pleasure to meet you."

"Likewise, Mrs. Montiago," Dolonda said, extending her hand.

"Girl, is you crazy, too? You don't shake my hand. We're family. Give me a hug." Vadaleen was queen of no filter. "I see you two body language. It says you love each other. So, tell me what you two gonna do. Get together or co-parent this grown daughter you got?"

"Mommy, do you think that's an appropriate question right now?"

"Yes. I think I deserve to know if you're finally getting rid of that no-good, life-sucking, trifling trollop."

Dolonda fell out rolling. "I love you already, Mama Montiago."

"Yeah, that damn Lilly... She just no good for my boy. I tell him long time kick her out on her ass. She lazy, lazy, and just lazy. What kind of woman don't work but don't cook a hot damn meal every night for she husband? No one but a trollop."

Holton's face told them both that he wasn't feeling this conversation.

"Mommy," Holton said very sternly. "Listen, would you... Me and Lilly are over. Now, be quiet."

Vadaleen just smiled because God had finally answered her prayers and the nonworking, lazy drug addict was finally no longer gonna be her daughter-in-law.

"I need you to just sit with Tavares. I gonna drop Dolonda off before I head to my meeting. When I'm done, we'll come back."

"No, I can stay here."

"No, you can't stay here. You haven't slept, eaten, or taken a shower. My mother got this covered."

"Yeah, you two go. I'm gonna sit with my granddaughter."

Holton and Dolonda updated Tavares's friends as they exited the building.

"I'm just glad my friend is gonna live to see another day," Leslie said, still a bit shaken up.

"We all are," Holton said, knowing they all shared the same feelings. "You ladies might as well go home and get some rest. Tavares won't be taking any visitors until tomorrow. She's in good hands—better than Allstate. My mother is going to sit with her until we get back."

Randee spoke for Leslie and herself when she said, "Okay. We'll be back first thing in the morning. We're just waiting for them to discharge Mona-Lisa."

"Do you ladies need a ride?" Holton questioned.

"No, we're good, but thanks."

Tavares's parents and best friends exchanged hugs and comforted one another before going their separate ways. Vadaleen was escorted to her granddaughter's room where she slept heavily sedated from the surgeries. She used the time to speak to Tavares. Rubbing her hands through Tavares's hair, she spoke to her as if she were awake.

"Hello, me beautiful granddaughter. It's your Glam-Ma Vadaleen. Your cousins call me Glam-Ma because they say I'm the flyest nana in town. I must admit that they're telling the truth. Your granfadah is Harvey Sr., but I call he White Boy because when I meet him I say 'What I do with you, White Boy?' We been in love for over forty years. He's so cool, laidback and a sweetie. Him just want to play golf, watch sports, smoke he cigar, and hang with the good ole boys every Friday. You have two aunties and two uncles. Auntie Veronica and Auntie Vanny. Auntie Ronica, as I call her, she's my pit-bull. Pretty, pretty, pretty but so frigid around the edges. She a lot like me in my day. She take no shit."

Vadaleen laughed at admitting where her oldest daughter got her ways.

"Ronica will slap someone quick and ask questions later. But, her heart big, so big for she family. Auntie Vanny is the pretty, pretty princess. She just so stuck up. I sometimes wonder if she mine. I like nice stuff, love to shop, and be glamorous, but that Vanny—she too much. Shops like a fashion whore, spends too much money and just bossy to she kids and she husband.

"Uncle Harvey is a lot like your pop-pop, your grandfadah. He boring and got them white genes. Then, there's Uncle Hayden. That damn ass Hayden... He just my pretty playboy. Only one not married, but always got he a hot young piece of tail. What do you think about your father's wife? I no like her. I haven't for a long time. She try to always make my Holton feel bad for the loss of your bruddah. But, she need to feel bad for all the damn drug she do. But guess what? She's kicked to the curb. You father look like a teenage boy when him look at your mother. She pretty. Very, very pretty, and you look like she. I just met her, and I can't wait to get to know both of you."

Vadaleen got comfortable in the recliner chair and planned to talk to her granddaughter until her son returned.

***

Dora somehow got stuck transporting not just his mother and grandmother, but Tavares's mother as well. They were all gonna shower and hang out at the Natick house until he came back to get them. How he was feeling, they better hope he came back for them at all. The grown women felt like school children listening to Dora chastise them for their behavior in the hospital. Dhara and Me-Ma didn't know how long this ride that seemed like forever was gonna take, but they were ready to be at Tavares's house already.

"Y'all was acting like senior citizen hoodrats in that hospital. Pops is long gone, Ma. Why would you even entertain some wack ass shit about who was fucking whose man and who was the side bitch?"

"Doll deserved what she was about to get, trying to call us side bitches," Tavares's mother defended herself.

"She was trying two real ass bitches," Dolonda said, opening the door for Dora to give her the business, too.

"Newsflash, Dolonda. You and my mother's real ass bitch days are over. Y'all are old now. How about y'all sit down and worry about being real ass grandmothers?"

"I heard that," Dora's grandmother chimed in like she was innocent.

"Me-Ma, you better cut it out because you was ready to swing, too. I'mma tell y'all like this. My girl has to be there, and she needs to recover in peace. Let that shit go. If y'all want to act like old lady hoodrats, it better not be at that hospital."

When they pulled up to Tavares's big, newly painted blue house in the suburbs, the ladies hurried out of the truck because they were sick of Abdora's mouth.

"Thank God we're finally here," Dolonda rolled her eyes.

"Feelings mutual," Dora said, letting his girl's mother know he was sick of them just like they were of him.

He got them settled with towels, washcloths, and take-out menus. Then, he was on his way. He wasn't sure what this meeting was all about that Holton was calling, but he hoped that it was about who had news on who shot Tavares. The real nigga in Abdora didn't give a fuck about much of anything else at the moment.

By the time Abdora arrived, the meeting was in full swing. He silently made his way to the one empty seat in the room. It was next to Holton. He looked around the room and noticed a few familiar faces. He only gave one of them a head nod. That was his right-hand man, Majors. Then, two faces caught Dora's attention. Unlike the other faces around the table that appeared settled, they didn't look at ease.

Dora made a mental note of that because body language speaks volumes.

"As an OG to the game," Holton schooled the new generation, "Fellas, getting money and violence just don't mix. The city, the cops, and the community won't fuck with you when you getting money. They tend to turn a blind eye because you ain't hurting no one—not anyone they care about, at least. But, when you add violence to the equation, things change and change fast. The police aren't going to have blood on their street when they allow you to hustle, and neither am I. No matter the money I've acquired or the many successful businesses I own, I'm from the streets," Holton said, looking around the table at each man so they could catch his drift. "I live by and play by the rules of the streets. So, street shit, I never take personal because it's a life we choose to live. But, when it's my daughter whose lying in a hospital, right, motherfucking right I take it personal. I asked you all to come here tonight because I need to know who's responsible for putting my daughter in that hospital bed. You fellas are the heavy hitters in the city. If anyone knows who was shooting last night, it would be one of you. Ratting is when you're helping the cops. Telling me is like helping an old friend."

The men at the table were quiet. Everyone knew what had happened the night before because the streets talked. Two of the gentlemen at the table, along with their boys, had been shooting at each other. Some of the gentlemen at the table were friends, others were enemies, and most were cordial. But, they all knew if they threw the two enemies under the bus, it would be a death sentence for them. Therefore, everyone continued to be speechless.

"I like that. You fellas want to stick to the G-code of not snitching. Okay, that works for me too," he chuckled viciously. "I thought at least one nigga in here would have enough love for me to tell me who possibly shot Tavares."

Hearing Tavares's name, every nigga in the room except Dora and Majors, who were aware who Holton's daughter was, damn near jumped out of their seats.

"From the shifts in body language and facial expressions, I see that y'all know my Baby Girl. Well yes," Holton said too calmly, "that's my daughter. Someone's gonna pay for putting her in that bed. I thought I could count on y'all for help. Since I couldn't, here's how things are going down. There will be no purchases or sales until I've received retribution."

"What!" "Oh shit," and "Fuck no" were a few of the shocked responses of the raw cocaine purchasers. Dora just laughed. He knew that didn't apply to him, so he would be monopolizing and moving in on a few niggas' territory. Holton wrapped the meeting up.

"You might can call me Tucker, but you won't ever call me sucker. Ain't no way in hell will a nigga who almost killed my daughter still eat off my product."

Niggas at the table was fuming mad. Because they were trying to stand on principle and not cost two of the men their lives, it was going to be a drought. Yeah, they could purchase product elsewhere, but it wasn't going to be anywhere close to the quality of Holton's white girl, cocaine. Quality was why they were able to move things wholesale at a rapid rate. Now everyone was fucked until the truth reached their connect.

"Holton, would you mind going to the house and checking on them senior citizen hoodrats? I wanna holla at my man for a little bit. Then, I'm going back to the hospital. So, you can call your mother and tell her she can get on the highway before it's too late. I'll be there long before Tavares wakes up."

"You got it, young blood. I'm going to catch some shut eye on y'all's couch. Then, me and them troublemaking ass old ladies will be back there bright and early in the morning."

"That works," Dora said, giving his girl's father dap and heading on his way.

Dora and Holton never saw the gentleman outside the door eavesdropping on their conversation. After hearing the bit that he did, the guy made a beeline to do what he needed to do.

Dora hopped in the car with Majors and said, "Shit's about to get real. Nigga, let's go get a drink."

Majors was making his way to Packy's, ready to hear what he already knew this talk was about.

"Yo, two of them niggaz was at the Roxy last night. It got hectic real fast once shots were fired, but I REMEMBER seeing two of their faces. Them sitting in that meeting looking tense and not even saying they was there, rubbed me wrong. My gut knows it was them busting at each other, and my girl caught a few of their stray bullets."

Majors didn't feel right throwing niggaz under the bus to Holton. Dora was a whole different story. Dora was his mans. At the end of the day, he was going ride with Dora and handle niggaz. That was more of Majors's speed than ratting.

"Nigga, you're right. Everyone in the streets is talking about last night. The whole hood and all them niggaz at the table know who's guilty for last night's shootout. Their hoods have no fucks given when it comes to where they'll whip out their hammers and start shooting. We'll probably never know whose gun actually shot Apple, but it was their recklessness that put her in that hospital bed. Let me do some research. We can't move reckless because the hood is on fire, but payback is coming."

"Bet," Dora said as they pulled up to Packy's.

Majors and Dora made it through the back door of the Black Cheers. They spotted Hawk, Bryce, Maniac, and Bam-Bam occupied at the round table for eight. They were murdering chicken wings, mac and cheese, collard greens, steak tips, French fries, and onion rings.

"You niggaz is greedy," Dora said, helping himself to a wing.

"Whatever, nigga," Bryce popped off.

"If we so greedy, don't eat our shit," Maniac co-signed.

"Nigga, after I covered your ass earlier, my drinks is on you," Dora laughed.

Majors gave his homies dap and made himself a plate before they got down to business.

Dora and his mans weren't the only ones plotting and planning. On the other side of Roxbury, two men who normally shot at each other were putting their differences aside for the time being. They put together a not well thought out plan. All they were waiting for was a phone call from their helper on the inside. Then, they'd be ready to make a move. They had to move quickly if they planned to save their lives. They also wanted to be sure Holton would never find out who was responsible for his daughter being in the hospital bed. They were waiting to do something they never thought they would do. They were actually working with their archenemy.

***

Tavares finally awakened after hours of being in a coma. Before she looked left and right, her nose told her where she was. She knew she was in the one place she hated more than anywhere. She wanted to scream, but seeing the melanin-free woman sound asleep next to her bed stopped her. She looked to her left and saw an overwhelming amount of flowers and balloons. Her eyes roamed until she found the clock on the wall. Seeing that it read 10:30, she wondered where her boyfriend, parents, and friends were. Why was she all alone in the one place every one of them knew she hated?

Tavares lay in bed looking at the ceiling for a long while. She was slightly high from the morphine drip that she was connected to, yet she was coherent enough to wrack her brain. It took her a minute, but everything started coming back to her. She remembered she was going to beat Damien's bitch up at the club. She wondered where Damien was. Tavares's thoughts were interrupted hearing her room buddy slide out of bed and make her way to the bathroom. She closed her eyes to continue piecing the puzzle together that ended with her in a hospital bed.

At a quarter to eleven, Kevin slipped in the hospital. Thanks to his cousin who did security at the hospital, he knew exactly which wing and room Tavares was located in. He was in scrubs, wearing a white doctor's jacket and a stethoscope around his neck. Blending in perfectly with the other doctors and nurses on the floor, he was cool, calm, and collected. He exited the elevator with a bright smile and waved to those still in the elevator. With no remorse for the vicious act he was going to commit, he made his way to Room 812.

Tavares heard the door crack open. When the bright light from the hallway illuminated the dark room, she squinted her eyes. As a doctor walked in backwards, Tavares prepared to pretend to be asleep. She hoped he was there for her roommate. If not, she prayed he saw her closed eyes and went away. The door shut behind him. After a few moments, the door didn't reopen. So, Tavares kept her eyes squinted so low that it was impossible to see that they weren't fully closed.

Hearing the doctor say, "Oh she's sleep. This is gonna be a piece of cake," caught the pretend sleeper's attention. Tavares knew that face and that voice. Her gut told her that she should be in panic mode as she lay in the bed defenseless. Yet, she lay still to see what his next move was gonna be. He pulled out a cell phone and made a call.

"She's asleep and has no one in here. This is gonna be quick. In ten minutes, meet me where you dropped me."

She watched him go to the vacant bed and grab a pillow. Tavares tried to feel for the call button on the bed, but there were four buttons. She didn't want to hit the wrong button and alert the disguised doctor that she was indeed awake. Then, what she felt next to her in the bed eased all her fear of dying where she lay. As Kevin stood over Tavares with the pillow preparing to put it over her face and shoot her, the bathroom door swung open. Tavares's roommate was immediately frightened seeing the pillow and gun. She screamed for dear life as the badly aimed shooter fired a shot at her and missed.

He quickly turned back around to do what he came to do and get out of dodge, but his finger wasn't quick enough on the trigger. Seizing the opportunity, Tavares fired the gun she discovered in the bed moments before. With two shots from the silenced nine-millimeter gun between the eyes, his brain exploded and his body hit the floor. Tavares's heart was racing, not because she'd just killed a man, but because he'd almost killed her. Tavares pushed the call button on the bed while the white girl was still in the bathroom scared, screaming, and literally shitting on herself.

"Hi, what do you need?" the nurse answered over the call button.

"Please send my nurse as soon as possible."

Upon entering the room, Charlene didn't know whether to run, scream, or piss her pants. She'd never experienced a murder on her shift, so she wasn't sure of the protocol. Tavares looked her straight in the eye. She didn't speak above a whisper or with any trembling in her voice.

"Please call someone to get this body off the floor and have us moved to a new room. But, can you please go check on the little frazzled white girl in the bathroom first? Oh, and I need my phone," Tavares said.

"Uhh, uhh, uhhh... Miss Del Gada, why is this dead body on your floor?" the nurse questioned before she moved.

"He shot at Suzy in there and tried to kill me. So, I shot him in self-defense."

***

Landell had waited more than thirty minutes for his partner in this crime to arrive at their meeting spot. In that time, he'd called a few times from his burner cell but got no answer. Now, there were tons of police flying past him. His brain told him something went very wrong and to get out of dodge. He didn't know if Kevin had gotten caught and dropped his name, and he wasn't about to stick around and find out. Landell had twenty thousand in cash on him. Instead of heading back to the hood, he hit the Mass Pike. He wasn't coming back until things had blown over.

Dora was fully intoxicated when he stepped off the elevator on the eighth floor. He quickly sobered up when he saw the million Boston police officers in the hallway. He raced toward Tavares's room, when he saw that there was yellow tape in front of the door. He flew to the nurse's station like a tornado.

"Where the fuck is my girlfriend? She was in room 812, and now there's yellow tape by the door. What the fuck has happened?"

The nurses were looking speechless at the big, tall, fine angry African-American man.

"Sir, she's been moved for her safety."

"Take me to her now." Abdora didn't ask; he commanded.

Charlene said, 'This way."

Dora was escorted one floor up. There were a million more police congregated outside Tavares's room. As Nurse Charlene approached the door, an officer stopped them.

"I need to see your ID."

"No, you don't," Dora said and pushed through the small crowd of officers.

When he entered the room, Tavares was lying in the bed like nothing had happened. She wasn't shaking like the white girl in the bed next to her. Dora gave no fucks that Tavares was talking to a detective. He cut the conversation off.

"Boo, what the fuck happened?"

"Excuse me, sir," Detective Andre Brown said, irritated that this man had just rudely interrupted him. "We're in the middle of a murder investigation."

Dora's eyes pierced the officer before turning to Tavares.

"Boo, what does he mean a murder investigation?"

"Like me and the snow bunny told him, he had a pillow about to cover my face and a gun about to shoot me. Snow bunny came out of the bathroom and startled him by screaming. That's when I shot the son of a bitch between the eyes and killed him."

"Boo, you just woke up and you killed someone?" Dora asked at the irony.

"Yeah, I did. If I didn't, me and ole snow bunny over there would be in the morgue instead of his ass."

"Miss Del Gada, where did you get the gun that you used to kill him?"

Tavares answered him drenched with sarcasm. "I woke up with it in my bed. Maybe my gun fairy left it for me because she knew harm was coming to me, and Boston's finest wasn't around to protect me."

"So, you're telling me on the record that someone left that gun in your bed?"

"That's exactly what I'm telling you."

Dora gave Tavares a side eye. He also wanted to know where the gun had come from.

"Before I go, I just have a few more questions for you."

"And, what would they be?" Tavares snapped because she was irritated and ready for him to go.

"Do you know the man who was trying to kill you? If you do, do you know the reason that he was here to kill you?"

"Officer Brown, let's cut the chitter chatter and bullshit. Of course, I know him. Have we sat down and ate tea and crumpets together? No, but he's from the same hood I'm from. Boston is small. Roxbury, Dorchester, and Mattapan are even smaller. So, everyone knows everyone. Why he was here to kill me, I really don't know," Tavares lied. "If you can speak to the dead, ask him. If not, you're going to have to do your job and find out."

"I will do that, Miss Del Gada. Per your story, the evidence, security cameras, and the witness's story, this is a clear case of self-defense. Therefore, no charges will be filed. I will be on my way now. If anything comes up, I'll be in touch."

Once the detective was gone, Abdora asked, "Boo, where did you get the gun?"

With skeptical eyes she answered, "Didn't you leave it for me?"

"Me? I didn't leave it for you. You weren't even in your room when I left here. Your grandmother was sitting with you while we were all gone. But, I know she ain't that gangster that she left you a gun."

"What grandmother? Boo, you're crazy. I don't have a grandmother."

"Holton's mother."

"Oh shit. She was here?"

"Yeah, we left her here with you while we handled some business."

"Let me find out I got a gangster granny, and she left a gun that saved my life."

Dora needed to make some quick calls to let his team and Holton know what had just taken place. One of the victims on his list was now a morgue resident.

"Boo, I'm not leaving. I have to go make some calls. I'll just be right outside the room. I'm going to call Bella, Cali, and Rocky to make sure they're settled at the hotel. They hit the highway when I told them what happened to you. Then, I gotta call our parents. They're at the house."

"What house?" Tavares yelled.

"You know what house. I know you just got shot and then killed someone all in twenty-four hours, but don't play retarded with me."

Dora knew what Tavares was about to ask. It was like they could read each other's minds.

"Yes, your mother is at the house, too. I wasn't going to tell her she couldn't stay there."

Rolling her eyes, Tavares said, "Don't you have calls to make?"

Alyssa was no longer shaken up from seeing a man get killed in front of her, so she sparked up a conversation with her murderous roommate.

"Is that the first person that you've killed?"

"Killed, yes; shot, no. Is that the first time you've seen someone killed?"

"Shot yes, but dead no," she said. "Wow, you're like a real gangster bitch, huh?"

"Excuse me?" Tavares snapped her neck.

"I don't mean any disrespect. But, that was the wildest shit I've ever seen, yo. I've never seen nothing jump off like that. That was wild crazy. You real busted off and saved our lives."

If Tavares had closed her eyes, she would have sworn she was talking to a black girl. The bad part was that she wasn't even trying too hard. She was simply being herself. Either she was from the hood or fucked black men.

"Alyssa, what's your story? Everyone has a story. So what's yours?"

"I'm the daughter of a wealthy, sick fuck of a doctor father and an alcoholic mother. Been molested and fucked before I was ten by my pedophile uncle. A drug addict since I was twelve. Been a mean booster since I was fourteen. I'm now twenty-four, and I haven't touched dope in thirteen months. Kicked that shit cold turkey. Hardest shit I ever did. Weighing eighty pounds and looking like a zombie was for the birds. My boyfriend brought dope to my house. When I told him to leave, he beat me up and broke a few ribs. That's why I'm here. You got a new nigga for me?"

Tavares almost fell out of the bed at the snow bunny's last sentence.

"Girl, no, and you can't say nigga to me while we're sharing a room."

"I don't mean it like that. I mean, I grew up with black people my whole life. I fuck with y'all. Come from money, but my soul is blacker than a bitch named Shaniqua. I ain't no wigger or no dumb shit like that."

"That's cool, Alyssa, but don't say nigga to me. You looking to meet someone... Fine and cool, but don't fucking say nigga."

By the time Abdora had returned, Tavares actually liked Alyssa and knew that they would kick it once they were out of the hospital. Dora hated to inform Tavares of everything she missed, but he didn't want her to feel like she was in the dark. He ran it to her in a nutshell and left her head spinning.

"Doll and Dhara were going to fight, and you and Damien are brothers? You have got to be kidding me."

Tavares felt like she was in the twilight zone.

"I left Damien for his brother," she chuckled even though she didn't find it funny whatsoever. "What are the odds that the one man I fall in love with and have children with is Damien's brother. This is crazy as crazy can get," Tavares said, totally in shock.

"Like I told everyone else, and I'm telling you, that bitch ass nigga ain't my brother. I don't give two fucks if my father's sperm made him. He AIN'T my brother. I don't give a fuck if he's lying in a coma. He AIN'T my brother."

Tavares could hear coldness in Abdora's words and decided she should leave well enough alone.

***

Monday morning at 9:00 a.m., it was like a party in Room 916. Tavares awoke to Belle yelling, "Wake your ass up. We came too far to check on you for you to be sleep."

"Well, waking me up with that big ass mouth, I wish you would go home," Tavares laughed, still half asleep.

It wasn't just Bella, Rocky, and Cali in the room. It was also Mona-Lisa, Leslie, Randee, her parents, her twins, Dhara, and Me-Ma.

"Damn, y'all could have warned me it was a party. I would have got up and washed my face and brushed my teeth."

"Dora knew we were coming, so blame your man, not us," Randee sassed.

Everyone got as comfortable as they could in the mediocre-sized hospital room. They had catered lunch and breakfast from local restaurants. Rebel ass

Randee had Patrón, Ciroc, and Remy deck. Mona-Lisa had her Bluetooth speaker. They laughed, trash talked, joked, danced, and sipped while Tavares just lay in the bed happy to be with the people she loved. They spent the day with her and Alyssa. Alyssa envied that Tavares had so many people who truly loved her. By early evening, Tavares was exhausted from the company, jokes, laughs, medications, and good time.

"Well, y'all ain't got to go home, but y'all got to get outta here," Tavares laughed. "I'm beat from you party animals."

"Yeah, my Baby Girl needs some rest. So say y'all goodbyes and let's go."

Randee, who always had no filter, said, "Before we leave, I gotta ask, where the fuck you get a gun and you're lying in bed crippled?"

"I thought Dora left it, but he didn't leave it. I have no clue who put that gun there." Holton and Dora's eyes met because they knew it was Holton's mother. She confirmed that she indeed left the gun because it didn't sit right with her just leaving Tavares with no one there. She said she didn't think Tavares would need it, but she wanted her to be safe. Therefore, she left her brand new gun by Tavares's side. Thank goodness, her intuition was right because she'd saved her granddaughter's life.

Dora hated to leave Tavares after what happened the night before, but he had to help take the twins home.

"Listen, mumma, I'm just gonna take the boys to the house, bathe them, and get them ready for bed before I come back. My mother said she could do it, but I just miss my boys and want to do it myself. Nas is right outside the door. He's your police detail's detail. Nothing is going to happen to you, and you aren't gonna kill anyone else," joked Dora.

"Oh, you got jokes. Just make sure I don't have to kill you," Tavares said with a grim smile. "Boo, you go ahead. I'm tired and will probably be knocked out when you come back. Kiss my babies a million times for me before you put them to bed."

"You got it," Dora said, kissing Tavares's eyes as he loved to do.

Everyone was gone and Tavares was enjoying the peace and quiet. It was just her and Alyssa chitchatting about the fun day with Tavares's friends and family.

"That's dope that your folks got so much love for you. I stopped getting high and lost all the people I thought were friends. My mother can't stop popping Xanax and drinking vodka long enough to come check on me. My father is so ashamed that I was a dope fiend that he just acts like I don't exist. He sends me monthly allowance checks so that he doesn't have to be bothered with me."

"Well, Alyssa, if it makes you feel any better, I just reunited with my mother and father some months ago. I never knew my father, and my mother was on a crack hiatus for about ten years. I know it's hard to tell, but we're just as dysfunctional. So, don't feel bad. I must admit, though, it's nice to have people who love me. They're always full of life and a big ball of fun. You'll see when you hang out with us."

"I would love that," Alyssa said, feeling like she was gaining her first real non-junkie friend.

CHAPTER 4

The door opened mid-conversation. Tavares was expecting it to be her doctor or Nurse Charlene. However, she was sadly mistaken. It was a surprise visit from an unwanted visitor that Tavares was sure was there to kill her vibe. They locked eyes and Alyssa instantly felt the tension in the room rise.

"Hello, Tavares. You don't look pleased to see me."

"Why would I be?" Tavares asked dryly as she rolled her eyes. "Alyssa, meet Carmen Vega, the wicked witch of Fed bitches."

Alyssa was wondering just what kind of stuff her roommate was into that she was being paid a visit from a federal agent.

"Hello, Alyssa. Be careful—your roommate here is somehow always around a dead body."

"Always is a far stretch, don't you think? I told you before. I never saw the last body that you accused me of seeing. So please don't come in here with your false accusations."

"Well, I hear that you landed in the presence of another dead body. I thought I would come check on you."

"Well, why would you do that? It was self-defense, and I'm out of your jurisdiction."

"Oh, no worries, Tavares. I know that it was self-defense. However, seeing that he almost killed you, I was wondering if you had a change of heart on wanting to talk to me."

"Absofuckinglutely NOT!"

"You think that man came here to kill you for no reason, and it had nothing to do with that gangbanger kingpin boyfriend of yours?"

"Like I told that other asshole, if you can talk to dead people, you ask him why he came here to kill me. I don't fucking know. But, what I do know is that I wish you'd hurry up and get to the point of your visit."

"I want to talk to you about your boyfriend."

"Well, Agent Vega, you wasted a plane, train, or bus ride, because I'm doing no such thing."

"Tavares, are you willing to go to jail or die, all because you think it's cute to be a ride or die chick for a gangbanger and a murdering drug dealer?"

"Hmm, let me think about it." Tavares acted like she was in deep thought. "Agent Vega, like I told you before... but, in case you forgot, let me remind you. You will fucking see pigs fly before I tell you a motherfucking thing about Abdora Santacosa. Even if I knew anything, which I DON'T, I wouldn't tell you. I would much rather take my chances on going to jail or dying before I ever wear the dishonorable badge of being a fucking rat bitch. Sorry, that's not something I would like to add to my resume. But, thanks for the offer."

Carmen hated to admit it, but as much as she hated Tavares and was going to enjoy destroying her, she was loyal to her man and the game.

"Well, Miss Del Gada, you seemed like a smart girl from the research I did. I guess it was wrong. You keep to the code of being a ride or die chick. But, you just remember that not once, but twice, I offered you the chance to help yourself. The third time we meet, you won't be so lucky. And, please don't be mistaken—there will be a third time."

"Well, Miss Vega, good luck. I look forward to the third meeting. Maybe then you'll do more than just blow smoke out your ass and actually have some legal proof or evidence to try to destroy Abdora. Now, if you could, please close my door when you leave."

Carmen dropped her business card on the table sitting in front of Tavares. As she turned to leave, Tavares picked the card up.

"Wait, Agent Vega." Tavares tore the card into pieces and said, "Have a nice night."

"I hope Abdora will be well worth the jail time that I'm going to make sure you receive for protecting him."

As the door closed, Tavares yelled, "I hate that fucking bitch."

"What was all that about?" Alyssa timidly questioned.

"A bitch with a hard-on for trying to destroy Abdora who has life fucked up if she thinks that I'll ever fold on him."

"Are the things she said about him true?"

Tavares knew better than to answer that so she gave a generic, "So she says." Then, she closed her eyes to try to calm down from the sight of Carmen Vega.

Carmen walked across the street to the Double Tree Hotel, checked in, and got settled before calling Holton. After trying him three times only to get no answer, she decided to take a shower. She was sure he would be coming through once he learned she was in town. She wanted to be fresh for his good loving. Holton saw Carmen come across his caller ID a few times and knew that he couldn't avoid her forever. Once Dolonda was settled at their daughter's house with Dhara and their grandsons, he was going to take a drive and call Carmen back. They were going to have a talk that he was sure she wasn't going to like.

Holton hated to break Carmen's heart, but he had his mind made up. He was going to cut her off, divorce Lilly, and get back with Dolonda. He knew the price he was going to pay: losing his airtight connect on drugs straight from the Dominican Republic. He would also lose his protection from all areas of law enforcement and the government meddling in his drug cartel. At this point, he was willing to start from scratch with a new plug. He had lucrative businesses and would be rich even if he never sold cocaine again.

Holton had loved Dolonda a long time. He made the mistake of letting her go once and he wasn't going to do it again now that he wasn't getting a second chance to follow his heart.

At 9:15 p.m., Dora was done playing with his sons. He'd loved all over them before bathing them and putting them to bed. He stood over Elijah and Jeremiah and watched them sleep. Being a father had changed him. It made him think even more calculatedly and decide more wisely. He wanted to be around to watch his boys grow up. He wanted to play ball with them and coach their football and basketball teams. As Dora watched his twins sleep, he knew that he wasn't getting out of the game immediately. He was planning to get out in the next year, though. Nothing was going to come between him and his family—not even the streets that he loved, controlled, and got rich from. Kissing his babies one last time, Dora prepared to go be by their mother's side.

When he went downstairs, Dora found his mother, Dolonda, Holton, and Me-Ma in the kitchen having drinks and shooting the shit.

"Alright, my boys are out. I'll be back in the morning to bring them to see their mother. Are y'all good before I head out?'

"Boy, we ain't no damn kids. We're just damn fine," Me-Ma playfully chastised. "Go be with your lady love. We got this covered."

Holton leaned in and kissed Dolonda. "Baby, I'll be back. I'm gonna roll out for a few."

"Oh, I didn't know you were leaving back out," Dolonda said sadly.

"Don't worry. I won't be gone too long."

"Jesus, y'all need to get a room," teased Dhara.

"Oh, hush your mouth," Dolonda said, throwing a potholder at Dhara.

As Holton and Dora left the house at the same time, Dora asked Tavares's father, "You good?"

"Yeah, young blood. I'm cool as a fan. I just got some business I need to take care of."

"Does it have anything to do with them sucker ass niggaz who tried to kill my baby? Because if so, I got that covered."

"Nah, I gotta end things with this bitch I been seeing and doing business with for years. I hate to sever the good pussy and sweet business deal, but I'm really in love with Dolonda. I can't have anything solid with her if I don't cut this off. Ole girl been blowing me up since Dolonda been here, so I'm just gonna do her a solid and tell her the truth. It's over."

"And, what about the business dealings?"

"There's no way I'm gonna break her heart and she's gonna still do business with me." Holton had to bellow out in laughter at the thought that Carmen wouldn't be so petty, but he knew better. "I got a shipment dropping Monday, so that gives me a few months to secure a new solid connect."

"Well, I got a plug that I never followed up with because I deal with you. I met him while me and Tavares was on vacation. If need be, just let me know, and I can reach out to him. He's a smooth Dominican nigga who's about that money."

"That's good to know, young blood, but let me get this over with so I can get back to my baby."

Giving each other dap, the men departed to their luxury cars and went on their way.

Holton retrieved his phone to call Carmen. He saw he had a missed text. It read: "I'm at the Double Tree downtown in Room 309."

Holton had to read the message several times. Did Carmen take it upon herself to pop up on him? He usually wouldn't have been mad, but he wasn't feeling her sneak move. He placed a call to her and went in as soon as she said, "Hey big daddy."

"Are you fucking doing pop-ups without speaking to me first?"

Carmen didn't like Holton's pitch.

"I had to come here on official business and decided to stay the night so that I could see you," she lied.

She actually got the call about what happened to Tavares and took the liberty of popping up on Tavares so she could have an excuse to be in Boston and see Holton.

"I'm on my way," Holton said, hanging up before Carmen could respond.

He cruised the Mass Pike listening to smooth R&B. Donnell Jones's "Where I Wanna Be" was coming through the speakers loud and clear. The lyrics were talking to him. *Oh, when you love someone, you just don't treat them bad. Oh, how I feel so sad now that I want to leave.* Only he wasn't leaving Carmen to be alone like the song was singing. He was severing ties because he knew exactly where he wanted to be. He wanted to be with Dolonda, and he was going to be the man that *she* needed him to be. Even if it meant being the bad guy to Carmen...

Holton was in deep thought trying to come up with a way he could amicably end things with Carmen without breaking her heart. The more he wracked his brain, the more he knew that wasn't possible. No matter what, she was going to be heartbroken. How could she not be? They had history and thought their futures were going to be spent together. Holton truly didn't want to hurt her. Yet, he knew that if he really wanted to be the man that intended to be with Dolonda, he had no other option but to end his decade-long relationship with his side chick.

He pulled into the parking lot of the Double Tree Hotel and climbed out of his car. He boarded the elevator ready to do the right thing. He knocked on the tall black door that read 309 and waited for it to open. Positioning herself in a sexy stance, Carmen swung the door open. She was in a red lace corset with matching panties, a garter belt, and black thigh-high stockings. Holton tried to ignore all her voluptuous curves in the enticing attire and matching red lips that looked so tasty. He reminded himself to think with his big head, not the little one. He came to end things and couldn't let Carmen's outfit or banging body sidetrack him.

Walking right past Carmen without blinking an eye, Holton said, "Carmen, we need to talk."

"Well, hello to you, too. And, the only thing I want to talk about is your fulfilling my sexual appetite," Carmen said as she tried to caress Holton's chest.

Him moving her hands away shocked her.

"Well, that's not what we're going to talk about. I need to talk about something a little more serious. So, if you could, I would appreciate it if you put on some clothes."

Becoming agitated with Holton's off behavior, Carmen tossed on a matching red silk robe and said, "Okay. Let's talk."

"I want to talk about us," he began.

Not liking the flat tone, Carmen cut him off.

"I want to talk about us as well," she snapped. "Is there a problem with us? You've been distant the last few months. You don't call like you used to. I used to get a few calls a day. Now, I'm lucky if you call at all. You don't come visit like you used to. Shit, we were together once a week or at least every other week. It was either me flying here or you flying to New York. Today, you had a problem when you thought I popped up. What's really going on?"

Holton knew Carmen was telling the truth. Since the escapade at Dhara's house when Tavares learned of him, he'd been trying to court and give all his attention to Dolonda. That left him to fall short with Carmen.

"Listen, there's no easy way to say this. I've fallen back in love with my lady."

Holton made sure not to say his wife because that would have been a blatant lie. However, he wasn't going to give Carmen any ammunition to go digging into his lady, trying to find out who she was and doing anything to come between them. He knew Carmen all too well. She had the resources to do so, and he knew it would only cause problems if she got wind it was someone new.

"I want to do right by her. The only way I can do so is if we end this affair."

Carmen's eyes welled up and her body tensed.

"What did you just say? You're leaving me? After ten years, this is way more than a fucking affair. We're in a relationship. The last eight years you've told me you love me and that I'm your woman. Let me quote you: 'She's just my wife on paper. You're my wife in real life.' Holton, you said that when you divorced Lilly, we were going to get married. What the fuck do you mean you've fallen back in love? After being out of fucking love for ten years, how do you just fall madly back in love? You sound fucking insane," Carmen said as her voice escalated and she began crying.

"Carmen, I don't know what to say. I hated to come here and have to do this. It hurts my heart that we're having this conversation, but you deserve more. You deserve someone that's going to give you all of them. I'm trying to do you a solid and not just lead you on. I can't continue to let you be the other woman, knowing that I'm in love and not going to have a future with you."

"Holton, I thought you loved me. I waited all this time for you. I love you. I wanted to spend my life with you. How could you do this to me?" Carmen sobbed.

"The things I said to you, I meant them. I never in a million years thought that I would fall back in love."

"Well, don't you love me?" the heart-aching woman questioned.

"Of course, I love you. The love I have for you is different, though. I love you because we have history. We were friends, insatiable lovers, and we made major power moves together. How can I not love you? But, with her... never mind."

"No. I want to fucking know. What's so fucking special about HER? Don't say never mind. You already crushed me, so tell me... With her, it's WHAT?"

"I'm totally *in* love with her. With her, my heart skips a beat. I feel like a teenage boy all over again. She makes me better. She makes me want to do better and be better. And, I can't do any of that if I still maintain a relationship with you. It wouldn't be fair to her and damn sure not to you. Especially when I know what you want and are expecting. I know you won't understand right now, but in the long run you will."

Carmen didn't know what to say, think, or how to feel. She wanted to appreciate that he was being honest, but the angry part of her wanted to take her gun from her purse and shoot him. She decided to use her trump card instead.

"I supply you with the rawest uncut cocaine that enters the United States. Do you really think that we're still going to do business together if you leave me? I'm the reason your business runs smoothly. I make it so that your operation stays afloat without local, state, and federal law enforcement fucking with you. Are you willing to give all that up? Are you, Holton?"

Without a second thought, Holton answered, "I am. For her and the life that we're building, I am. I'm not foolish enough to think that you could still do business without getting fucked." Holton fell out laughing as he hit Carmen below the belt with the truth. "But, make no mistake about it... Monday, I will get my shipment. I've already paid. So, unless you want me to kill you for fucking with my money, Monday my shit will be there. It better not be no bullshit, delays, or even a quarter of a brick short. Going forward, I don't give a fuck if you don't do business with me. I ate before I dealt with you, and I'm still going to eat."

Carmen couldn't believe what she was hearing. Holton was walking away completely. Letting their business go without a care in the world told her that he really was in love and turning over a new leaf. She began sobbing again. As cold as Holton was in the streets, it hurt his heart that he'd caused Carmen so much pain. He had to go.

"Carmen, I'm so sorry. Going forward, please don't contact me, and I'll do the same." Leaving his ten-year fling there crying, Holton left the hotel room knowing that he would be placing a call to his lawyer to file for divorce papers the next morning.

***

For hours, Carmen lay in bed weeping. Her heart hurt. Every time she tried to pull herself from the bed, she cried a little harder. For two hours straight she'd stained the pillows with her heavy flowing tears. She loved Holton so deeply. It wasn't until this moment that she realized just how much she really did love him. In the world that she lived in, working for the feds and the Cartel, she was required to wear a hard exterior. Holton was her soft spot. He was the reason she smiled. When Carmen's hurt shifted to anger, she promised herself that he would pay for breaking her heart. It was only fair, the spiteful woman rationalized.

The following morning, Tavares awoke to the sun beating her in the face. She hated waking up to that, but Alyssa loved to pull the blinds back. After

Alyssa's pancreatitis flared up, the ladies learned they would be together at least another few weeks. Tavares decided they were going to need some room rules. She looked over to Alyssa's bed to tell her to close the blinds, but the bed was empty. Looking to her right, she thought she was going to see Abdora still sleeping uncomfortably in the chair. What Tavares saw instead made her question whether she'd died and gone to hell or whether she was really witnessing the sight before her eyes.

Dolonda was sitting in Holton's lap. She was looking at him like a teenager experiencing love for the first time, and he was returning the look. They were cooing and kissing all over each other. Tavares's parents were so engrossed in one another that they didn't notice her watching them.

"I can't stomach another moment of this shit. Someone please shoot me."

Together, her parents both laughed.

"Good morning, sunshine," Dolonda greeted her.

"I know I got shot and damn near got killed over the last few days, but would someone like to fill me in on what all this lovey-dovey shit is between you two? And before y'all tell me some shit I'm not ready to hear, where's Abdora?"

Dolonda knew Tavares wasn't going to like what she was about to hear, so she was gonna let her father break the news to her.

"While you speak to this outspoken child of ours, I'm gonna go and get everyone breakfast. Tavares, should I bring Alyssa back something?"

"Uhh, yeah, that would only be right. It would be really rude of us to sit and eat right in front of her."

Tavares rolled her eyes. Holton didn't know whose personality she had more of, his or Dolonda's. She was truly a lethal combination of the two of them. She got her natural smart mouth and habit of honestly cutting straight to the point from both of them.

"Abdora is home with the boys. We came bright and early to sit with you while he went home to nap and get the boys ready to come to the hospital. Now about your mom and me. She's hesitant about us, because she thinks that you aren't going to approve."

"Well, at least she knows," snapped Tavares.

"Mija, I need you to cut her some slack. I love your mom. I always have. I fucked up the first go round. This time, I want to be every bit of the man I should've been when we were together two decades ago."

Tavares listened to her father intently. When he finished, she decided that she would let them be. Everyone deserved love, so if they were happy, she would at least try to be happy for them.

"Papi, what about Lilly?"

"Me and Lilly are a done deal. This morning, I called my lawyer to draw up the divorce papers. Lilly can have everything—the house, cars, and even a generous lump sum of alimony. I just want her to sign the papers. I want our marriage over so that I can move forward with your mother."

"Wow, Papi, you're dead ass serious."

"As a heart attack," laughed Holton. "I stayed with Lilly for so long because I felt guilty. I felt like if I'd been around when she needed me after your brother's death, she wouldn't have turned to crack. Once she got a habit that she never knew I was aware of, my heart and the love I had for her wouldn't let me walk out on her. But, Mija, I love Dolonda. I want to spend my life with the woman I love, not the woman I'm pretending I love out of guilt."

"Where is Lilly? She hasn't been here to see me. Not that I expect her to now that you and mommy are really like an item..."

"Well, your mother and Lilly had it out in the lobby when you first got here. Then, Lilly and I had it out."

"What?!" Tavares exclaimed.

"Yeah, it was crazy. I don't know where she is, but she hasn't been home. I'm sure she's some place getting high. Once the papers are drawn, I'm going to send my personal courier to find her and get her to sign the papers. If she acts like she doesn't want to sign them, I'm sure the money he's going to offer her will oblige her in her crack-induced state."

"Damn, Papi, I feel bad for Lilly. I got mad love for her. Word, I do. Our bond was more than her just buying from me. Over the years, we built a relationship."

Dolonda walked in on the tail end of the conversation. She couldn't resist jumping in. "You didn't feel bad for me, so don't feel bad for her."

"Dolonda, do me a favor. Don't fucking start with me," snapped Tavares. "Whatever smoke you got with Lilly is between you and her. At the end of the day, I do feel bad for her. Her husband is leaving her for his baby mama, and she got a habit that she can't kick. Forgive me, homewrecker, but I have a heart."

"I beg your pardon," Dolonda said, placing her hand on her baby-bearing hip.

"You heard me, but I'm going to let you live. Papi made it clear y'all are in love, so who am I to judge? Do what you do, but you're still a homewrecker," Tavares joked.

Alyssa returned from her CAT scan to find Tavares and her parents hanging out. She really admired her roommate.

"Wow, you guys brought me breakfast, too? Thanks so much."

"Yeah, my mom was gonna let you starve, though," Tavares said playfully.

"Oh, my God. No, I wasn't, Tavares. Why would you tell that lie?"

"Oh, relax. I was just playing. Alyssa, can you keep my mom company while my dad wheels me down to see Damien?"

"Absolutely, I might as well get to know your mom better since your parents might be adopting me once I get in good with the family."

"No worries... You can have them."

After Dolonda and the nurse washed Tavares up, Holton rolled her down to see Damien. As the father and daughter traveled two floors down, Tavares spoke to Holton about something that was weighing on her.

"Papi, do you know that Doll hasn't come up to visit me? I find that very odd."

"Yeah, I was surprised that we didn't see her either—especially since her family came to see you. I stopped in to see Damien, but she was kind of out of it. She was very quiet and looked very withdrawn. Maybe she's just trying to process Damien's current state. It's not looking too promising for him. So, don't take it personally. Right now, her focus is her son."

"I know, but me and Doll are mad close. She's been like a mother to me all these years, so why wouldn't she come check on me, too?"

When they arrived to Damien's room, Doll, Nana Dancy, and Rollo were sitting by his side. Tavares and Holton greeted everyone. Nana Dancy and Rollo replied, but Doll didn't even look up. Dancy tried to ease the stiffness in the room by making small talk. Tavares entertained her for a moment, thinking Doll would chime in. Then, anger welled up inside Tavares for the coldness Doll was showing her.

"I don't mean to be rude, but would you guys mind stepping out for a moment? I'd like to have a conversation with Doll in private." The trio obliged and headed to the hallway.

"Doll, do you have a problem with me?"

"Excuse me?" Doll replied with a deep nastiness. "Why would I have a problem with you?"

"Let's see. I'm two floors up, and you haven't even come by for thirty seconds. Then, I come in here, and you can't even bring yourself to speak to me. So, to me, that says you have a problem. If you do, let's clear the air," Tavares dished out the same tone she was receiving.

"Well, seeing that my son is lying in a coma, and you're alive and going to be just fine... Forgive me if I'm not running to be by your side like everyone else."

"Doll, you're beating around the bush. Why don't you come and tell me what's really on your mind?"

"What's on my mind?" Doll shouted. "What's on my mind is that my motherfucking son may never wake up, may never talk again, walk again, tell me he loves me, or see his kids grow up because of YOU! From the story I got, my son was out there trying to stop you from fighting his lady friend when he got shot. So, if he was never out there messing with your jealous bitter ass, I wouldn't be sitting here right now. I wouldn't be praying every moment, feeling like I'm in a fog and out of my mind."

Hearing the words that Doll was barking was like acid on Tavares's soul.

"So you blame me for this? Doll, I didn't put Damien in that bed. How fucking dare you say something so blatantly untrue and hurtful? Yes, we may have been outside that club going at it, but I'm not to blame. If you want to fault someone, blame the two hoods that were having a shootout. In case you haven't noticed, I got shot as well. And, I could have just as easily been lying in the same place that Damien is. We were at the wrong place at the wrong time. But, I get it—you have to point the finger at someone. No problem, I'll be your scapegoat."

"Fuck you," spat Doll as she began to cry. "This is your fault. All your fault."

Tavares was in total disbelief. She thought she'd literally just felt her heart break.

"Papiiiii!" Tavares yelled from the top of her lungs.

The heavy brown door swung open. Seeing that both women were now crying, Holton just grabbed Tavares and began to wheel her out.

"Wait a minute, Papi. Nana and Rollo, I'm sorry. Really sorry this happened to Damien. But, I won't bear the blame that Doll is trying to lay on me. I'm going to come back and see Damien later when she's gone."

Dancy felt bad for Tavares as she rubbed her back and said, "I know, baby."

She'd tried to reason with her daughter but no one could convince her differently. The rest of the day, Tavares was in a bad space. Nothing her parents, Dora, or Alyssa said to her eased the pain that Doll had inflicted on her. Even playing with her big bright-eyed babies, Tavares felt withdrawn. She understood that Doll was hurting and fearing the loss of her son, but to be so cruel and place the accountability on her pained Tavares in the deepest way. Dora was lying next to Tavares's bedside trying to comfort her, but she just wanted to be left alone.

"Babe, I know you mean well. I know you do, but can you go home?" Tavares said, having to chuckle at her own bluntness.

"Well, you ain't gotta tell me twice. I been kicked out of better places," teased Dora. "I'm going to go home and rock out with the boys. I'll give Holton and Dolonda a break. First you kicked them out, now me. You're a real sucker," Abdora said, kissing Tavares. "I'll be back later."

Shortly after Tavares cried herself to sleep, she felt someone gently waking her up.

"Hey, Rollo. What's up?"

"I just wanted to tell you that I'm taking Ma and Nana home. You can go down and see Damien and have some alone time with him. I'll be back in a little while. I already stopped at the nurse's station. Your nurse is coming in to take you down."

"Thanks," Tavares said, trying to find a smile.

"If it's of any comfort to you, I know you aren't to blame. We're from the streets, and sometimes shit happens. My mother is just in despair. Please don't let that shit she said to you weigh on you. Damien's gonna be fine."

Rollo kissed Tavares's forehead and headed out. Nurse Charlene came in with a big smile.

"You ready to get up out of that bed and go see your friend, pretty girl?'

"I am. Thank you."

"Tavares, you're one special lady. I see all these people coming to visit you. The floral arrangements haven't stopped. Not to mention the nurses are loving all the edible arrangements your boyfriend keeps giving us because you don't want them. And, that tells me just what kind of woman you are."

"Well, not everyone thinks I'm great," Tavares said, feeling the sadness coming back on.

"What do you mean?"

Tavares filled her nurse in on their journey to Damien's room.

"I don't have children, but I can only imagine what she's feeling. She's just grieving. But, you enjoy your time with him. Talk to him. I believe people in a coma need to feel love and energy to bring them back to life."

"I plan to. Thank you."

"When you're ready, press the call button, and the nurse at the station will bring you up."

Tavares sat and looked at Damien for a good twenty minutes through teary eyes. He was hooked up to a million tubes. He had a breathing machine and didn't even look like himself. The more Tavares sat and watched Damien totally unresponsive, the harder she cried. With her johnnie soaked from her waterworks, snot running down her face, she pulled it together.

"Damien, how did we get here? How? This wasn't how our love story was supposed to go. You were supposed to love me and be my happily ever after. The love and the bond that we had should have never allowed you to betray me. And, I should have never let myself come so far out of character that we ended up staring death in the face. Now I'm recovering from bullets, almost got murdered, and you're fighting for your life. Listen to me," Tavares sobbed. "I need you to fight. You're not no weak, wack sucker ass nigga. I need you to fight like you've never fought before. Please, Damien, I'm begging you. I never thought this was how that night would end. I wish I could turn back the hands of time." Tavares took an intermission to cry.

Wiping her tear-drenched face, she went from shattered to mad. "You better not fucking die on me. I'm not playing with you. If you die on me, I'll bring you back to life and fucking kill you again. It's not your time to go. I know they say God has a plan for us, but I don't believe this is His plan for you. You have to watch your kids grow up. You have to deal with that stupid ass baby's mother of yours. You have businesses to run. You have to take care of Doll. I don't want to do any of those things, so just cut the shit, get it together, and fight like hell to come back to us.

"Can you believe that Dora is your brother? I literally pissed my pants when he told me. How could the man that loved me when you broke me and picked me up when you kicked me down be your brother? That's some wild shit. Your papa was a rolling stone," laughed Tavares. "I see where you get it from, you trick dick bastard. Your mother and

Dhara was about to get it popping in the hospital, all because of my troublemaking ass mother. This is just too crazy for me. How are you gonna laugh at all this madness if you try to pass away? I'm going to stop speaking on death because like I told you, I will come to the pits of hell to bring you back and kill you again.

"Damien, I love you. We hit some low spots over the last year, but I promise I love you. You saved my life when I had no one or nothing. For that, I'm always going to love you. You did a lot of fucked up foul shit. You almost made me lose myself in the process of loving you, but the good you did outweighs the bad. I'm not sure where I'd be or how my life would've turned out had we not met. You made me the woman I am. You're why I know how to treat and love Abdora. You're why I'm such a book-smart, geeky hustler.

"We never got to clear the air after our breakup because it was just bullshit after bullshit. I wasn't creeping with Abdora while I was with you—at least not physically. Mentally and emotionally, he had me, though. And, that's where you lost me. Yet, I loved you so much that I maintained a platonic relationship with him. Then, I caught you fucking that trifling bitch in our spare bedroom. That's when enough was enough, and I threw in the towel. I just wanted to be loved the right way.

"I want to tell you that packing my bags, leaving the brownstone, and walking away from the life we had together was the hardest thing I ever did. But, I had to. I was loving you more than I was loving me. You were loving me with words, but your actions were breaking me. You damaged us beyond repair sleeping with that wack ass bitch in our house. I just wanted you to not only love me, but value me and appreciate me. However, that was too much for you. But, no worries, your brother is everything you weren't."

Tavares cracked up laughing, knowing that would have set Damien on fire. She just wanted to sit in silence with Damien and reminisce. She thought about how he rescued her the day they met in the Boston Commons. He tried to sell her crack because he thought she was a fiend. Noticing Tavares's beauty underneath the dirty clothes, he fell in love with the innocence he saw. So he took her home and wifed her. Together they built a whole life before she was even of age. He taught her to hustle, made her street smart, gave her a comfortable life, and put her through school. That was why she was able to blossom from a homeless caterpillar to a college-educated, self-sufficient, go-getter butterfly. They'd laughed, lived, loved, weathered storms, yelled, screamed, fought, and at times almost killed each other. Still, it was their love story, and Tavares wouldn't change it for anything in the world.

CHAPTER 5

Tavares had the same schedule for two weeks. She went to therapy and received visits from Abdora, her parents, sons, friends, and paternal side of the family. Even though Dhara and Me-Ma were back in Jersey, it felt like they were there since they called so much. They were as bad as her Jersey girls who literally called ten times a day to check on her. When Tavares wasn't being kept company, she was sitting with Damien or cracking jokes with Alyssa, who had left two days ago. She felt like she was in jail being confined to the hospital for two weeks. She was ready to go. Today the doctor was supposed to determine if she could go home and finish her therapy as an outpatient. If there was a God, Tavares would be limping out of the hospital on her crutches and back to her life.

Dora and her parents said Tavares was being a brat. So, they left together to let her sit alone. She didn't care because as far as she was concerned, they were smothering her. She wasn't being a brat, she just wanted to go the hell home. She wanted to be able to go outside and smell the fresh air, sleep in her own bed, be with her kids, and get some loving from her man.

"This doctor needs to come the fuck on," Tavares said to herself.

As if God heard her, the door opened. Tavares lit up like a Christmas tree. However, when she saw that it wasn't her doctor, the smile disappeared.

"Oh my, you not happy to see Glam-Ma?" Tavares's grandmother asked in her oh so thick accent.

"No Glam-Ma. It's not that. I'm always happy to see your pretty face."

Tavares's petite grandmother greatly resembled Lena Horne. The only difference was that she had long, thick hair to her butt and was always dressed immaculately.

"You coming to sit with me is the best part of my days. I love the time we spend together, getting to know each other more and more."

"Then, why de long face?"

"Because I thought you were my doctor. I'm ready to go home. I want out of this place. The doctor is supposed to come tell me if they're releasing me today as planned."

"Oh, no worries, baby. Dem letting you go home."

"Glammy, don't tease me like that."

"Dem are. I just hear 'em say so when I was coming in."

Tavares's face lit up again. While she was in her glory to be going home, the woman she thought about daily was in a crack house, wishing she could go home.

Lilly was no longer in control of her habit. She was cracked out. Rather than face her issues, she just kept making ATM runs to keep running from her problems. She couldn't believe that after smoking $500 a day for the last two weeks, she'd officially smoked through her bank account.

"What the fuck am I going to do when this is gone?" Lilly asked herself as she loaded one of her fifty rocks into the pipe.

The crack was working effectively. Lilly was in her numb place. She felt like she was floating in the clouds, only she couldn't stop her thoughts from confronting her. *Will Holton leave me? Can I survive if he does? How long can I stay in this crack house? Do I really want to smoke crack forever?* Lilly didn't know the answers to any of the questions running through her brain. They were interrupting the enjoyment of her high, so she reached for another fifty rock. With the purple BIC lighter in hand, she was ready to travel deeper into numbness. Lilly stopped mid-flick when she heard Stacey yelling her name.

Lilly asked herself, "Why is this bitch calling me? I gave her two fifty rocks already, she ain't getting shit else from me."

Lilly was trying to ignore Stacey, but she just continued yelling, "Lilllllly!"

Knowing Lilly could hear her, she yelled her name louder and louder with each call. Lilly put her pipe, rocks, and lighter in her purse to go see why Stacey was calling her like she'd lost her mind. As she traveled down the stairs, she found Stacey standing at the bottom with an unfamiliar gentleman.

"Why are you calling me like that?"

"This man is here to see you," Stacey said, so high that her eyes were closed.

Lilly eyed Lance, and he eyed her back even harder.

"I don't think you're here to see me. You don't even know me."

Lilly rolled her eyes.

"You're Lilly, right?"

"Yeah."

"Okay then. I mean, did I catch you at a bad time? Were you busy? Were you in the middle of something?" Lance said, not hiding that he had an idea of what she'd been doing.

Lilly became even more aggravated with the asshole that had interrupted her getting high.

"Listen, I don't know why you're looking for me, but I don't fuck or suck no one for no coke."

"Good, because I don't fuck crack-heads in exchange for crack. So now that we're on the same page, can we go someplace and talk in private? This stench of crack isn't really my thing," Lance said, throwing another low blow.

"Talk for what?" Lilly snapped.

"I have some papers for you."

With one eyebrow raised, Lilly asked, "Papers?"

Not waiting for a response, Lance opened the door knowing that Holton's soon-to-be ex-wife would follow. They stepped onto the small porch, and Lilly closed the door behind her. Lance passed the thick envelope to Lilly and patiently waited for her to open and read the enclosed documents. As Lilly read, her eyes grew bigger and bigger. She then looked from the papers to Lance, from Lance to the papers.

"A fucking divorce?" she bellowed from the top of her lungs. "Is Holton fucking kidding me?" she asked, enraged. "This motherfucker wants to leave me and is such a coward that he sends you."

Lilly's eyes wanted to cry, but she was so full of anger that the tears wouldn't come. "Listen, lady, I'm just the messenger. Don't shoot me."

Lilly did one better. She whipped her phone out of the back pocket of her jeans that were starting to sag. She called Holton and didn't even let him get a hello out before she went in.

"You coward ass motherfucker. I've been married to you for twenty years. I've given you my best and never cheated on your lowdown dirty dog ass. Now that I'm at my worst, you're going to just leave me. Leave me like I'm some bimbo bitch or one of your many mistresses. You don't even want to try and fix us? How fucking dare you just send some thug ass drug dealer over here to deliver the paperwork? You got a lot of fucking nerve, Holton Montiago. A lot of fucking nerve." Lilly continued her rant for another two minutes with Holton just listening.

As Holton stood in Tavares's hospital room with Dolonda, Vadaleen, and Abdora, he was listening to Lilly fuss about the divorce papers she'd just received. He knew the call would be coming once she got served, but he didn't care. He wanted what he wanted and that was a divorce. It was just that simple. Everyone in the room could hear someone on the other end of the phone screaming from the top of their lungs. While everyone just looked, outspoken Tavares asked, "Who the fuck is screaming at you like that, Papi?"

At the same time Tavares was questioning who was on the phone, Lilly was yelling, "Aren't you going to fucking say anything? Anything at fucking all?"

Holton remained calm, cool, and suave as always.

"What do you want me to say? What? I really don't want to disrespect you because that's not me, but we're over. You've stayed with me all these years because I take care of you and afford you the luxury to live like a boss and still get high. I've stayed with you all these years out of guilt, but those days are over. I'm a fucking boss, so how the fuck can I be with an active base head? It's time for you to stand on your own two feet and for me to live my life."

Lilly cut him off. "Are you fucking leaving me to be with that bitch Dolonda?"

"She's not a bitch, so please watch your mouth. And, you don't want me to answer that."

"Yes the fuck I do. Tell me the fucking truth! Is she the reason?" Lilly asked through her deep sobbing.

"She's a big part of the reason, but not the only reason. I want to be with her and do right by her. I want her to be my woman, not my mistress. We're married for show. We aren't in love. I do me and you do you. We live in separate quarters and have sex once every few months. This shit is played out."

Lilly started wailing with tears. Everyone was aware of who Holton was talking to on the phone. All three of the women in the room felt bad for Lilly— even the two who hated her guts. They were getting their wish of Holton leaving Lilly, but to hear her crying and screaming made them feel bad as women.

To make things less awkward, they continued talking to each other and packing Tavares's stuff up.

"Holton, please don't leave me. I love you. I promise I'll get clean. I can't live without you. You're the only man that I want. I give you my word that I'll get my shit together and be the wife that you used to love."

Holton wasn't moved by Lilly's tears or begging him to stay. "You have two options. Either sign the papers and take the generous offer that's in the papers, or don't sign the papers and I'll contest having to give you shit when it goes to court. Now, if you sign the papers right now, there's a signing bonus—a bonus that I'm sure you need since I checked your account, and it's on empty."

Lilly tried to get gangster and said, "I ain't signing a motherfucking thing. I'm gonna take you to the cleaners. Then, let's see if that bitch wants you when you're broke."

Holton broke out laughing.

"Lilly, don't sign the papers and watch you walk out of court with nothing but the clothes on your back. You better read them papers again and see that I'm being way more generous than I have to be. Remember, in twenty years you haven't contributed one red cent to this marriage. All that you've done is spend, spend, spend. And, I'm pretty sure you can use that ten-thousand-dollar signing bonus since your account is empty and you can't get shit else from me."

Holton didn't wait for a response. He powered his phone off. He knew his wife well enough to know she wasn't going to gamble walking away with absolutely nothing.

Lilly's heart stopped when she heard the notification of the call dropping. She felt like her world had just crashed, knowing that it was really over and Holton was leaving her. She cried and cried. She was so caught up in her sorrow that she forgot that she wasn't alone.

"Listen, I'm just a drug deal thug who delivers papers, so either you gonna sign or you aren't. I don't have all day. So, what you gonna do?"

"Where is your compassion?" Lilly sobbed.

"I'm not paid to deliver compassion. You gonna have to find that inside in the pipe that just got you served divorce papers. Either you're signing and taking this ten racks, or I'm out of here."

Lilly snatched the pen he was extending to her. She knew better than to think Holton was joking when he said she would get nothing. She signed the papers that would end her twenty-year marriage, staining them with her tears that wouldn't stop coming. When she was done, Lance took the papers and passed her ten thousand dollars in hundreds.

"Don't spend it all in one place," Lance said, laughing as he departed the porch and headed on his way to collect his fee for delivering the signed papers.

Lilly made her way back into Stacey's feeling like her legs were going to give out on her. She was weak and feeling discombobulated. Her mind and heart were both racing. She hurried up the dirty stained carpeted stairs to get high. She had to escape the shattered reality that she was living. The man she loved her whole life was finally ending things. Lilly didn't know how she would take care of herself because Holton had done it since she was twenty-one.

Picking up the crack pipe, she said, "You just cost me my life and my marriage. Now, you're all I have." She went to light the loaded pipe and stopped. She dropped the lighter and pipe, and then curled up in a ball and cried for hours.

While Lilly was sick with heartbreak, her mother-in-law was happy as a pig in shit. She couldn't wait to get out of the hospital to bask in her happiness from the conversation she'd had the pleasure of hearing. She called her daughter Veronica to share her good news.

"Hey, mommy. What's going on?"

"I'm just leaving the hospital."

"How's Tavares?"

"She's good. They released her, so I'm following your brother to her house. I have some good, good news. Call your sister, Vanibell, on the three-way."

"Hey sissy," Vanibell answered.

"It's me and mommy. She has some good news that she wants to share with us. Mommy, you there?" Veronica questioned, as she anxious to hear what had her mother sounding so happy.

"I just wanted to share with you girls that my Holton is finally leaving that damn ass Lilly. He served her with divorce papers. She called crying and crying, begging and pleading, but it's finally overrrr," Vadaleen sang.

"Oh, my God, mommy. Is that your good news?" Vanibell asked, in shock that her mother was so ecstatic for her brother leaving his wife.

"You damn right. Best damn news I had all year. I been waiting forever and ever for my son to leave that no good wench."

Veronica couldn't help but cry out in laughter.

"Vanibell, that's your mother."

"She was your mother first," Vanibell shot back.

"Mommy is foul, but Brother did need to leave her," Veronica co-signed. "Lilly was like a wife fixture rather than a wife. She hasn't done anything in all these years to contribute to the family or their marriage. Shit, she didn't even bring a dish when we had our family gatherings. What kind of shit is that? Vanny, you telling me you can remember once in twenty years her cooking something or even hosting something at their house? I sure as hell can't."

"You two are some foul heffas," Vanibell said on the other end of the phone, shaking her head.

"Foul me damn ass," Vadaleen snapped. "My son need him a good woman. A woman that can do more than smoke drugs and spend all him damn money."

"Mommy, Holton stayed all these years, so we can't blame her. Not only did he stay, he allowed her to not work and to not contribute."

"What the hell ever," Vadaleen said, not giving a good Goddamn what her youngest daughter was talking about.

They continued the debate for about twenty minutes with Vanibell in the minority.

"All I'm saying is she's a woman just like us. So, I can only imagine how she feels. Despite her habit and her flaws, she's still human, you two coldhearted heffas," Vanibell tried to reason.

"Hearing her cry, I really did feel bad for a quick moment. Then, I came to me senses. Well, listen. It was nice to share my great news with my two favorite girls and chitchat, but I'm pulling up to your niece's house. Holton, Dolonda, and Abdora have put together a small gathering to welcome Tavares home. Make sure y'all stop by when you get off." They both agreed and the women hung up.

Tavares and Abdora exited their car and entered the house with Vadaleen right behind them. Holton and Dolonda were in the driveway still in the car.

"You were quiet the whole ride here. Are you okay?" Holton inquired.

"Yeah, I'm fine."

"Then, why all the silence and the down look on your face?"

"I was just in deep thought."

"About what?" Holton asked, having a feeling he knew the answer to his own question.

"About the conversation you had with Lilly. Are you really going to divorce her?"

"Is water wet?" Holton asked Dolonda with a serious tone while looking her straight in the eyes. "Do you not want me to?" he asked, confused about why Dolonda seemed down rather than happy.

"Holton, that's a stupid question. I just never saw any of this coming. If someone had told me that we would be here at this very moment after our initial visit at my house before I got clean, I wouldn't have believed it. When you started calling me and trying to push up on me, I still didn't believe you were sincere. I thought it was all about you trying to get me in bed. But, the last few months, I've completely fallen for you, no matter how much I tried to fight it. Being with you, talking to you, touching you, and loving you brought me back to the happy place I used to be in before you walked out and I hit the lowest point of my life. I can't stand to go through that again. Not that I'm weak enough to turn back, but I just don't want to endure that kind of pain. I love you. I've always loved you, and I just don't want to get my hopes up for a future together if it's not real."

"Dolonda, let's have this conversation one time and one time only. I not only loved you twenty something years ago, I was madly IN love with you. I was young. I grew up in a culture where you stand by your woman, you marry her, you take care of her, and be a standup man for your family. Even though I was in love with you, it felt wrong to walk out on Lilly knowing she was having my baby, and we had planned a life together. I was young and didn't know any better. I married her because that's what I thought I was supposed to do, so to speak. I never stopped thinking about you, wondering about you, or even loving you—not even after I found out you was strung out.

"I cut my mistress off when I left here that night. In cutting her off, I didn't just lose pussy. I lost my business. But, I had to do it if I wanted to be a standup man to you. The next morning, I went and filed divorce papers. You're the woman that I want. I admire your fight to regain control of your life. I love your smile, your dimples, the way you walk, how smart you are, and that big ole butt of yours. I want to be your strength and for you to be my weakness. I want to be every bit of the man that you deserve and that I should've been to you back then. We can't change the past, but what we can do is live in the present and build together if you're up for it. I'm not no fairytale kind of nigga, but if you'll have me, I want to be your Prince Charming."

Holton laughed and Dolonda blushed.

"I know that was kind of corny, but I mean it. God makes no mistakes, and He's giving us a second chance. I'm running with it. So, you with it or not?"

Dolonda didn't answer with words. She used her lips to tell Holton yes.

***

Five weeks passed and Tavares couldn't believe that it was already the week before Christmas. Time had flown by her. She had a daily schedule of doing her in-home therapy. She was through the roof happy that it was done, and she'd made a full recovery. She was hanging with her grandmother and spending time with her parents when they were actually in town. She was also visiting Damien every day for an hour, spending time with her A-1s since day one, and keeping busy with Abdora and the boys. Tavares was happy that her favorite holiday had rolled around with all the chaos of the last few months.

Christmas was going to be at the Jersey estate. It took a lot of begging, pleading, and damn near bribing Dhara to let her host. Tavares had planned everything and didn't care if she didn't get one present. She was getting the one present that was priceless. All her family and friends would be traveling to New Jersey to spend the holiday with her, Abdora, and her kids. It would be the Montiagos, Dora's family, her crew from Boston, the Jersey girls, and all Abdora's friends. This was going to be a holiday they wouldn't forget if it was up to Tavares. She was ready to catch her flight to Jersey for the next two weeks. With Dora and the boys already gone, she had one stop before she caught her 6:00 p.m. flight.

When she arrived at Tuft's New England Medical Center, Tavares did her daily ritual. She stopped at the gift shop and got Damien some fresh flowers, made her way upstairs, and made a pit stop at the nurse's station.

"Merry Christmas, Charlene."

"Thanks, honey. Same to you. Do you have any big plans?"

"Actually, I do, and I'm so excited. Dora and I will be hosting Christmas at our house for all of our family and friends."

"Aweee, that sounds really nice."

"Do you have any special plans?"

"My husband and I will be going to my in-laws' to do the same thing we do every year."

"Well, I hope you guys have a very Merry Christmas," Tavares said, sliding Charlene an envelope.

"Oh you didn't have to give me anything," Charlene said with a big smile.

"I know I didn't, but I wanted to. You and I bonded when I was here. And, you take very great care of Damien. I just wanted to give you something to let you know how much I appreciate you. Please don't open it until Christmas, and do something nice for yourself."

Tavares was so grateful for Charlene, who went above and beyond in caring for Damien, and she hoped she did something nice for herself with the

$500 she'd put in the Christmas card. After giving Charlene a hug, Tavares went to sit with Damien. She changed the floral bouquet before taking a seat.

"Damien, I won't be here for Christmas, so I just wanted to come see you before I leave. I'll be back after the New Year, so you get a break from me. I would think you're tired of hearing my voice and would just wake your ass up. You've always been stubborn, though. You and I have to have a talk. I know I told you don't die on me, but with every day that I come here and see you like this, it tears me apart more and more. And, to be honest, I don't know how much more I can take of this. This isn't you. I'm used to you being full of life, cocky, talking shit, and living life to the fullest. This isn't you, and I don't think it's fair to make you live like this.

"I remember on several occasions you said if you were to die, don't bring you back to life and don't ever let you live on life support. So, I'm not sure why we're going against your wishes. I think everyone knows that those were your requests. However, because of the sensitive state that Doll is in, no one has mentioned it. The doctors are saying that your condition hasn't changed since you came in here almost two months ago. You have all these stupid ass tubes in you, and that machine is breathing for you. This isn't how you want to live. I know it isn't. I want to remember you for who you were, not like this. It's time to let you be free.

"I know Doll isn't going to like it, but I plan to bring it up to her when I come back. She hasn't spoken to me since we had it out and she blamed me for you being in this condition, but it's time someone bites the bullet and has this talk with her. She's going to yell, scream, and curse me out, but I just want to do what's right for you. She's holding on to hope, and I get that. Still, this just isn't what you wanted, and I want to obey your desires. If you'd made any sign, I mean one single sign of improvement, I wouldn't even be having this talk with you. However, you haven't. Doll can't make you live like this forever because she can't let go. Some may say I'm out of pocket since we aren't together and I'm not your wife, but I don't give a fuck. You made it clear what you wanted, and this ain't it."

Tavares talked to Damien for a little while longer before kissing his head. "Damien, I'm giving you two weeks to do something, and then it's going to be World War Three when I tell your mother my thoughts. Merry Christmas, Asshole." One more kiss and Tavares was heading to catch a cab to the airport.

In the days leading up to Christmas, Lilly was on Tavares's mind and heart. It was two days before Christmas and she so desperately wanted Lilly to answer her call and let her know she was at least alive. She'd been calling her day in and day out since she heard the conversation between Lilly and her father. Lilly wouldn't answer, though. Every time she saw Tavares calling, she wanted to pick up. However, her heart wouldn't allow it. She was wallowing at rock bottom in her addiction, and she wasn't ready to face the world—especially not Tavares. Tavares knew Lilly wouldn't answer, but she called her anyway. Getting no answer, she left the hundredth message.

"Lilly, I don't know where you are, but I just pray that you're okay. I want you to know that I'm here for you. If I can help you or you need anything, pleaseee don't hesitate to call me. I love you. You know that. And, no matter what goes on with you and my father, you're always going to be in my life. I love you, and please call me. I'm terribly worried about you." With tears coming down her eyes, Tavares wrapped up her message. "Please, Lilly, call me."

Tavares hung up and cried for Lilly as she continued to Jersey Gardens Mall. Her ringing phone broke her crying spell.

"Hello?"

"Boo, what's the matter?" Abdora questioned.

"I just tried to call Lilly. Of course, she didn't answer, but I'm just so worried about her."

"Boo, Lilly is going through it. You have to just let her be, and let her reach out to you when she's ready. She's battling addiction and trying to come to terms with the fact that your father walked out on her. That's a lot."

"I know it is, but I just need to know that she's okay. I've stopped at Stacey's house a million times since I came home from the hospital. Every time, they say she hasn't been there since the day she got the divorce papers."

"Boo, dry your eyes. Put a smile on your face, and try to cheer up. All our family and friends will be here tomorrow. I need you in a good space."

"I'm going to be okay."

"Where are you now?"

"I'm heading to Jersey Gardens Mall to grab a few things. Is there anything that you need me to do?"

"Me and the boys are heading to my mother's, but if you need me to do anything, just let me know."

"No, everything is covered. The event planners will be at the house at 7:00 p.m. to transform the indoor basketball court into the dining space. All the food is at the house. I seasoned the meats yesterday. My mother, Dhara, Glam-Ma, and Me-Ma are coming at 7:00 as well so we can do all the prep work. Oh shit," Tavares said, remembering that two extra stoves were being delivered. "They're dropping the two industrial stoves off in about an hour. Can you let them in?"

"I'm on it, Boo. Do you think those three stoves will be enough?"

"Yeah, because on top of those three stoves, we have the grill and the smoker. And, your mother and grandmother are going to take stuff to their houses and use their stoves. Listen, Boy, I planned this to a T. Once that food is in, all we have to do is wake up, open presents, and get this party started."

"Okay then," Dora laughed. "Let me get to the house to wait for the delivery people. I'll get with you later."

"Laterrrrr," Tavares said, hanging up the phone to get her shit done.

By 7:00 p.m. all the ladies were at the house with aprons, gloves, and hair nets on ready to get down to business. Tavares's kitchen was so massive that all the women were doing their thing without being in each other's way. Dolonda was on Spanish dishes. She was prepping her rice and beans, three pork shoulders, and seafood paella. Glam-Ma Vadaleen had the West Indian dishes on lock. She was making oxtails, steak, curry chicken, jerk chicken, and pigeon peas and rice. Me-Ma and Dhara had all the southern dishes. Christmas couldn't take place without mac-and-cheese, collard greens, cabbage, potato salad, and macaroni salad. Since Tavares had seasoned all the meats, she was only doing prep work and helped as she was needed. It didn't sound like a lot, but they were making five pans of every dish, so they were working hard.

Most people played Christmas carols while cooking, but they were listening to trap music and reggae, per Tavares's playlist. As they entered the kitchen, Dora and Holton looked at each other before Holton spoke.

"What in the hell are y'all listening to? Y'all in here listening to gangster rap. Where's the holiday music?"

"Listen, Papi. We're a family full of gangsters. Fuck that soft holiday shit," Tavares joked. "Glammy was just in here getting low to the snow man. You better stop playing."

"Tell him, baby. Tell him. Glammy still got them moves."

Dora just shook his head.

"Glammy, your granddaughter got you listening to Jeezy?"

"I thought he was the snow man?"

"Glammy, that's his nickname. Don't listen to Abdora. He's a hater."

"I have a suggestion," Dhara chimed in. "Won't y'all get out."

"I know that's right," Me-Ma co-signed. "I don't know what y'all in here for and ain't doing a lick of cooking."

"See Darlene, we came to help," Holton said, slapping Dolonda's butt.

"Y'all ain't needed," Me-Ma made clear. "So, just get the hell out."

Not having to be told twice, Holton and Dora returned to the man cave. By midnight, all the prep work was done. All the ladies poured themselves a drink and made their way to see the transformation of the indoor basketball court.

"Wow."

"Oh, my God."

"How beautiful."

"Damnnnn," were their responses.

"Oh, my goodness, they did exactly what I asked."

Tavares was jumping out of her skin with joy as she looked at the room. It was decorated red and gold. There were four long banquet tables to hold all the food, two bars, and three desert tables for all Cali's sweets she would be bringing. In each corner of the room were twelve-foot Christmas trees that were exquisitely decorated in red and gold decorations. The presents underneath the trees were wrapped to match the décor. Every other table had a red or gold linen tablecloth with elaborate centerpieces and formal place settings.

"Tavares, you really did an amazing job," her mother complimented.

"Thanks, mommy. Okay, ladies, let's get us a cat nap so we can get up at 4:00 a.m. and put the food in the oven."

"I like the sound of that," the ladies said as they made their way to their resting places.

By 11:00 a.m., everything was done. All the dinner food was cooked and laid out. The house was cleaned up. They had trashed the wrapping paper from the present exchange between Dora, Tavares, their parents, grandparents, and the literal one hundred unneeded presents they'd bought their children who weren't even old enough to open anything. The house was smelling and feeling like Christmas. Everyone was off to get dressed. Tavares and Dora snuck in a quickie while Tavares's parents dressed themselves and the twins.

After Abdora had bent and twisted Tavares every which way, giving her a mean dose of Christmas sex, they were ready to prepare to host what was going to be an amazing day.

"Boo, get in the shower, and I'll lay your clothes out."

"Sounds good to me," Dora said, walking to the shower with his Mandingo penis swinging.

Tavares laid out their clothes, wrapped her hair, and was ready to shower so they could get the party started. Dora came out of the shower, looked at the bed, and screamed.

"Ayo, come here, Boo!"

Returning to their master suite, Tavares looked at Abdora, who was staring at the bed.

"What's the matter?"

"Boo, what the fuck is that?"

"What do you mean? That's your outfit, what's wrong with it?"

Dora looked at Tavares and cracked up laughing.

"I ain't wearing that shit."

"Yes, you are."

"No the fuck I ain't. Boo, I'm not wearing no fucking button-up shirt, shoes, and slacks."

"Abdora, you can't fucking be serious. It's Christmas. Everyone else is going to be dressed. You're going to be wearing what exactly?"

"Boo, that outfit is stupid and I ain't doing it."

Tavares just folded her arms while giving Abdora the stare down.

"Matter of fact, I don't give a fuck. Look like a scrub on Christmas," Tavares said and left Abdora standing alone.

Dora yelled to the door that had just slammed behind Tavares, "I'm gonna be a fresh scrub. And, best believe ain't none of my niggaz coming dressed like this shit you got laid on this bed. I bet not even none of your uncles or father will have no shit on like that."

Tavares was ignoring Abdora by blasting music. Dora ripped the tags off and tossed on his gray Champion sweatpants, his crisp white tee, and fresh out the box red, white, and grey Jordans. Tavares could dress like she was going to a ball, but he wasn't having it. After getting dressed, he headed down to entertain the guests.

By 2:00 p.m., the house was popping. DJ Dex was rocking out, spinning all the hottest tracks. The hired staff was walking around serving appetizers and drinks. Dora was downstairs in the man cave with Bryce, Mid, Maniac, Hawk, Nas, and Bam-Bam blowing sour and shooting dice. Holton, his father, brother-in-laws, and his brothers, Harvey and Hayden, were in the movie theater sipping Remy 1738, sitting in the reclining seats watching football.

All the children and teenagers were running wild with no one bothering them or caring to tell them different. The old lady gang that consisted of Dolonda, Dhara, Tavares's aunts Veronica and Vanibell, along with Dhara's sisters, were two stepping like they still had it. Me-Ma and Glam-Ma were holding Jeremiah and Elijah hostage from all the guests while they hung out with the mothers of Tavares and Dora's friends in the meeting room. Tavares was in the kitchen with Bella, Randee, Leslie, Cali, Rocky, Ebony, and Mona-Lisa shooting the shit, smoking, taking mad pictures, and taking shots of Patrón. The house was full of people mixing and mingling and having a ball. Tavares couldn't wait to see all the pictures the photographer was taking and just capturing everyone in the moment.

At 4:00 p.m., the half-intoxicated adults and hungry children were ushered to the breathtaking makeshift event room for dinner. Every person who came in was blown away with the over-the-top Christmas décor. They had four serving lines, so everyone was sitting and eating in no time. Dex was still spinning and the energy in the room was a force to be reckoned with. Tavares was walking around checking on her guests and thanking everyone for spending their holiday with her and Abdora. Abdora was stuffing his face like he was a guest and not a host, leaving the social butterfly to do the hosting for both of them.

While dessert was being served, Holton excused himself from the table with his parents, siblings, brother-in-laws, and Dolonda. He made his way over to Dex.

"Could you kill the music for a moment and let me borrow your mic?"

Conceding to the request, Dex let Holton have the floor. Holton was half intoxicated and half nervous.

"Merry Christmas, everyone. If you don't know, I'm Holton, Tavares's father. I just wanted to take a few moments to thank my daughter and Abdora for welcoming us into their home on this beautiful day. They really went above and beyond for us. When I look around this room, it's a beautiful sight to see family and friends together having such a wonderful time. With all this joy, and love in the air, I couldn't think of a more perfect time to come up here. I... uhhh... have something that I would like do."

"Boy, would you spit it out for God's sake?" his father, Big Harvey, shouted playfully.

"Ma, you better get your husband before I give him these hands."

"Boy, please. They don't call me Big Harvey for nothing. Don't let this white skin and ole age get your ass knocked out."

Everyone in the room was laughing at the father and son joking.

"Okay, since the only man in the room wants to rush me, let me hurry up. Dolonda, would you come here for a moment?"

Dolonda hated being in the spotlight, but she got up from her seat and went to the front of the room where Holton was standing.

"Dolonda, I want to tell you in front of all these beautiful people that I love you. I've loved you a very long time."

Tavares's mother was blushing from ear to ear.

"I told you not too long ago, if you would have me, that even though I couldn't be the fairytale man, I wanted to be the man you so deserve. I want to be your strength while you be my weakness. I want to be your provider, protector, best friend, and biggest supporter. You make me feel like a teenager in love every moment that we're together. I want that feeling for the rest of my life," Holton said, taking a box out his sweat suit jacket and getting down on one knee.

Out of sheer shock Dolonda's mouth dropped, and she touched her chest with both hands.

"Will you spend the rest of your life with me?" Holton asked with a ring that even the furthest guest in the room could see because it was so big and sparkly.

"WHAT THE FUCK," Tavares said out loud.

It wasn't until every pair of eyes in the room turned and looked at her in disbelief did she realize that the outburst didn't take place in her head. It had actually come out of her mouth, and that wasn't her intention. Dolonda and Holton looked at their daughter with hurt in their eyes. Dora, who was standing by her side, had a look of fury on his face.

"I just can't with you two," Tavares said, not caring that everyone was looking at her.

Ignoring his daughter, Holton said, "Dolonda, look at me. I want to spend my whole life and world with you."

Dora grabbed Tavares and dragged her with force out the door that was a few feet away.

"Let's go. Me and you need to talk right fucking now."

Hearing the applause, Tavares looked at Dora and sarcastically said, "I guess she said yes."

Abdora was infuriated. "What the fuck was that? That was some real foul, raunchy ass disrespectful shit you just did. What is your fucking problem?" Dora asked through clenched teeth, which confirmed to Tavares just how enraged he was. "You owe them an apology for ruining what was supposed to be a special moment for them."

"I don't owe them shit," Tavares spat.

"Can we get to the root of the fucking issue here? I've never been as mad or as disappointed in you as I am right now! Those are your fucking parents!" Abdora screamed. "It's not hard to tell that they love each other and are head over heels for one another. So why the fuck can't you just be happy for them and support them?"

"I don't have to do shit but stay black and die."

"Yo for real, Tavares, you're pushing my buttons. You a spoiled fucking brat, and everything is NOT about you," Abdora said, taking his index finger and poking Tavares in the forehead. "Since you found them, they've been there for you, tried to build with you, and they were by your bedside and helping with the kids the whole time you were in the hospital. Even when you gave your mother your ass to kiss, she was there for you. They don't need your fucking approval. But, who the fuck are you to try and make them feel bad for loving each other? You need to grow the fuck up and get over yourself."

Dora left Tavares standing in the kitchen so he could go clean up the ignorance she'd just displayed. While Tavares was in the kitchen having a drink, in walked her parents and Glam-Ma.

"Tavares, we want to talk to you."

"I don't want to talk. Y'all want to get married, please do so. You don't need my blessing."

Through teary eyes, Dolonda asked, "Why can't you just be happy for us?"

Silence was all that you could hear.

"Tavares, I fucked up. I fucked up bad. I can't change the past, but I'm trying and fighting like hell to build with you. I love your father, and he loves me. Why can't you just be happy for us?" Dolonda sobbed.

Holton pulled Dolonda close to comfort her.

"Holton, why don't you take Dolonda and help her get herself together before everyone comes back in. I want to talk to my granddaughter in private."

"Glam-Ma, I'm fine."

"You're not fine, because what you said out there indicated that you don't approve of your parents' relationship. Can you just talk to me?"

"Glammy, why are they getting married? Just tell me why? I just feel like my mother needs to work on herself, rebuild herself, and not throw herself into Papi. And, Papi needs to be divorced before getting engaged to Mami."

"Tavares, sometimes life is complicated. The best way I can help you understand this is like this. You love Abdora. I see love when you're together, when you look at him, and even when you talk about him. How would you feel if your sons wanted to interrupt that love? The same love I see between you and Abdora, I see between Holton and Dolonda. I've never seen your father happier. He loves that woman, and she loves him. At the end of the day, nothing else should matter. You're grown with your own man and family. Allow them to have the same happiness that you're enjoying."

By the time Abdora had ripped her a new asshole and her grandmother gave her a big girl talk, she knew they were right. Her parents deserved to be in love and for her to be happy for them. Tavares pulled her big girl panties up and went to find her parents to apologize. She found them in the meeting room.

"I owe you guys an apology. I think I wanted you each to myself and not for each other, and that's not right. That's selfish and wrong. I apologize. You have my blessing on your engagement. I mean that from the bottom of my heart."

Dolonda jumped to her feet and wrapped her arms around Tavares. Holton was happy that he was finally gonna have peace between his two ladies. By the time everyone came inside, the party continued like nothing had ever happened. Dora saw Dolonda hugging her daughter and was happy that Tavares heard him loud and clear.

He congratulated the newly engaged couple while joking, "Damn, Holton, now you gonna make me have to put a ring on it."

"Don't do me no favors," Tavares fired back playfully.

The four spoke for a little bit before going back to partying hard. By the time the night ended, Tavares, Abdora, and all their guests had truly enjoyed a Christmas they would never forget. Tavares couldn't count her blessings enough for being able to spend Christmas in her home with all the people who truly meant the world to her. With the new year around the corner, she was ready to see what was in store. Hopefully, it wouldn't be as eventful a year as 2012 had been.

CHAPTER 6

New Year's Eve rolled around and Tavares opted out of partying. She believed in the old saying that how you brought the new year in would be what you would be doing all year. So, she just wanted peace and quiet. She was tired of chaos, shootings, drama, police, and all the things that she'd endured over the last few years. She wanted a year of calmness and just regular living. Therefore, she wanted to be home in bed with her babies when the ball dropped. She'd cleaned the house, finished the laundry, and had money in her wallet. She was following the old black saying of all the things you were supposed to do when the new year came in. She tried to convince Dora to go to King's and bring the new year in with their friends, popping bottles and partying like a rock star, but he declined. He said if Tavares was staying home with the boys, he was too.

After having lobster, shrimp, baked potatoes, and salad, Tavares cleaned up, showered, bathed her babies, and was in bed maxing and relaxing with Dora on the other side of the bed by 11:00 p.m.

"I think I like this," Dora laughed.

"You like what?"

"Just us home with the boys… No company, no partying, just us cooling like regular folks do. I think I could get used to this."

"No, you can't," Tavares said, pulling Abdora's card. "You and your team are used to living and balling like rock stars. You would go out of your mind doing this all the time."

"Well, you know what they say: new year, new beginnings. So, I'm going to try to be out less, not working at the club as often and not always in the streets."

"We'll see," Tavares chuckled. She didn't mind the life they lived. She just wanted some peace for a change.

At 11:30, Dora moved the boys to their rooms and returned to cuddle with his lady. When the ball dropped, they popped a bottle of Don P, toasted, kissed, and finished watching Dora's favorite movie, *Boyz In the Hood.*

"Boo, what time do you guys' flight leave in the morning?" Tavares questioned, knowing that her house would be hectic because Dora's boys were meeting at their house.

"We have to be at the airport at noon, so the fellas aren't coming here until probably 10:30 or 11."

"I can't believe y'all are going to Belize and not taking y'all's women."

"We needed a getaway with just the fellas, but don't worry. You and I are going to take a trip soon."

"Yeah, yeah, yeah," Tavares said, not mad at all. She was happy that Dora was going to enjoy himself with his friends.

"What time is the flight back to Boston for you and the boys?"

"We leave at 3:30 p.m., so we'll be heading to the airport right behind y'all. My parents are going to pick us up, because they want to see the boys before they head to whatever sunny destination they're off to now."

True to his word, the next morning Dora's boys were buzzing the gate at 10:45 a.m. Tavares had made a light breakfast for them, knowing they would need the food before they started pre-gaming with the Remy. Bryce came in as always talking shit.

"I knew breakfast better had been being cooked when I came through here."

"Nigga, don't start," Tavares said, waving the spatula in her hand at him. "You're the biggest nigga of them all, and I would hate for you to leave hungry."

"You wouldn't do that to your favorite brother."

"You're right, but I'll do it to you because you ain't my favorite," Tavares laughed.

"You a motherfucking liar," Bryce said, pulling Tavares's hair.

Within ten minutes, all the fellas had arrived and started making plates. Tavares had to talk her shit before they left.

"I want to know who the fuck do y'all think y'all are to be going to Belize?"

"Bosses, that's who," Maniac answered for everyone since they were busy trying not to come up for air out of their plates.

"Blah, blah, blah," Tavares said, rolling her eyes. "Most hood niggaz go to Vegas or Miami. Here you bougie ass hood niggaz want to go to Belize, and got the nerve to not be taking the women with y'all."

"Awweee man. Here you go," Hawk said, having heard that same statement at home all week. "We're always taking the wifeys on trips. We needed a fellas trip."

"I'm just giving y'all a hard time. Y'all have fun, but not before y'all clean my fucking kitchen up."

Tavares left them to devour the breakfast while she went to pack her and the boys' stuff for her trip back to Boston.

With Dora on his way to paradise, Tavares, Jeremiah, and Elijah were en route to Boston. The boys slept the whole flight, and Tavares tried to prepare herself for going back to the hell of having to deal with Damien still in his coma. At four o'clock, she arrived at Logan International Airport. Her parents were there waiting, still glowing and in love. They helped Tavares to the car with the babies and were on their way.

"Mija, what's the first stop?"

"Let's go to my house. I want to go grab my car. Y'all can either take the boys with y'all or stay at the house with them. I just want to run to the hospital and see Damien. I also plan to have a conversation with Doll."

"Is she still not speaking to you?" Dolonda asked.

"Nope."

"So, have a conversation with her about what?" Dolonda asked as she rolled her eyes for the woman she didn't care for.

"Mami, it's time she faces the fact that Damien isn't making any improvements. She needs to think about what to do next."

Holton didn't like where this was going.

"Mija, I know you aren't going to suggest she pull the plug on her son."

"I mean, you could put it like that, but those aren't the words I plan to use. I'm going to remind her of Damien's wishes, and it's not fair to keep him on life support against his wishes."

Holton looked at his daughter in the rearview mirror.

"Tavares, you're treading in dangerous waters. Be mindful of the words you use."

"I probably won't," Tavares responded nonchalantly. She was ready to face the music.

Ever since Damien's admittance into the hospital, Jazz had been reaching out to Doll asking if she could come visit. Doll didn't want any drama in her son's hospital room, though. If Tavares caught Jazz there, it was going to be a real bloodbath that Doll could do without. To avoid the bullshit, she just kept saying she didn't think it was a good time. Jazz didn't give up, though. She continued to call almost every other day. Tired of being rejected, she called again on Christmas Eve. When Doll once again told her it wasn't a good time, Jazz broke down in tears.

Through her half real, half acting tears Jazz said, "I'm carrying Damien's baby, and I just want to see him in case he doesn't pull through."

Doll was in shock hearing that Tavares's ex best friend was carrying her son's baby. She didn't see that coming and didn't know how to receive it. She didn't approve of what Jazz had done to Tavares by betraying her and sleeping with her son. Yet, hearing Jazz was carrying her son's baby made her feel torn. Doll indeed thought Jazz was a snake, but she didn't want to turn her back on her son's baby's mother and his unborn child. To her, it was no longer about Tavares, Jazz, and Damien. It was all about her unborn grandchild. Knowing that Tavares had gone to Jersey for the holidays, Doll told Jazz she could visit on Christmas Day. Since that day, Jazz had been coming to sit with Doll and Damien. She was in her glory feeling like she was a part of Damien's world and family. Neither of them thought about what they'd do when and if Tavares returned.

Before Tavares opened Damien's room door, she heard Doll's voice. Just when she prepared herself to go in and be cordial with Doll, she heard another voice, one she knew all too well. Tavares's heart stopped. Anger welled from the bottom of her feet to the top of her head. She busted the door open with all the force in her body. Caught off-guard, Jazz thought she'd seen a ghost. Doll was speechless.

"Doll, really? Like really? This is how the fuck you're moving? I leave town for a few weeks and you're sitting and laughing with a bitch who said she was my friend but was fucking my man? I know that you blame me for Damien being in that bed, but I can't believe that you would stoop so low as to be sitting with this snake in the grass. I thought we were better than this."

Doll turned to Jazz. "I think you should go."

"Doll, why do I have to leave when they aren't even together? I'm the one who—" Knowing what Jazz was about to say would get her body-slammed, Doll cut her off.

"Jazzlyn, please just go!"

With mayhem in her eyes and murder in her heart, Tavares asked, "You're the one who what?"

Trying to have one up on Tavares, Jazz blurted out, "I'm the one carrying Damien's baby!"

Tavares froze. Then, she laughed.

"Bullshit, bitch. Damien would never knock you up."

Jazz stood up, and the proof was in the pudding. Tavares blacked out.

"You lowdown cum guzzling, scum of the earth ass bitch. It wasn't enough for you to sneak your snake ass in bed with Damien! You had to get you a baby too. Huh? Newsflash, bitch. Damien is in a coma, and it doesn't look like he's going to wake up any time soon."

Hearing the hard truth, Doll screamed, "You just shut the fuck up! Shut the fuck up! Damien is going to wake up."

Tavares hadn't meant to let the painful truth fly out of her mouth, but sometimes her mouth got ahead of her brain.

"Jazz, do me a favor and get the fuck out," Tavares spat.

"I'm not going no fucking where. I have the right to be here with my child's father. You're nothing but an ex-girlfriend who can't let go."

Tavares burst out laughing. "Yeah, well you keep telling yourself that. I'm not mad that you got my sloppy leftovers. I'm a fan of giving to the less fortunate and needy."

With below-the-belt insults being hurled left and right, Doll was crying, "Would you two please just stop? Please stop! This isn't the time or place."

Hearing all the chaos, the nurses called security. When they entered, they asked if there was a problem.

"Yeah, this bitch has to go," Tavares said calmly with her arms folded against her chest.

"I'm not going anywhere. She has no legal standing to put me or anyone else out."

"See, Jazz, there you go talking what you don't know." Tavares pulled an envelope out of her purse and slid it to the security officer.

"Jazz, please just go," Doll begged.

Jazz felt like she had something to prove. Therefore, she wouldn't budge.

The security officer looked at her and said, "Ma'am, per these documents, Tavares Del Gada has the medical power of attorney for this patient. She has full authority of his care and indeed can decide who visits and who doesn't."

While Doll was in shock hearing this news for the first time, Jazz was paralyzed with embarrassment. Once again Tavares had won. Jazz grabbed her purse and began to cry as she looked at Doll with pleading eyes.

Doll responded, "Jazz, please just go. Don't upset yourself or the baby."

Tavares was laughing the whole time.

"Oh, and from this day forward, you're barred from being able to visit. But, best wishes to you and your baby." Tavares laughed again.

Jazz departed crying like a newborn baby. With victory in her eyes, Tavares sat in Jazz's seat, crossed her legs, smirked, and didn't give Doll a second look. As far as she was concerned Doll was rocking with the enemy, so she no longer had anything to say to her either.

Doll wasted no time asking, "Why would you make up those fake papers just to have that girl thrown out?"

However, she knew the question was farfetched. She really wanted to ask when and why Damien gave her his medical power of attorney.

"Doll, does that even make sense? One, I didn't even know she was here. Two, I'm not about to make some bogus power of attorney papers. I brought the papers to give them to *you*."

With a raised brow, Doll asked, "Give them to me for WHAT?"

"We need to talk."

"And, what the fuck do you think we need to talk about?" Doll asked with the volume of her voice climbing.

"We need to have a talk about Damien. But, first and foremost, I want you to know that I don't want the fate of Damien's life to come down to these papers."

Doll stood up, hand on her hip.

"What the fuck is that supposed to mean? Them papers ain't going to determine or decide a motherfucking thing when it comes to MY son. I don't give a flying, flaming fuck what them papers say. I'm the only one deciding anything about my son."

"Hmmmm okay, if you say so," Tavares responded, cool as a cucumber.

Her being so calm about something that was so serious pissed Doll off. She wanted to slap the shit out of Tavares. But Doll had betrayed Tavares in her eyes, so she wasn't going to watch her words as her father had suggested.

"Just how long do you plan to leave Damien hooked up to all these machines and this breathing tube? We all know that Damien is brain dead. He hasn't made one improvement in two months. Never in a million years would Dame want to live like this, and we both know it. He expressed it on more than one occasion. So really you're leaving him hooked up for your own selfish reasons. So again, how long do you plan to leave him like this? You do know that he's not breathing on his own, right?" a sarcastic Tavares asked.

"Who the fuck do you think you are?" Doll asked like a quiet storm. "That's my motherfucking son that I carried for nine months, nurtured, raised, and loved with everything in me. So, I would like to know who the fuck you think you are to come in here and question me about how long I plan to leave him hooked up to these machines? I don't give a flying fuck what Damien said about not letting him live on life support. It's my choice and my decision. I can leave him hooked up for a hundred years if I want to. You're out of line. You and my son aren't even together. You cheated on him, had babies, and moved on. So again, I ask, who the fuck do you think you are to inquire, ask, or try to discuss shit about me having my son hooked up to these machines?"

"Doll, what I'm not going to do is debate with you. I'm just the person that Damien legally left in charge to make medical decisions for him. Why he left me in charge, I don't know. Why he thought I would make better decisions than you is beyond me. Although these papers are what they are, I still want you to make this decision. I want you to free Damien's soul. I want you to decide that he had a full life, and it's time for him to rest in peace. I wanted you to do it. I don't want this to come down to me pulling rank as the power of attorney. I'm pretty sure if you have this conversation with Nana Dancy and Rollo, they'll tell you the same thing. I'm giving you a week, and then we're removing the breathing tube to see how long Damien lasts breathing on his own."

Doll was sobbing uncontrollably. She couldn't even muster words to try to cuss Tavares out. She knew what Tavares said was the truth. That didn't mean it hurt any less. She just wasn't ready to say goodbye to her eldest son. He was her best friend, the one who took care of her and had always been her main man. How could she take the breathing tube out and let him go?

Tavares let Doll cry and didn't try to console her. She knew there was nothing she could say to make the truth burn any less. Silently, Tavares gathered her belongings to allow Doll to face her reality on her own.

Tavares left the hospital feeling emotional from everything that took place in Damien's hospital room. She was ready to go to the Black Cheers of Roxbury and have a drink. As she was getting on the elevator, Rollo was stepping off.

"You okay, sis?"

"Nah, Rollo, I'm not. Can we talk for a moment?"

They stepped to a corner of the quiet, all white hallway, and Tavares spilled what she was feeling.

"Me and your mom had it out."

"Was Ma on her shit again?"

"No, I came in and your mother and Jazz were sitting and chopping it up."

Rollo's eyes expanded.

"Rollo, that shit rubbed me all the way wrong. I lost it. That shit made me feel so betrayed."

"Tavares, you know I ain't with the fuck shit. That bitch is grime ball, and my mother knew better than that shit."

"Oh, no, no, no. Bro, that ain't even the kicker. She's pregnant."

"Whaaaaat?" Rollo screamed. His laidback demeanor became angry. "That bitch is lying."

"No, Rollo, she isn't."

"This is some real-life Jerry Springer shit, sis. I'm so sorry. Dame should have known better from the gate. I'm just disgusted." Rollo dropped his head in shame.

"Look, there's no easy way for me to say this. I told Doll that Damien can't live on that breathing tube forever. Not just because she can't let go. I gave her the papers to show that I'm Damien's medical power of attorney, but I don't want to be forced to use them as a trump card. I want her to make the decision. I gave her two weeks. I'm sorry, but Damien made it clear to all of us he never wanted to be alive in this way. I think it's only right we obey his wishes."

Tavares expected Rollo to be upset. What he said next shocked her.

"Thank you. Nana and I have discussed it. Neither of us have had the heart to say it to my mother. I think two weeks is long enough for her to wrap her mind around the fact that it's time to let my bro be free. If she doesn't take the breathing tube out, do what you have to do. I hate seeing my brother like that. I want to remember my brother how he was, not like that. He's there just lifeless. That's Dame's body, but that ain't my brother, yo. Nana cries endlessly when she leaves here. Lil D and Ashaunda are heartbroken every time they visit. Only my mother is content with Damien being alive like that. It's been two months. It's time."

Tavares wrapped her arms around Rollo. He eased her heart and mind for making Doll face the truth.

***

Dora was in Belize having a ball with his mans. They rented bungalows on the beautiful turquoise waters and were enjoying their time of no business and all play. Lying on the beach smoking a blunt, Dora was thinking about Tavares and his boys. He couldn't stop thinking about how he was going to exit the game. He loved the money, the power, and giving back to his people, but his priorities had changed since he had a family now. He wanted to live his days loving his lady and watching his boys grow up. Thus far, he'd had a great run in the streets. Still, like anything else, he knew nothing lasted forever. Dora didn't know how he was going to do it, but he was getting out of the game. Being a boss and getting money was what he did, but he was ready to go straight legit. His friends weren't going to understand, and it was going to be a big shift, but Dora was ready. He was giving himself a year to make some major power moves and go a hundred percent legit. With Tavares on his mind, he rose from the white sand and went to call his lady.

Seeing the international number come across her phone, Tavares dropped the pink ballpoint pen on the legal pad and answered her phone.

"Hey sugar dick."

Dora laughed because his boo was such a trip.

"What's cracking, boobie? You was on my mind."

"Are you over in that foreign country with all those fine bitches behaving?"

"But of course I am. You know you're the only exotic mix breed for me."

"Watch your mouth now," Tavares laughed.

"What were you doing?" Dora inquired.

"I was just sitting here outlining everything that's gonna be needed for Damien's funeral."

"WHAT! Damien died?"

"Nah, but in less than a week, Doll will be pulling the plug."

"Damn, that's wild."

"Yeah, I told her she had to do it or I would."

Dora just dropped his head and took a deep breath. His whole lighthearted demeanor changed.

"What do you mean you told Doll she has to pull the plug on her wack ass son? Boo, you're out of pocket."

"Why am I outta pocket?"

"That's not your place."

"It is my place. Damien made it clear he never wanted to live on life support. I think it's wrong that she's keeping him on it just because she can't let go, so I told her so. Rollo and Nana Dancy agreed. So, next week she's pulling the breathing tube out."

"Sometimes you just need to fall back and mind your fucking business. That's HER son. Y'all ain't together, so you was outta pocket. You're my woman. I own you, so don't be trying to control the next nigga's life."

"One, you don't own me. Two, I ain't trying to control nothing. I just think it's wrong."

Dora wasn't about to let his woman ruin his vacation, so he changed the conversation to his kids. After talking to Tavares about the boys he expressed his love and got back to his good time. He would deal with Tavares when he got back.

***

After informing her family that she was going to be taking the breathing tube out in the coming weeks, Doll did what she needed to soften the painful blow. For thirteen days, she was glued to her son's side. She only moved to shower and brush her teeth. Other than that, she talked to Damien, prayed with him, laughed with him, reminisced with him, cried with him, and expressed her love for him. On the final day, she called all her family, her pastor, his closest friends, and Tavares to the hospital. With everyone crammed into Damien's room, they prayed with him, cried, and watched the doctor remove the tube. After breathing on his own for thirty-seven minutes, Damien took his last breath at 11:11 a.m. on January 16, 2012.

Dora had constantly asked Tavares if she was okay since his return from his trip. Every time, her answer was the same: "I'm fine now that Damien will be free."

On the day of the services, Tavares awoke feeling numb. Sadness hadn't hit her yet, nor had she cried. Even with all the planning because Doll wasn't mentally strong enough, she hadn't shed one tear. She climbed out of bed and left her stubborn boyfriend sleeping. He refused to attend the services of his half-brother. Dora said he didn't care that his mother and Mid were attending. Tavares had a better chance of getting the twelve apostles to show up before he would. Tavares simply said a silent prayer for strength and guidance and made her way to the shower to get ready for what was going to be one of the longest days of her life. When she was halfway through getting dressed, Dora awoke and didn't say a word. He went to the shower mad that he was doing something he really didn't want to do. He was going to a bitch ass nigga's funeral just because he wanted to support the woman he loved.

"What's his fucking problem?" Tavares asked herself.

When Dora emerged from the shower looking like a biscuit that Tavares wanted to sop up, she asked, "Are we beefing?"

"Nah, not at all, Boo. I'm just feeling some kinda way that I'm going to this nigga's funeral."

"You're going?" Tavares asked, swept off her feet with shock.

"Not because I give a fuck to pay my respects. I'm going for you. I always want to be there for you, even if it means going to this nigga's funeral. So please do me a favor and just let me smoke a blunt and get dressed."

Respecting the love he had for her, Tavares adhered to Dora's wishes. Less than an hour later, they were walking into Concord Baptist Church. Tavares felt her knees get weak, even though Dora was by her side. The wraparound stairs to the left had a long line and the stairs on the right had an even longer one.

Tavares said, "Y'all come on," to Dhara, Mid, Dolonda, and Holton. They bypassed the line on the right and entered the double doors to a full house. She had to look around to make sure she wasn't dreaming. *Who are all these people?* she wondered. Tavares couldn't believe that Damien had literally brought the city out and filled one of the biggest churches in the city. Taking seats in the rear of the church, Dora, Dhara, Holton, and Mid, along with the rest of the church, watched Tavares naturally strut to the front in her cobalt blue dress and matching peplum jacket. She was with the immediate family, who were also dressed in Damien's favorite color.

Tavares took a seat next to Rollo and waited for the services to begin. She looked around and was proud of how everything turned out. When she and Rollo did the planning, all she wanted was for Damien to be laid to rest immaculately. Together they had surpassed the goal. Damien was in a beautiful, luxurious silver-toned copper casket with a platinum finish. They'd ordered all white roses, lilies, and blue orchards to surround his casket. He was in an all black perfectly tailored Armani suit with a fresh haircut, and his makeup was to perfection to make him reflect his natural self.

When the services ended, Damien wouldn't be leaving in a hearse like the average person. He would be traveling to the cemetery in a horse-drawn carriage. During the burial service, they would release one hundred white doves in the air. Even the repast hall was professionally decorated white and cobalt and being catered. There wasn't one thing that Tavares had failed to go over the top with for Damien's final goodbye.

When the service began, the pastor announced, "Before we get started, we'll have a few words from Tavares Del Gada."

Tavares got up from her seat, full of life and strength, and walked to the podium.

"For those of you who don't know me, which I'm sure there aren't many, I'm Damien's ex-girlfriend. On behalf of myself and the family, I would like to thank everyone in this jam-packed church for coming out today. I look around, and I see just how loved Damien was and how many people's lives he touched. I see family, friends, acquaintances, associates, and admirers. All of you are appreciated.

But, there is one group of people in particular that I would like to thank for showing up. You deserve special recognition.

"This group has a lot in common. They share a devout admiration and love for Damien. They texted the same caring messages, sent similar photos to him, and expressed their love and desire to hold him down. Never did they miss a day checking on him, calling him, or wanting to be in his company. While each of them believes they're more special than any other, indeed they're the same. So, I would like to thank all Damien's side chicks and jump offs for showing up."

When Tavares finished her last sentence, there wasn't an eye in the church that didn't get big or a person who didn't gasp.

"I believe since you ladies were so special and sharing Damien at the same time, you should have your own section for the funeral. If you will, please each stand and meet Big Jay, the head of security, in the rear. He will lead you to the basement. And, please don't mistake this for me being mean and cruel. The whole time Damien and I were apart, I expressed to him that I wanted him to find someone great to be his friend, for him to build with and level up with. I wanted him to find someone as amazing as the person that God blessed me with after we parted ways. And, Damien did. He found all five of you. So, I thought it was only right that you come together and console each other during the loss of y'all's man."

People were in disbelief at what they were listening to. Unfortunately, Tavares didn't care. What she wasn't about to do was sit and listen to all Damien's sidepieces cry, scream, and sob during his service. She'd dealt with enough shit when they were together, and she wasn't having it today. The five women Tavares was referring to didn't bat their eyes. Instead, they were praying that they weren't one of the women that Tavares was putting on blast. Some people were giving her crazy looks. Others were chuckling, and the majority had their mouths open in shock. When the women didn't move, Tavares proceeded.

"Ladies, I don't want to go so far as to call your names. However, if you don't get up in the next thirty seconds, your designated security officer will help you to your designated place for the service."

Still, none of them moved. Jazzlyn, Chasity, Talia, Amya, and Rhonda thought it was a game until five big black solid-faced security officers walked to where they were seated and said, "Let's go."

Not wanting to be embarrassed any further, they got up and took the walk of shame.

Dolonda and Holton looked at Dora, not knowing what to think of this lady they called their daughter.

He shook his head and said, "Don't look at me. She's just my savage girlfriend. Y'all made her."

Randee was sitting between Leslie and Mona-Lisa, trying to mask her laughter. She whispered, "That's my boo."

"Your boo is ridiculous," Mona-Lisa said, palming her face with her hand in disbelief.

Leslie was speechless, just shaking her head back and forth. Rollo wasn't mad. Tavares had earned the right to go out as a boss as far as he was concerned. Doll was livid. She was already a mess, but the circus act that Tavares had just pulled turned her pain to anger.

After the sister wives were lead to the basement, the service officially began. Everything was just beautiful, from the words people spoke of memories with Damien to the eulogy and the poem Lil Damien had written. The soloist who sang "His Eye Is on the Sparrow" created a waterworks show. There wasn't a dry eye in the church when she finished, except cold ass Abdora's, who was there but not really there.

When they arrived at the hall decorated in vibrant blue, white, and black, Tavares needed to get herself together before she celebrated Damien's life, partied, and mixed and mingled with the hundreds of people that would be there soon enough. She excused herself from her family and went to the private, empty lounge on the lower level. She was having a drink alone, just trying to gather her thoughts and get her mind together. After she'd been gone for more than twenty minutes, her family grew worried and went to search for her in unison. They found her all alone at the bar and each took a seat in the long row of empty chairs.

"Damn, boo. That's how you do it? You come have your own private party and leave us upstairs."

"I'm sorry," Tavares said, leaning in and kissing Abdora. "I just needed a little time alone."

"Oh, we thought you were down here feeling bad for putting all those side chicks on blast," Dhara joked.

The newly blended family sat together laughing, talking, and joking until a storm blew a big bad wolf mother and her pregnant snake sidekick through the door.

All everyone heard was, "How dare your jealous, bitter, gold-digging ass make a circus act of my son's funeral by embarrassing those women."

Tavares and her family were in utter shock. Doll didn't stop there.

"That was disrespectful. My son took you in when you had nothing and no one. No one wanted you, not even those two people you're sitting here with and call parents. Damien took care of you, loved you, made you who you are, and you fucking make his funeral some sort of three-ring circus. How dare you!" Doll cried. "Your ass was nothing, and the only person made you into something, you make a fucking joke of his funeral. That was my fucking son, and he didn't deserve that. And, I want all my son's money, because I know you got it. We've been looking and looking, and there's nothing. I know Damien had more than the few punk dollars in his bank account."

When Doll stopped smacking her gums talking shit, Tavares tried to gather her words so she didn't plain and simply tell Doll "Fuck you and your son" before she went back to her drink. However, she didn't get a chance to let anything come out of her mouth. Her mother jumped up out of her seat. Dhara tried to grab her back and missed. She was in Doll's face in no time.

"I don't give a fuck if you just buried your son, who, mind you, cheated on my daughter the whole time they were together. If you say another fucking slanderous ass word to my daughter, I will drag your ass all up and down this hall."

Doll tried to swing and didn't connect. Holton and Abdora jumped and separated the two because it was about to get brutal without a doubt.

"Get the fuck off of me!" Dhara screamed. "This bitch got me fucked up. You got a problem with my daughter's actions, oh the fuck well."

With praying hands, Tavares said, "Stop, Mami, stop. I got this."

She didn't scream or talk above a whisper. "Doll, let's get something clear. Your son didn't make me. I made me. He showed me the way. Because I'm me, a go-getter at heart, I made it do what it do. I hustled and made my own fucking money. I ain't never needed and wanted shit from your son but loyalty, and his trick dick ass couldn't even get that right. And, whatever my parents didn't do don't got shit to do with nothing.

"I paid for that funeral, not you, not your family, not them bitches, and for damn sure not this snake ass bitch standing next to you. So, you cut me a check for thirty-two thousand, and then you can talk shit to me. If my memory serves me right, you couldn't even give me five stacks on that twenty thousand-dollar casket I laid YOUR son to rest in. If you thought I was about to sit and listen to all them bitches who was fucking my man when he was with me crying and sobbing, you got me fucked up.

"Where's your son's money? Where? Please let me know. Because trust me, the last thing I wanted to do was drop thirty racks on my old nigga. I could have let y'all cremate that nigga or put him in a box from the state, but I didn't. So, when you find his money, please make sure I'm the first person you call, because you owe me thirty thousand as of right now. Yeah, Damien was hustling, but that nigga wasn't Nino Brown or Larry Hover. I don't know what you thought, but if your son had money, I sure as fuck don't have it and don't need it. I got my own bread. Furthermore, I got a man who takes very good care of me. Therefore, I don't need Damien's money."

Jazz jumped in. "Tavares, why would you do that to me? You're my friend. You're my best friend. And, just because Damien loved me and we're having a baby doesn't mean you have to be so cold and bitter. That was the foulest shit in the world that you did today."

Tavares squinted her eyes and tilted her head sideways to figure out if Jazz was crazy or delusional.

"Jazz, let me tell you something. We aren't friends. We will never be friends again. I don't give a fuck about you or that baby. You think Damien loved you? Newsflash, Damien didn't know what love was. And, fucking up with a solid bitch like me should tell you that. You think you won because Damien fucked you and you got pregnant? Baby Girl, you're on a real life episode of the biggest loser right now. Damien is dead and never gonna see that baby or give a fuck about that baby. All you won was a one-way struggle to being a single mother."

Tavares's words stung like hot grease on Jazz's skin, and she ran out crying. Immediately, Doll and Tavares picked back up their throwing low blows at one another until the door of the lounge opened. Not wanting to air all their dirty laundry to the person entering, the women halted their spats.

In walked a frail woman in a pretty black sequin dress that looked like it once fit but was now two sizes two big. Tavares gasped and instantly started to cry for the woman who didn't even look like herself. It was Lilly.

Doll's heart was pained seeing her friend who had never looked so bad in her life. Lilly had always maintained her image through her addiction, so this told Doll that she was truly at rock bottom. Holton and Dora were in shock at Lilly's appearance too, by the looks on their faces. Dolonda rolled her eyes and sucked her teeth, while Dhara felt sympathy for the woman who looked like she lost a major fight with her crack addiction.

Lilly could feel the awkward stares, and it made her cringe inside with humiliation. When she learned from the streets that Damien had passed, her heart hurt for Tavares, and she just wanted to see her. Her plan was to just see Tavares and go, but she now regretted that she came. Tavares ran and wrapped her arms tightly around Lilly.

"OMG, Lilly, you're okay. I've been so worried about you. I've been looking for you everywhere. Thank you for coming."

"I know how much you cared for Damien, so I just wanted to see you face to face and give my condolences to you and Doll. I'm going to go now," Lilly said, not even having the heart to look at Holton.

"Lilly, I love you. You know I love you, so please let me help you."

"I'm fine, Tavares," Lilly said with her head low, looking at the ground and trying to avoid the eyes of the people in the room.

"Lilly, hold your head up and look at me," Tavares said, cupping her face. "You aren't fine, and it's time you decide to take control of your life. If you don't, the addiction will kill you. You're a size zero now, your faced is sucked in, your skin isn't glowing, and you just look broken. This isn't you, and don't let the break up with you and my father allow you to just not have any fight left in you."

Tavares turned to look at her father, who had a face of sadness. Holton never thought that it would get this bad with Lilly. He didn't even know the woman standing a few feet from him.

"Papi, I need you to pay to send Lilly to a top-notch rehab."

Dolonda screamed, "Bullshit! My man... my fiancé will be doing no such fucking thing. Miss high and mighty ain't no better than any other addict. If she wants to get clean, then let her do it. But, Holton is my man now, and he isn't paying to send her any fucking where."

Dolonda was fuming with rage at what Tavares had just asked.

"Mami, are you fucking kidding me? The ink isn't even dry on their divorce and you're asking Papi to be a piece of shit ass nigga. Papi," Tavares said with pleading eyes, "please do this. Do this for me."

Holton was caught between a rock and a hard place. He hurt for Lilly, but he knew helping her was going to hurt Dolonda.

After hearing no words, Lilly said with tears falling down her face, "Tavares, it's okay. I'm going to be fine."

"I know you're going to be fine, because Papi's going to send you to rehab. Aren't you, Papi?" Tavares was talking to her father but looking at her flaming mad mother.

Doll looked at Holton and said, "What kind of man are you? She was your wife for two decades. Now that you're engaged to your piece, you're going to leave Lilly high and dry?"

Doll opened the door for what was to come next.

"Doll, you gave her the first hit of crack and started this addiction. So why the fuck don't you send her?"

"That's not true! That's not fucking true!" Doll said, screaming and getting defensive. "I told Lilly she couldn't have any, and she snatched the pipe and tried it anyway. I would have never given her that shit knowing that she couldn't come back from it. Furthermore, when I got clean I tried to get Lilly clean, too. So fuck you, Holton."

Tavares was blown away at what she'd just learned but didn't get sidetracked.

"Papi, listen to me. You stand for something. You're a standup kind of man. Don't let Mami make you be someone you're not. You're not a piece of shit, so don't start just to appease my selfish ass mother."

Holton knew that Tavares was right. He loved Dolonda and was going to spend his life with her, but he would never sleep at night knowing he could have saved Lilly and didn't.

"Find a rehab, and I'll write a check."

Dolonda went slap dead the fuck off. "How fucking dare you save this bitch that made you turn your back on me and your daughter. Holton, fuck you and fuck her. You want to be captain and save a crack-head bitch, then you should have stayed with that bitch."

Dolonda called Holton every name except for a child of God before storming out. While Dhara and Dora went after Dolonda to calm her down and console her, Tavares just shook her head in disgust. She couldn't believe her mother, who knew firsthand the grips of addiction, would want Holton to just leave Lilly fucked up.

"Papi, don't feel bad for doing the right thing. Mami will be just fine. She just has to calm down. This doesn't mean that you love her any less. It just means you're a stand-up nigga."

"I know, Mija. I'm not worried about your mother. This isn't going to change us. I'm not worried at all. Her anger will pass."

Doll hugged Lilly and said, "Baby, you got this. You got this, and I'm going to be here every step of the way to walk this path with you."

Tavares felt like someone had dropped a ton of bricks on her head after her argument with Doll, having to hurt Jazz's feelings, and having to check her mother. All three of them had just about sucked the life out of her with their bullshit. Tavares was over it. She was going to get through this day. She would find Lilly a rehab in the coming days, and then she was packing her bags. Tavares realized that it was time for her to leave Boston for a while. She was going to make New Jersey her permanent residence and continue building her life with Abdora and her boys.

True to her word, Tavares did as she said. She got through the repast, mixing, mingling, hugging, smiling, and doing her best to avoid Doll. She went home mentally drained. Her mother decided she wasn't staying at her house since she was so Team Lilly. She and Holton went to a hotel and that was okay with Tavares because she wanted to call her mother a million bitches. Dhara stepped up and told Tavares to take the night off.

"You had a long day, Miss Thing. I got my grandbabies covered."

Tavares didn't dare put up a fight. She took a shower and climbed in bed.

Abdora asked, "Baby Girl, you okay?"

Tavares wanted to say she was, but she wasn't. Instead, she cried. Dora understood and just held his baby close and allowed her to cry out all her hurt, pain, and anger until she fell asleep.

***

It took Tavares three days to research and find Lilly a rehab. Three days after that, they were on a plane to Puerto Rico. While Tavares was starting the journey to getting clean with Lilly, Dora was being her better half. He'd packed up his truck with everything Tavares wanted to take. He, his mother, and the twins were on their way back to Jersey. Dora was happy that Tavares was finally ready to settle into a life in Jersey and stop living in two places. It had been a long time coming, and he was happy it was finally happening. With Tavares gone for the next few days, Dora was going to take the time to plan something very special as they started a new chapter of their lives.

While on the three-hour flight, Tavares and Lilly had a very heartfelt conversation.

"Lilly, you got this. You've been masking your pain through your habit, and now is your second chance at life. You can't change the past and you don't know the future, so seize the moment to fight for your life. Use this time to find Lilly again. Find the Lilly that you lost through that pipe—the Lilly that you were before Holton, Jr. passed away and you lost yourself. The Lilly that existed before you stopped living and were only existing. I'm going to be here every step of the way. I don't care what it is that you need. You can call me morning, noon, or night, and I'm going to drop everything. I can't explain our bond or the love that I have for you, but what's understood doesn't need to be explained."

"Tavares, there are no words that can express my gratitude. I love you, sweetie. And, I give you my word that I'm not looking backwards. I'm taking my life back. I never imagined life without your father, but I'm going to take this time to be gentle with myself. I'm going to learn myself, find me, and build myself a life. Again, thank you for being my strength when I was at my lowest point."

After two days of getting Lilly settled, Tavares was back on a plane heading home to her family.

CHAPTER 7

Tavares had been back in Jersey for almost two weeks. She was finally getting back to some sort of normality. With all the drama that had taken place at the funeral with her and Doll, her mother and Lilly, and learning that her ex-friend was having a baby with her dead ex-boyfriend, Tavares left Boston completely drained. She was glad that what seemed like the calm after the storm was finally starting. It was Friday, and she was ready for a day of pampering followed by a night out with Bella, Cali, and Rocky. She couldn't wait to see her Jersey Girls. Laughter, trash talking, good food, and strong drinks were long overdue with her friends.

She was at Me-Ma's door at 8:30 a.m. sharp with Jeremiah and Elijah. She rang the loud bell and patiently waited for Dora's grandmother to retrieve her great-grandsons and all their belongings. They had clothes, pajamas, bathing products, blankets, toys, Pampers, wipes, bottles, food, formula, pack-n-plays, and their walkers. Me-Ma wasn't going to need a single thing while she was babysitting for the weekend.

Me-Ma opened the door with a huge smile on her face. "Hey, sweetie pie. Bring them precious babies on in here. I been up all morning excitedly waiting for y'all to get here."

"Me-Ma, you grab the bags, and I'll carry their heavy butts inside."

Together they headed to the decked-out living room. Dora's grandmother was hood, but she surely liked nice stuff. Tavares chuckled looking around the living room. It reminded her of a room of the rich and famous. It was decorated with expensive art on the walls, crystal vases, an angora rug, and mustard yellow Italian leather living room furniture. This was definitely a woman who had some expensive taste.

"Thank you so much for keeping them for the weekend. I just really needed some me time."

"Girl, you don't have to thank me. These are my babies," Me-Ma said in a way that only a grandmother's love for her grandchildren could convey. "Tell your mommy we're going to have us a good ole time this weekend. Ain't we?"

The twins were smiling just as big as could be like they understood their gangster great-grandmother.

"Dhara's going to be jealous that I got her grandsons."

"Who are you telling?" Tavares said, laughing. "She hates sharing them. She'll be calling to cuss me out for not asking her to keep them."

"That's why I didn't even tell her selfish ass that I was keeping them," Me-Ma said with a sly grin. "They're all mine for the weekend, and she better not bring her stank ass over here trying to invade my time with them."

"Y'all are too crazy when it comes to these boys."

"Because that heffa daughter of mine think these twins belong to her and only her. How are you holding up since you been back?"

"I been good, Me-Ma."

"I know that you and Damien were together for a long time, so it's going to take some time to adjust to him being gone."

"It's odd, but I feel like Damien is finally at peace in a better place. I hated seeing him in that coma. That wasn't him I was looking at. It was his body, but it wasn't him. It was killing me seeing him like that. And, now he's finally in a better place, even if some beg to differ," Tavares stated, referring to Doll. "More than anything, I'm just glad to be out of Boston away from all the drama."

"I hear you, sweetie pie. Don't no one have time for all that foolishness. And, where is my handsome grandson?"

"We left him curled up in bed. He was sleeping peacefully, so I left him as is, did what I had to do, and here we are. He didn't even wake his big head self up when I was dressing us and prepping all their stuff."

"Well, Baby Girl, I want you to enjoy baby-free weekend. Now, get out."

Tavares laughed, kissed her kids, hugged Me-Ma, and was out the door. She climbed into her blood-red Lamborghini truck and headed down South Orange Avenue to Newark. The clock read 9:16 a.m. She was gonna be right on time for her hair appointment and not running late as she usually was. Bree's Beauty Bar was the only place you could get a full-service manicure and pedicure from the Asians, a massage from a Swedish white girl, and your hair slayed by a black woman. Tavares couldn't see herself going anywhere other than this one-stop pampering palace.

By 2:00 p.m., she was looking and feeling like a new lady. Not only had she received a massage, a manicure, and a pedicure, but her hair friend and stylist Bree had fried, dyed, and laid her hair to the side.

"Goddamn, Bree. I feel like a new woman."

"Shit, you should," Bree responded in her high-pitched squeaky voice. "Your nails were chipped, and your hair was nappy as all hell. And, that's impossible for someone who has your hair texture," she laughed. "I just can't with you. Don't you ever come in here with those nails looking so ratchet or with that head so matted again."

"I know, I know. Shut up. These last few weeks since my ex's funeral, I just didn't want to do anything but relax."

"Well, now you're looking like a diva again, so tip me accordingly," Bree joked, because Tavares always overpaid her. "Wait, girl. Get in this chair and lay your head back so I can do them bushy ass eyebrows."

By the time Tavares got up, she was officially herself again. She gave Bree $300 for her services that tallied $200, knowing that she would tip her staff. Then, she was out the door to Jersey Gardens Mall for some retail therapy. Tavares was on the New Jersey Turnpike when it hit her that Abdora hadn't called her all day. She picked her phone up, scrolled to "My Other Half," and pressed talk.

"Yo," Abdora answered.

"Don't 'yo' me when I haven't heard from you all day. Someone could have kidnapped me and the kids. You wouldn't even know because you haven't called me all day."

"Kidnapped you and my kids?" Abdora had to laugh at his dramatic girlfriend. "Babe, that's a real force. No one is crazy enough to kidnap my family. They know the backlash would mean going ten feet under. And, if someone did kidnap YOU, trust and believe they would bring you back when they realized how high-maintenance your bougie, shit talking ass is," Abdora said matter-of-factly. "I know my kids are okay because Me-Ma has sent me a million pictures since you dropped them off. When I woke up, I was like what the fuck. I don't know who taught her how to text, but I owe their ass a slap."

"OMG, Me-Ma sent you pictures? She didn't send me any."

"Of course she didn't because she don't like you like that," Abdora said, falling out laughing.

"You're right. She doesn't like me like that. She loves me, chump. Anyway, what're you doing?"

"I just got up not too long ago, got dressed, and left the house. I rolled over and you were gone. Who told you to leave like a thief in the morning?"

"I had stuff to do."

"Stuff to do like what?"

"I had to get my life together! I went to get my hair and nails done."

"You were at the Beauty Bar giving Bree all your money, you mean."

"Shut up. Bree earned every dollar I paid her."

"And, what are you doing now? Want to meet me at home for a quickie?" Abdora suggested with a sneaky tone.

"Absolutely not, because a quickie with you is always an hour or longer. Shit don't even be a quickie. So nope, I'm not messing with you. I'm about to go shopping," Tavares responded with a long pause, knowing she said the wrong thing.

It was about to be war now.

"For what? Just tell me for what, Tavares. You have a whole two-level walk-in closet. It's filled damn near to capacity with shoes and clothes. Half of the stuff still has tags on it. I know my sons don't need shit because they outgrow all the shit we buy them before they get a chance to wear it. Hell, they don't even wear the same outfit twice, they have so much shit. So, tell me again what the hell you're going shopping for."

Tavares had to pull the phone from her ear and look at it because Abdora was talking pure craziness.

"Do I say anything when you come home with new sneakers every week or come in with a bag from Gucci just because you felt like buying it?" She didn't even give her other half a chance to answer. She beat him to the punch. "NO. So, leave me alone. I can shop if I feel like it."

"You know what, you're absolutely right, Baby Girl. It's your money. You can shop all you want."

"Well, actually, it's your money," Tavares said sarcastically.

"What? My money? How you figure? I didn't give you any money."

"Well, I was doing laundry and found a couple thousand in your pocket. I figured you wanted me to have it to go shopping."

Abdora bellowed over in laughter. "Yeah, that's what you figured. You found money in my pockets and just figured I left it for you to shop? Girl, you're fucking nuts, but do you. I swear you're one of a kind."

"I absolutely said he don't want this because who tosses their jeans in the laundry with that kind of money in it?" Tavares said, grinning on the other end of the phone.

"And, just how much was it?" Abdora asked, not really caring but still curious. He knew the more Tavares found, the more shit she would be coming home with that she, he, and the kids didn't need.

"It was—" she began, and then stopped. She caught herself about to tell how much she had to blow. "Now you asking too many questions, player," she said and busted out laughing.

"You got that, shopaholic. Just don't ask me to carry your bags in."

"I will. Don't worry."

"Tavares, I'm telling your ass right now. I don't care how much money you have; your ass better not walk in here with a million bags," Abdora said, trying to sound half serious with his girlfriend who he knew wasn't paying him the least bit of mind.

"Oh yeah? I'll keep that in mind," Tavares said, her response drizzled in sarcasm. "Actually, I really won't, but we'll pretend."

"Girl, don't play with me."

"Alright, alright. I hear you."

"Don't come home with a million bags."

"Well, how long before you make it home?" Abdora's spoiled wifey asked.

"I got some business to handle, gonna go see my kids at Me-Ma's, and then I'll be home. So, meet me at home about 7:00 or 8:00 p.m."

"Sounds good. I love you," Tavares said, ending the call.

Just as she pulled into the parking lot of the mall, the Bluetooth in the car said, "Rocky is calling."

Pushing talk on the screen, she answered, "Hey bitch. What's going on?"

"Ain't shit. I'm starving; let's go get something to eat."

"I just pulled into the mall. Come meet me because I'm starving, too."

"What mall you at, Jersey Gardens or Short Hills?"

"I'm at Jersey Gardens. I started to go to Short Hills so I could splurge on some high-end shit, but because they have more stuff for the kids, I came here. I came up, so I figured I might as well blow it wisely."

"Hmm, I know that's right, bitch! What was the come up?"

"Abdora's pocket," Tavares answered flatly like she'd really come up.

"Bitch, you stupppid," laughed Rocky. "That ain't no come up."

Tavares explained and together they laughed because she really did come up. She found six thousand in her man's pocket a week ago, and he'd yet to even blink or say a word about losing or misplacing so much money. Tavares was even nice enough to put it in his night stand when she found it, but when it was there a week later, it became finders keepers losers weepers. She did the right thing and told Abdora she took it, but he surely wasn't getting it back after a week of not even missing it.

"OMG, you know what I can go for?" Tavares said, damn near tasting it in her mouth. "A seafood casserole from Legal Sea Foods."

"Yes, bitch, that sounds like the move," Rocky said with matching excitement for the restaurant with the freshest seafood. "I can get me some crab cakes and sangria. That'll set my day straight."

"Let me run in here, and then I'll meet you at Short Hills."

"Tavares, me and my stomach don't got time for your shit. Once you go in that mall, you'll be in there forever."

"Shut up, no I'm not. I'm gonna just run in the Gap and Kid Footlocker, and then I'm hitting the highway."

"Bitch, I swear to God if you have me waiting, you're paying the whole bill," Rocky said, giving Tavares incentive to hurry her slow ass up.

"Okay, so how long?" Tavares said, knowing now she had to get in and get out and not get sidetracked and run in a million stores.

"You have an hour because I have to run two errands. I just gotta throw my boots on and I'm walking out the door now."

"Cool, call me when you're heading my way. I'm going in the mall now."

***

Doll was in Boston thinking about Tavares. *I miss my Baby Girl,* she thought to herself as she stood at her stove making Tavares's favorite meal of smothered chicken, white rice, and collard greens. She knew that she'd said some pretty hurtful things in their heated argument, but she was upset and in pain from losing her son. She knew deep down in her soul Tavares loved Damien more than anything in the world, and they shared a similar pain from his passing. She'd said some things that cut deep and she didn't know if Tavares would come around anytime in the near future. The more Doll thought of Tavares, the more she thought of her son, who was her world and her everything.

Missing Damien was an understatement. Doll broke down crying like she did every day since they'd buried him. Taking a seat at her kitchen table, she began to sob uncontrollably. Her crying session was interrupted by her phone ringing. When she looked at the (862) area code, she couldn't believe that God heard her, and just like that Tavares was calling. She wiped her tears with her shirt and pulled it together to speak to Tavares.

"Hello," she answered with her voice shaky from the crying.

"This is Dhara. How are you?"

Hearing the voice on the other end, she was shocked and angry at the same damn time.

"Fine," Doll said with a slight attitude.

"Listen, I know we got a little out of control in the hospital. But, at the end of the day, I'm a mother and a woman just like you. So, while I can't say I know the pain that you're in, I do know that no mother should have to bury her child. I just wanted to reach out and check on you."

Doll took down her ready-for-war attitude hearing the genuine voice coming from the other end of the phone.

"I appreciate that. I really do. Thank you for calling."

The women spoke for a good while, laying their differences on the table.

"Doll, we were two young girls not even women yet who fell in love. We fell in love with a man, who, I hate to admit it, fell in love with two different women. I never thought it was possible to truly love two women at once, but Dorian did. And, rather than be a man about his shit, he played on both our hearts for his own selfish reasons. The worst part is that he fathered our set of youngest and oldest boys only a year apart from each other. No man should ever hide, deny, or keep his kids apart, no matter what."

"Dhara, I agree with you wholeheartedly. It's really sad that our children are grown and never had a relationship. Now, Damien is gone and will never experience knowing his brothers, but I hope Rollo is blessed enough to build a relationship with your boys. I'll never forget the day Dorian called me and told me that he'd got married," Doll said like it was just yesterday. "Crushed me and broke me beyond my wildest dreams. Felt like he ripped my heart right from my body. Shit, it drove me to a crack pipe for damn's sake."

Doll had to laugh at her own weakness and be grateful how far she'd come with over eighteen years clean.

"When he started going to Jersey, he would always say it was for us. It was business, not pleasure, so just ride with him. He would always say he was moving back to Boston when his business could run itself from Jersey, and he never did. I never stopped to think he had a family over there. In the same conversation of him saying he got married, he said when the boys were a little older, he would start taking them regularly on weekends, vacations, and for the summers. I cussed his ass out and called him every no good, lowdown, two-timing, coke-pushing, nigga, bastard, and bitch in the book."

They cracked up laughing together.

"No, I did. Because I gave him two children and believed WE were gonna be married and have a family. Rollo was only one year old, and just like that you call me and say you got married and to hell with my boys and me. I changed my Goddamn number on him and tried to figure my life out now that it was shattered. Somehow, he got my new number and called to check on the kids and to see if I needed anything. I cussed his ass out again, hung up, and changed my number again.

"After changing my number a dozen times, he got the hint. But, he always had someone deliver me a package of money every month. Still, I would never take his calls. I was broken and damaged. As a woman who loved him so purely, I just felt stupid. When the money stopped, I knew something happened to him. It was maybe three months that I didn't get the money that I'd been getting for ten years. Then, Booga came to see me and told me that Dorian was killed.

"Initially, I was like fuck him, but then it hit me. I was wrong all those years and just a scorned woman. The bigger picture was my children would never know their father, and I was partly to blame for them not seeing him. He never just came for them or fought to see them, so he's liable, too. But, I never made him feel like he could when he would try to call and be cordial with me for his kids' sake.

"When the kids were older and asked about him, I would just say he moved out of town and he couldn't contact them because my number changed. And, to this day, I've never told them he walked out. I just told them that he loved them and supported them with child support until the day he died, because he did."

"Doll, we don't choose the cards that we're dealt. We just make the best of the hand we're given. I'm very sorry for Dorian's lack of manhood. If at any time he'd ever mentioned your boys to me, I would have picked the phone up as a woman and called you so that we could figure it out and do what we had to for our children's sake. Children don't ask to come here. Through all the mess, if nothing else, our children deserved a relationship.

"From our disgusting showdown at the hospital, I'm positive that we would've yelled, screamed, cussed, and been nasty to each other initially. However, I would like to believe that eventually we would've put the bullshit aside for our children. And, even all these years later, it's heartbreaking to me that my children experienced so many things, growing up in the house with Dorian, and your kids missed out on those memories. But, the blessing is that it was by God's choice. Although, in a crazy way, we now know and our children will hopefully build going forward. Oddly enough, we have to thank Tavares for that."

"Dhara, I can't thank you enough for calling. God is so good. He always knows what we need and when we need it. He used you as a vessel today. I was just sitting here thinking about my son and Tavares and bawling my eyes out when you called. You really lifted my spirits. More than anything, it warms my heart that although Rollo lost his big brother, he's gained two more. Of course, they may never be as close as he and Damien were, but I'm going to pray that they receive him and allow him into their lives."

"No need to pray. It's claimed. I know my sons, and nothing matters more to them than family. Which reminds me that I would like to invite you and your whole family down tomorrow. Abdora is putting together a night of love in celebration of Valentine's Day. I know that it's short notice, and for that, I apologize. Between running my sober houses and my damn son working me like a runaway slave for this party, I don't know if I'm coming or going.

"This morning we were going over the guest list, and it hit me I forgot to reach out to you. He really wants you guys here, so he'll pay for your whole family's airfares and accommodations. Just tell me how many and the names, and it will be booked in the next hour."

"That's very sweet and kind of Abdora, but I don't think that Tavares wants to see me. We had a very bad falling out after the services that I'm sure you heard about. I said some quite painful things to her. I didn't mean them. I was just angry and in the moment of hurt. So, I think that my family and I will decline."

"Doll, we all say things we don't mean out of hurt and anger. Tavares loves you. She loves you probably more than she loves her own damn mama. So, I really wish that you guys would come down. It's actually a surprise, so she has no idea my son is putting together this party. But, it's going to be an absolutely beautiful night of love. I'm positive that since we're celebrating love, she would want her family here. No matter what, you, and your family are her family. Think about it. Call your family and see who can come, and call me back. Oh, and one more thing. It's a formal occasion."

"Goddamn it, Dhara. You want us to get formal on less than a day's notice."

"I know, I know. I'm beyond sorry, Doll. It doesn't have to be a ball gown, just not casual."

"Okay. I'm gonna think on it and call you back."

***

Tavares was in the mall flying from store to store for an hour and forty-five minutes, racking up bags from Kids Foot Locker, Adidas, Carters, True Religion, Timberland, Ann Taylor Loft, Saks, and the Gap Outlet when she realized Rocky still hadn't called her. She was ecstatic Rocky hadn't called because she'd accomplished way more shopping than she planned on, but now she was hungry. She stopped in front of the Bed Bath & Beyond and dropped her bags. She opened her oversized black on black Gucci purse and rumbled to the bottom to find her phone. Looking at the home screen that held a picture of Abdora and her twins, she saw she had no missed calls. So, she called her lunch date because her stomach was growling.

Rocky picked up, not even saying hello but, "I know, bitch. I'm running late. I got all the way to Jersey City to run my first errand and realized my wallet wasn't in my bag but on the kitchen fucking counter. So, I had to drive all the way back home. I've already been to Jersey City. Now, I'm in Newark, running in this store to pick something up, and I'm heading your way."

"Rocky, bitch you play too much. I'm ready to eat. Now, it's after 4:00 p.m., and we're gonna hit mad traffic on 78," Tavares said, hardly mad. She was just talking shit.

"It wasn't my fault, so shut up. I'm heading your way right now. Just sit in traffic and imagine how good our food is gonna be," the late lunch date joked.

"You make me sick. I'm walking out of this mall right now. I'm going to beat you there, so I'll just sit at the bar and have a drink until you get there."

"Cool, that works. I'll be heading that way in about ten minutes flat."

Tavares loaded her trunk and thought about Abdora saying not to come home with a million bags.

"Well, it's not a million," she told herself, but she knew he was still going to talk shit. Her defense was going to be that she caught some mean ass sales and at least she came home with stuff for him, too. Popping on Pandora through her Bluetooth, she exited the mall and got ready to fight rush-hour traffic on a Friday. When she made it to the freeway, she was happy that traffic was flowing and not stuck bumper to bumper. In her car jamming to K-Michelle, who she'd come to love like Keisha Cole, her song was interrupted with the same odd (617) number that had been calling for the last few days. They'd even left messages, but due to the unfortunate fact that Tavares never checked her voicemail, she had no idea who it was calling. Never answering numbers she didn't know, she was hesitant to answer, but she did.

"Hello? May I please speak with Miss Tavares Del Gada?" the well-spoken, deep voice asked.

"May I ask who's calling?" Tavares asked, curious as hell who this man was asking for her by her whole name.

"Yes, my name is Attorney Dylan James."

"Speaking."

"Hello, Miss Del Gada. How are you?"

"Well, thank you. What can I do for you, Mr. James?"

"First, I would like to express my deepest condolences on Damien passing away. I'm actually calling in regards to a legal matter with Damien."

He got no further before Tavares went left on him.

"Listen sir. I don't know what case Damien owed you money for, but I'm not paying any of his unpaid debt. If he didn't pay you before he went under, guess what? You're shit out of luck. Damien is gone, and your legal matter was with him, not me."

"No, no, no," the lawyer said, seeing that she was as sharp-tongued as Damien described her. "Damien didn't owe me any money preceding his ill-fated death. I'm calling in regards to his estate and will."

"Will and estate?" Tavares stated with her tone expressing just how lost she really was. "Damien has a will and an estate?" she questioned, hearing this information for the first time.

"Yes, ma'am."

"Mr. James, I truly apologize for flying off the handle. I truly do. I just thought that I was once again being called on to be the cleanup woman for Damien. But, I think you called the wrong person. Damien and I weren't together at the time of his passing, so I'm sure his will has nothing to do with me. I think that you should call his mother, Devin."

"I can call her as well, if you would be so kind as to give me her contact information. But, Miss Del

Gada, it's YOU that I should be contacting in regards to setting up the reading of the will. You're listed on all the paperwork as the beneficiary."

Tavares was baffled, seeing that they hadn't even been on the best of terms.

"I understand, Mr. James, but I'm sure it's his mother that you should contact. Whatever Damien had for me, I don't want it. So, if you're ready, I'll give you Devin's number."

Grabbing his 24-karat gold pen from the holder and his initialed writing pad, he stated, "Ready."

"It's (617)-555-8322. I'm sure whatever business that needs to be rectified can be handled with her."

"Miss Del Gada, it's not that simple. Seeing that you're executor of the will, nothing can take place without you. So, if you could give me a date that you can come into my office, we can set up a time for the will reading."

"Actually, I'm in New Jersey where I currently live. I'm not too sure when I'll be returning to Boston. But, this is what we can do. If you call Devin and just set everything up with her as far as the details of the date and time, I'll make it my priority to be there."

"That sounds like a plan. I will contact her, and once everything is confirmed, I'll give you a call back with the date and time."

"Thank you, Mr. James."

"No, thank you," he replied and the line went silent.

"What the fuck," Tavares said out loud. "When did street niggaz start having wills and estates?" she questioned to herself.

Yes, Damien had the brownstone and the corner store, but for the life of her, she couldn't wrap her head around all this will and estate business this lawyer had just called her about.

"I don't know, and I'm sure as hell not about to attempt to even try to figure it out," Tavares told herself.

When she realized that she was only two exits away from Short Hills Mall, Tavares went back into Happy Friday mode and was ready to have a late lunch/early dinner with her friend. In no time, she pulled up to the luxury mall that housed the majority of her favorite stores such as Bloomingdales, Neiman Marcus, Gucci, Louis Vuitton, Victoria's Secret, Pandora, White House Black Market, Banana Republic, Ann Taylor, and a few more. Tavares had to say a prayer while she waited in line for her car to be valet parked.

"Father God, I'm calling on the shopping Gods far and near. Please have them watch over me, my debit card, this cash in my pocket, and my credit cards. I'm an addict. Knowing is half the battle, and I do know that I've got a real shopping addiction. So please, Father, direct the shopping Gods to not let me get in this dang mall and spend any more than $5,000 of my own money. Amen."

Tavares hoped her prayer worked because she already had a million bags. If she came home with a million more, she was for sure going to have to fight with Abdora. That was a fight that she had no desire to have, seeing that it was Valentine's Day weekend. All she wanted to do was curl up in bed, cuddle, eat, have sex, and do it all over again. But, if she dared to come home with a million more bags, the only thing that she was going to be doing was walking around with an attitude from hearing Abdora's mouth.

As she pulled into valet, a suave Hispanic man with two long cornrows wearing a big smile that displayed perfect white teeth approached Tavares. She took the valet ticket and slipped him a $50 bill.

"Keep the change. Please just take care of my baby," she said as she hopped out of her truck and walked into her heaven.

CHAPTER 8

Tavares had almost made her way to Legal Sea Foods. However, her lunch date still hadn't called, so she detoured to the Gucci store. Upon entering the bright, well-displayed, oversized store, she saw her girl showing bags to a woman. The customer looked like a walking billboard for True Religion as she was sporting a full sweat suit and t-shirt with their name plastered on it. Tavares screwed her face up because she hated logos and stood in the corner waiting to get her favorite Asian's attention.

Ever since Tavares and Dora started dating, she'd become a fan of Short Hills Mall. It was during her first visit to Gucci that she met Kimmy Xu, who had a little too much soul. From their initial meeting, Tavares knew Kimmy was hood and loved black men. Everything about her soul, demeanor, and personality said it. The more she frequented her second favorite pocketbook store, the more she and Kimmy built a rapport. It got to the point where Tavares wouldn't let anyone else get her commission because she'd fallen in love with the Black Asian, as Tavares had nicknamed her.

During one of her regular visits, Kimmy invited her to lunch. From there, they became friends. It was over lunch that Tavares had learned that she was absolutely right about homie. Kimmy only dated black men. She'd never been with an Asian man in her life, and she didn't care what her Asian Mafia family thought.

Tavares made eye contact with Kimmy and jokingly gave her the middle finger. The sales associate laughed and smiled at her crazy always hefty-spending customer and homegirl. The woman didn't notice Tavares and got nasty with the sales associate.

"Is a black woman shopping here funny to you? Because I don't see anything funny about me asking you prices. My money spends just like your chink cousins and them white women over there at that register."

Kimmy almost let the hood come out of her and wanted to respond with "Bitch shut up, buy something or get the fuck out." She was over this ghetto heffa the moment she started asking why certain bags that were the same size were so much more expensive than others. But Kimmy caught herself. Instead of coming down to the woman's level, she flagged her new employee.

"Bethyl, please help this customer, please."

"And, why can't you help me?" the ghetto fabulous woman snapped.

"Ma'am, because I just had a customer come in who needs to pick up an order and that's something that only I can do," Kimmy said, lying through her perfect, pretty white teeth.

With no further explanation, she walked away and let Bethyl earn the commission that she didn't even want if she had to deal with this woman another moment.

"Black Girl, Black Girl," Kimmy said, smiling and giving Tavares a hug. "How are you? I've missed you."

"Yeah, you missed me and my commission," Tavares joked. "I'm doing a lot better. Thanks for asking."

"I knew something was wrong when I didn't see you in here for over a month. I was like where is this Gucci-addict and we got all this new stuff. I started calling you and blowing up your phone. When you didn't answer, I was worried because it's not like you to not answer my calls. I was so happy to hear your voice when you finally called me back."

"Yeah, Kimmy, it was crazy. But, I'm good now. Trying to bounce back and move forward from the craziness. What you been up to, Black Asian?"

"You know me, Black Girl. Just selling these bags, traveling, and loving all over my chocolate Mandingo."

Tavares fell out laughing at Kimmy blushing over her long-time square boyfriend who she would cut a bitch over if they dared looked his way. The ladies were making small talk when the ghetto princess caught their attention. She was now on her phone while she waited for her purse to be rung up. The two ladies kept chatting, but their ears were on the unbelievable conversation that was taking place.

"Girl, I love him. That's my boo. I don't care if he got a girl. That's his headache, not mine. As far as I'm concerned, he's both our man," the happy mistress laughed. "That nigga is just getting on his feet, stacking his paper, and then he's moving down to Philly with me. She slipped up and let a bitch like me get a hold of her man. I ain't going nowhere. I'm playing for keeps with this Jersey boy. He's feeling me hard body, too. Shit, it's Valentine's Day, and he just gave me two stacks and said buy something nice."

Kimmy and Tavares were in a trance listening to this woman's stupidity when Tavares's phone interrupted their ear hustling.

"Take that call, and I'm going to go get your stuff," Kimmy said, shaking her head at the trash she'd just listened to.

When Tavares answered the call, she said, "Rocky, I'm starving. Where the hell are you?"

"Girl, I don't know why the heavens above are trying to stop me from having my sangria and crab cakes, but I'm coming. I'm stuck in goddamn traffic. There was a three-car pile-up, and I'm stuck in bumper to bumper traffic. I'm only an exit away so I'm gonna just hop off and cut through the city to get there. Are you at Legal?"

"Nah, I'm in Gucci. I had to come get two of Dora's Valentine's Day gifts. Unfortunately, I got stuck listening to a wack ass self-proclaimed side bitch. You know I hate a side bitch more than I hate synthetic weave," Tavares said loudly enough for the woman to hear the two shots she busted at her.

The girl heard Tavares but she just mumbled under her breath, "Bitches stay hating."

Rocky was laughing her ass off. "Why you hating on that side bitch? Leave her happy for sloppy leftovers ass alone."

"You're right. Now hurry the fuck up because I'm starving. I'm heading to Legal now. I'll be at the bar waiting because I'm gonna have a drink for the both of us."

"Cool, I'll be there soon."

The ladies ended their call. Then, Tavares paid for Dora's gifts and made her way to the famous New England seafood restaurant.

Entering Legal Sea Foods, Tavares was elated that the bar was completely empty. As she took a seat, the slender redhead bartender came over.

"Hi, my name is Holley. Do you know what you'd like?"

"Yes, may I please have a glass of red sangria with a shot of patron on the side?"

"That kind of day?" the woman asked playfully.

"No, it's been a great day, Holley. I'm just kick-starting what's going to be an even better night."

"Got you," Holley chuckled and high-fived Tavares before making her drink.

***

Doll gave Dhara's invitation some long thought before deciding that she was going to New Jersey. After checking with her family to see who was in, she called Dhara back.

"Hey, Doll. I hope that you're calling to tell me that you and your family are coming down."

"Actually, I am. We'll be there. I'm going to text you the names of everyone for the plane tickets. Once you have the reservations, just forward the confirmations to my email."

"Sounds good, sounds good," Dhara said. "Do you have a hotel that you prefer to be at?"

"Honey, as long as it isn't a motel but a hotel, it doesn't make a bit of difference. We just want to take hot showers and rest our heads. Hold on, Dhara. Someone's beeping in... Hello?"

"Hi, may I please speak with Devin Seastasher?"

"Speaking," Doll responded skeptically.

"My name is Attorney Dylan James, and I'm calling in regards to your son Damien's will."

"Will you please hold on, Mr. James?"

"Sure."

As she clicked back over to Dhara, Doll was in total shock.

"Dhara, I've gotta take this call. But, I'll get you the names and just email me everything."

"Okay, and I'm so glad you're coming."

Doll rushed back to the lawyer on her other line.

"I'm sorry. Now, what did you say? This was in regards to my son's will?" she asked for confirmation that she'd heard him right.

"Your son has an estate and a will. The executor of the will is Miss Tavares Del Gada, but she suggested that I go through you to set up everything as far as setting up a time for the reading."

Doll was fuming inside that her deceased son had trusted whatever he'd left behind to Tavares and not her. She loved Tavares without a doubt, but she couldn't understand what would make Damien leave her in charge of his will.

"Mr. James, I'd like to do this sooner than later. When can we get it done?"

The proper-speaking lawyer stated, "I'll be out of town next week, but you guys are more than welcome to come in any day the following week."

They mutually agreed that a week from Monday, Doll, her family, and Tavares would meet at his office at noon. Doll hung up with the lawyer and her mind was racing as she got dressed to go find something to wear to the party the following the day.

Damien had a will? What did he have that I don't know about that he'd need to leave a will? Why would he make Tavares the executor instead of my mother or me? Doll was thrown for a loop by the call she'd just received. More than anything, she felt horrible for the accusations she'd nastily hurled at Tavares about having and hiding Damien's money. She couldn't wait to see Tavares to wrap her arms around her and apologize from the bottom of her heart.

CHAPTER 9

Tavares downed her shot and was savoring the taste of her sangria when she heard a loud voice say, "Daddy, you so crazy, but I love me some you."

She instantly recognized the irritating voice from the Gucci store.

As she scanned the room, she found the side chick sitting at a booth not too far behind her. With disbelief at who the chick was with, Tavares thought her eyes were deceiving her. She blinked a few times.

"I know that's not who I think it is," Tavares said, knowing she had to be trippin'. However, she realized that she was looking at exactly who she thought it was. Now she understood why God was trying to keep her and Rocky from coming to lunch. Things were about to go from zero to a hundred if Rocky's irrational self walked in and witnessed what she was looking at.

Tavares waved the redheaded freckle-faced adult Annie lookalike down.

"Hey, hun. You ready for another double dose already? You haven't even finished that sangria."

"No, Holley, not yet. Could you just watch my stuff for a minute?"

"Sure, hun. No problem!"

Tavares gathered her thoughts swiftly because she knew if Rocky walked in, they'd for sure be going to jail. Rocky whooped ass first and asked questions and figured things out second. The last thing Tavares felt like doing was sitting in a jail cell, so she had to move and move fast. Sliding off the tall bar stool chair, she walked toward the couple who were so busy boo-loving that they didn't even notice her coming. It wasn't until she pulled out a chair and sat down uninvited did they look up and notice her. The ghetto rat was confused, then angry that the shit-talking woman from the Gucci store was sitting at their table. The gentleman looked like he'd seen a ghost. He knew being caught by your girl's friend was just as good as being caught red-handed by your girl herself.

"What the fuck? Do you know me? Do you know my man? Do you know US to just be sitting at our table interrupting our Valentine's Day lunch?"

"Listen here, you loud-mouth gutter rat. I don't know who the fuck you're talking to, but don't let that liquid courage of cognac get you snatched back in your lane."

"Do I know you?" the girl questioned with less attitude.

"No, I don't fucking know you, because you ain't my breed of bitch," Tavares snarled. "I'm a wifey kinda bitch, and you, hunny… You're a side bitch, which means that you ain't even in my life class. You for damn sure ain't on my level you $9.99 no-tax, synthetic track wearing ass wench."

"Bitch, fuck you. You don't know me. I'm from north Philly and will fuck you up."

Tavares was so amused she had to genuinely laugh.

"As I said… Bitch, I don't know you. But, this nigga right here, I for damn sure know. Isn't that right, Javan? Go ahead and tell side chick Shaquita you know me."

Rocky was so happy to have finally made it to Legal that she powered her phone off upon making her way to the bar. She just wanted to eat, drink, and kick the shit with her girl after all that she'd gone through to get there. As she approached the bar, Rocky found only two older white gentlemen. She was confused as to where her friend was.

"Excuse me," she said, waving the bartender down.

"Hi, what can I get you, sweetie?"

"I'm actually looking for my friend. A pretty mixed girl, blond hair, blue eyes."

"Uhh, there was a young lady there with that description," Holley said, pointing to Tavares's stuff and empty seat, "but her hair is far from blond." Looking around, the bartender spotted Tavares and said, "She's right back there. It looks like she's joined some friends."

Rocky looked in the direction that the overly pale bartender was pointing and realized that she knew two of the three people. And, Tavares's hair for damn sure wasn't blonde. Based on the body language from where she was standing, it didn't look too friendly. So, she scurried over to the table in the back corner.

"What the fuck is going on?"

Tavares knew this was where everything was about to go sour.

"Is this your friend?" Rocky asked Tavares while rolling her eyes at the woman sitting close to her best friend's man.

Tavares looked over her shoulder at her ticking time bomb friend.

"Bitch, knock it off."

With that said, Rocky turned her attention to her best friend's man.

"Javan, what's really good? Who the fuck is this bucket ass bitch fresh off a stripper pole?"

"Javan, like who the fuck are these chicks? They just coming over here out the cut tryna bum rush us and shit."

"Chill, Kamari. I got this."

"Nigga, you ain't got a motherfucking thing," screamed Rocky. "Only thing you BETTER have is bail money when I beat the fucking brakes off this chicken head ass side bitch."

Javan had to think fast. He had to get Kamari out fast because he knew his wifey's girls were gonna fuck her up. Beyond beating her ass, they were going to fuck shit up, not only with Kamari but with his wifey.

"Listen, ladies. I loved Cali, but I'm leaving her."

"What the fuck you just say?" Rocky snapped. "My bitch just held you down while you did a five piece, Nigga. And, she took care of your kid like he was hers with his monkey-looking ass. You might motherfucking wish you were leaving her."

Rocky was about to give Javan a two piece and a biscuit.

"Rocky, it is what it is. This is my baby. We fell in love while I was locked up. I'm gonna tell Cali as soon as the time is right. Y'all ain't gotta hurt her and tell her. Let me do it. I at least owe her that much. I mean, as you said, she did hold my monkey-looking ass son down, right?"

"Nigga, have you lost what little bit of mind you walked out of jail with?" Tavares barked.

"Humph," the chick chuckled, feeling like she'd won after what Javan said.

That humph got her cap snatched back. Rocky wrapped her hands tightly around Kamari's cheap hair that was pulled back in a weave ponytail.

"Bitch, I'll bag and drag you up and down this mall. Shut the fuck up and stay in a side bitch's place."

Tavares shockingly said, "Oh, my God. Rocky, let her go."

She hadn't even seen it coming because Rocky reacted so fast.

"Yo, chilllll," Javan said.

Rocky had fire in her eyes.

"Shut the fuck up. You got this bitch out at Legal like she's your bitch. You're supposed to be kissing my girl's ass right now after all she did for you. And, you got the balls to be sitting here with this skeezer."

Rocky was fuming but knew that fucking around in Short Hills Mall they would go to jail. She let Javan's mistress go but used her other hand to pick up a glass of water and throw it in the hoodrat's face. The chick jumped out of shock. She instantly went to reach for her bag to get her knife and stab Rocky. She was disappointed when she realized she'd placed it in the seat next to Tavares.

"Rocky, you're wildin', sis. Let her leave. We ain't doing this here," Javan said, putting his gangster in his voice. "I need to holler at y'all."

Rocky got his drift. She rolled her eyes, stepped aside, and let wet head out. Kamari grabbed her bags and waited until she was out of reach to say, "Y'all fucked with the wrong bitch." She left devastated that her man's main chick's friends had just run up on them and gave her the business.

As soon as Kamari was gone, Javan busted out laughing.

"I don't find shit fucking funny," Tavares said, snapping her neck and rolling her eyes. "You got a good bitch, and you running around with that monkey face bum bitch."

Rocky was so mad her nose was flaring. She didn't say anything. She just took a seat next to her girl and debated if she should reach across the table and punch Cali's man in the face, as he also happened to be her boyfriend's boy. Not wanting to explain to the two people she loved why she'd given Javan a black eye, Rocky took deep breaths to calm down.

Then, she said, "Javan, you got shit all the way fucked up. You gonna leave Cali after all these years to wife a top-tier hoodrat like that?"

He looked at his wifey's friends, and from their still angry faces, he could sincerely appreciate the love they had for his better half.

"Listen, Dumb and Dumber. You two dingbats should KNOW better. You leave rats in the gutter, not bring them home. It's not what y'all think."

"Get the fuck outta here," Tavares said, getting mad that Javan was trying to play them for suckers.

"Then, what the fuck was it?" Rocky asked through clenched teeth, still steaming. "Because that bitch just swore you're in love with her, and your ass just had the nerve to tell us you're leaving our girl for her. So, what's really good, Javan?" Rocky said, using all her inner strength not to punch him in the face.

"That bitch be moving work for me. And, I do mean she be moving it. She's a stripper that works at the Big Daddy's down in Philly. She comes in contact and knows all the major players state to state. I'm eating and taking no risk. She has it in her mind that she's doing this for us to help me get back right, so we can live happily ever after—like I really want to wife a stripper trap queen. My girl is part hood, all classy, strong, and has a solid thriving business. Most importantly, she held me and my seed down while I was away. I ain't never leaving Cali. I don't care how much money a broad drops in an account for me. This ain't nothing but a come up. Nothing."

"And, where did you find that ole extra stupid hoe?" questioned Tavares skeptically.

"I met her when I was doing my time down Rahway. My man said he had someone to bring me that work. She came up a few times, and it was all business. Off the rip, I could tell what kinda bitch she was—a trap queen, just tryna lock a baller down. Next thing I know, our conversations go from trapping and brief on the visits to someplace else. She said she's digging me, has fallen in love with me, would do anything for me, including help me move the work on the outside because she has connections in her profession. She been doing just that," laughed Javan. "She was bringing me work, so I could do my one-two on the inside while she was hustling and stacking my bread on the outside. Not to mention, she was filling my canteen up. But, hell fucking no, I ain't leaving my girl for her."

Sometimes the truth was hard to hide. Although Javan was doing this bucket head stripper dirty, they knew he was telling the truth.

"Javan, you're playing with fire," Tavares tried to warn him.

"Nah, I ain't. I ain't even giving her the pipe. I got her believing that she's so special that I don't even wanna dick her down until I leave Cali. She thinks I want us to be together before we even have sex because she's the one I'm gonna spend my life with."

Javan was cracking up from the bottom of his soul at the game Kamari was falling for.

"Nigga, you can laugh all you want," Rocky said with a stone-cold face, "but, trust me when I tell you, you're playing with fire. What are you gonna do when she becomes a woman scorned and reaches out to Cali or even worse, drops a dime on you?"

"Nah, I'mma end it soon. Real soon. I got three drops I need her to make, and I'm done with that bitch. I'll have made three hundred thousand without seeing anyone or touching anything."

"You doing the most," Tavares said, rolling her eyes as far back as they would go in her head. "I don't want to keep this from Cali, but since it's business and not pleasure, I'mma keep my mouth shut and mind my business."

"Like you should," Javan said with a strong voice and firm eyes.

"Fuck you," Rocky responded for her friend. "Now, you owe us lunch for dragging us into your bullshit."

"Will do," he said, smirking.

"And, let me tell you one motherfucking thing," Rocky said, pissed that she had to keep this kind of thing from her friend. "Don't let this come back to bite you in the ass. Because if that bitch dare gets out of pocket and tries to disrespect my friend, she's going in a fucking trunk, and I'm not playing."

"Listen, gangster... If that bitch ever tried to come for Cali, I'd put her in a trunk my Goddamn self."

While Kamari was being the joke of lunch, she was in her cobalt blue Mustang devastated at what had just taken place. She cried for a second out of embarrassment, but then convinced herself it didn't matter because she was getting the man. So, she thought... Once she dried the tears from her face, she called her cousin who she was staying with while visiting Jersey for the weekend.

"Hey cousin, how was lunch with your boo thang?"

"Oh, my God, cousin, you'll never guess what happened," Kamari said, informing her of what happened from start to finish.

"What in the fuck, cousin? That was some real fucking bullshit, and he didn't even come to your rescue. Something about him I ain't feeling. I told you from the gate. If he was fucking with you like that, why didn't he get released and come down there to Philly with you?"

"I know, I know, cuz... But, he said that him and ole girl had major history and he just didn't want to shit on her like that."

"Hmmmm, yeah. That don't sound like he's on the up and up to me. I don't like the way this shit sounds. And, I told your ass from the beginning if he still got a girl, don't fuck with him. In no way am I condoning what her girls did. But real talk, what did you want them to do? Was they supposed to sit at the table with you and act like shit was all good?"

"I know it sounds bad, but he told them he's leaving their friend and going to be with me because he loves me."

Kamari's cousin listened, but she didn't like that sound of things. However, she wasn't going to hurt her cousin's feelings.

"Cuz, I don't know who them bitches thought they was fucking with, but we don't play that shit out in Philly. No disrespect. I got something for them. When they least expect it, I'm gonna come for them bitches and make them wish they never fucked with me."

"Chill, K. You came down here for a good weekend, so we gonna leave that shit alone right now. We're going to hit club King's tonight and party like rock stars. I'm at work about to leave, so I'll meet you at my house in about an hour."

Kamari was letting it go for now, but she for sure wasn't gonna let them two bitches get a pass on what they did to her. As of now, she was ready to turn up and enjoy her weekend in Jersey.

***

Tavares, Rocky, and Javan had lunch and sipped on drinks while shooting the shit.

"I'm glad I cleared with you two killers what was really going on, because y'all was acting like y'all was gonna jump a nigga," Javan half-joked.

"Oh, trust me. We wasn't too far from the thought," Rocky confirmed, sipping her sangria.

"So what's y'all plans for tomorrow?" he asked the ladies, knowing that since it was Valentine's Day it was a big deal to women, overrated as it was.

"You got me beat," Rocky said, lying.

Tavares rolled her eyes before responding. "Abdora said we have to attend some stupid event. Like who the fuck has something on Valentine's Day?" she asked, annoyed at the thought.

Almost two hours had passed before the bill came and Rocky politely slid it to Javan.

"This is all you, playboy."

Tavares was weak and rolling.

"Y'all got that, Tweedle Dee and Tweedle Dum," he said, dropping three crisp hundred-dollar bills down before they headed out.

Tavares was heading home and couldn't shake the thought of the call from the lawyer regarding Damien's will. She picked up the phone and called her father.

Before he could say hello, Tavares screamed with excitement, "Papiiiiiii."

"Mijaaaa," he responded, giving his daughter the same energy. "What's shaking, Baby Girl? Nice of you to give your father a call. What you up to? Is everything alright?"

"Yeah, everything is fine. I was just driving home and wanted to call and ask you if you have a will."

Holton chuckled. "Why? Do you plan on killing me for my money? If so, don't waste your time. You ain't getting shit. Everything is going to my grandsons," Tavares's smooth-talking father answered her.

"Damn, that's how you do your long-lost beautiful daughter," Tavares joked.

"No, seriously. I do have a last will and testament. When I found out about you and the boys, I changed a lot of things. Should anything ever happen to me, you guys are set for life."

"And, what about me?" Dolonda asked, sitting across from the love of her life.

"Is that mommy?" Tavares asked.

"Who else would it be?"

Holton wanted his daughter to realize that her parents were back together and going to stay that way.

"Tell mommy I said fall back, she ain't getting nothing."

"Your daughter said, fall back because you ain't getting nothing."

"Tell her wives trump kids. Boom!" Dolonda said, joking back with their daughter. "Tell her I said first become a wife and not a mistress."

Tavares bellowed over in laughter.

"That ain't funny, Baby Girl."

"What the heffa say?" Dolonda asked, cutting her eyes at her daughter's father. "I know that wench said something smart because she has both our mouths put together."

"Alright, enough of you two. Why are you asking me about a will?" Holton asked, curious about the random question.

"Well, Papi... I got a call from this lawyer who told me Damien has a will, and I need to be present for him to do the reading."

"Damien had a will?" Holton questioned.

He was half shocked and half proud that the young man thought about if something ever happened to him.

"Okay, so what's the problem?"

"There is no problem. I directed him to Doll because I really don't care to be bothered. Truthfully, I don't want anything to do with her."

"Tavares, hear me out. Okay? You and Doll had an ugly falling out."

"Fuck that bitch," Tavares heard her mother say in the background.

Holton gave her a look that made it clear for her to shut the fuck up.

"Y'all fell out, but you have to remember that she was hurt and mourning the loss of her son. Sometimes people lash out when they're hurting. By no means do I condone the shit she said to you, because I know it wasn't true. But, try and cut her a little slack."

"No," Tavares said dryly.

"Baby Girl, losing Damien should show you that life is too short. Go to the will reading. If you want, I'll even come with you. Who's the lawyer?"

"Dylan James, I think he said his name was."

Hearing the lawyer's name made the wheels in Holton's head spin.

"Whoa, whoa, whoa... Damien had business with Dylan James? What type of shit was Damien into that he could afford to do business with Dylan?"

"Papi, you know him?"

"Yeah, I know him personally. He's done a lot of work with your grandparents and some friends of mine, as well as a few things for me. He's big time, though. You don't just go to Dylan James for a few thousand dollars or some minor bullshit. Damien must have had some major cash or property you don't know about."

"I don't fucking know. But, I know he wasn't Gotti, getting it in the streets like that."

"Well, there must be some shit you don't know because to even go see Dylan James, you have to be in the million-dollar club of the underworld. He's straight up and legit, no back-door bullshit. He don't mess around in the small-time world when it comes to money. So, let me know when you have to go, and I'll be there with you if you'd like."

"Thanks, Papi. Where are you and mommy?"

"In the Berkshires."

"Do y'all ever sit still? I feel like since I got out the hospital all y'all do is travel."

"Well, what the hell else do we have to do? I have a fully capable and trusted staff to run my businesses. Your mom is done with school, and our child is grown. All we have to do is spoil our grandchildren and see the world. It's called living life, Sweet Pea."

"It must be nice," Tavares said, half sarcastic but half happy her parents found love. "Hold on, Papi," Tavares said, entering her estate that had such sleek, modern architecture.

She was scanning the perimeter for Abdora's car. He usually parked in the circular roundabout in front of the house. When she didn't see his car, Tavares got excited.

"Word, I don't have to sneak my shit in the house. Yesssss!"

"Sneak what shit in the house?"

"My stuff I bought at the mall today."

Holton didn't know what else to do but laugh.

"Why would you be sneaking stuff you bought in the house?"

"Because Abdora told me don't come home with a whole bunch of shit I don't need. Of course, I don't know how to leave anything at the mall. So, his words went in one ear and out the other. I just don't feel like hearing his mouth, so I was gonna sneak it in."

"Y'all are crazy," Holton laughed, but he loved his daughter and hopefully soon-to-be son-in-law.

The sensor on the six-car garage recognized Tavares's car and began to open. The moment she spotted Abdora's black Lamborghini truck, silver Lexus GS, cocaine white BMW 745, and cherry red old school, she screamed, "FUCK, FUCK, FUCK!" and startled Holton.

"What's the matter, Tavares?"

"Abdora is home. That means I'm gonna have to hide my stuff."

"Baby Girl, you can't be serious," her father said while giving his soul mate a kiss. She was feeling neglected as he talked to their daughter.

"Papi, I'm dead serious. And, can you and mommy knock the mushy mushy shit off? This is a real crisis."

Holton turned to Dolonda and said, "I don't know who this girl gets her crazy from, me or you, but she's for sure crazy. Your daughter's having a mental break down because Abdora is home. She wasn't supposed to buy the whole mall, and now she has to hide her stuff."

"That's your child," Dolonda said, shaking her head at her daughter. "Because I'm a boss and would have walked in with it."

Tavares couldn't hear what her mother said, but she knew it was some fly shit.

"Papi, tell Mami to close her mouth."

As she was kicking it with her father about the boys, how she was holding up, and just conversing, Tavares popped her trunk and began stashing her stuff. She put some in the trunk of her Acura, some in the recycling bins, and prepared to carry another fourteen bags in the house. Walking up the short set of stairs that led into the house, Tavares prayed Abdora wasn't looking at one of the eight security cameras in the house that toggled various places on their estate. If he was, she was caught in the act. As she crept in the house, her first stop was the lower-level laundry room. She knew six of her bags would be safe there because Abdora never set foot in there. She breathed a sigh of relief.

"Papi, I'm good."

Tavares busted out laughing at the tactics she had to go through to enjoy her retail therapy.

Sarcastically her dad responded, "I'm so happy you didn't get caught committing your crime."

"I'm true to this, not new to this."

The shopping addict could joke now that the coast was clear. She walked through her basement where the movie theater, game room, and lady and man caves were and headed up to the kitchen. As Tavares opened the tall double-door stainless-steel refrigerator, an oversized trash bag that was sitting on one of her marble counters caught her attention. Holton was telling Tavares that he and her mother would be there soon to visit, but Tavares cut him off.

"Papi, I know Abdora has lost his mind. He has a damn trash bag sitting on my Goddamn counter."

"Why would he leave trash on the counter?" Holton asked, confused.

"Good Goddamn question. We're about to find out. Abbbdora!" Tavares screamed from the top of her lungs. With no response, she screamed again.

"Don't lose your damn voice screaming like a madwoman."

"I am a madwoman, daddy. But, I don't even know why I wasted my damn breath like he can hear me in this stupidly humungous house."

"Girl, who complains about a huge mansion?"

"Papi, don't get me wrong. This house is gorgeous—the dope architecture, the customized state of the art décor, and the million amenities—but it's just too damn big for me. I feel like we're in a hotel instead of a home. It's so fancy."

"Well, let's trade," Holton joked with his daughter about the home that Abdora had paid millions to purchase and customize every angle of for his daughter and grandsons.

Tavares walked over to the hunter green trash bag to try to understand why her boyfriend would put nasty, funky ass trash on her Italian marble counter. When she opened it, she got the shock of her life.

"What in the entire fuck?" she said, annoyed. "Papi, how about it's not trash. It's money. Looks to be about a couple hundred thousand."

Holton just cracked up laughing.

"What am I going to do with you two? No, the question is what are you going to do with that damn fool because who puts that kinda money in a trash bag and just leaves it on their kitchen counter? A boss, that's who," Holton answered his daughter with nothing but seriousness.

"We're gonna see who's the boss, because I'm about to lay his ass out. Papi, I love you. Kiss mommy for me, and if I don't speak to y'all tomorrow, have a very Happy Valentine's Day. Wait, speaking of

Valentine's Day, what did you get *me*, because I'm the real love of your life."

"What did I get you for Valentine's Day?" her father asked rhetorically.

Dolonda knew that her man was totally in love with his daughter and probably did get her something, but she answered for him.

"NOTHING. My man got you nothing, girl. That's why you got your own damn man."

"Babe, she can't hear you."

"Yes, I can. And, tell mommy to stop hating and mind her business. She ain't gotta be mad because her man *and mine* got me something," Tavares joked.

"Will do, and I guess you'll have to wait and see what I got you. Love you, Baby Girl. Go easy on my man."

CHAPTER 10

Tavares grabbed her bags and headed to the foyer of her luxury home. She looked at the spiral stairs and decided she wasn't trekking up approximately a hundred stairs to get to the fourth floor of her house. Instead, she was getting on the bronze and glass elevator that was hidden in the spiral stairs. As much as Tavares loathed having an indoor elevator, in her lazy moments like now, she hated to admit that she appreciated it. Still, it seemed too bougie—even for her.

When Tavares got off the elevator, she walked across the glazed white ceramic tile floors that went through the whole house. She made her way down the hallway that led to the wing where their master suite was located. It was more like a small apartment. She barged through the twelve-foot-tall white frosted glass French doors ready to give her boyfriend a verbal lashing, but he caught her off-guard. He was sitting up on the California king-sized bed comfortably watching T.V. while wrapped in nothing but a towel.

When he saw her, he immediately asked, "What in the fuck happened to your hair?"

Tavares rolled her eyes and asked, "Do you love it? I'm sure you do."

Her tone dared Abdora to talk shit.

"You left this morning with blonde hair that was damn near to your ass. Now, you come home with it all chopped off and colored turquoise with pink highlights. So, I'm just asking what the fuck happened to your hair."

"It's only hair. Relax, why don't you. I wanted something different."

"Don't get me wrong, Babe. Your shit is hot, but I didn't expect you to come home looking like a My Little Pony doll."

"Fuck you. Just know I can do this. I march to my own beat, and best believe ain't another bitch walking around here that can pull this off. But, can you tell me why the fuck there's an oversized trash bag full of money on the kitchen counter?"

"It's for the wedding."

Tavares was dumbfounded and confused, and her face said it before her words did. "What Goddamn wedding?"

"Ours, girl. Duhhhh," Abdora said sarcastically.

Waving her ring finger in the air, she stood at the bottom of the four stairs that led up to her bed.

"In case you haven't noticed, I'm not wearing a ring, so I don't know how you think we're getting married."

"Hell, take some money out of the bag and go buy whatever ring you want," Abdora said straight-faced, knowing he was making Tavares mad.

"I'll be doing no such stupid ass thing like that. In case you aren't sure how the order of operations works, let me help you out. First, YOU buy a ring. Then, you propose, and if I say yes, then we plan a wedding."

"IF you say yes?" Abdora laughed.

"Yeah... Who said I want to be married to you? I mean you're fine, rich, my baby daddy, and you got the best dick around... But, who said that means I want to be with you forever?" Tavares said straight-faced while walking up the stairs to their bed.

Before she made it to the last step, Abdora reached out and slammed her on the bed. Mounting her, he leaned down and kissed the woman he loved with everything inside him. Her body felt like he'd set it on fire from how passionately he'd kissed her.

"I love you, and you will be Mrs. Santacosa whether you like it or not."

"Abdora, I don't got time for this," Tavares yelled, knowing where his sweet, passionate kisses were heading. "OH, MY GOD, you're gonna fuck my hair up!" Tavares yelled.

"So what? You're bald-headed now anyway," he laughed and leaned down. He kissed her lips and then her neck while whispering, "Of course, you have time for this."

He slipped her shirt over her head, unhooked her pink lace bra, pushed her DD breasts together, and began slowly sucking her fully erect nipples. The fight was over from there. Tavares lay back and moaned, while her center was moist and ready.

"Wait… At least let me wrap my hair and take a quick shower."

He released her breast from his mouth and said, "Deal."

Tavares wrapped her perfectly symmetrically cut hair and made her way to her mind-bogglingly designed all-white bathroom. It had his and hers amenities. From wall to wall on the left and right sides were glass mirrors with chocolate brown vanities that ran the length of the full wall. Each side had its own double bowl sink, and each vanity had a chocolate brown chair. Their bowl-shaped tub was in the center of the bathroom. Behind the tub was a sixty by sixty steam glass shower. The his and hers shower heads were separated with a built-in marble seat that was arranged perfectly in the middle of the shower.

Tavares hated to get out of the shower that she loved more than any other place in her house, but she'd been in for thirty-five minutes and knew Abdora was going to be talking shit. She lathered her body one more time, caressing each body part as she went. Then she rinsed off and prepared to get out and get ready to get dicked down before she painted the town.

When the shower went off, Abdora yelled, "Goddamn, you been in there so long my man done went down."

"Shut up. When he sees this body, we both know he'll stand right back up to full attention."

As she dried off, Tavares said to hell with the clothes she planned to slip on. Instead, she exited the bathroom naked from head to toe. On the way back into the room, she made a pit stop in the closet and slipped on a pair of six-inch charcoal gray Dior pumps. Then, she made her way to the bed. True to what she'd said, the moment Abdora laid eyes on the perfect thickness in front of him, his dick went straight up in the air. Tavares wasted not another minute. She went to town on her man who had waited on her. She kissed him, sucked his bottom lip, and began massaging his dick at the same time with the baby oil she put on her hand right before she left the bathroom.

Then she whispered, "I told you he would get excited the moment he saw me."

She went back to kissing Abdora with the same passion he'd given her a little while ago. She kissed his mouth, his ears, and his neck, never releasing his rock-hard dick from her hand. She leaned in and kissed his chest and made her way down. Before she could even put his masculinity in her mouth, his eyes were rolling in the back of his head. Tavares loved catering to the man who had softened her heart and showed her what true love was. She gratified him mentally and emotionally, but what she did to him sexually blew his mind. Their passion in the bedroom was indescribable. It was never anything less than fireworks or sparks flying. Abdora couldn't do anything but brag about his woman. He loved that she was a classy woman in the street but his own personal freak in the sheets.

With no hands, Tavares made love to Abdora's manhood while he watched. With her warm, wet mouth, she kissed and sucked just the head. Then, she slowly took him in inch by inch, kissing and sucking each previous inch.

"Oh, my God!" Abdora yelled and tried to touch Tavares's shoulders.

Using her hands that were still free, she slapped his hands away and said, "Don't touch me. Take it like a big boy."

After he did just that, he turned Tavares around and made her grab her ankles. He gave her long, slow strokes until she was wet like an erupted volcano. Abdora was doing the work, but Tavares was bouncing her ass like she was one of the strippers they'd seen one time too many.

"Damn, baby... You're throwing it back," he moaned.

"That's how I keep you. I got kryptonite in my pussy," laughed Tavares.

They went from standing to the window seat to their desk and finally to the bed. They were moving with matched rhythm on the edge of the bed, getting it in doggy style until Abdora's phone interrupted them. He ignored it the first four times. After the fifth call, he leaned over and picked his phone up and saw that it was his mother calling. He finally pressed talk and speaker.

"What's up, Ma?" he answered, trying to conceal his moans.

Tavares didn't stop, and Abdora was even more turned on.

CHAPTER 11

Dhara wasn't paying any attention to the heavy breathing her son was doing when he answered the phone.

"Boy, you'll never guess who just left here."

"Hmmm," Abdora said.

His mother thought he was trying to figure it out, but he was concentrating on the fact that his girl had got up in the middle of doggy style and whispered for him to sit on the edge of the bed. She dropped to her knees and went back to making love to his penis with her mouth. Dora was fighting not to bust while Tavares was looking him straight in the eye. Abdora slowed his breathing down. He was trying to focus on Tavares and talk to his mother at the same time.

"Ma, Mason just left there. I sent him."

"No, Mason was here earlier. And, thanks for the smokey smoke," Dhara laughed. "Pretty Priscilla just left here," Dhara sang to the tune of Michael Jackson's song "Dirty Diana." The moment the name rolled off his mother's tongue, Tavares felt Dora's whole body tense up, and he instantly ejaculated in her mouth.

"What the fuck?" Tavares yelled, not caring that his mother heard her.

"Oh, my God, I didn't know that you had me on speaker."

Tavares wasn't mad that he came in her mouth; that was nothing new, but she didn't see it coming. However, she wasn't sure if he came at the sound of the name Priscilla or because she'd pleased him until he climaxed. Something told her it wasn't the latter of the two. She got up and made her way to the bathroom to wash her face and brush her teeth. The look of death on her face told Abdora just how mad she was.

"Ma, it's cool."

He truly didn't want to have this conversation and for damn sure not on speakerphone. Although, if he took his mother off speaker now, he knew Tavares would have something to say.

"Are you sure? I heard Tavares and she sounded mad."

"No, she's fine. I just spilt something on her," Abdora chuckled at the half truth. "What do you mean Priscilla just left there?"

"Yes, she was here for a few hours with me. She's back in town for a while."

Tavares made it her business to hurry up in the bathroom so she wouldn't miss too much of the conversation. She walked back in on Dhara saying, "Penny is sick. Really sick, and they don't expect her to live too long. So Priscilla is back to take care of her."

"Oh, damn. I didn't know Miss Penny was sick. I was wondering why I haven't heard from her."

"Prissy said she has cancer that has spread all over her body and there's nothing else they can do for her."

Abdora was truly sad, he had a lot of love for Miss Penny.

"Damn, Ma. I gotta go see her. I would hate for her to leave this world without me seeing her."

"Well, she's home right now with around-the-clock care. Priscilla asked for your number."

"And, I hope you told her he's taken," Tavares snapped, letting herself into the conversation.

Abdora just looked at Tavares because he knew there would be no restraint once his mother said that.

"No worries, Missy. I didn't give your man's number out."

"Appreciate it," Tavares sang.

"Ma, let me get with you a little later," Dora said, ending the call before his mother said any more. "But, I'm gonna go check on Miss Penny ASAP."

"Bye, Mama Dhara," Tavares said, waiting to cut into Abdora.

Dhara felt bad because she knew her son was about to catch hell, so she simply said, "Good night. Love you guys," and hung up.

Abdora hadn't even laid his phone down before Tavares cut into him.

"Who in the fuck is Priscilla?"

Dora really wasn't up for this conversation. He knew it was coming, but the last thing he wanted to do was explain to Tavares who Priscilla was. She was a sore topic that he didn't talk about. He wasn't ready to talk to the woman he loved about the only other woman he'd loved, who had broken his heart and whom he never got closure with.

"Priscilla is Miss Penny's daughter."

"Yeah, I figured that much from the conversation. So, let's cut through the bullshit and get down to what I'm really fucking asking you. Who the fuck is Priscilla to you?"

"No one," Dora said straight-faced with a dehydrated tone.

"Is that your fucking answer?"

Tavares was standing naked with her hands on her hips, ready to slap the shit out of Abdora.

"Babe, Priscilla is no one. At least she's no one worth us discussing."

"Bull motherfucking shit. Priscilla *is* someone," Tavares said, feeling herself about to go from zero to a hundred. "The moment your mother said her fucking name, you tensed up and busted in my fucking mouth, motherfucker."

Dora laughed, "Cut the shit, Baby Girl. My mother saying that girl's name didn't have shit to do with me cummin'."

Dora knew Tavares wasn't buying it. But that wasn't stopping him from trying his best to convince her she was wrong.

"I was on the verge of cummin' before my mother called, and you know it. You're the one that swallowed deep, and I couldn't hold it anymore."

He was only half lying. Tavares had more than pleased him. However, Dora couldn't admit that hearing that name had pushed his mind to over five years ago and caught him so far off-guard that it made him climax.

"Abdora, you're full of fucking shit. I want to know who the fuck Priscilla is because I don't recall you ever mentioning her. Your body language was a dead giveaway that you were uncomfortable talking to your mother about whoever she is in front of me. So, what's really good?"

Dora was trying not to get mad that his boo was pressing him so hard, but this conversation wasn't happening.

"Babe, just fucking let it go. I told you she's no one, and she isn't. This conversation is over," he said firmly.

He got up off the bed and walked to Tavares. He tried to embrace her and pull her close, but she wasn't having it.

"No, nigga, fuck you. Don't touch me. I have nothing to say until you're ready to tell me who the fuck Priscilla is."

Not saying another word, Tavares went in the bathroom and slammed the door behind her. She was fuming inside. Yet, when she left the house looking like a million bucks, it was gonna be Abdora who was mad.

***

Carmen missed Holton terribly. With Valentine's Day the next day, she couldn't help but be down and miss him even more. This would be the first time in ten years that she wouldn't have someone to put a smile on her face, make her feel special, and make it all about her. She was mad, hurt, and angry that he broke things off between them. She couldn't believe after a decade he'd ended things.

Carmen truly believed eventually Holton would leave his wife and marry her. He always told her how much he loved her and when the time was right he was gonna make an honest woman of her. She'd waited and waited, simply enjoying their ride together. Now, she was home trying to keep her mind off the man she'd truly grown to love. *How could he leave me and go back to his wife*, Carmen kept asking herself over and over again. *He went back to a woman he acted like he hated all these years. Something just doesn't add up*, she told herself.

After dwelling on her heartache, Carmen redirected her thoughts to the fact that the ninety days was up from the last time they received their last big shipment. It was time to prepare for the next one, and she and Holton weren't even on speaking terms. The last thing she planned to do was orchestrate the deal for her ex-lover to get millions of dollars' worth of raw, uncut cocaine in the country. If he could say fuck her, her heart, and her feelings, then she was being petty and saying fuck his business and his money. It was an eye for an eye as far as far as she was concerned. So far, he hadn't called her. But, one thing for sure, Holton Montiago didn't play about his money. So, even though he hadn't called since he broke her heart, she knew for sure that he would be calling in the next forty-eight hours. Then, she was gonna take great pleasure in hurting his feelings just like he'd hurt hers.

What Carmen didn't know was that she was going to be holding her breath waiting on Holton's call. He'd already made power moves to secure a new connect. When he told Carmen he was done with her, he meant that, and not even her connects in the drug underworld would pull him back. That was the blessing of being a stand-up businessman with a reputation that preceded him. It only took one phone call and he was good.

***

When Tavares stepped out of the bathroom, she was nothing short of breathtaking. Abdora eyed her from head to toe, wanting to rip her clothes off, toss her on the bed, and make love to her. Though seeing that he could still see steam coming from her ears, he didn't push his luck.

Instead he said, "Boo, you look beautiful."

His future wife was killing the black leather baby doll dress that hugged her to perfection. She also wore black designed lace stockings and simple black red-bottom pumps.

"I know," Tavares said, overly dry, to let him know she was all set on his conversation.

She applied her bright red lipstick and shook her hair out. Then, she grabbed her Louis Vuitton clutch and headed for the door.

"Don't wait up."

Abdora half chuckled and said, "Yeah, aight. Don't get beside yourself. My chick don't let the sun beat her home. So, don't get it fucked up."

Saying nothing, Tavares walked out of her room and left Abdora standing there feeling some kind of way that she didn't say bye, give him a kiss, or anything.

By the time Tavares arrived at Justine's, she was past fashionably late. She was an hour late. Rocky, Cali, and Bella were drinking and appeared to be well past their first drink from how loud they were.

"Well, look who the fuck decided to show up and join us," Bella said, talking shit and sipping her Remy at the same time.

Tavares paid her friend no mind and made her way around the table, giving each of them a kiss on the cheek before taking a seat.

"Oh God. Who let this witch drink Remy? Y'all know damn well the night never ends well when she drinks that brown monster," Tavares said, not joking.

"Bitch, I let me drink Remy. I'm always on my best behavior, Remy or not," Bella laughed, knowing she was lying through her teeth.

"What did I miss?" Tavares asked, looking for a recap.

"Yeah, Bella. What did Tavares miss?" Rocky said, being sarcastic about what Bella had shared with them a few minutes prior.

Bella sat straight up and asked Tavares, "How would you feel about getting with some of the other girlfriends of the Murder Mafia?"

Tavares looked to her left and her right at Rocky and Cali before looking straight ahead at Bella.

"Why the fuck would I want to do that dumb shit? 1st Wives Club is for us and only us. We ain't looking for no new friends. We don't even like each other half the time. So why am I interested in meeting some new bitches?"

Her partners on the left and right burst out laughing, because even Tavares thought this was stupid. Bella tried to convince them before Tavares's arrival that she wouldn't be against it like they were. However, Tavares's response had just gunned her all the way down.

"When did we start socializing with the girlfriends of the mafia? They ain't even on our level or life class to try to hang with us."

"Rigggghtt," yelled Rocky, giving Tavares a high five.

"You bitches are so fucking mean," Bella said, joking. She was just as mean, but she was trying to do what her man asked of her.

"Listen, it's not me. I told Mason that we would meet Bam-Bam's chick at the club tonight."

"And, who told you to agree to that foolish shit?" Cali asked, looking at her cousin waiting for a legitimate explanation.

"Mason said that we have our own mean girl club, aka the 1st Wives Club, and Bam-Bam is really feeling this chick. He said that he's probably gonna wife her and wanted us to just let her hang out with us."

Rocky just shook her head. Cali spoke what she knew her friends were thinking. "Why does whoever Bam-Bam decides to wife have to hang out with us?"

Rocky cut Cali off before she could say anything else. "Every brother in the organization knows we don't hang out with anyone except each other. Hell, Tavares was a stretch Rocky threw out there."

She was joking but serious at the same time. No one at the table cared what Mason had convinced Bella to do. They had no desire to hang out with any new chicks. Rocky tossed her shot of Patrón back before speaking again.

"So when we get to the club, we have to entertain, hang out, and kick it with retarded ass Bam-Bam's girl?"

Bella replied in a low tone, "Yes. So, you bitches need to put on your nice girl faces and get ready."

They just shook their heads because they all hated making friends with the other girlfriends. They had their own circle and liked it that way.

"I hope Mason or Bam-Bam is footing the bill tonight, because I ain't spending one red cent for this set up," laughed Tavares.

The ladies caught up over more drinks and appetizers. Right before dinner was due to come out,

Tavares caught everyone off-guard like she hoped to do.

"Who the fuck is Priscilla?"

Rocky dropped the ice out of her mouth. Cali and Bella looked at each other with bulging eyes.

"Rocky said, "Uhhh, who is Priscilla?"

"Cut the shit, bitches. Mama D called talking about she'd come to visit her, and Abdora's whole body language changed. He refused to talk about it. So now, which one of you bitches is gonna give me the drop on who the fuck Priscilla is?"

Cali, Rocky, and Bella exchanged eyes to see who was going to spill all the history. "You bitches is killing me. It doesn't matter who tells me, but someone better start talking," Tavares said, grabbing a knife and waving it around the table.

"Okay," Rocky said, taking a long breath and sipping her freshly delivered double shot of chilled Patrón. "First off, Abdora would kill each and every one of us for sharing this info with you. So, Bitch, whatever you do, just don't tell him where you got your intel."

"No problem," Tavares agreed, smiling from ear to ear because the disclaimer told her it was juicy. "And, don't ever insinuate I would rat on y'all, because bitch you know I don't move like that. The last thing I am is a cheese eater. Now spill it," she said, sitting upright in the leather dinner chair.

"Priscilla was Abdora's childhood honey, teenage sweetheart, and the love of his life."

Tavares screwed her face up at the last part.

"Well... until he met you," Rocky said, cleaning the last part of her statement up. "He knew at thirteen years old he wanted to marry that skeezer. When he got on in the streets, she was the flyest bitch walking around here. Her hair and nails were done regularly, she always had new sneakers and fly clothes, and there was nothing he wouldn't do for her. There was something about that girl he just loved to no end. He was going to marry her."

Bella and Cali thought Rocky could have stopped at the last sentence but they didn't say anything.

"She wasn't really a mix of both worlds—street and school. She was all school, and I think that was what Abdora loved about her. She was an honors student, on the debate team, class president, and a whole bunch of other stupid square bitch shit. She got accepted to a lot of big colleges and was gonna stay here and just commute to NYU. But, Abdora told her to go, explore the world past the tri-state area. He told her that he would be there every step of the way. Then, he said they would get married once she graduated. She got a scholarship, so Dora did everything else to set her straight."

Tavares was sucking it all up to hold in the arsenal for when she needed it.

'He bought her a new car, flew her to school, got her a crib, furnished it, and made sure she was good. All her mama had to do was wave goodbye, thanks to Dora."

"But, her and her mother are a whole another book," Cali chimed in. "Dora took care of her all the way through school. Word is that at some point, she lost her scholarship due to lack of funding. Her mom was gonna sell her house to cover her tuition costs, but Abdora bought the house and let her mother stay in it."

"Can't confirm or deny that... Just the streets talking," Rocky made clear.

"Okay," Tavares said, wanting to get to why they weren't together. "Why did they break up?"

Bella took over from there.

"We aren't too sure what went down exactly. But, Dora flew out there for her college graduation and was ready to propose to her. He was excited, proud, and bragging how he was gonna propose to the love of his life. He bought the ring and everything. However, he came back and said it was over and that Priscilla didn't exist anymore. We all knew whatever happened must have been deep for him to say that, and no one ever mentioned her name again. Not until you just brought it up."

"Interesting," Tavares responded to all the information she'd just ingested. "Well, that bitch is back because her mama is about to kick the bucket."

"Tavareeesss," Cali screeched at her friend for her cold emotionless words for someone about to lose their mother.

"WHAT? Don't Tavares me. She is. That bitch went by Mama D's house. But, if she knows like I know, she better stay in her lane and not be checking for my man before her and the mother be lying side by side in a casket."

The ladies laughed, but they knew Tavares wasn't playing when it came to Abdora. They all changed the subject and enjoyed the rest of dinner. They were in their zone, laughing, joking, talking shit, and just enjoying each other's company.

"So, what's y'all's plans for tomorrow?" Tavares inquired about her friends' Valentine's Day plans.

"We're going on a triple date. Duh," Bella teased.

"Oh, fuck me and my man, huh?"

"Listen," Cali said, "talk to your man. He was the ninja acting like y'all was too good to hang out with us like this ain't what we do on a regular day."

"He makes me fucking sick," Tavares said, sucking her teeth and rolling her eyes as she thought back to their argument before she left the house. "I can't believe he has us going to someone's stupid ass party on Valentine's Day. He gets on my nerves. Word he does."

Cali decided to fuck with Tavares.

"Damn, Booski. That sucks for you. We're going to be all the way turned up tomorrow. We're going to that new Ice Bar where the whole thing is made out of ice. Then, we're going to dinner, doing a Valentine scavenger hunt, and we have a luxury party bus taking us to Atlantic City."

"I hate you bitches," Tavares said, steaming inside.

"Maybe next time," Cali said, blushing.

The vertically challenged, plump smiling waiter delivered the bill. The ladies all looked to Tavares.

"What the fuck are y'all looking at? I know the rules," Tavares said, rolling her eyes and grabbing her wallet.

They had an unwritten rule that when you were more than an hour late, you paid the bill. With no hesitation, she dropped $400 on the table.

"It's always a pleasure, bitches," Tavares said, giving them the middle finger.

As the crew made their way to the garage, Cali asked, "Are we taking one car or driving our own cars?"

"No one is gonna want to come back and get their cars after we've been drinking. We might as well park at your house, Cali, and just hop in one car," Rocky said, dropping logic.

Cali told her cousin whom she rode with, "You know it's going to be smoke if Tavares and Priscilla cross paths."

"I doubt it, cuzzo. They have no reason to have beef. Prissy is old news, and Tavares is Dora's present and future."

"Bish, please," laughed Cali. "That mature shit sounds good in logic, but you and I both know that if those two cross paths, it's not going to be gumdrops and lollipops."

"Well, thank God they have no reason to be near or around each other," laughed Bella, because she knew Cali was right.

Tavares was in her car listening to Jennifer Hudson trying to not feel some kind of way that she had to learn about Priscilla from her girls instead of her man. They always had an open line of communication, so this was rubbing her wrong that he'd been so tight-lipped about his ex. She trusted Dora and wasn't insecure. She just knew Priscilla better stay in her lane.

Before the ladies knew it, they were at Cali's house. Rocky and Tavares hopped in Bella's black on black Range Rover where the two cousins awaited. They drove to King's talking shit and laughing.

"Tavares, who the fuck are you texting or are you on social media? You social media whore," joked Rocky.

"No, I'm not on social media, nor am I a social media whore. I just post and tag Dora for his aggravating ass groupies. I like them to see and know they can follow and like all they want, but he got a wife in real life," Tavares said with a vengeful laugh.

"I hate them thirsty ass hoes. That nigga will post some dry ass cornflakes, and them hungry follower bitches will like and comment dumb shit like "Yessss, so dope, looks yummy, love it, I want some!" and I be like really, Abdora!"

Everyone fell out rolling because Tavares wasn't lying. Dora's social media was crazy like he was a celebrity.

"I'm actually texting Ebony. She said she guesses dark girls weren't invited tonight. Why y'all didn't invite her?" questioned Tavares.

"Tell Ebony I said to go kill herself," Bella answered flatly. "I invited that dingbat and she said she was on stepmom duty with Bryce's daughter, so she better cut the shit."

"Y'all know Ebony is sweet, but she's slow as fuck," bellowed Tavares. "Well, she's meeting us at the club. Actually, she's already there," Tavares informed them, putting her phone back in her bag.

"Why is the line always around the corner?" Rocky asked, aggravated at the sight. Although she and her friends would never in a million years stand in a line, she just didn't get why it was always so damn long.

"We need a club," Tavares informed them matter-of-factly.

"Well, tell your boyfriend," Cali half-joked.

"We can call it Queens," Rocky added.

"I'm on it," Tavares said, making a mental note to get serious with Abdora about opening another club or buying her a club and letting them become each other's competition.

As the ladies were bypassing the line, engaging in conversation, they were forced to stop when they heard, "Ole stuck up bitches think they can cut the line." The four stooges turned around ready to bring the smoke. Then, they saw it was Ebony and burst out laughing.

"Fuck you, bitch," Bella said for all of them.

Then, everyone looked at Ebony baffled. Even though there was no possible logical answer she could give them, Cali asked what they were all thinking. "Ebony, what the fuck are you doing standing in line?"

Bella, Rocky, and Tavares just fell over in laughter because there was nothing Ebony could say that would make sense.

"Well, there was a new door guy, and I didn't know if he was gonna let me in, even though Bryce owns the club," Ebony naively stated.

In unison, the ladies just shook their heads at her. "Bitch, let's fucking go," Cali yelled.

As they approached the door, Tavares told her co-defendants, "I got this."

"Please do, because if we leave this to Ebony, we'd not only be in line but also paying," Bella said, shaking her head, laughing, and rolling her eyes.

"Hi, what's your name?" Tavares asked the chocolate bouncer with an acne-covered face.

"Line is around the corner," he responded.

"I didn't ask you where the line was. I asked you your name," Tavares snapped.

"Listen, no one charms or slides me any extra money to cut the line. So, you ladies might as well turn around and go to the back of the line."

"Excuse you," Tavares snapped. "We don't pay to get in, so we sure as hell ain't sliding you nothing extra. My man owns the club."

Rolling his half-crossed eyes, the bouncer said, "Is that right? Well, I wasn't informed of no girlfriends, side chicks, or baby mamas getting in free. So, again, the line is back there," the ignorant bouncer said, pointing to the line like he was talking to toddlers and not grown ass women.

"Oh, this nigga is disrespectful," Rocky said, almost choking.

Tavares looked at the bouncer and said, "Nigga, you done lost your mafucking mind."

She almost slapped the dog shit out of him but decided acting trashy at Dora's club wasn't the route to take.

"Let me call Abdora, because now you being disrespectful."

Hearing Abdora, the bouncer said to himself, "Oh shit... She might be telling the truth."

When Tavares whipped her phone out, she realized she couldn't call her other half. "Fuck!" she yelled out loud.

She was still pissed with him and wasn't giving in that easy.

"Oh, let me guess. You don't have Abdora's number in that phone," the half fat, half buff bouncer taunted.

"Motherfucker, what I *AM* gonna have is your job. So, enjoy tonight because I promise it will be your last."

When she looked at her friends, Tavares's face said what she was thinking before she stated it.

"I ain't calling Dora. I'm still pissed."

Rocky said, "Bitch, we're at this door like we ain't Boss Bitches. You better call him."

"Nope."

"You're just mean and stubborn," Cali tossed in.

"Ebony, give me your phone," Tavares said, extending her hand but looking straight at the bouncer.

She dialed the already programmed number, and he answered, "Hey baby."

"Not your baby. It's your best friend's wife."

"Tavares, what you want? I thought you was my baby."

"No, she's standing right here. We're at the front door, and your new security man doesn't want his job seeing that he's treating us like we're groupies trying to bypass the line."

"Pass him the phone."

Tavares gave a devilish smirk and did just that.

"What's up, Boss?"

"Are there five women in front of you?"

"Yes."

"Look at their faces very well. Hell, take a picture if you have to. The Godiva chocolate one is my wife. The blue-eyed devil is Abdora's wife. Those are the three stooges with them. They don't pay, and they don't wait in line. If you see them coming, just step aside and let them in."

"Okay, Boss."

"Doesn't matter who comes with them, just let them in. They're all family. Just save yourself the aggravation and know them pain-in-the-asses don't pay and don't wait in line. Got it?"

"Yeah, I got it."

After returning the phone to the owner, the bouncer stepped aside and let the ladies in.

"Thanks, asshole," Tavares said, rolling her eyes.

"Next time, we gonna fuck you up," Rocky joked as she walked by and pinched his cheek.

CHAPTER 12

Tavares felt a little chill and tried to roll over in the uncomfortable position she was balled up in. When she looked down, she saw bright green toes on her. She jumped when she saw Rocky stretched out on the other side of the couch.

"What the hell? We fell asleep," Rocky said.

"What the fuck," Tavares yelled while scurrying trying to find her phone.

Everyone opened their eyes looking at Tavares like she was crazy.

"Bitch, what's your problem?" Cali questioned.

"What time is it?" Bella asked.

Spotting her phone under the rubbish of weed and empty blunt boxes, Tavares went to check the time only to find that her phone was dead.

"What fucking time is it!" she yelled.

"It's 8:18," Rocky answered.

"Tavares, if you don't lie back on that couch and shut the fuck up," Bella said from the other side of the sectional couch.

"I gotta go, y'all. Abdora is gonna bug the fuck out when I get home."

"Oh, Miss I'm so mad, fuck him. Now, you worried about being in trouble," Cali teased. "Tell him you fell asleep over here. He'll be okay," Cali said, reaching for the un-smoked blunt they left in the ashtray.

"Damn, we must have been to the meat that we left a fully un-smoked blunt," Bella said, sitting up for some morning wake and bake.

As she grabbed her shoes, purse, and coat, Tavares said, "Happy Valentine's Day, heffas. I love y'all, but I'm out."

"Oh, shit. It is Valentine's Day," Rocky said, knowing that she too was going to catch hell for staying out all night.

"Damn, bitches. We all might as well get up because them niggaz is gonna be trippin' that we stayed out all night on Valentine's Day," Bella said, knowing that Mason was probably at the front door waiting on her.

Tavares drove home with mixed emotions. It was Valentine's Day, and she felt some type of way about the previous night of what went down with Dora's first love. Priscilla had tried her. And, now she was gonna have to face some bullshit when she got home because she got so high she passed out.

She raced home and parked in the semi-circle driveway in front of the house. As she rushed out of the brisk morning air, she wondered if Dora was even home. As she got to the elevator, she could hear Tupac playing and got the answer to her question. Following the music and the aroma of breakfast, Tavares entered the kitchen. Her man was standing over the twelve burner stove with his back to her. He was wearing some sweats and a wife-beater looking sexy as hell. She didn't even know what to say.

"Happy Valentine's Day, babe."

Abdora didn't respond or turn around from the stove.

"Abdora, I know you hear me talking to you."

He still made no acknowledgement of her presence.

"Don't be like that."

Still, silence was all Tavares got.

"Oh, you're going hard, huh?" Tavares asked while steaming inside.

Ding dong, Abdora's phone chimed. He ignored it and kept making breakfast. Dora thought that he was going to start the day by bringing Tavares breakfast in bed after he made love to her. Yet, when he woke up, she still wasn't home. He was flaming mad, but had a long day and decided to avoid being aggravated. He wanted to turn around, but he wasn't sure he could do it without disrespecting the woman he loved. So, it was best that he just ignored her.

"Abdora, you're being a real live fucking asshole. I know I said don't wait up, but what the fuck. I fell asleep at Cali's. I didn't stay out all night on purpose. All the fucking nights you're ripping and running, I don't say anything. Now, you want ignore me because I didn't come home one time."

Still no response. She was pissed even harder with the continued silence. However, she didn't know how to leave well enough alone.

"Well, I'm not about to kiss your ass. I fucking said I fell asleep. If you want to be on sucker ass nigga shit, by all means do so."

Abdora had tried long enough. Then, he turned around and let loose.

"Tavares, do me a favor and leave me the fuck alone. And, I do mean the fuck alone," Abdora said with a moderate but freezing cold tone. "I don't know where the fuck you was for you to claim you fell asleep. But, what I do know is I told you my woman don't let the sun beat her home. So fucking what I rip and run and come in late. You can't do what I do. It pays the cost to be the boss, and I ain't never came home and told you I fell asleep no fucking place. If I'm out the house, it's money- or business-related. I don't give a flying fuck about what you went outta here mad about. You still should have brought your motherfucking ass home last night. You fell asleep. Well, guess what.... You should have fell the fuck asleep at home with your man on Valentine's Day. I went to sleep and woke up to my woman still not next to me. I don't know where the fuck you were. And, to be honest, I don't give a fuck. But, do me a favor and leave me the fuck alone," Abdora said with a razor-sharp attitude. "Matter of fact, I got shit to do. You can eat this breakfast I planned to bring you in bed. I'm about to get dressed and get up outta here before this gets a lot uglier." Grabbing his phone, Abdora stormed out of the kitchen without another word.

Tavares's eyes were out of her head. Her mouth was wide open and she thought she was about to do the matrix. She was in utter shock. Never had Abdora talked to her in such a way. She didn't know what was worse: his words or the frostbitten pitch he'd taken. Abdora hated that he'd just spoken in such a harsh way to the woman that he loved. He planned on making her his wife soon, but she'd just pulled his ugly side out. Her mouth and not coming home had gotten the best of him. Abdora had shit to do, so he would have to let well enough be for now. When he checked his phone, he saw the ignored text was a group message from Javan.

When he opened it, Abdora almost felt like shit. It was a picture of Tavares, Cali, Bella, and Rocky all passed out on the sectional couch in Javan's basement.

"You niggaz owe me a night's rent for the space and heat y'all women took up. Don't worry, I'm covered these high heffas up and didn't let them freeze," Abdora read.

Looking at the picture and caption, Dora realized that Tavares had indeed told the truth. She was passed out, mouth open, and truly looked like falling asleep hadn't been her intention. Still, Abdora didn't give a fuck. The fact still remained that she left mad and didn't make it home like she should have. Not that he ever questioned, wondered, or thought she was out cheating, but he swore she stayed out on purpose, even though the picture proved different. He put his phone down and dressed in one of his favorite ensembles of the season—a Champion sweat suit, puffy vest, some black and white foams, and a fitted cap. Then, he bounced to take care of his business without so much as a "goodbye" or an "I love you" for Tavares.

After making sure the night he planned was going to be perfect, he drove to Eighth Street to Miss Penny's house. Dora wasn't sure if he was ready to see Priscilla, but he knew he couldn't avoid her forever. He rang the doorbell and braced himself for a blast from his past. To his surprise, it was a young woman he recognized that answered.

"I know you from somewhere," Dora stated to the face that greeted him.

"I met you while I was with Bam-Bam. Are you here about last night?" the girl asked nervously, because everyone knew that Dora didn't play.

Clueless, Abdora said, "Last night? I'm not sure I know what you're talking about."

"The big blowout with Priscilla and Tavares," Brooklyn answered, realizing Dora was clueless.

"Fuck is you talking about, Shorty?"

Brooklyn played the eventful evening back and Dora took in each word. He couldn't wait to get home and give Tavares's ass the business.

"Shorty, good looking out on the replay, but I wasn't here for that at all. I had no idea that my wifey and Priscilla was at my club acting like hoodrats. If you'll excuse me, though, I'm gonna go see Miss Penny."

As he entered Miss Penny's room, Dora could feel death around the corner. He felt a piece of his heart chip away for the woman he had mad love for. He and Penny had been close since he and her daughter were children. Seeing her lying in a hospital bed inside her bedroom looking lifeless got the best of him. However, Dora pulled it together. He kicked it for a good long time with Miss Penny about any and everything. They both knew it would be the last time they had a talk of this kind. She was frail, weak, and the complete opposite of everything Dora had ever known her to be.

"Dora, I'm happy that you found real love. You deserve it," Penny said faintly with her eyes barely open as she lay in the hospital bed. "Take good care of her and them precious twins of yours."

"Thanks, Miss Penny. I plan to. She's everything I've ever wanted."

"Well, you remember that and don't let Prissy change your heart," Penny said, trying to muster up a laugh, but her body wouldn't allow it.

"Miss Penny, I loved your daughter. I would have given her my life, but what she did to me would never allow me to open that chapter of my life again. I'm head over heels in love with my girl. She got a way that surpasses anything I ever had for your daughter. You know me, so you know I say what I mean and mean what I say."

"Well, Dora, do me a favor. Just do me one favor: take care of my daughter and your maybe baby."

Abdora almost choked.

"Miss Penny, stop. That beautiful little girl isn't mine."

"Maybe," Penny said and left it there, but Dora knew better. "Abdora, give me a hug. I'm just so tired, baby. Tired. And, I need a nap."

Abdora kissed Miss Penny's forehead and whispered, "Everything is all set when you're ready to go home."

Then, he let himself out and said goodbye to Brooklyn. When he turned to leave, he bumped into Priscilla. They stared at one another, each not knowing what to say.

"Hello, Abdora," the once love of his life said, breaking the silence.

"What's going on, Prissy? I mean Priscilla. I just came to check on your moms."

"I appreciate it, thanks. I'm sure she was glad to see you."

"No thanks needed. I also heard about you and my girl acting like gutter rats. But, I apologize if she started it."

"Yeah, she's a feisty bitch, but no need to be sorry for her. I thought we was gonna kill each other last night," Prissy said, shaking her head at how the night took a turn for the worse.

"I'm glad the night didn't end with one of y'all needing bail money. I have to run, but grab my number from Brooklyn. Call me if your moms needs anything, and I do mean anything."

Priscilla's mouth spoke, "Okay," but her thoughts were saying, *how did you walk out on this fine specimen of a man?* Abdora had always been handsome, but with age and the maturity of his physical features, fine was an understatement. Priscilla was in bed with the devil, but seeing Abdora just made her mind up that this was no longer business. She wanted Abdora back for keeps.

She didn't know what she'd gotten herself into agreeing to come back to get close to Abdora. The reason had been undisclosed to her, but the amount of money had been worth it at the time. Now, the money wasn't the real payoff. Getting Abdora back was gonna be the real jackpot. Seeing his face had just made her heart stop. In thirty seconds, she thought about the past and what her present life would be like had she not walked out on the man she'd loved for all the wrong reasons.

Due to the incident the night before, Priscilla knew that Tavares was gonna be a real headache and give her a run for her money. She for sure had her work cut out for her with trying to get close to Abdora, and most importantly, getting him to come back to her. She just smiled because she was gonna work her magic and get what she wanted.

Before she went to sit with her mother, she called her boss to inform her that she'd crossed paths with Abdora and to tell her about the fiasco from the night prior.

CHAPTER 13

Since Dora had left Miss Penny's house, Priscilla kept creeping into his thoughts. He couldn't figure out if it was because of the irony that she and Tavares had bumped heads already, or if it was because the life he was planning with Tavares was one that he'd only wanted with Prissy once upon a time. He was trying to push Priscilla from his head. God must have heard him because his phone rang.

"What up, Bro?" Dora asked his best friend.

"Ain't shit. I'm just about done shaking and baking for this evening. I'm gonna be dapper as a motherfuckerrrrr," Bryce sang. "I know it's about you and Tavares tonight, but don't be hating on a nigga," he joked.

"Nigga, you couldn't be flyer than me if I dressed you myself!" Dora shot back.

The lifelong best friends were rolling as they usually did when talking shit to each other.

"Nigga, what you calling me for, because I know it ain't to tell me how your ugly ass is gonna be fly at my party tonight."

"Fuck you! I'm the flyest fat nigga you know. I was calling to see if you was Gucci or if you needed me to do anything."

"Nah, we good money. All we gotta do is show up and show out. But, wait... Nigga, why you didn't call and tell me Prissy and Tavares was acting up at the club last night?"

"Nigggggaaa," Bryce said with his voice rising with every syllable. "After that shit died down, I had to finish the club business. When I looked up to call you, it was four in the morning. Today, I didn't even bother because I knew you had your plate full. But, Dawg, your women showed the fuck out. They got hoodrats of the night awards last night."

"Yo, B, I had no clue. I went by Miss Penny's and Bam-Bam's girl filled me in because she thought that was why I was there. I was stunned as fuck, but I'm not surprised at Tavares. She'll set shit off. That sweet shit is just her alter ego," laughed Dora.

"I thought it was about to be a royal rumble match. It took three of us to hold back that bolt of lightning that you call a girlfriend. She was gonna whoop the brown off Prissy."

"Well, what the fuck happened?"

"I don't know what took place upstairs in the private room because Ebony didn't want to talk about it, but whatever it was started in there. They were all leaving after destroying the private lounge. Prissy said something slick as they got in the foyer, and Tavares stone-cold charged at her. She just kept yelling, 'Bitch I'll lay you in a casket next to your half dead mother.'"

Abdora thought that was real low of Tavares to talk about someone's dying mother, and she was gonna know it soon enough.

"Tavares was hungry last night, and she was gonna eat Prissy alive."

Dora didn't even know what to say.

"Nigga, you know she didn't make it home? And, when she did, she failed to tell me this."

"Oh, shit... Gangster Boo didn't make it home. Get the fuck outta here," he said, not believing that Tavares would cheat on his best friend.

"Nah, she fell asleep at Javan and Cali's. Javan sent everyone a text this morning talking shit about our wives taking up his heat last night."

"She was in hot water with the boss. That's why she didn't tell you she was about to tear the club up," Bryce joked.

"Nah, she didn't, but I got a trick for her ass. I'm about to go home and lay her out."

Dora shot the shit with Bryce until he made it home. Pulling up in his garage, he was ready for war. Dora was gonna teach Tavares a lesson that she wouldn't forget. He didn't care about the beautiful night that he had planned for them. He grabbed his gun and crept in the house. He listened to see if he could hear Tavares on the first floor. With no trace of her voice, he stopped in the kitchen to load the ammunition in his weapon of choice. Dora checked the security camera, and with no sight of his lady, he knew she had to be in their suite.

When Abdora made his way to the master suite, he found Tavares knocked out. He watched her sleep for a lengthy moment. Thoughts about his past, present, and future filled his mind. He slowly pulled the covers back to find that Miss Stay Out All Night was covered in only a wife-beater and boy shorts. He let out his infamous chuckle, and then he pulled the trigger. Tavares felt her body being hit. Her subconscious told her she was dreaming. She was cold and couldn't move. Finally, she managed to roll over on her back.

She faintly mumbled, "Stop, please stop."

The next shot was between her legs, and she felt like she released fluid. Tavares came to and realized she wasn't dreaming. Abdora was shooting her with a water gun.

She instantly popped up and yelled, "What the fuck, Abdora! Like, seriously, what the fuck?"

"Shut up," Dora said, pointing the gun at Tavares's face and shooting again.

"Are you fucking kidding me?" Tavares screamed from the top of her lungs.

She got sprayed again.

"What is your fucking problem?"

Spray.

"Why the fuck are you shooting me with a water gun?"

Spray.

"Are you still talking?"

Tavares didn't say a word. She was heated.

"Now, do you have anything you want to tell me?"

Silence filled their room. Spray. This time Tavares moved, and he missed.

"Why didn't you tell me about you setting it off with Priscilla?"

Tavares didn't know if she was more heated that her man had just awakened her with a water gun or that he was questioning her about his ex. She went from zero to a hundred with the water gun, but asking her about Priscilla had just sent her to a million. That's when she blacked out.

"Motherfucker, I know that's not why the fuck you're up here fucking waking me up with no motherfucking water gun. Have you lost your cotton picking ass mind? Abdora, you got me fucked up. *ALL* the way fucked up. Like you told me this morning, I better leave you alone. You better leave me all the fuck the way alone. Fuck her, and fuck you even more for waking me up with this foolish ass shit."

"Geesh, so hostile," Dora taunted and sprayed the last of the water from the gun.

"Ughhhh, you fucking get on my nerves," Tavares said, now with her body, pussy, and head wet.

"Damn, Gangster Boo. Tell me why you mad. I just want to know why you were at my club acting crazy," Abdora said with his arms folded across his chest, looking at his soaked bed and girlfriend trying to maintain a straight face.

"Let's see... I'm mad because it's fucking Valentine's Day and you gave me attitude this morning. You didn't buy me a gift, and now you want to be fucking with me because of your wack ass ex. Just leave me the fuck alone," Tavares said wet, mad, and cold at the same damn time.

"No, I'm not leaving you alone. I want to know what made you come out of character at my place of business," Dora said, no longer joking but wanting an answer.

"Blame Bella."

"Bella?"

Dora was lost.

"How is this Bella's fault that you was acting like a hoodrat?"

"Because she should have never signed us up for no group fucking fieldtrip to hang with Bam-Bam's girlfriend. Like, who wanted to do that?" Tavares rolled her eyes. "Not fucking me or anyone else in the 1st Wives Club. Then, Bam-Bam's bitch comes in with side Bitch Sally and Punk Ass Priscilla."

"Who is Side Bitch Sally?" Dora said, totally confused now.

"Long story, but it's a bitch Javan is fucking."

"Tavares, cut the shit."

With no smile, she looked Dora in the face and said, "I busted them together yesterday. I just haven't told Cakes because Javan says he's ending it. So, you want to blame someone for last night going wrong? Blame Bella for dragging us there or Brooklyn for coming with them trash ass bitches."

"Babe, you can blame whoever you want. I just want to know from my woman's mouth what happened."

"That punk bitch Priscilla realized I was your girl. Then, she thought she could take shots at me by continuously referencing back in the day and how you used to love her. She let these blue eyes and turquoise hair fool her. She must have thought you had you some punk ass white or Spanish bitch and that I wouldn't bust her fucking ass. After I let her live for a while, I said, 'Well y'all let me go because my man is at home waiting to rub on my butt.' When I was leaving, she gonna tell me, 'Tavares, tell Abdora that I'm staying at my mother's house.'"

Dora choked because he knew that was what sent Tavares to the left.

"I didn't stoop to her level and get trashy right there. I told that bitch, 'We'll gladly stop by to see your soon-to-be dead mother' and laughed."

"Tavares, you didn't say that shit."

"Why the fuck didn't I? Fuck her."

"That girl's mother is about to die. That was cruel."

"Sorry, but her ill mother became a casualty of war. That bitch hopped up like she was ready for what I was handing out, and it was on from there. I told that bitch don't be fooled by my skin color and if she was feeling froggy, LEAP. She tried it. I'll give her that. But, I charged her first to clothesline the shit out of her. Bella and Ebony tackled her to save her. It just went crazy from there. Your security team came and broke up the flying chairs and bottles. When we were all leaving, she tried to get cute again. And, you know I don't play getting cute, and for damn sure not when it comes to my man. The bitch had the nerve to say, 'Enjoy my leftovers for *now*.'"

Dora was speechless.

"That's when I went charging at her. I told that hoe her and her mother was going to be buried together. Thank God for your boys because I should have woken up in jail and not on Cali and Javan's couch. It took like three of them to get me. I wanted to murder that bitch. So, if she knows what's good for her, she'll stay far in her lane and away from you."

Dora knew this wasn't over, not even by a long shot. He didn't want to deal with this bullshit right now. Instead, he leaned down to kiss Tavares. Meanwhile, he caught her off-guard, sliding his middle finger inside her center.

"Shit, my baby got a gushy pussy," he joked.

"Fuck you, asshole."

Dora knew it wasn't an invitation, but he took it as one. He grabbed Tavares by both of her feet and pulled her to the edge of the bed. As he pulled her boy shorts off, he commanded, "Spread them." Tavares obliged, and he opened her legs straight up in the air and went in head first. He used his tongue with meticulousness to take Tavares's pussy on a roller coaster ride. He was up, down, and around at various speeds inside her wet middle. She couldn't help but shiver, quiver, and damn near cry.

"OMG, stop, stop, stop," she was pleading.

After letting Tavares beg a few moments longer, he got up, scooped her off the bed, and slid her down on his long, thick penis. Fucking her standing up, Dora was hitting every inch of her g-spot. Tavares was cummin' left and right and screaming with each warm orgasm she released.

By the time Abdora was done with his makeup sex, he'd flipped, tossed, and twisted Tavares in positions that made her head spin. He'd fucked her, had sex with her, and made love to her all in one session. With exhaustion consuming her, Tavares lay on the floor wrapped in a sheet.

"Now, get your sticky pussy ass up."

"Hell no. I'm beat."

"Get up, Boo."

"Get up for what?"

"Because we have the party tonight, so stop playing with me."

"I don't want to go. Take Priscilla, your ex-girlfriend you failed to tell me about."

"Here you go. I just gave you all this loving, and you're starting. Just shut it up."

"Hell, I ain't even got started."

"Tavares, I ain't playing with you. Get your ass up."

"Abdora, you fucked my hair up so I'm going nowhere," she said, returning the serious tone that was just thrown at her.

"Bree is on her way to do your hair and makeup."

"How the fuck you get Bree to come to the house on a busy day like this?"

"Come on, Boo. You know I'm the man. Money talks; bullshit walks. So, get your ass up and get to walking to that bathroom."

Tavares got up, but she was talking shit the whole time.

"Like, who the fuck has a Valentine's Day Party? We aren't kids or teenagers. No one wants to spend their time at a party on fucking Valentine's Day. This is some stupid, selfish shit. I want to be on a triple date with the 1st Wives Club, but nooooo. You want to drag me to some stupid ass party. Whose party is it anyway?" Tavares asked, wrapping her robe around her nude body.

"My man's," Dora responded dryly.

"And, what does that tell me? Everyone is your mans," Tavares screwed her face up.

"Just get in the shower. Bree's on her way and the photographer will be here at 6:00 p.m."

Tavares was almost to the bathroom when the word *photographer* made her stop in her tracks and look over her shoulder.

"You're doing the most. A photographer for what?"

"Because I'm gonna be sharp as a motherfucker," Dora said, giving his lady the beg-your-pardon face.

"Yeah right, dude."

"You're such a hater," Dora laughed. "Lady, just be glad I'm letting you be in my pictures."

Tavares just rolled her eyes and kept going.

***

Two hours later, Bree had earned the thousand dollars Dora paid her for the home visit. She could have made more at work with it being Valentine's Day, but she liked working smarter, not harder. All she did was blow dry, curl, and slay Tavares's face flawlessly, so she was happy to make the easy money.

As Tavares looked in the mirror, she was overly pleased with the finished product.

"Damnnnnnn, Bree. You did that!"

"Girl, you have to be slayed for your big night!"

Bree caught what she'd said and cussed herself inside.

"Girl, please. It ain't my night. I'm just being dragged to this stupid ass party."

Bree sighed in silent relief that Tavares was really clueless that it was her and Dora's party.

"Well, honey, with this hair and makeup, you might as well be the lady of the night. Where's your dress, so I can help you in it?"

"Good damn question, Bree. I told Dora since he was dragging me, he'd better get me everything I need. I have no idea what my dress even looks like."

"Now, stop it," Bree said with her tiny voice that was identical to the 80s singer Michel'le. "I know you didn't trust Abdora to go get you no dress. What if you don't like it? What if it doesn't fit?"

Bree's client just cracked up laughing.

"Now stoppp, Tavares."

"Well, if it don't fit, that's my way out."

Tavares reached over to the phone on the wall and paged the house intercom.

"Yooooo," Dora answered.

"Babe, can you please bring my dress to the hair salon? Bree is gonna help me finish getting ready," she said, and then she asked Bree, "Do me a favor and meet that crazy ass man of mine at the door. He's gonna give you my shoes and dress."

"Girl, you and this man are something special because I can't believe you trusted him to buy you a dress and haven't even seen it or tried it on."

As she made her way back with the dress, Bree said, "Damn, this shit is heavy."

She admired the beautiful gown as she hung it on the bathroom door and unzipped it. She and Tavares both looked at each other.

"Wow," Bree said with her mouth literally needing to be picked up off the ground. "It's absolutely beautiful," she said, pulling it from the bag.

"See, he's to be trusted," Tavares stated, not having been worried at all.

Tavares was magazine ready when Bree was done helping her get dressed. Her hair, makeup, and dress were beyond drop dead gorgeous.

"My Lord, Tavares. You are past perfect."

"Thanks, but I would much rather be in the bed. The kids are gone for the weekend, and I just wanted to lay up with my man. So, I just know that after this stupid ass party, Abdora better rip me out this dress and give me the damn business."

They both fell out laughing because as beautiful as Tavares was, she was only thinking about making sweet love. The ladies made their way upstairs to the first floor of the house. Abdora was in the foyer talking to the photographer when they stepped off the elevator. When he saw Tavares, his eyes jumped, his mouth fell open, and he was speechless. The photographer quickly snapped Abdora's face, and then he caught a candid shot of Tavares walking toward them.

"Uhhhhh, uhhhh," Dora stuttered.

He was at a loss for words looking at the woman that he knew he wanted to spend his life with.

"Why are you stuttering and blushing all crazy?" Tavares asked.

"Boo, you look mind-blowing."

"Thanks, considering this dress was your doing," Tavares said, spinning under the chandelier.

The photographer didn't miss a beat capturing the beautiful shot. Bree loved that they were so in love.

"You two have fun tonight."

She hugged each of them and hurried out the door so she could make it home to get dressed and not miss the party. Tavares was breathtaking in her dress that appeared to be two pieces but was indeed one. The top was a lace corset that fit to the T. The bottom was floor-length tulle that was so full that it could have easily been a wedding dress. Dora matched her, fly in his cream Kenneth Cole tuxedo that was trimmed in black. He'd searched high and low until he found the dress that he wanted to see Tavares in. Looking at her, he was more than pleased with his choice.

The photographer continued snapping a million pictures and poses from candid shots to in love, dope, fresh, romantic to just free-styling. Tavares had gotten in the mood to enjoy the evening and was all smiles when their car arrived.

CHAPTER 14

A few minutes before the car arrived at the venue, Abdora looked at Tavares and said, "I need you to put this on."

Looking at the eye mask, she fell out laughing.

"What is that for? I'm so not putting that thing on, Abdora."

"You have to."

"No, I don't! I want to see where you're taking me and what's going on."

Abdora extended the cream-colored satin sleep mask.

"I have a surprise for you."

"I don't even know why anything you do surprises me anymore."

Tavares snatched the mask, only pretending she was mad. As she covered her eyes with the mask, the old-school Rolls Royce stopped.

"OMG, Abdora, what's going on?"

"Don't worry about it. Just hold my hand. You're gonna feel the driver lift the bottom of your dress so it doesn't drag."

As Tavares followed her man's instructions, she felt a beautiful, warmer than usual breeze go across her face on what should have been an artic February evening. Dora removed the satin mask. They were on the side of the road in the middle of the country. A couple of miles ahead was a massive piece land with a castle in the middle of it. A horse-drawn carriage was parked next to the Rolls Royce.

"Here we go!" Tavares screamed.

"Tonight is going to be magical for you, so what other way would we really show up?"

Tavares just blushed because Abdora was always a step ahead with something up his sleeve.

"Once we get in the chariot, you have to put the mask back on."

Tavares did as she was told. She didn't know what to expect when the carriage stopped.

"Can you at least tell me what's going on?"

"No. Don't worry about it. Just hold my hand and follow my lead."

Tavares didn't even put up a fuss. She simply followed his lead for a change. The next thing Tavares heard was Jessie Powell's "You" being sung by someone live.

"May I have this dance?" Abdora asked.

"This is so my song."

She was still clueless about where they were and why that song was playing.

"Babe, can I take this thing off?"

"No, leave it on."

They were dancing in a ballroom under a spotlight with everyone watching them in silence.

When the song stopped, Abdora said, "Hold my hand and use the other one to take the mask off."

When Tavares pulled the mask off, she looked around and her whole body froze with shock. She was on a dance floor in the middle of a stunning ballroom decorated like a winter wonderland with approximately two hundred spectators. The oversized space had white drapery from the cathedral ceilings, white chandeliers, and artificial white trees and snow, all of which were illuminated with red lighting. It was modern, chic, and breathtaking. Tavares was confused and felt weird that a room full of people had just watched her dance intimately with her boyfriend.

"Abdora, what is going on?"

He wasted no time with what he'd been waiting to say. "Tavares, you are my best friend, my ride or die, my homie, my lover, my baby mama, and my world. The moment I saw you, I knew that I wanted to be your everything."

"He sure did!" Majors yelled from the crowd. People laughed.

"You changed my world. First, by blessing me with the gift of true love, and then with our beautiful boys. You're breathtaking on the outside, but incomparably even more beautiful on the inside. I want to spend my life being your provider, your protector, and the king of your castle. You make me laugh, live to the fullest, and love in a way that I never imagined to be possible."

Finally, it hit Tavares like a ton of bricks where this was going. She grabbed her chest and began crying. Abdora softly brushed her face with his hand to wipe her tears. Then, he used his lips to kiss the rest of them away.

"You don't have to cry. I want to continue to show you that love doesn't hurt. I want to always have your back. I want to give you the world because you mean the world to me."

The soloist started singing "Let's Get Married" by Jagged Edge. Simultaneously her friends walked from each side of the long staircase that led down into the ballroom. They were dressed in different but cohesively designed black dresses. Each one was escorted by one of Dora's friends. Each lady was carrying a single rose and the gentlemen were carrying signs. As each couple reached the center of the floor where the couple of the hour was standing, each lady passed Tavares her rose and retrieved the concealed sign from her escort. The fellas, who looked dapper in their all black suits, stood behind Dora, and the ladies stood behind Tavares.

As Tavares watched and listened to the soloist, she used all her might to fight back the tears that were welling up in her eyes. Dora leaned in and kissed the lady who had stolen his heart. Instead of kissing her lips, he kissed each eyelid.

"I told you the eyes are the window to your soul. The moment I took one look into yours, I knew you were my soul mate and that God had created you for me. Turn around."

Each lady had her sign up to form the statement that read: "Tavares, I love you. Will you be my wife? Let's get married!" Tavares used her hands to cup her cheeks as she turned around with an open mouth to see Abdora down on one knee holding a ring. She instantly screamed. Then, she cried again. Finally, she pinched herself because this wasn't real. When she looked around, there wasn't a dry eye in the room. She was stuck in shock as she kept blinking and looking around through her tears. This couldn't be real. How did Abdora pull this off? Abdora was not proposing to her in such a fairy-tale way.

Everyone was in the same position wiping their eyes until Doll yelled, "You better say yes to that man!"

Everyone was chanting, "Say yes! Say yes!"

Tavares knew this was real; she wasn't dreaming.

"No, I don't want to be your wife."

Every single person in the room gasped. Abdora got up with a look of shock and heartbreak. He looked like that sentence had shattered his heart. Tavares turned around to her friends and gave them back the roses. She walked toward Abdora, whose face was hurt. Then, she stood on her tippy toes and reached for his face, bringing it down to hers. She kissed him before speaking.

"Abdora, I want to be more than your wife. I want to be your life partner. I want to be your partner in crime. When life goes left, I want to be your right. When the world is cold, I want to be the one who keeps you warm. When you have bad days, I want to give you brighter nights. When you fall, I want to be the one to catch you. You are everything and more than I could ever ask for in a man. I don't know what I did to deserve you, but I'll never leave you. I want to spend my life with you, being everything you deserve. If I could give you one thing, it would be my eyes so that you could see yourself through my view and see just how special and amazing you are to me. I love you, and YES, I will marry you."

The sound of applause and screaming filled the room as the couple kissed.

After what felt like forever for the crowd to stop cheering and screaming, Tavares asked, "Where is the pastor?"

"Oh no, no, no, Baby Girl. This is your practice wedding."

"What?" Tavares said, looking at the love of her life like he was crazy.

"We're going to do everything except actually get married. Today, we will commit our love. When *you* plan your dream wedding that you so deserve, we'll legally get married. Today you're getting an engagement, practice wedding."

Tavares grabbed her face, laughed, and shook her head. Within ten minutes their mock wedding was going down. There were flower girls and even boys in suits like their fathers. The soloist sang "Crazy Love" by Brian McKnight, and Angelica read a poem entitled "Love." When it was time to exchange vows, Abdora pledged his love further. Then, he slipped the ten-carat single stone princess-cut diamond that was set in a two-carat diamond band on his love's finger.

"Everyone, when I met Tavares, she had a beautiful ring on her finger. It wasn't as ill as this, but it was aight."

The crowd laughed at his sarcasm.

"And, I told her that one day I would be putting something better on her finger. Tell me I didn't come through."

Everyone was cracking up because, even in the moment, he still had jokes. Dora grabbed Tavares and kissed her with so much passion that they could have started a nine-alarm fire. The crowd started screaming. They were clapping without a dry eye amongst them. Every onlooker had just gotten a glimpse of real love. People who didn't believe in love had just received a glimmer of hope.

Tavares and Abdora spent the evening hugging people, taking pictures, and celebrating the next chapter of their life together.

Tavares was in awe at all the people that Dora had reached out to for this surprise. Her girls from back home, her college road dawgs, and her new friends from Jersey were all there. Majors, Kimmy her Asian sensation, her parents, and even Doll and her family had come through. Tavares didn't have many people who were near and dear to her. However, each one who held a special place in her heart was there, except one person.

It was more than a magical night for her. If she didn't get a dream wedding, Abdora had just given it to her. There was food that was ridiculously good, just as it should have been for one hundred dollars a plate. They also had a chocolate fountain, a dessert bar, an open bar for the alcohol, a photo booth, and amazing vibes flying around. Love was truly in the air.

Tavares tried her best to spend a few moments with everyone who came out to celebrate with them. Abdora hugged the bar, congregated with his boys, and glowed and basked in happiness at how his surprise engagement was more beautiful than he could have ever imagined. After an hour of working the crowd, Tavares rounded up her mock bridesmaids and led them into the lobby. She gave Mona-Lisa, Randee, Leslie, Bella, Cali, Rocky, and Ebony all hugs.

"I can't believe you heffas knew about this and not one of you, not one single one of you dropped a dime."

"Girl, are you crazzzzzy?" Ebony asked. "That man of yours would have had our heads and our asses."

Everyone laughed because when Dora reached out to each of them, he made it clear that if anyone told Tavares, they were in deep shit with him.

"Well, I want to thank you beautiful ladies for being part of such a memorable night for me. You women are the epitome of what great friends should be. Can I just ask who picked out the dresses, because each dress is different yet so cohesive?"

"Bitch, don't even get me started on these fucking dresses!" yelled Rocky. "This is why I had you waiting yesterday. I was slow getting it altered, and it was a big ole mess."

"Oh, shut up and stop complaining," Cali said. "To answer you, though... Mona-Lisa informed your event planners, who picked the dresses out, which not one of us was feeling. We wanted say so, but Dora said they were in charge. That damn Chelsee... Good Lord, is she a picky bitch with great taste."

Everyone laughed in unison.

"She had no problem saying, 'that ain't for you, you look frumpy, that ain't your cut, nah, I don't like it, try again.' But, in the end, her vision turned out beautiful."

Tavares held her bridesmaids hostage until she looked up and saw Doll coming toward them.

"Ladies, I love you guys, and I can't thank you enough. Let me holler at Doll, and y'all go take full advantage of all that free liquor in there."

She and Doll were alone face to face. Doll reached out for Tavares and wrapped her arms around her before she spoke.

"Baby, you are beautiful, and tonight is your night. I just want to tell you that I love you, and I'm sorry. I said some things that I can never take back, as hurtful as they were, but I was wrong. I was so wrong. I know you loved Damien. I just want to tell you I love you, and I hope that you can forgive me."

Tavares kept it simple and said, "I love you more, and I forgive you." Then, she returned the hug. With the hug, her anger melted away because she understood what her father had said to her. She did love Doll like a mother. Hand in hand, they returned to the party. When Dora saw his fiancée return to the party, he excused himself from the people he was standing with.

"Goodness, lady. I give you a ring like that, and you just disappear on me."

"Oh, hush up. If you want some of my time, just say so, because you know I'm popping and whatnot," Tavares teased.

The beautiful couple stole a few minutes for themselves.

"Well, Miss-I-Don't-Want-To-Go-To-This-Stupid-Party, are you happy you came now?"

Tavares knew she'd gone hard, so she couldn't do anything but laugh.

"I so didn't want to come. But, had you told me you were gonna propose, I would have gotten dressed with a smile," she said, blowing the fine man in front of her a kiss. "I just don't even know how you pulled this off without me having the slightest idea."

"Honest, boo, it wasn't much work keeping it from you because I didn't do anything. I only had to get a guest list. That was it. It was all Chic and Classy Events. You always brag about them. so I said let's see how good they really are. I didn't think they'd be able to pull it off because we're here in Jersey, but I called them anyways. Chelsee said you would kill me and them if they didn't do the party. Chanae asked me my budget. I laughed and told her to make it as magical as she could because it was your surprise engagement party. She was so excited for you. I don't think she really knew I meant spend whatever because she kept calling asking me is five thousand too much for this or is three thousand too much for that. So you know me, Boo. I didn't have time for her. She's a sweetheart, but I didn't have time."

Tavares laughed because Chanae was very picky and got excited over event planning. She could only imagine her calling Dora to spend money he didn't care about.

"I told her there was an account with two hundred thousand in it. But, they went above and beyond anything I could have ever imagined and didn't even spend anywhere near what I gave them. My kind of girls," laughed Dora.

"Babe, I just love you," Tavares said, totally in love with the man looking at her. "It was truly a surprise, and I can't wait to do the real thing."

"Well, you better top this, because then they gonna be saying your man plans a better wedding than you," joked Dora.

After an enchanted evening with the people they loved, and a night full of passionate love-making, Tavares woke up still floating on air. She slid her curvy naked body from under the sexy, sleeping man who was snoring like a bear. Then, she showered to wash all his bodily fluids off her. After that, she got dressed and reconfirmed her orders for the evening. Tavares cooked breakfast and was smiling from ear to ear, looking at the beautiful rock on her finger. Once breakfast was done, she used her soft lips to plant kisses all over Abdora's face until he woke.

"Rise and shine, Sleepy Head."

"Good morning. pretty girl. Why you all dressed and not in bed naked for another round of love-making?" Abdora asked, stretching.

"Maybe because you decided that you wanted to continue the celebration and invited all our family and close friends over for part two to watch the showdown between the Patriots and the Giants. You were bragging about how we were going to get it popping because you weren't a broke nigga. So now I gotta make that happen."

"Oh shit, I did do that, huh. I mean it's true, but the liquor was talking. What's the plan? What do you need me to get up and do?"

"I don't need YOU to do anything. Stay right there in bed all day if you want," Abdora's fiancée smirked. "But, I need your credit card."

"Of course, you do," Abdora chuckled, getting out of bed to grab his wallet.

"You know I can make a party happen with my eyes closed. Thanks to the best event planners ever being in town, magic is about to happen. Bryce is getting the liquor from the club. Cali is making a cake and one hundred cupcakes. I got Weezy G the grill master coming through to cater. I've got just a few other things to do and we're good."

"Oh boy," Dora said, seeing where this was going.

Small was turning to over the top messing with Tavares.

As she grabbed the black card, Tavares said, "I have some moves to make so we can entertain properly, so you just let Chanae and Chelsee in when they get here. They'll take it from there. And, do me a favor... Don't be giving them no hard time."

"Now why would I be giving them a hard time?"

"Because that's what you do. Always think you have to be the boss and in control. Just get out of the way and let me do what I do because YOU created this shit. I have to pull it together in hours, so let my event planners do what they do."

Tavares kissed her boo with his morning breath and said, "Breakfast is waiting for you downstairs." Then, she was on her way.

***

In Jersey City, Brooklyn was having brunch with Jade, Priscilla, and Kamari. She was giving them the lowdown on the previous night's event.

"When I say Dora murdered that proposal, that dude did the damn thing. It was beautiful. She was clueless, and he did everything from planning it to picking out her dress."

The more they sucked it up, the more Jade and Priscilla were steaming inside. They were both aware that each had dealt with Dora. However, seeing that they only knew each other from Brooklyn, they had no beef. Instead, they both shared a serious dislike for Tavares.

"Fuck that bitch," Kamari said, still fuming at how Tavares had ruined her lunch with Javan and came for her.

"Fucking right. Fuck that wack ass bitch," Jade interjected. "She took that night nigga right from under my nose. He should've been proposing to me last night."

"You know what they say," Priscilla added. "How you find them is how you lose them. So no worries… She won't have him long," she said, not letting the girls know this wasn't a general statement. She was actually plotting to get her old boo back.

"What was even more beautiful was when Tavares's parents got up to congratulate the couple. They told them if they don't believe in anything, they should believe in love. After twenty years, they had rekindled and nothing was greater than true love."

"Aweeee, that was sweet," Prissy had to admit. "And, that girl's father is finnne. Do y'all hear me? Fine!"

Jade's mother caught the last sentence as she walked in the house from the night prior.

"Whose father is fine? Because mama need a new man," she joked.

"Oh, last night I went to a surprise engagement party with my boyfriend, and the future bride's father, Mr. Montiago, was fineeeee, Ma."

Jade's mother froze. She was quick on her feet to not let the surprise of the name show on her face, but now she was curious.

"Oh, nice, sweetie. So how was it? Tell me all about it."

Brooklyn gave Jade's mother the same playback. When she got to the parents' speech, Jade's mother's heart stopped. Her eyes bulged, and things that were unclear made perfect sense now.

"That's absolutely beautiful the way he proposed," she said to play things off. "And, after twenty-two years, her parents are still together."

"No, Ma. They just got back together after twenty-two years. I must say, you can tell just how in love they are."

Jade was over this love story.

"Ma, fuck that bitch Tavares. Ain't nothing beautiful about the fact that she's marrying the love of my life. You know I hate her. Abdora should have been my man and he would have, had that bitch never come in the picture. I wish someone would just off that bitch."

"Watch your mouth," Jade's mother snapped. However, she was thinking *that makes two of us.*

After looking at her watch, Brooklyn hated to leave her friends, but she had a date with her man.

"Brunch was nice, ladies, but Bam-Bam is dragging me to Abdora and Tavares's house for part two."

"You're a traitor," snarled Kamari.

"Really, Kamari... Oh, trust me. After you fucked one girl's man and these two hussies are plotting on Tavares's fiancé, I have no desire to go to this woman's house. Bam-Bam wants me to go, so what the fuck am I to do?"

"Stand for something or fall for anything. Tell his ass NO!" yelled Prissy.

"You petty heffas are just being selfish. I can't shut my man down because y'all ain't shit," joked Brooklyn.

"That's fine. Go hang out with your new best friend," Jade said, really feeling some kind of way.

Brooklyn wasn't about to defend herself. She simply said, "Fuck it." Then, she grabbed her purse and slammed the door behind her. She couldn't believe her cousin and friends. They had her in between a rock and a hard place. Her loyalty was to them, but how was she gonna tell her man she couldn't roll with him when these people were his circle? They would have to get over it, as far as Brooklyn was concerned.

Jade, Priscilla, and Kamari were downstairs feeling some kind of way, and Jade's mother, Special Agent Carmen Vega, was upstairs on a million. She'd paced her large bedroom so many times that she probably had walked to Boston and back.

Talking to the thin air, she spoke, "I can't believe this motherfucker. This motherfucker. Holton left me for that crack-head Dolonda Del Gada. What in the hell!" screamed Carmen.

She was beyond angry, mad, on fire, and livid. She couldn't believe that all this time she was right when she felt something was right with Holton falling madly in love with his wife. He hadn't cut her off for his wife. He cut her for his crack pipe blowing daughter's mother. Carmen already had a personal vendetta with Abdora and Tavares. She hated Abdora for leaving her baby hurt and Tavares for snaking her daughter's man. Now that she learned Holton had left her for Dolonda, she was in take-down mode. She was going to watch each and every one of them hurt the way she and her daughter had been hurt. Her goal was to make everyone pay. If she had her way, Holton would never get to see a major shipment of cocaine.

Even worse, he and Abdora would be going to jail forever. Then, Dolonda and Tavares would be a wreck for the rest of their lives after losing the men they oh so loved.

Carmen had to do some research, but after a few hours, she finally tracked down her hopefully soon-to-be co-conspirator to ruining Holton. The next day she would be going to see her daughter's great aunt to ask her to check in on Jade while she was gone. She was hoping this plane ride wasn't going to be for nothing and that she was going to land a partnership that would make this plan go a lot smoother. No matter what, operation take Holton and his crack-head bitch down was in full effect.

CHAPTER 15

When Tavares arrived home, she was in great spirits that she'd accomplished everything she'd set out to do in such a short time.

Walking in the front door with a million bags, she yelled, "Yessssss, yessss, yessssss!"

The red, cobalt blue, and white balloons along with handmade signs for the Patriots and Giants told her that her event planners hadn't let her down. Excited to see what the outside looked like, Tavares made it a few feet before Abdora popped out of the elevator.

"Excuse me, party queen. Uhhh, is your phone broken?"

"No."

"Did you lose your phone?"

"No."

"Well, I've been calling your ass for the last few hours."

"Boo, I know. But, if I'd answered your calls, I would've gotten sidetracked, and I had shit to do."

Dora just looked at Tavares and shook his head.

"Remind me to use the same line when you're calling me and I'm busy. I'm just glad it wasn't an emergency."

"Oh, shut your face. I knew it wasn't because you didn't text me," Tavares laughed.

"Well, I made your wish my command and didn't get in the way of your party planners."

Tavares stood on her tippy toes, grabbed Abdora down to her five-foot height, and kissed his forehead.

"You're the best. How does the outside look?"

"Let's go look and you can decide if it's everything you shouldn't have spent my money on."

Tavares laughed hard at the last part.

"Of course, I should have. I don't like no half-ass shit, Dora, and you know that. Wait, can you get the boxes out of the car first?"

"No."

Tavares frowned her face up, not expecting the love of her life to say that mean, nasty word.

"All the money this party cost me in a matter of hours, I'm not doing nothing." Abdora laughed hard as hell because he was getting the last laugh this time.

When they made it outside to their terrace, Tavares was literally jumping up and down.

"Oh, my God! It's exactly what I told Chelsee and Chanae I wanted—a reproduction of a football stadium."

"They for sure made it happen. I came out here and was shocked. Not jumping like your crazy ass, but for sure had to give them credit for doing their thing."

The ladies had rented bleachers and set them up around the perimeter of the grass. They'd used white spray paint to make the yard look like a football field. Giants and Patriots signs were everywhere. In each zone, there was a movie theater-sized projector screen to watch the game on. Tavares had heated lamps around the bleachers and heated tents. There was food under one tent, a bar under another, and the third was just for people to hang out.

"I'm more than pleased," Tavares said, smiling from ear to ear. "Now, can you please get the boxes out of my car?"

"No."

"Why not?" the brat whined.

"I already told you why, and what boxes?"

"The t-shirts."

"What t-shirts?"

"I had Patriots t-shirts made for my people and Giants t-shirts made for yours."

"How did you pull that off?" Dora cracked up, loving how hard she went.

"My t-shirt guy at home, Lloyd, has a shop in Harlem as well. It wasn't cheap, but I was able to get enough shirts for the whole crew."

"Boo, you might be the shit. Just might..."

"Bullshit... Ain't no *might* about it. I am the shit," laughed Tavares. "Now, please go get the t-shirts!" she asked nicely with a puppy dog face.

Everything turned out as Tavares hoped. They had a DJ and photographer. Warren G was doing his thing on the grills with his staff. He'd suggested that they keep the food to what a stadium would sell, and he was right. There was a variety of soups, hot dogs or sausages with onions and peppers, burgers, fries, nachos, and wings. It was simple, but it was perfect for the ambiance. People loved the t-shirts, and Tavares was just happy everyone was having such a great time. She was on the sidelines with her Boston Besties, the Diva Squad, and her Jersey Jezebels just laughing, blowing it down, and watching the game when she saw her mother walk up on Doll.

"Oh, shit," she said mid-conversation.

"What's wrong?" Mona-Lisa asked.

She pointed but never took her eyes off the two women who were like oil and water.

"From their body language it appears to me that they're just fine," Rocky said. "So mind your business and smoke this blunt."

"Devin, I want us to bury the hatchet. My daughter loves you very much, and it seems like neither of us is going anywhere. We can't be a part of her life and not be adult enough to get along. So, we both need to leave the past in the past."

"I totally agree," Doll responded.

She knew that it was the right thing to do for Tavares. They sealed their burying of the hatchet with a hug, but Doll got the last laugh.

"I'm sill gonna be the cuter Mama of the Bride at the real wedding."

Dolonda just cried in laughter.

"We'll see about that."

As Tavares watched, she didn't know what they'd spoken about, but it made her heart cry tears of joy that her mother and second mother had just hugged and were smiling while engaging in a conversation.

Dora snuck up behind Tavares, wrapped his arms around her, and whispered, "You're cute as fuck, but this shirt you got on is wack as hell."

Tavares just laughed.

"You're just a hater, because you know in Brady we trust."

"You better tell him," Tavares's grandmother Vadaleen yelled.

"See... Even Grammy knows," Tavares said, throwing her butt back.

Leaning in, Abdora whispered, "You playing games, and you know I'll take you right in a bathroom and fuck you with all our family and friends here."

"Don't threaten me with a good time," Tavares said and cracked up laughing before making her rounds to check on her guests.

By the time Bam-Bam and Brooklyn arrived, Tavares and Dora had just made their way back outside. They slid into a bathroom for a quickie that turned into them being MIA for forty-five minutes. Tavares was halfway intoxicated, and she wasn't feeling Brooklyn. She wasn't sure if it was the alcohol or the events from the other night, but she didn't know how to take this girl that Bam-Bam was proudly introducing to everyone. The curvaceous, pretty young girl was very polite and cordial to everyone throughout the party, but Tavares wasn't moved.

In her eyes, Brooklyn was on the enemies' team, and she didn't fuck with bitches who fucked with her enemies. Just that simple. So, she wasn't sure how she was gonna rock with this woman who she knew she would be seeing on the regular. Tavares's thoughts were interrupted.

"Yo, sis, can you take my shorty to the kitchen so she can grab our plates? Dora said you put some food in the house," Bam-Bam yelled.

"Gladly," Tavares responded.

As they made their way back into the house, Brooklyn tried to make small talk with Tavares as she retrieved the food.

"You have such a beautiful home. Thank you for the invite."

Tavares's response caught Brooklyn off-guard.

"Do me a favor and miss me with the bullshit. What's your deal?"

"Excuse me, Tavares?" Brooklyn responded, the least bit intimidated.

"Well, I'm just confused about how you have the balls to come to my house after I was gonna bust your thirsty ass girl's ass the other night."

"Actually, who was gonna bust whose ass is to be determined."

"You keep thinking that," Tavares chuckled. "Your girl is all bark and no bite. Me, I'm no bark and all bite."

"My deal is this. I'm not here trying to be your friend, BFF, or none of that shit. I know where my loyalty lies. But, my man works for, rolls with, and admires your fiancé. So, as his woman, I'm here being cordial and respectful."

Tavares didn't get a chance to respond because in walked Dora and Bam-Bam.

"Yo, what's taking y'all so long?" asked Bam-Bam. "Y'all got a nigga out there starving."

"Oh, I'm sorry, baby. I was just telling Tavares how much I admired her and Abdora's home."

Abdora could read Tavares's face and body language and knew it was more.

"Babe, you good?"

"Oh, I'm always good," Tavares said, looking straight at Brooklyn. "I was just telling Brooklyn she's always welcome on the strength of Bam-Bam because I don't usually fuck with bitches that fuck with bitches I don't fuck with."

Bam-Bam was clueless.

"What's that supposed to mean, sis?"

"Oh, ask your woman," Tavares said with a sly grin. "I have to go check on my boys."

Abdora just shook his head at the low blow and exited the kitchen with his troublemaking fiancée.

"What was Tavares just talking about?" Bam-Bam asked, totally out of the loop.

Brooklyn hadn't told Bam-Bam about the drama because it wasn't her beef. However, thanks to the bitch of the house, she was gonna have to spill it. After she gave him every detail of the night at the club and Kamari sleeping with one of the guys outside, Bam-Bam just shook his head.

"Ladybug, this puts me between a rock and a hard place. You know I rock with you hard body. But, how can I bring you around my man's wives and shit when you got beef with them?"

"Bam-Bam, I don't have beef with them. Prissy, Jade, and Kamari are grown women. Don't you dare fucking try to hold me accountable for their actions."

Bam-Bam knew his shorty was right, but bringing her around the wolf pack wives wasn't going to be easy. He just wanted his girl to get along with the other wives.

Tavares and Abdora made their way upstairs to the nursery where they found her grandmother and Me-Ma playing with the boys and reminiscing.

Me-Ma, who was always slick at the tongue, asked, "What y'all want? We don't need no wet-behind-the-ears new parents checking up on us and our great-grands."

"Me-Ma, you gonna get put out my house messing with my boo," joked Tavares.

"Girl, I'll beat the hell outta you and Abdora in y'all's own house," joked Me-Ma, causing all four of them to share a good laugh.

Abdora's phone started chiming like crazy. After reading the messages, he looked flushed.

"You okay, baby?" Me-Ma asked, concerned.

"Uhhh yeah." He kissed Tavares and said, "I have to go handle something."

"What? Where you going?" Tavares questioned, just as discombobulated as the face Abdora had just been wearing.

"I'll be back, boo."

He kissed his grandmother, Tavares's grandmother, and his sons before he disappeared. Dora wasn't the only one who had to leave in an instant. Brooklyn received a call that made her tell Bam-Bam she had to leave immediately too. She also had an emergency.

CHAPTER 16

As they hopped in the Range Rover, Abdora was silent while Mid and Bryce were trying to figure out where he was rushing them to. Someone had to break the silence, so Mid helped himself.

"Nigga, where in the fuck are we going?"

"Say word, my nigga," Bryce co-signed the question. "It was on and popping at your spot so where the fuck are we going?"

Dora knew the backlash was about to come, but he told them anyways.

"To the hospital. Priscilla texted and said Miss Penny took a turn for the worse and asked me to come."

Mid turned around and looked at Bryce in the backseat. Bryce's face said everything that he wasn't going to say.

"Nigga, what the fuck you want to say?" Dora asked, peeping at his friend's facial expression. "I know you just like you know me, so go ahead and say it."

"Nah, my nigga. I ain't saying shit."

Bryce was truly upset with his friend. Mid didn't hold back.

"You dragged us from a good time with our family and friends for this shit. You left your new fiancée to go be by the side of a bitch who shitted on you. Nigga, you done lost your mafucking mind. You always told me and taught me when a nigga know better, he do better. So, tell me what part of the game is this? You're outta pocket, big bro."

Bryce was boiling inside more and more and couldn't hold back.

"This shit is going to come back to bite you in the ass. Before we walk in this hospital to be by the side of a no-good ass bitch, just remember this. Don't lose what you have for a bitch who didn't appreciate you when she had you. Tavares is the woman you love—your ride or die. She just had it out with this chick at the club the other night, and now you're going to be by her side. Yeah, my G, you're in direct violation."

"What the fuck is you niggaz talking about?" Dora said, spazzing out. "Y'all know damn well I would never, ever do anything to betray Tavares. That's my queen. She has my heart, and I'm going to spend my life with her. I'm not going here because I'm at Prissy's beck and call. You niggaz know better. Y'all know me better than anyone. Me and Miss Penny is dumb close. What kind of nigga would I be to not go to this hospital?"

They heard Dora but still weren't feeling this trip. Tavares wasn't even their lady, but she was their sister and they felt like they were betraying her. Maybe Abdora's intentions were pure, but neither his best friend nor his little brother believed the same of Priscilla's motives. She always had Dora wrapped around her finger, so it wasn't sitting well with them that she was back in town calling on him, knowing he had a woman, twins, and a family. Bryce wasn't going to call the spade a spade just yet, but he knew it wouldn't be long before he was able to do so.

Tavares didn't let one monkey stop a show, not even her fiancé. She hung with her and Abdora's crazy grandmothers for a little bit before returning to the festivities.

"Where the hell did Dora, Bryce, and Mid rush out of here to?" questioned Rocky with her nosey butt.

"Girl, your guess is as good as mine. Dora got a text, his face looked crazy, and he said he had to take care of something. So, don't get me to lying. I just know the party shall continue without his ass."

"Humph, I know that's right," Chelsee said, throwing a Remy shot back.

"I just want to know who's gonna help me clean up," Tavares asked her friends she was politicking with.

There was nothing but silence.

"Y'all ain't shit," Tavares said, laughing at all the lazy ass friends she had. "Thank God I have the cleaners coming in the morning."

***

The trio entered the hospital in silence and stopped at the front desk. Dora was about to ask for Penny Hamilton's room when he spotted Bam-Bam and Brooklyn in the waiting room. They made their way over to where the couple was.

Bryce said, "What up, fool?" to Bam-Bam, who was all in his phone on social media. Brooklyn and Bam-Bam were both in utter shock to see the gentlemen standing before them.

"What y'all doing here?" Bam-Bam asked, confused.

"Same thing I want to know," Bryce said.

"We'll let Dora answer that while me and Mid go get coffee for everyone."

Prissy came out to inform Brooklyn, her mother's caretaker, that it wasn't looking good. She noticed Abdora before she noticed anyone else.

She immediately threw her arms around him and said, "Thank you for coming, Dora. Thank you so much. I really needed you here. Thank you for coming."

Bryce and Mid were just sitting in the corner watching the snake in the grass trying to slither her way back into Dora's life. They weren't buying what she was selling even if Abdora was. After hearing the update that Miss Penny had taken a turn for a worse and it wasn't looking like she had long to live, Dora consoled Prissy. He told her not to worry, everything was going to be okay, and she wasn't alone in this.

She began to cry, and he put his arms around her and held her tight. Bryce was sick to his stomach watching this bootleg episode of *The Young and the Restless*. He couldn't stand it another moment.

"Bam-Bam and Mid, can I holler at y'all for a second?"

The three gentlemen walked away and left only Brooklyn to watch what even she knew was a dramatic scene on Prissy's part. She knew that Prissy was hurting, but thus far she hadn't seen her so hurt or torn apart about her mother's failing health. It had actually been the opposite, so she was watching the waterworks show in awe.

"Bam-Bam, I know your girl and Priscilla are friends, but I ain't with this bullshit, yo," Bryce made clear.

"What you mean, my nigga?"

"Priscilla is a fraud."

"Word, she is," laughed Mid.

"I don't give a fuck what my brother says. She's up to no good. She could have called her friends, her family, or anyone, but she calls my fucking brother when they don't even rock like that. She knows he has kids, a fiancée, and a family now. I don't trust her intentions," Mid said, staring at Priscilla like he was looking through her.

Bam-Bam scratched his beard and said, "Yeah, I was shocked as fuck when y'all rolled up on me. I knew they used to rock, but I couldn't figure out why Dora would leave his own party to come here."

"Easy," Bryce said, getting madder by the moment. "He wants Tavares to kill him and us when she finds out we was here with him."

Dora spotted his mans and them conversing and decided to let himself in on the conversation.

"Excuse me for a moment, ladies."

When Dora was out of earshot, Brooklyn asked, "What the fuck is going on, Priscilla?"

Acting appalled, she responded, "What do you mean?"

"I mean what the fuck is Abdora doing here? The other night you just had a catfight with his now fiancée, and you called him here to console you."

"Me and Abdora had something long before he met that half-breed bitch. He's here because we have history and because he's my friend."

Prissy pulled out her phone and snapped a few pics of Dora and his boys standing a few feet away. Brooklyn shook her head in pure disgust.

"You're playing with fire. When you get burnt, don't say I didn't warn you."

***

Tavares spent the rest of the night with her family and friends drinking, laughing, trash-talking, eating, smoking, taking pictures, and simply having a great time. Besides the fact that Abdora, Bryce, and Mid had to leave, it turned out to be a great night. People loved the food, enjoyed the ambiance, and were all smiles. Seeing her guests having such a great time made Tavares smile too. She wrapped the night up giving big hugs to all her Boston people who would be leaving in the morning. Her parents were the last people there. While Dolonda was in the ladies' room, Tavares was chopping it up with her father.

"Papi, where are you and Mami staying? You guys are more than welcome to stay in one of the many guest rooms."

"Oh, no, we're good, Mija. We got a room at the Marriott Marquis in Time Square for the week."

"Why do y'all have a room for a week?"

"Because I had some business to handle. Plus, your mother is still torn between staying here and taking a job that Dhara offered her or moving back to Boston with me."

"Although I don't want Mami here nagging me, it would be a good idea if she took the job and stayed here."

"What would be a good idea?" Dolonda asked, entering the kitchen.

"If my Papi found a new woman," Tavares answered and keeled over in laughter.

Only, her mother wasn't laughing.

"Holton, you better get your daughter and her fly ass mouth"

"Tavares, leave your mother alone. You know she's the love of my life."

"Blah, blah, blah," Tavares said, still cracking up from her own joke.

"No, baby, I was telling Mija that we have a room for a week because you're undecided about staying here or moving to Boston with me."

Dolonda was truly torn, and it showed in her face.

"Mami, why don't you just take the job and stay here for a while? It'll be good for your sobriety, and not to mention, you can be here with me and the boys. Papi is only an hour plane ride away or a five-hour drive."

"I know, Tavares, it makes all the logical sense in the world, but I don't want to be away from your father."

Tavares rolled her eyes in the hard way that she did when she was making a statement with her eyes instead of her mouth.

"Is there something wrong with your eyes?" Dolonda questioned.

"Yeah. You sound exceptionally crazy. You left Boston to escape a life and to get back on track. Now, you've fallen head over heels for Papi and are ready to run right back. That shit sounds stupid as hell to me."

"Just because it sounds stupid to you doesn't mean that it is. I love your father just as you love your man, and I want to be with him. I don't want to just see him every other weekend or a few days a week. I want to be with him every day."

Holton just sat back and said nothing because he understood both of them. He badly wanted Dolonda with him, but he wanted her to keep her sobriety more.

"Well, Mami, you're grown. I told you my thoughts and my opinion, but you're right. Who am I to tell you something sounds stupid, even if it does?" Tavares slid in. "You do what you think is best for you. At the end of the day, it's your life and your decision."

Tavares left well enough alone and simply kicked it with her parents about the good weekend, her engagement, and how the shift in her life felt wonderful. It was damn near one o'clock in the morning when they left.

Tavares hated being home alone. Dora still wasn't back, and Grammy Vadaleen had packed her kids up and taken them to Me-Ma's where she was staying. She said in her thick Trini accent, "Let us enjoy them for the night. You and Dora have them for a lifetime."

Tavares had been drinking and had no desire to fight with her grandmother, so she simply packed their bags, kissed them goodnight, and said she would retrieve them in the morning. In an attempt to make things easier for the cleaning people, Tavares straightened up a little. She was officially exhausted after such a long but successful and fun-filled day.

By the time she showered and got in bed, she realized that it was 2:07 a.m. and Abdora still wasn't home. She called him twice but she got no answer. *I guess payback is a bitch*, she thought before she drifted off to sleep.

When Tavares opened her eyes again, the sun was shining, the birds were chirping, but she couldn't move. Abdora had his legs locked over hers and his chiseled arms wrapped around her from behind. As she peeled herself from the tight hold, she was wondering, how this damn near seven-foot-tall man wrapped his whole body around her.

"Did I really sleep through this big ass monster getting in the bed?" Tavares asked herself?

The chrome clock on her nightstand read 9:28 a.m. Tavares thought her eyes were playing tricks on her. She never slept past seven in the morning, no matter how late she was up.

"Damn, I slept good," she thought to herself, feeling rejuvenated.

The party rental people along with the cleaning service would be there at 10:00 a.m., so she had to get a real move on things. The special ringtone for the phone at the front gate sounded on the house phone at 10:00 sharp.

"Goddamn, these people are prompt."

She was on her side of the bed sliding in her jeans and remotely opening the gate at the same time. Abdora hadn't even rolled over since she got up. Tavares slipped on her bra and Boston Girl t-shirt, kissed the snoring bear on the forehead, and made a dash out of the bedroom, down what felt like a hundred stairs to the front door.

By the time Enchanted Party Rental retrieved all the benches, movie projector screens, heated tents, tables, and chairs and the cleaning people had wrapped up making everything spic and span clean, it was half past eleven.

"I knew I felt naked," Tavares said, having felt all her pockets and realizing she didn't have her phone. After seeing everyone out, she hopped the elevator to grab her hoodie, Timbs, and a phone so she could make moves to go get her boys. Tavares knew that upon entering her room she was going to find Abdora awake just lying in bed, relaxing, watching TV, smoking a blunt, or doing anything except what he was doing, still sleeping. She just shook her head and looked around for her phone. As she retrieved it off the footrest, she saw that she had nineteen missed calls and eight text messages.

"Like really?" she said out loud.

Why had Cali, Rocky, and Bella called her so many times? The last message was from Rocky, and it read: *Call me FIRST.*

Tavares didn't know what was going on, but something was up. Just as she was about to start returning calls, the low battery indicator started beeping. So, she grabbed her socks, Timbs, and the cordless phone. As she was powering the phone on to call Rocky, she heard, "Hello?" on the other end.

"What the fuck?" Tavares said, not knowing how someone was on the other end of the phone that didn't ring.

"Right, bitch. That's the same shit I was about to say because the phone didn't even ring."

"That's because I was picking it up to call Rocky. But, what's up? Y'all called me mad times."

"Uhhh, yeah, we did. We been blowing you up. Where was you that you ain't been answering your phone?"

"I was downstairs with the cleaning and party rental people. I forgot my phone up here."

"You good?" asked Bella.

"Uhhh, to my knowledge, I am," Tavares responded, being sarcastic. "Hold on, I was supposed to call Rocky. Let me call her on the three-way."

"Yeah, you do that. I'm gonna merge Cali in."

Tavares clicked over and called Rocky.

Rocky saw *My Boston Boo* come across her caller ID and snatched the phone up.

"Bitchhhh," Rocky said, having been anticipating a call back for well over an hour.

Tavares merged the call.

"What, bitch? And, Bella and Cali are on the phone."

Hearing Tavares's voice, Cali said, "Heyyyy, cupcake. How are you?"

"I'm good, muffin face. What's up with you bitches, yo!? Y'all called me a million times, texted me like crazy, and now y'all acting all weird. What the fuck is going on?"

The line went silent.

"Helllllo," Tavares yelled. "What is going on with you heffas?"

"Soooo, we take it you haven't been on social media today," Cali said, breaking the silence.

"Nope. Why? What did I miss?" Tavares asked, now curious.

"Well, maybe you should go look at Dora's page," Bella suggested.

She knew that as calm as Tavares was, there was no way she'd seen what they'd seen that prompted all their calls and texts.

"I would, but my phone is on the charger. What the fuck is on Dora's page? What did one of his groupies post now? I stopped letting his page, the groupies, and their dick-riding posts get to me. I used to work myself up, but I had to tell myself this is what groupies do, and he ain't thinking about them."

Rocky hated to be the bearer of bad news, but she knew Tavares needed full warning before she logged online. The post on Dora's page was gonna set her off.

"Priscilla posted a picture of Abdora at the hospital last night. It appears that's where he went when he left the party. It's a picture of him and his boys, but it's the caption on the picture that blew our minds. It's like she's trying to bust a shot at you."

"Oh, is that right?" Tavares questioned nonchalantly.

She felt the inside of her body burning with fire. "This motherfucker was at the hospital with that bitch last night? I have the good fucking nerve to stab him in his sleep, but I'm going to wait until I look at this post."

Cali played devil's advocate. "Tavares, it's just a picture of him and the fellas. No need in catching a case just weeks before Bella's wedding. I promise the picture isn't a big deal. It's the caption that's a little much," Cali tried to reason.

Tavares grabbed her phone that she realized died because she never plugged the charger into the wall. Not wanting to wait for her phone to power up, she grabbed Abdora's phone. Before she logged on to social media, she went through her fiancé's phone. The only thing she saw was text messages from Priscilla, who was saved in Dora's phone as Penny's Daughter. The messages weren't worth getting upset about because Dora's hadn't even responded to any of them. She logged on to Abdora's social media. Priscilla had posted and tagged a picture of Abdora, Bryce, Bam-Bam, and Middeon in what appeared to be a hospital hallway. She read the caption out loud.

"'When your ex-boyfriend still treats you like his number one girl because he stops and drops EVERYONE to come be by your side in your time of need....' No the fuck this raggedy ass thirsty bitch didn't!" Tavares yelled.

Then, she had to laugh. To her, the caption showed the thirst was real.

"Yeah, that shit is crazy," Rocky said.

"She's trying to get to you," Cali chimed in, stating the obvious.

"Don't even fall for it," Bella said. "Level up. Post your engagement ring and let that bitch know she's not relevant."

Tavares was on fire. Not because Abdora was simply at the hospital, but because she didn't like being in the dark. Now, this bum ass ex-bitch of his was trying her on social media. Tavares heard her friends, but she wasn't listening to them. She was reading the comments, and it was clear everyone was hip to Priscilla's shenanigans. Tavares posted under the picture: *Priscilla, you really aren't that special. I came because you begged me to. I put a ring on my number one lady's finger two days ago. I got love for your moms, but don't come for my fiancée and get your feelings hurt. Stay in your lane.* ☺

Then, she busted out laughing as she hit POST.

"Yeah, bitch. Now, eat that."

"What the fuck you laughing at so hard?" Rocky questioned.

"I posted under the pic, but it looks like Abdora posted it."

"Oh, shit," Bella screamed. "You ain't playing!" she screeched as she was reading the comment with her own eyes.

Next, Tavares posted her engagement ring and wrote under it: *My favorite girl wears this.* Lastly, she posted the screenshot of the text messages and captioned it: *When you tell a story, learn to tell the whole story.*

"Where is Abdora?" inquired Bella. "He's a little too quiet to be in such hot water."

"His ass is in the bed knocked out. I guess he had a long night being by his bitch's side in her time of need. I'm letting him sleep until I decide to stab him to death or not," Tavares answered dryly, but sounding a little too serious.

"Tavareeesss," Cali shrieked.

"Don't fucking Tavares me. But, you know what? I don't got time for this shit. I'm going to leave Abdora lying right the fuck where he is while I put my shit on and go on about my day. Abdora's engaged, and that foolish ass girl looks stupid putting that pic up. It's clearly a pic that she took without them knowing."

"That's right, girl. Fuck that bitch," Rocky said.

"I had a good two days, and this shit is not about to ruin my fresh engagement. Although, I am going to check the shit out of Dora when he wakes up. Let me get my shit on so I can go get the twins. I'll holler at y'all later."

Tavares said her goodbyes to her girls and threw her Timberlands on. Abdora's phone was blowing up. She knew it was people calling because of what she'd just written on his page.

"Oh well. He'll deal with that shit when he wakes up."

Without a second thought Tavares grabbed her red Canada Goose ski jacket and Chanel purse and was out the door.

***

Abdora was wrestling in and out of sleep. He kept dreaming that his phone was going off. The more he wrestled, the more he realized his phone was indeed ringing nonstop. The text message notifications were blowing up too. Not to mention his social media notifications were booming. He was up and irritated that his phone had ruined his sleep. He found an empty spot as he rolled over to the right side of the king-sized bed. It was a little past noon, so he figured Tavares was somewhere around the house. She couldn't lie down for too long when the sun was up.

Abdora pushed the intercom on the side of the bed and tried to page Tavares throughout the house. When he got no response, he screamed, 'Tavaressss!"

Still no answer.

"What the fuck? I know she didn't leave and not wake me up."

***

Looking at what Abdora wrote under the picture, Prissy's mouth was wide open. She couldn't believe Abdora would check her like that on a social network. After she read all his posts again, she couldn't help but feel a little crushed. She was being a bitch when she put the pic up, but she hadn't expected Abdora to come for her bad. They had history, and once upon a time, he loved her more than anyone in the world.

"Should I call him?" she asked herself.

Prissy toggled with the thought for about thirty minutes and decided she was calling.

Abdora picked up his phone to find out where his fiancée had disappeared to. He didn't get a chance to call her, though. His attention was caught by the twenty-six text messages and sixteen missed calls.

"Damn, what the fuck happened while I was asleep? Shit must be deep the way my phone was blowing up."

Bryce, Bam-Bam, Middeon, Nas, Javan, and Hawk had been blowing him up for about two hours. He was reading the text messages, puzzled. His secretary Talia had texted: *Are you kidding me, Dora? Isn't it kind of early for 100 comments? Who is that chick? She tried it!*

"What the fuck is Talia talking about?" he asked himself, clueless.

Next, he opened the four texts from Bryce. The first one read: *I told you it was a mistake going there. Tavares is gonna kill all of us. Did you write that or did Tavares?* Abdora didn't read any further or get a chance to read his other texts because "Penny's Daughter" came across his caller ID.

"What's up, Prissy?"

"Uhhh, you tell me," she answered with a bit of an attitude.

"Yo, I just rolled over. So what's up?"

She didn't beat around the bush.

"Abdora, why did you write those comments on World Playground? They were real harsh and cold and made me feel some way."

"What the fuck are you talking about?"

"Underneath the picture I tagged you in."

"Priscilla, I don't know what comments or picture you're talking about," Abdora said with a tone that made it clear he was annoyed. "I just rolled over less than ten minutes ago. I haven't even been on WP. My life doesn't revolve around that social media bullshit. I have a REAL life off social media. So, what the fuck is this all about?"

"Well, Abdora, the comments have your name and your profile picture."

"Yo, look here, Priscilla. I just fucking told you I have no idea what you're talking about. So, either you fill me in, or we can hang up because what you aren't going to do is sit here and insinuate that I'm lying. You know better than that. I don't lie to kick it about a motherfucking thing."

"You go look on World Playground and call me back."

Abdora was mad he was awakened with all his phone notifications, but Priscilla had just worked his last fucking nerve. As he logged into his World Playground page, he damn near dropped his phone when he saw the picture and read the caption of the photo Priscilla had tagged him in.

"No wonder my phone was blowing up," Dora said to himself, reading the comments.

When he got to the comments that he allegedly wrote, he just shook his head. Dora read them over and over. He looked at the picture of Tavares's engagement ring and didn't know whether to be upset at her for stooping to Prissy's level or to laugh at her comeback. He had a very busy day ahead of him and wasn't in the mood for this stupid social media shit. This wasn't his speed and it wasn't even worth entertaining, but he decided he would call Priscilla back before he made any moves.

"Hello," Priscilla answered like she truly had an attitude.

"Prissy, I went on World Playground and saw the picture along with the comments. I didn't write the shit. That was my wifey."

"Your girl is petty."

"Is she, Priscilla? Is she really?" Dora asked, offended. "Priscilla, YOU started this petty shit by posting that picture—a picture I didn't even know you took. A picture that you added a real disrespectful caption to like you had something to prove or was trying to make my girl feel a way. My girl just finished it. Why did you feel the need to put that picture up and tag me? Fuck the picture because I don't have shit to hide. But, that caption was a straight shot at my girl. It was outta pocket, so miss me with the bullshit."

"Abdora, I wasn't trying to be petty," Priscilla said with a low, sad tone, trying to use her voice to deflect her behavior. She knew she was guilty as charged. "I was only giving you credit and a compliment for being there for me after all this time."

"Well, I don't know what you want me to tell you. Yes, I have love for you and Miss Penny, but you know I have a lady. You know I just got engaged. So, I don't know why you would post that picture and not think some bullshit was gonna come from it. You did what you did, and she did what she did. I don't have time for this childish shit. How's your mother?"

"She's still hanging in there. This morning when I came home to take a shower, they told me that I need to be prepared that she might be leaving soon and to make sure her affairs are in order."

Dora wasn't sure how much she knew about Miss Penny's insurance policies, so he just left it at, "Well, we'll cross that bridge when we get there. I have to make some moves, but keep me posted."

"I will," Priscilla said, feeling shot down because of how Abdora had defended his new lady like she wasn't once the love of his life. However, the game was on, and she was determined to take Tavares's man.

Now that Dora had checked Priscilla, he had to track down his wifey and clear the smoke with her. More importantly than social media drama, he had to find Tavares because he had business moves to handle and he needed her. He dialed her number and hoped it wasn't about to be a major blowout because he needed his business matter to run smoothly. That wasn't going to happen without his fiancée.

Just as Tavares was pulling into Me-Ma's driveway, she heard Abdora's special ringtone, Beyoncé's "My Rock." She rolled her eyes.

"Now this asshole wants to be calling me," she said out loud.

She put on her poker face and voice before answering.

"Hello?" Tavares answered her phone as bubbly as she wanted to be.

"Hey, Pretty Lady. Where are you?"

"In my skin. When I jump out you can jump in."

Abdora had to laugh.

"Mumma, cut the shit. Where are you?"

"Why?"

"Don't fucking ask me why. I can ask my fiancée where she is. Secondly, you left without saying a word to me."

"I was just following your lead. That's exactly what you did last night, right?"

"I told you I was leaving."

"Did you say where you were going? Speaking of which... where did you go?"

Abdora knew the bullshit was coming and it had just started.

"Did you go see a dog about a bone, a Mexican about some yayo, or a hoe about her dying mother?" Tavares asked straight-laced with no chaser.

Abdora knew it wasn't funny, but he fell out rolling.

"Babe, that was rude."

She knew it was and didn't give a fuck, so she kindly pushed his comment to the side.

"No, what she did was rude."

"It was, but you didn't have to retaliate with your post or just make that comment about her dying mother. Boo, you're crazy," he laughed.

"Oh, you think I'm hilarious, huh? Hmmm, okay. I promise you I'll get the last laugh."

Tavares didn't say another word. Instead, she hung up and let Abdora brew in anger because she didn't pick up any of the five times he called back. Dora was past mad. In fact, he was livid. That stupid ass picture Priscilla put up started all this dumb shit. Now, it had the potential to fuck with his business at hand because Tavares wasn't answering her phone and he needed her. His business transaction couldn't take place without her. Abdora could feel fire coming off his body, so he got dressed and prepared to track down his fiancée.

Tavares walked to Me-Ma's door and was trying her best to calm down.

"Hey there, baby," Me-Ma said when she swung the door open.

"Who raised that fool of a grandson of yours? Who, Me-Ma? Just who?"

"Well, hello to you, too."

"Sorry," Tavares said as she leaned in and kissed Abdora's grandmother.

Together they entered the living room, where Glam-Ma and Dhara were playing with the boys. Tavares smiled at the sight of her boys. Her face lit up as she bent down and kissed them and they got excited. After kissing her boys and cooing over them, Tavares instantly went back to going in on Abdora.

"Mama D and Me-Ma, Abdora is just crazy and stupid."

All three of the older women gave their attention to the fuming young lady. She wasn't letting up on Abdora.

"He's lost his mind. I don't know what's wrong with him, but he's just crazy. Do you hear me? Crazy."

"Oh no, not my sweet baby," Me-Ma said, grabbing her chest and gasping as if she couldn't believe the words that Tavares was saying.

If looks could kill, Tavares would have knocked Me-Ma down for that comment.

"Now, what did my sweet grandson do that would make you say such a thing?"

Dhara chuckled, "Now, daughter-in-law, you know you can't come for her grandson because in her eyes, he does no wrong."

Glam-Ma jumped in because she could see that her granddaughter was obviously upset.

"Baby, what's wrong?" Vadaleen inquired.

"Glam-Ma, last night when Abdora left, he went to console his ex at the hospital because her mother is dying."

Me-Ma, Dhara, and Vadaleen's eyes all got big. As women, they quickly understood why Tavares was going off.

"Oh, y'all can fix y'all's faces because that isn't even the worst. Today, she tried to put a picture up online being funny. When I broke her ass down, Abdora really tried to call me about it. He's just crazy," Tavares said, steaming even more at the moment.

Me-Ma was no longer riding with her grandson.

"You mean to tell me Abdora went to console that no good ass Priscilla while we were still celebrating y'all's engagement?"

"Ma!" Dhara yelled.

"Don't Ma, me. You know I don't like that trifling ass heffa. Tavares, you did right. Don't trust that tramp as far as you can see her."

Tavares hated to laugh, but she couldn't help it.

"Do you think his intentions were impure?" asked Dhara.

"Miss D, it doesn't even matter. Don't try to check me because I checked the next chick."

"I know that's damn right," Vadaleen said with her thick accent.

CHAPTER 17

By the time Abdora was slipping on his black North Face hoodie and matching puffy, his mother was calling him.

"What's cracking, Ma?"

"Boy, where you at?"

"Home getting dressed about to try to find my mad fiancée."

"Oh, you don't have to look too far."

"Why, she's at your house?" Abdora asked, getting a little less aggravated now that his mother was going to save his search.

"Nope, we at Ma's house, and boy she's mad. And, I do mean mad."

"I'm sure her stubborn ass is. She hung up on me and wouldn't even answer her phone. I'm on my way, but don't tell her."

Abdora hopped in his black on black Range Rover and got comfortable before placing his warning call.

"What's up, youngin?" Dora's mentor answered his phone.

"I wanted to call you and give you a heads up that we may have a problem."

"The fuck is the problem? I know my bread wasn't a dollar short."

"Nah, nah, Holton. It's nothing like that. It's not the paper or the play. It's your spoiled rotten daughter. She's mad at me. I don't think she's going to go for going with me. Adios motherfucking mios."

"What the fuck? I don't have time for this shit, Abdora. I really fucking don't. You know I need this deal like yesterday."

"Holton, it's not me. What I need for you to do is meet me at my grandmother's house and try to get her stubborn ass to see how important this is. She's gonna shut me down. You're my only hope to get her to go with me."

Hearing Holton yell in Spanish, Dolonda came out of the bathroom.

"What's wrong, baby?"

"Your daughter. I need her to bust a quick move with Abdora. He thinks because she's mad that she isn't gonna go."

"What the fuck?"

"I don't have time for the pretty princess today."

Dolonda laughed. "She is our daughter, but mainly she's your spoiled princess. So, good luck with that," Dolonda said, heading back to the bathroom to blow-dry her hair and get dressed.

"Baby, hurry up. We have to go talk to her," Holton said, now pacing the floor.

Dolonda was sick of her daughter, but she was going to go for the entertainment because she knew Tavares was going to shut her father and fiancé down.

***

Carmen was ready to take the trip the following day. She needed an alliance in taking Holton down and crushing his new lady to pieces. Who would be better than the person she was pursuing? There was just one loose end she needed to tie up before she headed out in the morning. Jade was grown, but she still wanted her daughter's great aunt to check on her while she was gone. Carmen finished packing, tossed on her snug GAP jeans and sweater, and got ready to go see her ex's aunt.

***

Dora used his key to let himself into his grandmother's house. As he walked toward the living room, he could hear the laughter.

"Hey, hey, hey, you beautiful ladies," Dora said, greeting his mother, grandmother, fiancée, and her grandmother.

Everyone spoke but Tavares. She only rolled her eyes.

"So is this where y'all are housing the runaway fiancée?" Dora joked.

"Ain't no one housing me," Tavares snapped. "And, at the rate you're going, I'm going to be your baby mama and not your fiancée because you got me all the way twisted with your stupid ass."

The tension in the room was thick.

"Listen, Mumma, I don't want to fight with you. Not today, and for certain not right now. You win, so can you please do me a favor? Drop the attitude, cut the bullshit, and go get dressed."

"Get dressed for what?" Tavares's neck snapped and her eyes rolled.

"Because I need you to come with me. This is serious. It's a big deal I need to close. I don't have time to play with you."

"Well, guess what. I ain't playing when I say, why the fuck would I go anywhere with you? You better call that hoe you was consoling last night."

Abdora had known this was how this conversation was going to take place. Yet, the level of anger Tavares was embodying told him this was about to be a losing battle. Me-Ma and Glam-Ma each picked a twin up.

"We're gonna let y'all talk," Dhara said, excusing all three women.

Tavares and Abdora were in a stare-down match.

"Tavares, I need you to cut the shit. This is millions we're talking about. So, get the chip off your shoulder and put the clothes on I left in the front hallway for you."

"No."

"No?"

"That's what I said, right? You have me entirely fucked up, Abdora. You spent the night with that hoe, and now you need me. Fuck outta here."

"Yo, Mumma, your mouth is getting real greasy. I'm trying to let you live, but you're pushing it. I didn't spend the night with anyone. I was at the hospital and came home to you."

"You were consoling that bitch, so you better call that bitch."

The doorbell broke the extra thick tension of their debate. In walked Tavares's parents. Tavares looked at her mother and father, and then to Abdora.

"What, you called my mommy and daddy? Newsflash, asshole, they can't make me do shit. I'm grown, and they don't run me. I just fucking found their asses, so they damn sure don't have no pull."

"I didn't come here to make you do a motherfucking thing," Dolonda said, making it clear that she wasn't there to do any such thing. "I came because your father thought he could. Trust me, here is the last place I want to be," Dolonda said, wounded by her daughter's last comment.

"Mija, listen to me. This is for Abdora, but it's really for me. He's doing this for me. I had a plug for years. When I decided to be with your mother and be the man that she needs me to be, I had to let my connect go because she was a woman that I was involved with. Dora secured this deal for me. And, I really just need you to go have dinner with him. Just dinner, Mija. That's all I need."

"No," Tavares said flatly.

Holton was shocked. Tavares seemed like she wasn't going to budge, not even for him.

"Did you just tell me no?"

"Papi, I ain't going nowhere with him. If this is for you, send your bitch."

Everyone looked at Tavares like she was crazy.

"Watch your mouth!" Abdora screamed.

Tavares was heated, but she hadn't meant to call her mother a bitch.

"Mami, I'm sorry," Tavares said emotionlessly. She meant what she said, but not to call her mother out by name.

"You know, Tavares, I've made my mistakes. But, I'm truly sick of your funky little all-about-you attitude."

"Mami, I said I was sorry."

Dolonda ignored her child. "You two fools sit here and plead your case. I'm going to see my grandkids," Dolonda said, excusing herself because she really wanted to smack the shit out of her mini-me.

"Papi, I'm sorry. Abdora did some shit that I'm not with. So, now he can't come to me needing me, and I'm supposed to just hop up."

"Can't you be mad tomorrow?" Abdora asked sarcastically.

Tavares wanted to slap the shit out of him, but she held back.

"Abdora, won't you tell my Papi what you did?" she said with daggers in her blue eyes.

"Holton, I went to the hospital last night to see my ex's mother who's dying. I didn't go for my ex. I went because me and her mother are very close."

Holton could see why his daughter was mad, but not mad enough to fuck up a five-million-dollar deal.

"Tavares, you're being stubborn," her father said. "I need you."

Out of nowhere Holton's mother appeared.

"You two let me talk to my granddaughter."

The two gentlemen shook their heads at how coldblooded Tavares was and left the room.

"Glam-Ma, I'm not going."

"You are going." Tavares's grandmother spoke with love and authority. "Sometimes when you are part of a Boss Family, you have to bite the bullet and do things you don't want to. Yes, Abdora made you mad, but now isn't the time to let your father and fiancé down. This is business, not pleasure. Your grandfather is a boss, your father is a boss, and now you're marrying a boss. So you need to put on your boss lady panties and get it together. There've been plenty of times your when Papito made me mad, but I would never let the family or the business down to prove my point. Please pick your face and pride up, and do what you have to for the men that you love."

Glam-Ma saw Tavares's face and knew that she'd gotten through to her. Tavares knew her grandmother was right. She was pissed, but it was time to do as she was told. She decided to put her big girl boss panties on and get this deal done.

Tavares took a long deep breath and said, "Okay."

Vadaleen opened her arms and gave her granddaughter a big hug. Tavares was fuming because Abdora had won the battle. Vadaleen went to the kitchen and informed Abdora and Holton everything was all set. They were in utter disbelief.

"Mommy, how did you pull that off?"

"I'm the grandmother. I gave her the lady boss talk from the head lady boss," Vadaleen winked. "Now, Abdora, hurry up before my charm wears off and she changes her mind."

Tavares changed into the ensemble Abdora had brought her. When she emerged from the bathroom, she was date-ready in her black cocktail dress, black lace tights, and simple but sexy black leather Valentino heels. Abdora matched her fly in a black suit that was tailored to perfection, a crisp black button-up shirt, and black Gucci loafers.

"Don't you guys look like a perfect couple," Dolonda said, trying to lighten the mood.

"Yes, you guys are picture perfect," Dhara said, giving her son dap.

"I guess," Tavares said, not feeling the fact that she'd gotten suckered when she was trying to be on her bullshit.

Holton gave his mentee dap and hugged his daughter. While giving her a tight embrace, he whispered, "Papi is gonna get you something special."

Tavares just whispered in return, "I love you, Papi."

Abdora knew his boo was mad, so he tried to ease the tension on the ride.

"Honey Babyyy, you look beautiful."

"Thank you," she replied dryly, still looking straight ahead.

"My sweet pumpkinnn, you smell great."

"Thanks," was all Dora got with an even drier tone.

"I really appreciate you coming through for us."

"Yep."

Abdora said fuck the sweet shit because it wasn't getting him anywhere. He pulled his gangster back out.

"You know what, nigga. I'm sick of your shit. You giving me them fucking dry ass responses, fuck it. You don't look good, you don't smell great, and fuck you."

His better half cracked up laughing.

"Oh, you mad, huh? Well, that sounds like your business," Tavares said with the driest tone she could muster.

"I thought I was rude, yo, but you'll make a nigga choke you," Abdora said to the woman who was absolutely his match.

She was the only one who gave him a run for his money, and she did a damn good job at it, too. Tavares curled her lips up, rolled her eyes, and went back to looking out the window.

As they pulled up to their destination, she got it all the way together. Money was emotionless, and this was about business. It was time to push her personal feelings aside. Hand in hand with big smiles they entered Nina O's upscale 5-star authentic Dominican restaurant.

"Damn, this is nice," Tavares said, admiring the ambiance, especially the colossal crystal chandelier that welcomed patrons upon entering.

The dim ambiance with candles lit on the tables and a live band made it feel sexy and intimate. Looking around actually brightened her mood as they waited to be seated. A woman in the far back was seating a couple and raised one finger, indicating that she would be with them in one moment. Tavares did a double take when she looked at the couple.

"Damn, that old lady is what you call the original bad bitch," she stated, giving the elderly Dominican woman a compliment.

Abdora leaned into Tavares and whispered, "Yeah she's a GILF."

"What the fuck is a GILF?" Tavares said with her eyes squinted in confusion.

"A grandma I'd like to fuck. She's a nana that these niggaz my age would give the business."

Tavares hated to laugh but she knew Abdora was telling the truth.

"You ain't nothing but a creep," Tavares said, playfully pushing Abdora away from her.

The hostess who was walking toward them had to be in her sixties, but she looked like she wasn't a day over forty. Her stomach was flat, her boobs were sitting high, and she was the perfect amount of thickness for the black pencil skirt, matching peplum blazer, and cream blouse she was doing major justice. The fact that she was wrinkle-free and strutting in six-inch Givenchy pumps was priceless.

Dora and Tavares were greeting her with a polite smile as she walked their way, but she wasn't doing the same. The closer she got to them, she looked like she'd seen a ghost. The color from her face was slowly disappearing.

"Hi, uhhh, uhh, I'm Nina Ortega. Welcome to Nina O's," she stuttered.

"Are you alright?" Abdora asked the woman, who truly looked startled.

"Yes, I'm fine," the woman said, pulling it together, but truly she was shaken inside. "Young lady, you have a candid resemblance to my daughter. That's all."

"Oh, well, she must be beautiful," Tavares said, not understanding why her resemblance to the woman's daughter had rattled her so badly.

Abdora was just as puzzled as his sidekick.

"No, honey, my Dee-Dee was beautiful. She's been deceased a long, long time."

Now the couple fully understood why she looked the way she did.

"My Dee-Dee was beautiful just like you. She was vibrant, gifted, and had a promising future ahead of her. But, now she gone," the elderly woman stated with sadness taking over her voice.

"I'm so very sorry to hear that," Tavares said, wanting to reach out and wrap her arms around the woman.

"No, no, don't be sorry. I have so many memories of her and us. Seeing you just knocked me off my feet because you reminded me of her in her younger days."

Nina felt tears coming and fought them back.

"Okay, now that we got that out of the way, tell me what are your names?" she asked with a forced smile.

"I'm Abdora, and this is my fiancée Tavares. We have seven o'clock reservations. Donnie O told me to ask for the best table in the house."

"Ohhh, okay. I'll be sure to take special care of you since my nephew sent you."

Nina knew that asking for the best table in the house meant he was there dropping off a large sum of money. Once his money was counted, she would call Donnie and tell him thanks for sending such stand up people over. That would tell him that the money counted the drop, and it was all set. Donnie didn't actually sell any drugs out of his aunt's restaurant. It was just a place where his selective heavyweight clients had dinner and dropped their payments off. When their car was valet parked in the adjacent lot, the valet, aka Donnie's workers, would retrieve the cash and drop it in another trunk. It was usually the trunk of someone who appeared to be in the restaurant having dinner but was indeed just waiting for the drop.

Nina showed the beautiful young couple to their table and made her way to her office to get herself together. She sat in her tall leather chair and cupped her face, allowing her tears to flow.

"Dee-Dee, I miss you so much. Just so much. And, I'm so sorry I wasn't there when you needed me."

It had been well over twenty years since Nina's daughter had left the earth. Yet, every day still felt like she was just hearing the news for the first time that her daughter overdosed and her body was so badly decomposed that there was no recognizing her. Nina hated that she never got to say goodbye. She never got to hug her one and only child before she crossed to the other side. She said a prayer, made her way to her bathroom, washed her face, reapplied her makeup, and got back to business as normal.

Tavares was actually enjoying dinner. She and the fine, overly sexy man she was with were like school kids on their first date again. They were laughing, blushing, joking, and kissing the whole time.

"How is all this going down?"

"I'm telling you nothing. Just know that we're having a beautiful, romantic dinner after you acted like you was leaving me," Abdora said, being sarcastic.

"Nigga, don't get cute because you still ain't out the clear," Tavares laughed as she scanned the beautiful restaurant.

Tavares dropped her head low and said, "Oh my fucking God. Oh, my motherfucking God."

Dora saw the panic in his lady's face, and it threw him into protector mode.

"Babe, what's wrong? What the fuck is the matter?"

"Don't look directly at the reception booth, but that's the fed bitch who was harassing me about you and who popped up at the hospital after I shot homeboy."

"Babe, you're trippin'. I'm sure this place is just a front for Donnie's business, so what the fuck would she be doing in here?"

"Dora, you fucking tell me. I don't know what she's doing here, but I do know that's her."

The wheels in Tavares's head were spinning now.

"How did she know we were here? Do you think that man set you up?"

"Ma, I don't know what the fuck is going on, but Donnie is legit as legit gets. That nigga ain't no rat. He has cocoa fields in the DR. He's importing cocaine straight from the Dominican Republic. And, no one other than your pops knows that we're here. Something ain't adding up. No one in this triangle of business is a rat for her to know we were going to be here."

Just like Abdora always protected Tavares, it was her natural instinct to protect him. She adjusted her crown, pulled it together, and thought fast.

"Listen, baby, I don't know who's who and what's what, but the deal is off. Call that man and tell him you want nothing."

Abdora thought he'd heard the woman who was his true Bonnie all wrong.

"Mumma, I ain't doing that. Fuck that bitch. Me or your father will have her put in a trunk and tossed in the ocean before we let her fuck this up. There's no way we're calling the plug like, 'Oh sorry. That five million in cash, we gonna need that back because we think the fed bitch is on to us.'"

Tavares gasped at Dora's words. Now she knew this man she planned to spend her life with was crazy.

"Are you fucking stupid, dumb, or retarded? We have two fucking kids. Not one, but two fucking kids. If we go to jail, yes, they'll be good, but are you willing to risk leaving our children parentless for some fucking drugs, you big ass dumb gangster?"

Just the thought of her kids going through what she went through infuriated her.

"Mumma, chill the fuck out. No one is going to jail. Not me, not you, and no one is going to be raising our fucking kids but me and you. Okay, that bitch is here. She might just be here socially. I don't think she's here for us."

"That woman is gunning for you. I don't know what her real personal is, but she has one. It's not who you are, the money you make, the streets you run, but something more personal. I heard it each time she came to see me. Not only does she have a personal with you, she has one with me now. So, the moment she spots our asses, you best believe no sooner than we leave here, probable cause or not, she's going to fuck with us. So, either you call the motherfucker or I will."

Abdora was silent and giving Tavares a blank stare. But, she wasn't paying him any mind as she was now texting on her phone. Nina was talking to Carmen, whom she didn't care for a whole lot. She tolerated her on the strength of her nephew that she loved a great deal. When she lost her daughter, it was

Donnie who'd been her rock. That time took her to her lowest and weakest, and Donnie was there every day, every step of the way. Seeing that she was his mother's twin sister, he loved her just as much as he loved his own mother. Their close relationship was the one and only reason she dealt with Carmen, who seemed to use their daughter as a reason to be a part of their family.

"TT Nina. Earth to TT Nina. Do you hear me?"

"Yes, I heard you. You have to go out of town and want me to just call and check in on Jade while you're gone. I'm sorry if I seem a little out of it."

"You don't seem a little out of it. You seem a lot out of it. What's the matter?"

"Yes, yes, yes, this is gonna work out," Tavares said optimistically.

Dora wasn't worried like Tavares, but he was going to appease her.

"Who were you texting?"

"I was texting Bella, Rocky, and Cali to see who was close enough to help me push this plan in motion."

Slightly looking over her shoulder, she could see the two women still talking.

"Babe, listen and listen fast because in about five minutes it's lights, camera, action. From the fact that they're still talking, it says the nature of the relationship and conversation is personal. That means that lady Nina is going to tell that bitch Agent Vega about me looking like her daughter, if she hasn't already. It's going to spark her to want to know who it is. Then, she's going to bring her ass over here. She's gonna see your face and suspect it's me, but my new hair color is going to throw her off. When you see her looking this way, blow me a kiss. Is she looking yet?"

"Nah, she's looking shocked right about now, so maybe they're discussing it like you said."

"When she does come this way, I'm going to get up and go to the bathroom. And, mark my words, that punk bitch is gonna follow. When I'm in the bathroom, I'm going to stall her. Tell Nina you had an emergency and for valet to give me the car. Rocky is gonna be in the parking lot in ten minutes or less. Get in her car and drive the opposite direction of Newark. I don't care if you drive to New York, Connecticut, or South Africa. Just don't go toward Newark. When we touch down, I'll call you. And, in the meantime, asshole," Tavares looked Dora straight in the eye, "call the man and tell him simply hold the drop. I don't trust the fed bitch. I just don't, but we need that coke. So just tell him to give you a week to throw her off."

Listening to what had TT Nina's nerves bad, Carmen's response was, "Oh my, Nina. Are you serious?"

At the same time, she was looking around to see who Nina was talking about. Seeing Abdora's face, her stomach almost came out of her asshole. She had her poker face on, but she didn't like seeing Abdora because that meant Nina could only be talking about Tavares. However, the lady she was looking at from the back had bright turquoise and pink blunt, short blonde hair. Was it Tavares?

Abdora leaned in, kissed Tavares's lips, and then nibbled on her ear.

"That cunt bitch is staring me down. When she starts to walk this way, I'm gonna tap your foot."

Abdora kissed Tavares and tapped her foot that fast. Tavares wiped her mouth, grabbed her purse and phone, and strutted to the bathroom. Nina and Carmen approached the table.

"Hi, Abdora. This is Carmen. I was just telling her about your girlfriend."

"Oh, Miss Nina, she just went to the ladies' room."

"Abdora, it's a pleasure to meet you."

"Is it? I feel like we've met before. Have we met before?" Dora said, drizzling every last word in sarcasm.

"No, we haven't, but I'm sure it won't be the last time we see one another," Carmen returned the sarcasm. "As a matter of fact, Nina, I'm going to run to the bathroom myself before I head out. Abdora, the pleasure was all mine, and I look forward to seeing your and your girlfriend here next time."

Carmen walked to the bathroom in more of a panic than any of the parties involved. Abdora and Tavares knew what her profession on paper was, so seeing her must have raised a red flag. Even worse, they were getting too close for comfort. They had the potential to open Pandora's box and take everything from her, including her life, if she didn't make her next move her best move. As she scurried to the ladies' room, Abdora received a text. It read: *Your ride is waiting*. Sticking to the plan, he did as Tavares said.

"Ahhh, Miss Nina, I'm so sorry I have to go. I have an emergency. Tell my sweet lady to take the car."

"I'll give your beautiful fiancée your message. Please come back sooner rather than later."

"I absolutely will," Dora said, reaching down and giving the beautiful, pleasant woman a hug that she'd opened her arms looking for.

Carmen entered the modern-styled bathroom and waited to startle Tavares with her presence. Exiting the stall, Tavares was anything but startled when she came around the corner to wash her hands.

"Well, well, well, Miss Del Gada, I guess three times is the charm." With a smirk like she struck gold, she asked Tavares, "What exactly are you doing here?"

"We're in a bathroom," Tavares said dryly, stating the obvious as she looked around. "It's safe to assume that I was just taking a piss. And, if you would get out of my way, I'm going to exhibit proper hygiene and wash my fucking hands."

"Don't fucking play me. You know what I mean. What are you doing at Nina O's? Are you here buying drugs?"

With no fear or nervousness, Tavares chuckled while looking through the mirror at the woman who foolishly thought Tavares was gonna answer that and incriminate herself.

"Hmm, Agent Vega... You might need to return to grade school. This is a restaurant, not a trap house. What do people do at restaurants? They eat. I ordered Arroz con Pollo, but I don't recall the waitress saying it was coming with a side order of a brick of dope," Tavares laughed.

"Little girl, don't fucking play with me. I know what you're here for. I finally got you and that no good, gang lord boyfriend of yours. You're going down."

"Oh, is that right, Agent Vega?" Tavares asked with a grim smile that let the double agent know she wasn't worried one bit. "If you know what I'm here for, then arrest me. Whip out your pretty little silver bracelets and cuff me."

Tavares extended her wrists. When Agent Vega didn't accept the invitation, Tavares bellowed in laughter.

"Because you have nothing and know nothing. But, the real question, Carmen, is it? What are *YOU* doing here? How do you know Nina O? Why would you, as a federal government agent, be where you think that anyone is purchasing drugs? Are you here purchasing drugs?" taunted Tavares.

"I don't buy drugs. Nina is my family. But, I know for a fact that's what you and that criminal boyfriend of yours are here doing."

Tavares cut her off. "Miss Vega, I don't know who the fuck you think you're fooling. You only THINK you know that. If you knew that for a fact, which you don't, it would be because you're here for the same reason. So, miss me with the fucking bullshit."

Agent Vega switched lanes. "I hear you got engaged. Congrats. I hope you make it to get married before I toss y'all's asses in jail and take down Abdora's whole organization. Speaking of drug organizations, how is your father? Holton, is it?" Carmen said, giving Tavares the same sarcasm she'd been giving her.

Tavares's smile disappeared, but in the process of it fading away, something hit her. She didn't know why God had blessed her with such a strong sixth sense, but He did. She knew for a fact that this bitch was the plug her father had lost when he stopped fucking her. Tavares's smile reappeared as she prepared to hit this no-good bitch where it hurt.

"My father, oh, he's great. Got him a bad Dominican bitch that he's head over heels for. She actually reminds me of you, but with a better body and she doesn't look as aged," Holton's daughter said, busting a low blow. "He spends all his time traveling with her. Truth be told, my Papi is in love. Oh, did I forget to mention that the woman he's in love with is my mother?"

Carmen's body language changed. She thought she had her poker face on and that Tavares didn't notice the shift, but she was wrong about both.

"But wait, how is it that you know my father again?"

Carmen's feelings were hurt, and it showed as she tripped and stuttered over her words.

"Uhh, uhhh... I uhh know, know... Matter of fact, I don't know him personally. I only know he's a piece of shit, drug dealing asshole just like your fiancé. I did my homework. All the men in your life seem to be the same."

Tavares cracked up laughing uncontrollably. Carmen was looking at her with mayhem in her eyes.

"Something funny? I find nothing funny that you, your father, and your fiancé are pieces of shit flooding drugs everywhere."

Before Tavares could answer, her text indicator went off. *The man is in the wind and I'm in the parking lot.*

She was about to wrap this meeting in the ladies' room up.

"Lady, you're funny. Oh, trust and believe you know my father. You know him well enough that you were swallowing his dick and supplying him with millions of dollars in cocaine. He has you to thank for having such a lucrative cocaine business. You were supplying, sucking, and fucking him until he kicked you to the curb. He got him a woman that he wanted to wife, not just fuck because she was the plug who sucked a mean dick." Tavares gave an evil laugh. "Must suck that he left his wife and still didn't wife you. Sucks to be you," she said before she laughed until she cried real tears. After regaining her composure, she said, "I wonder how your job would react knowing all that?"

Carmen's stomach dropped so low she thought she was about to shit her panties. Tavares knew everything.

"Little girl, you're fucking with the wrong bitch. You don't know shit. I'm a federal agent. I would never supply your father or anyone else with cocaine, nor was I your father's side bitch, contrary to what he may have told you."

"Sure, you're right," Tavares said, rolling her eyes. "Tell yourself what you want, but I'm sure it won't be hard to dig up a little evidence if need be."

'I'm the wrong bitch to play with," snarled Carmen. "You want to go to war with me? Then, let's go to war. But, I promise you, you won't win. I have more power and connections than your street boyfriend could ever dream of having."

"Actually, bitch, I will win because I'm a savage when it comes to the people I love. And, your law enforcement connects don't scare me, because my mob connections have a way further reach than YOU could ever think of. Every time you walk out your door, ask yourself if you'll make it home tonight," Tavares winked. "I haven't ever met a challenge that I didn't accept. I promise you on my kids, I'm going to get the last laugh. And, third time wasn't the charm. It was more like three strikes and you're out, bitch."

Tavares didn't say another word. She'd talked long enough. She brushed by Agent Carmen Vega, looking her straight in the eye to let her know she didn't pump any fear in her. It was the complete opposite; she'd met her match. Tavares was smiling inside and out as she made her way to the front of the restaurant to say her goodbyes to Miss Nina.

"First, Abdora. Now, you, too," Miss Nina said, still in awe at the resemblance Tavares had to her deceased daughter.

"Yeah, Miss Nina, I have to run, but I promise we'll be back."

"I'm gonna hold you to it, pretty girl. "

Tavares was just exiting the building when Carmen took a last look at her.

"That little bitch has to go once and for all. She will not take everything I worked so hard for."

"Carmen, I thought you were long gone."

"No, TT Nina. I was in the ladies' room. I got to chat with the young lady Tavares. Isn't she just lovely?"

"Oh, yes, she is."

"I'm gonna get out of here. Please remember to call Jade at least three times a day. I don't care if she acts aggravated or annoyed that I have you

288 | Acid Connections 3

checking in on her. Please just do it until I get back in a few days."

Carmen made a pit stop to the garage before getting in her car.

"Hey, Kenny. Can you tell me what kind of car that the couple that just left was in?"

Kenny hated Carmen. No one cared if she was Donnie's baby's mother. They still hated her. In the employees' eyes, she was worse than a rat.

"Nah, I don't know."

"What do you mean you don't know? You're sitting in the booth. All the cars pull up here, and you hit a button to let them out. Cut the shit."

"I don't know, yo."

"Do you have a problem, Kenny?"

Bluntly he answered, "My problem is that I don't answer to you. I answer to Donnie. These other niggaz let you son them because you're the police, but I don't give a fuck."

Before Carmen could rip Kenny a new asshole, Jason tried to keep the peace.

"It wasn't a couple. It was two chicks. One had crazy pink hair. They were in a black on black Range Rover."

Carmen didn't even say thanks as she spun around and placed a call to be on the lookout for Dora's Range Rover. Sadly, she had all his license plate numbers stored in her phone. So, it wasn't hard to give to her friend who was a state trooper.

"Christine, I have another call coming in. But, once they pull that car over, give me a call back ASAP."

CHAPTER 18

Carmen clicked over and answered her phone.

"What do you want, Donnie?"

"Carmen, Carmen, Carmen. Trust me. It pains me just as much as it pains you that I have to use my valuable, priceless air to call and talk to you. The feelings of dislike are beyond mutual."

"Okay, then what do you want?"

"I just got a call from TT Nina and Abdora Santacosa. The second call disturbed me a little. Would you like to tell me what's going on?"

"Only if you want to tell me what Abdora was doing in your aunt's restaurant. I didn't know gang banger killers were on the list of clients. Last time I checked, we service low-profile people, not his kind."

Donnie laughed before he got ignorant.

"Carmen, I don't fucking answer to you about who's on my client roster. We aren't partners. Bitch, you work for me, not the other way around. You're a federal agent to help me grease palms and get shit done. At the end of the day, I'm your real boss."

"Fuck you."

"No, that's the problem. I fucked you and got stuck with you for the rest of my life when I got you pregnant. So no. Fuck you. Now, back to what I called for. I don't know why your pussy gets wet harassing Abdora and his lady, but back the fuck off. As long as he does business with me, he's protected just like my other clients."

"No, he's not protected. He's a gang banger, a murderer."

"Bitch, don't fucking play with me. I already know you were lying when you said your loyal customer of over ten years was short this go round. So, instead of cutting your tongue out for lying, I let Abdora take that slot so I don't lose any money."

"I'm not protecting that fucker. I hope the agency throws him in jail."

"Carmen, you think this is a game. Do I sound like this is up for a fucking debate? You think because you're my daughter's mother it makes you special? Well, it doesn't! I don't play games when it comes to my money. You know this better than anyone else. Play me with me if you want, and I'll be burying you. Then, I'll stand over your casket and cry with our daughter as I console her."

Carmen was fuming inside because she did know that Donnie killed people for sport. Fucking with his money was the fastest way to earn yourself a one-way ticket into a grave.

"Abdora is already on the radar of the Jersey Field office."

"Well, you'd better keep him off. He's going to bring me too much money to let your bitter bitch ass fuck him over."

"What the fuck ever, Donnie. Are you done?"

"No."

"TT Nina called me all worked up about Abdora's girlfriend looking like Dee-Dee. She said that if one didn't know any better, they would have thought it was Dee-Dee reincarnated."

"Uhh yeah, the girlfriend resembles Dee-Dee. No big deal."

"Well, the resemblance was candid enough to frazzle my TT. What do you know about this young woman?"

"Nothing. I know she's a gold-digging whore who likes drug dealers."

"A lot like you," laughed Donnie.

"What the fuck does that mean?"

"It means I know for a fact you were seeing the man who was your loyal customer for the last ten years. You bent a lot of rules, and you were loving that drug dealer. So, Carmen, you should really refrain from putting your nose in the air at people.

Yes, you may be at a corporate level, but you're no better than that woman. Y'all move the same and love the same kind of men. Now, do a background check on her and get back to me."

***

Rocky was blown away after Tavares brought her up to speed on what had transpired.

"Bitch, you really are Dora's ride or die. Nah, more like his partner in crime."

"I don't know what the Fed bitch's deal is, but word up I'm gonna drag that bitch. Mark my words. She came for the wrong person. Don't play with my man or my kids. By trying to take us to jail, she's doing both."

Flashing police lights brought the conversation to a halt.

"What the fuck?" Rocky said, looking in the rearview mirror.

"No worries, bitch. We ain't riding dirty. I bet you this is that Fed bitch's doing."

They pulled over and waited for the motions to take place. When they saw what was at the side of Rocky's window, in unison they burst out rolling.

"Yo, Tavares, this is some shit we're gonna forever laugh at. This one is going down in history."

The officer knocked on the window, and Rocky tried to suppress her laughter as she asked, "Can I help you, officer?"

"License and registration, please?"

"Sure, no problem. As soon as you inform me why you pulled us over."

Looking in the car, the officer questioned Tavares. "Ma'am, is there a reason you're recording this?"

"Yes, sir. I plan to use it against you and the bitch Carmen Vega when I take y'all before internal affairs."

Tavares was polite and smiling with her response.

"Ma'am, I don't know who Carmen Vega is," he lied. He and Carmen were friends and did a lot of dirty business together.

"I pulled you over because you were going slower than the flow of traffic, which is suspicious."

The two girls looked at each other and laughed again, while Tavares continued recording. Rocky appeased the officer. While she reached for the registration, he questioned them.

"Do you ladies have any illegal narcotics or weapons in the vehicle?"

"No," Rocky said, rolling her eyes, passing over her license and the car registration.

"Do you mind if I check?"

That was it.

"I absolutely mind if you check my car without a warrant or probable cause," Tavares screamed. "Listen here, you fake ass Mr. T lookalike. I don't know if it's that outdated fucking mohawk or all that Goddamn gold you're wearing that's slowing down your brain function, but you got the wrong black girls. I'm not just some dumb black ghetto bitch. I'm a double major in Criminal Justice and Pre-law. Therefore, I know this traffic stop is bullshit. That bitch put you up to this shit, and now she's gonna get your ass fired."

"Young lady, you're walking a dangerously fine line. You need to watch your mouth. This is a routine traffic stop, and you ladies are making it worse than it has to be. So, again, I need you to just watch your mouth."

"I'm going to do no such thing. What YOU should do is think twice before taking directions from that dirty federal agent. She's going to cause you to be fired and receive no pension. Once I show this video of you illegally pulling us over and illegally searching my car, and I dig up the proof that you're a dirty cop like she is, I promise I'll have you by the balls, fired, and I'll be getting the last laugh."

State Trooper Thomas had never in his seventeen years on the job been checked that way.

"You ladies wait right here while I run your license and registration."

He returned to his vehicle, but instead of doing what he said, he called Carmen.

"Hey, Jerry. You got them? Were there drugs stashed in the car?"

"Carmen, who are these young ladies?"

"Young ladies? It should have been a couple."

"Well, it's two ladies and that turquoise head little bitch is real slick with her tongue."

"That's the main little bitch that I'm looking to send to jail."

"I don't know who she is, but she knows her shit. She knows I gave a bullshit reason for pulling them over and that it's illegal to just search the car. She even threatened to show the video she's recording to internal affairs."

"What fucking video?" screamed Carmen.

"The video she started recording when I approached the car. She told me not to let you get me fired because she'll find proof that I'm dirty like you. Carmen, sorry baby, you're on your own with this one. I ain't taking the chance that she does what she says. We've done too much dirt over the years."

"Fuck, fuck, fuck," Carmen hollered. "This bitch. This little fucking bitch. Fine, let them go, Jerry."

Carmen hung up her phone and thought she could feel fire seeping through her skin. Jerry returned to the vehicle and released the women. Riding off feeling like they'd won, Tavares phoned her father.

"Hey, Mija. How did things go?"

"Not good, Papi. Not good at fucking all. I need to get with you ASAP."

Holton was worried by the urgency in his daughter's voice.

"Me, your mom, your grandmother, and Dhara are in Harlem at your Uncle Hayden's house."

"I'm on my way."

"Where's Dora?"

"It's a long story. I'll tell you when I get there."

Tavares and Rocky were cracking up about Mr. T when an unfamiliar number phoned Tavares. She skeptically answered.

"Hello?"

"Tavares."

The sound of the voice on the other end of the phone infuriated her in seconds.

"Why are you calling me?"

Rocky was mouthing, "Who is that?" as she watched Tavares's pale face quickly turn fire engine red. She put her phone on speaker.

"I made it clear at Dame's funeral. We aren't friends. We will never be friends again. You fucked him. You got pregnant, and he died on you. That's your problem, not mine. I want NO parts of you or that baby."

"Please, Tavares, I need you. I wish I could turn back the hands of time. I'm sorry. I'm so sorry. I want your support with my first child. I'm living in my own hell for what I did to you. Please don't turn your back on me and the baby, because I need you."

Tavares keeled over crying from laughter.

"Is Ashton on the three-way and gonna tell me I'm being Punk'd? This can't be serious. Either you're crazy or have lost your fucking mind. I don't know which one, but bitch, I'm not fucking with you. I don't care what happens to you or that baby. I would have given you my last—even my life—but you crossed me. Envy and jealousy allowed you to betray me. So, guess what. You figure it the fuck out. I don't care if you go hungry, broke, or homeless. That shit ain't my problem."

Tavares hung up in Jazz's face, leaving her on the other end of the phone sobbing at her reality. She was having a baby with a deceased man who didn't want her, didn't want her baby, and had made that very clear before he passed. Her family shamed her for having a baby out of wedlock, and his family told her point blank period they would fuck with the baby but not her. She was living in her own hell for sure.

***

Bryce was damn near to Philly when it hit him that he hadn't heard from Dora since the morning fiasco on World Playground. He hit Dora to see if everything was good. Dora picked up on the first ring.

"What up, fool?"

"Just calling to make sure my sister didn't kill you and bury you in the backyard," Bryce joked.

"Nah, my nigga, but it's been a hell of a day. A hell of a fucking day. But, you niggaz is in the doghouse, too. The picture looked like y'all was team Priscilla. So, good luck," laughed Dora.

"Niggga, get the fuck outta here. How the fuck you gonna throw me and Mid under the bus? We told you we wasn't with that shit."

"Nigga, let me find out you scared of my wife. Pull your gangsta pants up, nigga."

"Fuck you. Tavares is a bulldog in heels. I don't want no smoke with her. Shit, buy her something nice. I'm sure she'll forgive you. It works for me all the time."

"Where you at?"

"I'm about to go meet Javan, Maniac, Bam-Bam, and Hawk at Big Daddy's in Philly."

"You niggaz love to throw y'all money away on strippers. Fuck that. I got my wifey taking enough of my bread that I ain't about to just toss it away to no other bitches just because they showing me pussy. I see pussy all day at home."

The best friends laughed together.

"Aight, I'm gonna meet y'all there in about an hour."

***

By the time Tavares and Rocky made it uptown to Harlem, Tavares was mentally exhausted.

"Rocky, I really feel like the devil is riding my back with everything that has gone on. Getting shot, Dame's gone, the drama, Priscilla, now this shit. The only bright side has been my engagement."

"Girl, that outshines all the bad in my book. Let's go in here and see what your pops says about the agent bitch. Then, you gotta make your next move your best move."

"Before we go in here, let me warn you. My uncle Hayden is fine and a flirt. He means no harm, though."

"Girl, please. Let's go."

The ladies walked up the steep stairs of the brownstone, and then Tavares rang the bell. The brisk New York air was slapping them left and right as they waited. It felt like forever, but only a minute later, Tavares's uncle swung the tall red door open.

"Oh, now you wanna come visit your fine ass uncle just because your mother and father are here with your grandmother and kids."

"Uncle Hayden, shut up and let us in. That's my girlfriend Rocky."

"Rocky, hmmm, nice to meet you."

"Pleasure is all mine," Rocky said, seeing that Tavares wasn't lying when she said her uncle was fine. He looked like a younger version of her handsome mulatto father, just tanner and taller. As they all walked to the second floor where everyone was, Hayden teased Rocky.

"Rocky, you're cute, girl. You looking for a sugar daddy or a daddy who wants no sugar, because I ain't that second nigga," laughed Hayden.

"Uncle Haaaydeen," screeched Tavares.

"Girl, relax. I mean, I am fine and your friend is my type with her pretty face, wide hips, and small waist, but I was just playing."

As the ladies entered the family room, the spectators waited for Tavares to spill what had happened.

"Geesh, can I breathe?" she joked, knowing what the cold stares were for.

She took her jacket off and then kissed all over her babies for a few moments before spilling the beans.

"Shit didn't go as planned because there was a glitch. A federal agent who's been gunning for Abdora came in, so I wasn't taking no chances. I made Dora stop the deal, but he called the man. Hopefully, it's still gonna happen, just not today."

Dhara, Dolonda, and Vadaleen's eyes were big upon hearing "federal agent," while Holton and Hayden were giving one another their own suspect look.

"Papi, I need to speak with you in private."

"Niece, you go on and talk to your father. I'm gonna keep your friend company," Hayden joked as he licked his luscious LL Cool J lips.

"Glam-Ma, watch your son, please."

"I got my eye on him, baby. Your uncle is a big ole mess. Rocky don't want his old butt," her grandmother said, only half right.

Dhara chimed in. "You're gonna need Viagra for that young thang, Hayden."

Everyone in the room laughed.

As soon as they entered the study and closed the door, Tavares wasted no time.

"What's the deal with the lady Carmen Vega?"

"She walked in the restaurant?" Holton asked, looking puzzled.

"She tried to come for me, you, and Abdora. That's where she fucked up. I don't give a fuck if she's the feds, she's a snake, a double agent, and I'm gonna drag that hoe for every person she's ever sent to jail."

"Listen to me. She's a manipulative, conniving snake in the grass. You can drag her, and she's no competition for what me or Abdora will do to her on a street level. Here's the problem. She has the law behind her, and she will play dirty as dirty gets."

"She called you and Abdora no good ass drug dealers."

"A drug dealer she was sweating for years," Holton responded.

"She told me she was sending me and Abdora to jail before we get married."

"Trust me, my brain and evilness are no competition for that bitch."

There was a light knock at the door.

"It's Hayden."

"Uncle Hayden, whatttt do you want?" joked Tavares.

"I want to know what we gonna do with that problem ass dog bitch Carmen Vega. I never ever liked that bitch. She would come around with your father acting like she didn't know her place. I hate when a bitch acts like she doesn't know her lane. Now it's time that she gets shown where her lane is."

Tavares was blindsided by her uncle's words.

"Uncle, were you listening to our conversation?"

"Not at all, Baby Girl. When you said a fed agent walked in, I already knew. What other federal agent walks in a drug establishment and you're standing here to tell us about it? Her snake in the grass ass was the first person that popped in my head. I told your father about her years and years ago. I don't like cops, so a federal agent for sure ain't my cup of tea. Holton, I told you she was good for what she did for the moment, but the day you decided to cut her ass off she would become a liability. I like to live the high life, so liabilities don't suit my life well. That liability has to go."

"She's outta here, bro. You already know that. When and how matter because at the end of the day, she is still a Fed. We have too much to lose to be sloppy. We ain't doing life in jail at our ages."

"Yeah, Unc, y'all are too old to be someone's girlfriends in jail."

Tavares was cracking up while her father and uncle looked at her like she'd lost her damn mind.

"Where's Dora?" her father asked.

"I don't know. I had him take Rocky's car and get in the wind. Then, we took the Range Rover. So, I'm here on family time for the rest of the day."

Hayden grabbed his niece and put her in a headlock.

"Out of all my nieces and nephews, you're my favorite now. You're about that life like your father, aunts, and uncles—not like our spoiled ass, silver-spoon-in-the-mouth kids."

"Bout that life?" Tavares said with a side eye. "Uncle Hayden, I thought you owned a construction company with Papi."

"Oh yeah, I do that, too," laughed Hayden.

He didn't think he niece needed to know that he was one of the biggest loan sharks around and that he had gambling rings and chop shops.

"Girl, you're from a family of bosses. Your Papa and Glam-Ma raised us to go out into the world and take it. Fuck waiting on someone to give us some shit. All our illegal affairs are protected by legal means. Now, let's go hang. I think your friend is feeling me."

"Papi, get your brother. Get him now," laughed Tavares.

Abdora was damn near to his house. He placed a call to his lady to make sure everything was okay.

"Hello?" Tavares answered in a low voice, sounding extremely tired.

"Hey, pretty lady."

"Hey, babe. What's going on?"

"I was heading to the house and was like damn my baby didn't even call me to come home?"

Tavares had to chuckle. "Call you for what? You're a grown ass man, not a lost puppy who doesn't know his way home."

"Shut up, stupid face. I know I'm a grown ass man, but you were supposed to call me."

"Me and Rocky ended up going to my Uncle Hayden's."

"Oh, and your phone stopped working?"

"No, smart ass. After hollering at him and my papi, it just slipped my mind. But, somehow, we ended up with my parents and Glam-Ma at the house. They're in the second-floor right wing. Them and the boys were all knocked when I left the house."

"Wait, what you mean? They're at the house, but you ain't there?"

"Nope."

"It's two in the morning. Where the fuck are you?"

Abdora's whole tone had just changed.

"Pump your brakes, killer. I'm on my way to the gym."

"The gym? Tavares, why in the fuck are you going to the gym this time of the morning when we have a fully equipped state-of-the-art gym downstairs?"

"Abdora, really? Because I wanted to get out of the house and clear my head. It's been a long fucking day, starting with your bullshit."

"Yeah, aight," he responded, treading lightly. "Don't forget your way home."

"Bye, Stupid Face," Tavares said.

"Later, Dummy Brain," Dora said before hanging up.

Tavares pulled into the damn near empty parking lot of the state-of-the-art twenty-four-hour gym owned by a friend of Abdora. There was one car in the lot and another pulling in as she retrieved her gym bag and hustled out in the cold toward the entrance. She quickly got into her groove listening to Lil Wayne while jogging on the treadmill when she saw someone next to her. She wasn't in the mood, so she rolled her eyes at the gentleman trying to get her attention.

"Hey, Miss."

With a bone-dry tone, Tavares said, "Hello."

"What's your name?" the physically fit, handsome man asked.

"Not interested."

"That's a different name."

"What do you want?"

"I just wanted to chit-chat since we're the only ones here."

"Sir, this is a place where people come to work out. If you're looking to make friends, go on a dating site. Or, you could even try Starbucks."

"Well, aren't you feisty," the gentleman with pretty white teeth smiled. "Your man lets you come to the gym all by yourself this time of night?"

"I'm grown. By the nature of this conversation, I see your lady let you off a leash to come to the gym and harass women like me."

"I guess you're not in the mood to be bothered, so I'll leave you alone."

"Thanks."

Tavares returned her headphones to her head and didn't give him a second look. After jogging for an hour, lifting some weights, and doing squats and sit-ups, she felt good. She released some well needed steam, did some thinking, and felt refreshed. Now, she was ready for a long hot shower and some time in the sauna before she headed home and crawled in bed.

The whole time she was working out, she noticed the man who had been harassing her staring at her. As she retrieved her bag, she gave him the middle finger and made her way upstairs to the shower.

She stripped out of her wet gym clothes, turned the shower on, and let the steaming hot water marinate all over her body. She was in pure bliss, lathering her body, listening to her portable speaker blaring Monica's "Still Standing." She never heard the locker room door open. She had an onlooker watching her sing in the shower as she washed her voluptuous hips, backside, and breasts. He watched for about a minute before he decided to help himself to what he liked.

Quietly creeping toward the small body that he towered over by more than a foot and a half, he cupped his hand tightly over Tavares's mouth. She tried to yell, but his massive hand muffled the sound.

"Don't fight it. Just spread your legs and make this easy," he whispered.

With his free hand, he slid his middle and index finger inside her center. Tavares's tense body loosened as he kissed the nape of her neck. Each kiss was softer than the previous one. He went down her wet back with his soft lips and didn't stop kissing until he got to her hind side. Quivering from the intensity of the hot water with fingers using her insides as a playground and the warm lips caressing her, Tavares's center was drizzling. With firmness, he grabbed her wide hips and turned Tavares around.

"Look at me. I wanna see your face while I eat this sweet pussy."

Doing as she was told, Tavares looked the pussy monster in the eyes. While on his knees, he took her right leg and positioned it over his shoulder. Then, he began to make love to her with his mouth. The mischievous pleasure that was taking place caused the happy victim to grab and massage her on succulent DD breasts. Tavares was shaking and quivering while looking him straight in the eye. As she began to burst, her head fell backwards under the waterspout, and she screamed.

The pussy monster wasn't done with her just yet. He didn't like how she'd spoken to him earlier, so he had to teach her a lesson. He continued using his tongue to slow dance on the center of her tootsie pop. The more she moaned, begged him to stop, and continued cummin' like a water faucet, the more he intensified his tongue game. With his penis fully erect, he stood up and looked Tavares in her ocean blue eyes.

"We shouldn't be doing this," Tavares said.

"Of course, we should. Don't worry. I won't tell your man if you don't tell my lady."

"My man is probably fucking your lady as we speak."

"I like how you think. Let's see if that mouth is good for more than talking shit."

Tavares looked down at the chocolate dick that was perfect in size and width. When God was passing out dicks, He showed up and showed out on what he'd given this fine, chiseled man. Tavares squatted down under the showerhead and held the fully erect nine-and-a-half-inch penis in her hand. While holding the shaft, she lubricated his manhood with her saliva. After she spit on his dick extra sloppily, she started at the head and slowly took all of him in her mouth. Looking him in the eye the whole time, she slowly used her mouth and tongue as a weapon of sexual mass destruction. After ten minutes his eyes began rolling backwards.

"Damn, girl. Your man must be a happy man."

No longer able to take it, he pulled Tavares up. With force, he turned her around and threw her up against the wall. The water poured down on both of them, and neither seemed to mind. He slid himself inside her slowly, one inch at a time. She moaned, screamed, and came all at the same time. With matched intensity, he stroked her and she threw her ass back, slowing fucking him the same way he fucked her. For well over an hour, he gave Tavares a dick down she didn't see coming. He bent her over doggy style on the bench in the shower. He made her ride him frontwards and backwards. He even stood her up, made her grab her ankles, and fucked her until she begged for mercy. For a finale, he lifted her small frame into the air and gave her slow, long strokes. She continued to cum on him, and he exploded inside her. As fast as he released, his dick immediately stiffened again. That dick was for sure one of a kind.

Just when Tavares thought the sexcapade was coming to an end, he picked her up off his penis and tossed her over his shoulder.

"Oh, my God! Put me down. Put me down," she said, kicking.

"I'm not done with you just yet, pretty lady," he said, spanking her. "Be a good girl, and it will be over soon enough."

Tavares continued to say, "No, no, no! It's over now."

Paying her no mind, he walked into the steam room and laid her on the bench that extended off the wall. It allowed more than enough room to take advantage of her. He grabbed Tavares's ankles and held them straight up in the air with a firm grip. Using his free hand, he slid one finger and then two fingers into her pussy. His fingers found the on button, and Tavares stiffened and squirted.

"I like that."

Tavares was lost in her orgasm. She couldn't speak words; only moans and screams were coming out. Replacing his fingers with his manhood, he unhurriedly caressed Tavares's insides.

"Cum for me," he whispered.

To his surprise, she did. He repeated himself, and like clockwork, she did it again.

"Damnnnnn," he said, feeling the powerful orgasm erupt.

Tavares was shaking and screaming, "Stop, stop, stop. I can't take another orgasm."

Intensifying his speed, he fucked her until she was screaming bloody murder. Ready to grant her wish, he let off one last time in the warmest pussy he'd ever encountered. Then, he dropped her legs and backed up.

The dick slayer asked, "Why you did you keep cummin' on me like that?"

"Why did you keep fucking me like that?"

"Because you liked it."

"Oh, well, there's your answer, sir."

"You're a naughty girl."

"You're right, I am. My fiancé told me every lady should be an inner porn star."

"He's a smart man. That's why he's keeping you forever."

Kissing her lips and grabbing her butt, the pussy monster whispered, "Meet me at home, and let's go for round two and three."

"Abdora, that's all your nasty ass is getting. You disturbed my gym time. You took my pussy in the shower and this steam room. I'm done. I'm going home for no more rounds. I'm gonna have a threesome with the blankets and the pillows."

"Knock it off."

Soaking wet, they made their way back to the shower.

"You loved every minute of it," Abdora said matter-of-factly as he lathered Tavares's back and washed her up. "You're such a naughty girl, and that's why I love you."

"I bet."

After showering together, conversing about the agent bitch and the long day they had, they dressed together but headed out as strangers. As they were leaving the gym, Tavares was a few feet ahead of Dora. They passed two women coming in.

"Damn, that dude is fine as fuck," the blunter, prettier of the two women stated.

Without stopping or making eye contact Tavares stated, "He's taken. Don't waste your breath."

As they reached Abdora, the less pretty woman flirtatiously asked, "You leaving so soon?"

"Yeah, ladies, I had a hell of a workout. It's time for me to go, but y'all enjoy."

"Did you know that woman that just left? She said you were taken, and I would like to get your number," the blunter woman said with no reservation.

"Nah, I didn't know her. She was trying to seduce me. But, I am taken. Sorry."

Dora kept it pushing without another word. Tavares waited in her car to see how long it was gonna take for Dora to walk out of the gym. Seeing that he walked out a minute right behind her, he was spared a verbal lashing. She started her car and headed home. As she drove, she tried to process the deal with Carmen Vega. Something besides the fact that she was a dirty federal agent didn't add up with her. Tavares didn't know what her deal was or what her real problem with her and Abdora was, but she was gonna get to the bottom of it.

She thought she was gonna beat Dora home and be in bed long before he could get the third round of the day that he was looking for. To her surprise, Mr. Hell of Handsome himself was in the garage leaning against his Range Rover when the garage door went up. The moment Tavares parked, he was on her like white on rice.

"Oh, my God. How did you get home before me? I was speeding," Tavares yelled as she hopped out of her truck.

"You want to be spontaneous and give it to me on the recycling bin?"

Tavares hated to laugh and had no energy to even do it, but Dora's silliness pulled it out of her.

"I hate you, and no."

"Don't act classy now, girl. You know you're a freak. You just took advantage of me at the gym."

"The devil is a lie... The devil is a lie."

Paying the borderline sex addict no attention, Tavares grabbed her gym bag and made her way into the house.

"Oh, you want to do it in the house? I mean, your family won't hear us, so that's cool, too."

"Oh, my God. We're doing nothing else. I'm tired, my pussy is sore, and you better get your ass in bed, wrap your arms around me, and hold me until I pass out."

Dora didn't like the sound of not having one last round of mind-blowing sex, but he obliged his woman anyway. After three hours of resting her eyes, Tavares was up bright-eyed. She didn't know how to sleep when the sun was up. On the other hand, Dora was dead to the world. He hadn't rolled over one time to answer his phone that seemed to have rung fifty times in the last twenty minutes.

"What the fuck?" Tavares cursed at the nonstop ringing. "Abdorrrra," she yelled.

Tossing and turning, still tired with closed eyes, he mumbled, "Hmmmm?"

"Get your ass up and answer that phone."

"Hell no."

"Look, whoever it is must really want something. Since I been lying here, awake it has rung at least fifty times."

With one eye open, Dora peeked at the platinum clock that read 8:13 a.m.

"Someone has lost their fucking mind calling me that many times and it ain't even 9 a.m. yet."

"I don't know, but it's getting on my nerves so get up and get it."

Following the boss's orders, Dora retrieved his phone off his nightstand. He sucked his teeth when he saw that he had thirty-three missed calls from Penny's Daughter. It was too early for smoke, and the moment he told Tavares who it was, that was all it was gonna be. Placing the phone back down, he rolled up and snuggled up with the nude body that was making his dick rock hard.

"Aren't you going to call them back?"

"Nope. I'll deal with it when I get up."

"Well, who is that calling like a fucking crazy person early in the morning?"

"Do you really want to know?"

"I asked you, right?"

"It's Priscilla."

Tavares's body stiffened, and she rolled her eyes.

"Like for real, Abdora. We've had smoke about this bitch all weekend. Today is a new day, and I'm not doing this. I'm just not doing it."

Abdora let out a long sigh, released Tavares, and rolled back over. Then, he grabbed his phone. To show his lady he had nothing to hide, he called Priscilla back.

Seeing Abdora calling, Priscilla answered before it had fully rung one time. She spoke through tears and sobbing.

"Dora, I called you all night and all morning. Why didn't you answer?"

Hearing the tears didn't stop him from checking Prissy.

"Priscilla, I have a woman. I was with my woman all night, and I'm lying here with her right now. Why are you calling me all crazy? What's up?"

Hearing the words coming through the phone made Priscilla sizzle. She knew Dora wasn't being shady. He was just being honest, but she didn't like hearing that he ignored HER because of his lady.

"I was calling to tell you that my mom passed last night."

Dora's heart skipped a beat at the sad news.

"Damn, Prissy, my deepest condolences. There's no words I can say, except I'm really sorry."

CHAPTER 19

As she lay in bed listening to Dora's sympathetic conversation, Tavares had an angel on one shoulder and the devil on the other. As much as she disliked Dora's ex-girlfriend, one part of her felt bad that she'd lost her mom. On the contrary, her devilish side was saying, *"Good, your mother finally kicked the bucket. Now you can kick rocks and go away."* Dora saw Tavares's face and could only imagine the thoughts that were running through her head considering she despised the woman to whom he was showing sympathy. She left him in bed to play Captain Sympathy while she went to get her life.

After washing her face and brushing her teeth, she exited the over-sized bedroom without any contact with Dora. She made her way to the second-floor wing where her parents and grandmother were with her twins. Seeing the rooms were empty, she made her way to the first floor. It wasn't hard to find them since the aroma of breakfast and music indicated that there was an early morning party in her kitchen. As she entered the colossal state-of-the-art kitchen, she saw her mother and father each holding a baby while they two-stepped to oldies but goodies. Glam-Ma was burning it down on the kitchen grill.

"What in the world is this?" Tavares joked.

"Girl, we're here having a good ole time," Glam-Ma said like it was 8 p.m. instead of 8 a.m.

"And, you two with all that sinful dancing with my kids in your arms. I'mma need y'all to put my kids down," Tavares teased.

"We were just showing them the pre-game to how they got here," Dolonda shot back.

Tavares just rolled her eyes and helped herself to a piece of bacon and a few sausages. She joined in the family party, loved all over her handsome babies, and started her day off right. While they laughed and talked, her phone started ringing.

"Mommy, pass me my phone."

Seeing *Dylan James*, Tavares wiped her hands and excused herself from the kitchen.

"Good morning, Mr. James."

"Hey Miss Del Gada. I'm sorry to bother you so early in the morning."

"It's no problem. I was just having breakfast with my family. Speaking of which, my father told me that you two know one another."

"Is that so? Who's your father?"

"Holton Montiago."

"Oh, wow. Holton's your father?" Dylan asked, sounding shocked, because to his knowledge, Holton had no children. "Holton's a very stand up man."

"Yeah, he really is," Tavares co-signed. "But, what's going on?"

"I was calling to see if we could move the will reading up by a day. I had some very unexpected family business come up, and I need to fly out of town Thursday evening. If it's not a major inconvenience, would you be able to come Thursday? If that doesn't work, we can reschedule when I return."

"No, that's fine. I can come in town a day early."

"I appreciate it and apologize for the inconvenience."

"No worries. I look forward to seeing you."

Tavares hopped on the elevator ready for World War III if Abdora was still talking to the newly motherless child. After busting the double frosted glass doors open, she was happy that she wasn't going to get to set it off on her man. She didn't want to beef with him. She smiled, seeing that he'd actually been in the shower and was getting dressed.

"I see how you looking at Andy. What, you want a quickie?"

"Noooo, but let me kiss him."

"That's why you're my baby," Abdora said, putting his hands behind his head and swinging his lengthy penis from side to side.

Tavares kissing Abdora's penis that she'd nicknamed Andy almost turned into morning sex, but she fought him and his owner off. Instead, she sat on the end of the stairs of her bed and watched the fine specimen clothe himself.

"Boo, we have to go to Boston tomorrow."

"What? For what?"

"I totally forgot with all the weekend events and the constant smoke over the orphan, but a lawyer called me Friday. I have to go to Damien's will reading."

"Tavares, I'm not going to Boston for no lawyer to tell you what that wack ass nigga left you."

"You mean your brother," she said cynically.

"No, I meant what I said—that wack ass nigga."

"Ughhh, you're so disrespectful."

"Why do you have to be present?"

"I said the same thing at first, but he told me the will can't be read without me because I'm the executor."

"Trust me, that nigga didn't leave you much that it's worth the trip," laughed Abdora.

He was the only one laughing, though.

"Abdora, I need to go to Boston, and I need you to come with me."

"Listen, pretty lady. Even if I wanted to come to Boston with you, I can't."

"Excuse me? Why can't you?"

"Miss Penny's funeral is Thursday."

To avoid the gasket that she was about to blow, Tavares counted backwards from five in her head. Then, she gave Abdora a blank stare.

"Why you looking at me all crazy?"

"Because you're talking crazy. Real crazy. Did you just tell me you can't come with me because you need to go to Priscilla's mother's funeral? Send your mother. Send Bryce. Hell, send the whole murder mafia with some flowers. Do something, but being at the woman's funeral isn't more important than being with me when I'm telling you I need you."

"I have known and had a close relationship with Miss Penny since I was a kid. How can you ask me not to attend just so we can go to a will reading? A will reading for a wack ass nigga who shitted on you and left you some shit that you don't need and shouldn't even want."

"It's not about me needing or wanting it. I just have to be there for it to take place."

"And, I'm not telling you not to go. I'm telling you that I can't go with you."

"So, you being there to support Priscilla is more important than you being there to support me?"

"Now you're talking crazy. I didn't say that. Didn't say that at all. This isn't about Priscilla. So please don't make it. It's about me going to pay my last respects to a woman who I have a lot of love for. I'd do anything for you. I give you anything you want, and I go above and beyond to be the man you need me to be. I try to give you the world, so please don't give me your ass to kiss and make me feel bad."

Tavares didn't know if she was hurt or just being petty. What she did know was that she wasn't going to beg Dora to come with her.

"You know what, you're right. Going to Miss Penny's funeral is important to you, so you go. I'll go to Boston and do what I need to do."

Tavares got up off the stairs to go back downstairs. When she reached the door, she said, "Kiss your kids before you leave because we won't be here when we you get back."

"What's that supposed to mean?"

"It means exactly what I said. You have your priorities fucked up. Real fucked up. What I'm not going to do is sit here until tomorrow with you and act like I don't feel some kind of way. What's important to me should be important to you because that's how I move with you. But, what you just said to me was that Priscilla and her mother are more important. I'm not going to yell, scream, fuss, or fight with you. But, no, I won't be here when you get back."

Watching the door close and seeing the hurt in Tavares's face made Dora feel bad. It wasn't his intention to hurt his love's feelings, but this was one time that he wasn't going to bend. He wasn't putting Priscilla first. He was putting the kind of stand-up man he was first. Because of the love he had for Miss Penny, it would have been wrong of him to just blow her funeral off. He knew Tavares was mad, but her spoiled ass would have to get over it this time around.

Tavares returned to the kitchen and the look on her face told her parents and grandmother something was wrong.

"What's the matter, Baby Girl?" her father questioned.

Because she didn't want anyone in their personal business, she lied and said, "Nothing. I have to go to Boston for the will reading a day early. I'm going to book flights, but I need someone to fly with me to help me with the boys. So, who's it gonna be?" Tavares asked, looking around the room.

Vadaleen had a bright idea.

"Dolonda, I'm really enjoying my time getting to know you. How about you and I hang with Dhara and Darlene for an extra day? It can be just the four of us with the boys, and then we can fly up and meet Tavares after the will reading."

"Wow, Mrs. Montiago. I think that would be so nice. I'm in."

"Uhhhh, hello? Does anyone care that I want my babies with me?" Tavares asked, only half serious.

In unison, both women answered, "No."

"Papi, Dora can't come with me to the will reading because he has more important engagements, so I'm going to need you to come with me."

"You got it, Mija."

"Mommy, what are you going to do long-term? Have you decided to stay here or are you going back to Boston for good with Papi?"

"I've decided to stay here, but I don't start work for another week. When your grandmother and I fly up, I'm just gonna hang with my boo until I start work."

"Good decision," Tavares chastised her mother like she was the parent and not the child.

Dora entered the kitchen and everyone, including him, could feel the vibe change.

"Good morning."

Everyone returned the morning greeting.

"Your plate is in the oven," Tavares's grandmother informed him.

"Thanks, Glam-Ma. Boo, I have to run out to handle some business. I'll be back in a little while. Don't make any power moves, please."

That was Dora's way of telling her not to leave until he got back.

She simply responded, "Okay." However, she knew that she was true to her words and wouldn't be there when he returned.

Abdora had learned early in life that he was different. God blessed him with the brain of a genius and gave him the coyness of the boy next door. He also gave him the heart of a lion. So, when he decided to be a boss and run the streets, he knew he could do it effortlessly. The first thing he mastered was that cash had no emotion. Therefore, every move he made was off logic and rationale. However, Tavares had tapped his emotional side with how they'd left off. Consequently, he was cruising the highway in deep thought about his future wife.

The last thing he wanted to do was hurt her. She was the Ying to his Yang, lime to his tequila, and sunshine on the cloudiest days. Her being hurt didn't sit well with him. There wasn't a doubt in his mind that he'd made the right decision to attend Miss Penny's funeral, but being uneasy about his decision had him feeling some kind of way. Dora hoped that when it was said and done, she could understand his logic. He wasn't putting Prissy before her. He was simply paying his last respects to someone he had a lot of love for.

While Dora was doing what he thought was right, Tavares was doing the same. She wasted no time disobeying his wishes to wait until he returned to leave.

"Glam-Ma, will you and my mom clean the kitchen while I get myself and the boys ready to go?"

"No problem, me baby."

Dolonda gave her daughter a skeptical look.

"Aren't you going to wait until Abdora returns before you leave?"

Tavares gave her mother a look of death and answered her, "Nope."

Everyone got her drift with that one word and prepared to head out. Within the hour, she'd bathed her boys, packed all they would need for their few days with their grandmother and great-Glam-Ma, and was getting dressed herself. When she came downstairs, she found her parents in the meeting room looking totally in love as they played with their grandchildren.

"Uhhh, are you two love birds ready? Where is Glam-Ma?"

"Yes," Holton answered, not looking up from playing with Elijah. "Your grandmother is mopping the kitchen floor. I told her she didn't need to, but she's old school West Indian."

Dolonda rose from the floor with her blue-eyed grandson and said, "You just think you are too cute."

"I mean, Mami, I am what I am. Don't hate, congratulate. Truth be told, I got most of these good looks from you."

Tavares's older twin just smirked.

"And, why you twinning with my man in a sweat suit and a mink?"

"You're aggy, Ma. A sweat suit is travel clothes. Ask your man why he tryna look like me."

Dolonda couldn't help but have fun teasing her daughter, who really was beautiful. Even in a simple grey PINK line Victoria sweat suit, black UGGs, and a mid-length black mink coat, her Baby Girl was stunning.

"Everyone's bags are in my truck. Where's your luggage?"

"Luggage for what? In case you forgot, I am going home to my house where I have a full wardrobe. I don't need anything except my purse and my shades."

"Okay, I got you, smart ass."

Tavares laughed because she knew she came off as being smart, but she wasn't trying to be. In no time, she and her clan were off to have brunch and hang out with her Uncle Hayden before she and her father caught their flight to Boston. Taking full advantage of the nice weather on a February day, they strolled the twins through Harlem. They were walking, talking, and laughing. The family had lunch at the famous soul food restaurant Sylvia's and spent a little time at Hayden's before the car arrived to transport her and her father to the airport. She had a great afternoon of fun, laughter, and family time. When the car arrived, she gave her boys a million kisses while her parents did the same to each other.

"Okay, okay, okay, that's enough," Tavares said, wanting to gag at the lovers.

"Oh, now you rushing me and my baby now that you're done," her father joked.

"Yes, let's go. We'll see them in two days."

Tavares's mind had been occupied the whole day. Now that she was comfy in the back seat of the Denali, she couldn't help but slip back into her feelings that Abdora had chosen Prissy over her. Holton could see that something was weighing on his daughter.

"Baby Girl, you alright over there?"

"Yeah, I'm fine, Papi."

"No, you're not. Talk to your old man."

"I was just thinking about Dora," Tavares said, letting her eyes drop to the massive rock on her finger.

"That's a beautiful ring you got there. Is everything okay with you two?"

"I guess," she answered with no enthusiasm. "I needed him to come with me. He told me he couldn't because he needed to go to Miss Penny's funeral. I get that he knew her for years, had a relationship with her, and wanted to pay his respects, but I needed him. He got me feeling like he put Priscilla before me, and I'm just not feeling that."

"Mija, you're being selfish."

"Papiii," screeched Tavares. "Whose team are you playing for?"

"Girl, I am the team. You and Abdora are both on my team," laughed Holton. "I'm a man of reason, so just hear me out. Abdora loves you. He doesn't just say it. He goes above and beyond to show you with his actions. He treats you like a queen. Just look at the ring on your finger. I'm sure that was someone's down payment on their house. You have to cut the man some slack. You want him to not pay respects to someone who meant a lot to him to support you for something with your ex. That's not fair. He's not putting that girl before you. He's doing what he should as a stand-up man. There's nothing worse than a broke pretty girl. Since you're the woman of a wealthy man and the daughter of a wealthier man, you'll never be that. But, what's far worse than being pretty and broke is being pretty and insecure. Don't be that woman."

"Insecure? Papi, are you crazzzzzy? I am not insecure. I just see through that heffa. And, I feel like Abdora being there through her mother's death is just another reason for her to feel like she's relevant."

"Don't worry about her. You might be right, but at the end of the day, Dora is more than a real nigga. He ain't gonna betray you for what was."

Tavares hated to not be right, but she could accept when she was wrong. Her father was dead on. She didn't have a leg to stand on, and she knew it after he set her straight.

"You're right. Dora loves me, and I just wanted him to not go so I could have one up on Priscilla. That was selfish, especially knowing how he felt about Miss Penny. He's a good dude, and I don't want him to be anything less for my own selfish reason."

"That's my girl. If she gets out of line, he'll put her in her place. Trust me. I raised him."

Tavares needed that. As they pulled up to JFK, she tossed on her Jackie-O shades and was ready to take this trip.

Across the Hudson, Abdora was sitting in front of Miss Penny's house. Tavares was on his mind and heart. He called her three times and got no answer. After sitting for a second longer, he grabbed the flowers and food from the back seat and climbed out of his Range Rover. Prior to ringing the bell, he could hear the loud music and voices on the other side of the door. His family was hood, but Priscilla's family was downright ghetto. Therefore, he prepared himself before he even pushed the bell.

Upon entering, Dora was greeted with major love. He received hellos, cognac-smelling hugs, and cheap vodka-brazen kisses. After setting the food down, he made his way over to Priscilla to give her the gorgeous floral arrangement he'd bought. Before he could extend the vibrantly colored flowers with his condolences, Priscilla set into him.

Rolling her eyes with her arms folded across her chest, she said, "Nice of you to join us six hours later. Seeing that when I called, you were in bed with your ladyyyyy." She cynically stressed her last word. "I'm surprised your little girlfriend gave you permission to come over here. Or, did you have to sneak?"

That was one, two, three shots fired. Priscilla had officially fucked up, and Dora's face said it. She busted her guns at the wrong person. The music went off, and the room got so quiet that you could have heard a pen drop. People's eyes popped and their mouths dropped at the way Priscilla had just come for Dora. He was on the spot, and since he had the floor, he took it. He almost disrespected Priscilla with no chill. He wanted to ask, "Bitch, who the fuck are you talking to?" However, looking around and seeing all the people congregated there, he remembered the reason they were there. He quickly caught his tongue and decided to respectfully disrespect Priscilla.

"I can't respect that fly shit you just let tear out your mouth, so I'mma check it right here at the gate. Since you THOUGHT you could belittle me in front of everyone, I'mma check you in front of everyone. I don't know who the fuck you thought you was talking to, but I'm still the same ole nigga. That nigga who doesn't tolerate disrespect. I'm a fucking grown ass man. I don't sneak nowhere. And my lady's name is TAVARES, but you knew that. Furthermore, she's not my little girlfriend. She's the mother of my children, my fiancée, and my soon-to-be WIFE. In case you forgot, I put a ring on it over the weekend.

Oh, but you knew that too, when she posted her ten-carat ring on my World Playground page. So, if you're gonna address her, address her by name and the title that she carries—my fiancée, not my little girlfriend."

There were oohs and aahs flying around the room after Dora put Priscilla in her place with his razor-sharp tone.

"Hmmm, do you got on a pair of Nikes?" Priscilla's closet crack-head Aunt Mya questioned like she was serious. "Dora just checked the shit out of you," she cracked up laughing.

"I know that's right," Mya's little sister Mariah said, putting her glass of rum to her lips.

Everyone in the small living room laughed because Miss Bougie was rightfully put in her lane.

"I don't find a Goddamn thing funny. So, shut the fuck up before I put y'all out my mama's house."

"Well, baby, it appears this ain't your mama's house after them papers we just read. Now is it?" Mariah fired back. "Only person that can toss us out of here is Abdora Santacosa," she sneered. "Abdora, are you tossing us out of your house?"

"Yo, Priscilla, let me talk to you in private."

With all eyes on them, the two made their way upstairs to talk in seclusion. They weren't even out of earshot before the snickering and whispering over Priscilla getting checked started. She was always acting like she was better than the rest of the family, so that was the highlight of the day.

Quickly closing the door behind her, Priscilla immediately asked, "Did you have to talk to me like that in front of them? Did you? You already know they hate me because I'm not like their bum ghetto asses. Did you really need to embarrass me like that in front of them and give them something to talk about?"

Abdora snapped his neck back, indicating to Priscilla that she'd lost her mind.

"Did you hesitate to demean my fiancée and me in front of them? Nah, you didn't. You got checked right where you tried it."

"Abdora, are you really going to marry that girl?"

Dora was losing his patience with Prissy. Considering that she was still in mourning, he was trying to hold back from snapping on her.

"What?" he responded with the nastiest tone he could speak. "Is that what your problem is? Priscilla, I'm absolutely gonna marry that woman. I love her. Didn't you marry the man you love?" Dora questioned with a mocking tone.

Priscilla could only drop her head.

"What papers did y'all find for your aunt to say what she said about this being my house?"

"We found a copy of a deed that says you're the owner. Then, when I found her insurance policy, it says you're the beneficiary. I'm confused. Were you and my mother having some kind of affair after I left?"

If Dora thought Prissy had lost her mind before, she'd co-signed it with the stupid ass question she'd just asked him.

"What the fuck are you talking about? Seriously, what in the entire fuck are you talking about? Why the fuck would I be having an affair with your MOTHER? Not only were you once the love of my life, your mother was like a second mother to me. Do me a favor and shut the dumb shit up. Actually, it's time you put your big girl panties on because I'm about to set you straight once and for all.

"I own your mother's house because she was going to sell the house outright to pay for you to go to school when you lost your scholarship that you lied about the reason for losing. When she did her research, she learned that your bitch ass father had been deep in debt with the loan sharks. Before he disappeared, he signed the deed over to them. She couldn't fucking sell the house in order to pay for your education at that expensive ass school. She called me upset and in distress. Seeing that you were going to be my future wife, no doubt I did what I had to do to help her help you."

Dora had to shake his head at the irony.

"I bought the house back from the loan sharks. But then, I figured if she sold the house, where the fuck was she gonna go."

Dora had no chill or fucks giving with the irritable voice he was using.

"So what did I do? I kept the house and let her live here. Then, I gave her the money each semester to cover what the loans didn't. She made me promise to never tell anyone. And, until this moment, I haven't."

Priscilla's intoxication was subsiding as she was listening to the information she'd never known. Her face confirmed it the more she listened. Now, she felt guilty that she never asked her mother how she was paying for her school and that she went as far to sell her house to help her go to school.

"It's money. Just money. I had mad love for you and mad love for your moms, God rest her soul. So, it was nothing to help. She would always tell me she couldn't pay me back in this lifetime, but she promised to pay me back in the next life. I never got it. Never fucking got it, until about a year and a half ago. She called me and said she needed to speak with me about something important. I came through here, and she told me that I was the beneficiary on her insurance if anything ever happened to her.

"I told her no a million times. But, she said it was already done. She informed me that she always pays her debts and when she went to her next life, I was indeed going to get every dime she owed me. Then, she showed me every amount I'd given her since you went to school. She even wrote down rent that I never charged her. I'm assuming this was about the time she found out about the cancer, but she never mentioned that part.

"After she told me about the insurance, we sat and talked. She gave me every detail of what she wanted when she passed. I mean, from the songs played to the church and the flowers. She even had picked out a casket. I didn't really think much of it. I just took the written details and put them in my safe. So, if you want to know why the fuck it took me six hours to get here, I was fulfilling all her wishes. Every single thing she wanted is ALL SET. All you need to do is go get her a dress and drop it off at the funeral home."

Priscilla was now sobbing uncontrollably.

"I can't believe my mother trusted you with everything. I'm her only child, and she didn't even think I could bury her. Instead of trusting me, she trusted you. She even left you my money."

Dora had to take a step back to make sure he'd heard Priscilla correctly. Disgust oozed from his voice.

"Are you crying because your mother is gone or because you aren't going to get her money?"

"It's not about the money!" Priscilla screamed, only half telling the truth.

She was banking on the five hundred thousand she knew her mother had in a policy. Dora felt like he was staring at a devil in jeans and a blouse.

"You didn't deserve your mother. You really are a selfish bitch who only gives a fuck about you. Just like I loved you and went above and beyond for you, you shitted on me. Your mother did the same. She's not even cold yet and you're shitting on her. I see why she trusted me. She knew in her absence the money wasn't going to matter to me and that I was going to lay her to rest exactly how she wanted, in style. Her services are going to be Thursday. My secretary will drop the obituaries off when they're ready. Don't forget the dress, or I'll have my secretary get one. Two limos will be here at 8:30 a.m. My condolences, Prissy. I'm out of here."

"Oh, my God Abdora. Please don't treat me like a monster. I'm not. I'm just in shock about all this. I had no idea. Just because I thought she was leaving the house and money to me doesn't make me a monster. So, please don't look at me so repulsed."

Dora didn't know what other way to look at her.

"Are you going to ride in the limo with us?"

"No, I won't be there. I'm going to have a private service with her tomorrow. I have to fly to Boston because my *little girlfriend* needs me."

Priscilla began to sob even more uncontrollably. With no sympathy for the woman who'd just shown her true colors, Dora exited the room without uttering a goodbye or a single word. He hadn't even hit the alarm to his car when his cell phone began ringing yet again. With the sour taste that Priscilla had just left in his mouth, he wasn't in the mood to talk to anyone. Whoever was calling would be sure to get the backlash if he picked up the phone. Seeing Donnie O on the caller ID, Dora had no choice but to pick up.

"What's up. Donnie?"

"Abdora mi friend. Did I catch you at a bad time?"

"Nah, what's going on?"

"I want to apologize again for the other day. Things are all set for next week. You'll have no more problems out of her going forward. But, I would like to speak to you face to face just to set things straight man to man and solidify all our future business."

"Cool, we can do that. But, I have to be on the up and up. I was subcontracting for my father-in-law. He's a stand-up man. He raised me to this game, so I vouch for him with my life. I would like you to meet him because he's the investor, not me. It's only right we clarify that because at the end of the day, I contract with him. Y'all should deal directly."

"Well, Abdora, you seem to speak highly of him. So yes, we can do that. Can you meet Thursday?"

"Fuck," Dora cursed.

"What's wrong, mi friend?"

"I have to fly to Boston to meet my girl."

"Oh, no problem, no problem at all. We can meet there. I can kill two birds with one stone by seeing you and handling some personal business."

"Bet," Dora said, happy that things were falling into place. "Just call me and give me a time and place. I will for sure be in Boston Thursday."

"Okay mi friend, no problem."

Dora ended his call and headed home to tell the love of his life he was coming with her to Boston.

***

After what felt like forever checking in and standing in line to go through the checkpoints, Tavares was back in her UGGs, mink coat, and Jackie O shades with her father twinning on her side. As they walked through the terminal with a boss air to them, people were looking at them thinking they were a couple. Holton looked like a dapper, slightly young sugar daddy with a young bad bitch. Oblivious to the looks, they were shooting the shit and minding their business. That was until Holton recognized an ass in front of him. He'd bent the ass over in so many ways, shapes, forms, and places over the years that he recognized it a mile away even if it was wearing simple clothes with a long sweater and leggings. Holton needed to have a conversation with the woman, so he needed Tavares gone for a second.

"Mija, do me a favor. Run in that Starbucks and get us something to drink."

"Papi, why you want that expensive ass coffee?"

"Because I don't like cheap shit and you get what you pay for. So, take this $20 and go," Holton said, reaching in his pocket and coming out with a money clip full of money and peeling off a crisp bill.

"Papi, you're aggy."

"Yeah, yeah, yeah... Just go."

Looking down at her phone, Carmen's heart skipped a beat seeing Montiago come across the screen. She'd waited for the call for so many days, weeks, and months that she didn't know how to feel now that he was actually calling. She was on a mission to take him down and here he was calling. Was she making a mistake taking this trip? She pondered too long because her phone stopped ringing. It instantly rang again.

"Hello?"

"Hey there, lady," the phone echoed. "I need to talk to you for a quick second."

"I can't talk right now."

"Yes, you can. Just stop right there."

"Excuse me?"

"Stop and turn around."

Doing as she was instructed, Carmen got the shock of her life to see that her ex-lover she missed so much was behind her.

"Are you following me now?"

Holton had to chuckle a bit at the credit this snake was giving herself.

"It's nothing but a coincidence, Carmen."

"Hmmm," she said, trying not to look as uncomfortable as she felt. "How are you?" she questioned.

"I'm doing as best as a no-good drug dealer can be doing."

Not expecting her words to slap her in the face, she knew that Tavares had told him everything.

"What do you want, Holton? I have a flight to catch and really don't have time for this shit."

"No worries. I'mma keep this short and sweet," Holton said, looking over Carmen's shoulder seeing that Tavares was still in the long line. "I hear that you met my daughter, and you said some not-so-nice things and made some not-so-nice threats."

"I didn't make any threats. I would call them promises," Carmen said, feeling herself.

"When you threaten my daughter, you might as well threaten me, because my money and my family are two things I don't play with."

"Your daughter acted like she wanted to go to war with me. I tried to warn her that wouldn't be wise. So, if I were you, I would keep her on a short leash."

"Bitch, my daughter ain't a dog, so she ain't on no leash. What you should do is be mindful who the fuck you're playing with. I've killed people for less."

"Are you threatening a federal agent?" Carmen asked, tossing her title around like it meant something to Holton.

"No, not at all. I don't make threats. I'm making a promise to a cum-guzzling, coke-pushing bitch who better leave my daughter the fuck alone. If you want to go child for child, I promise yours will end up in a trunk first."

Holton was so engulfed in the disrespectful tongue-lashing he was laying on Carmen that he never saw Tavares coming out of Starbucks. As she exited the top-notch coffee chain, she saw her father looking mad as fuck as he talked to some woman.

"Who the fuck is that?" she asked herself.

As she got closer Tavares recognized the woman from behind.

"Oh, Carmen, you met my drug-dealing father whose dick you haven't been fucking?"

Spinning around, Carmen was once again face to face with the young girl who she loathed.

"Should we clarify now that you've been sucking his dick and was his plug for the yayo?"

Carmen's face turned beet red but no words would come out.

"Mija, Mija, be nice," Holton taunted before he cracked up laughing. "Ms. Vega and I were just finishing up our conversation."

Holton wrapped his arm his daughter and escorted her away. Looking over his shoulder, he said, "Safe travels, Carmen. And, remember, I'm always ready for war."

Carmen watched the father and daughter walk away. "Laugh now and cry later. I'll laugh last," she said.

Then, she made her way to her gate and boarded her flight. She told herself that she wasn't taking no for an answer from the person she was trying to enlist as her partner in the takedown. She didn't care if she had to pay, beg, or flex her work power, but the partnership was going to happen. Laying her head back, Carmen tried to relax her brain. She had a two-hour flight until she was in Puerto Rico and heading to New Life Recovery Center.

CHAPTER 20

Tavares opened her eyes, happy that she wasn't hung-over from a long evening of drinking. When she rolled over, she realized she wasn't alone. Immediately, she screamed for dear life and hopped up. Hearing the scream that sounded like bloody murder, the stiff body that was on the other side of the bed jumped up.

"Boo, why the fuck are you screaming?"

"No, what the fuck are you doing in my bed?"

"Your bed? Girl, any bed you have is my bed, so this is *our* bed. And, I'm in our bed because you told me you needed me today, so I came."

"Abdora, you just scared the living shit out of me. I literally just pissed on myself."

"Why would you be scared? Who else would be in the bed besides me?"

"When did you get here?"

"At like four this morning. You were passed out snoring like a bear, so I didn't bother to wake you."

"Bullshit, I don't snore."

"Fuck, hell, damn if you don't," Abdora responded with a cut-the-shit face. "I was like look at my baby looking all cute but sounding like a big black grizzly bear."

"You know what, it's too damn early for your shit," laughed Tavares.

"I spoke to you all day yesterday. We texted a million times, and you never even said you were coming. Geesh, thank God I didn't bring my side nigga home with me," teased Tavares.

"You ain't crazy. Get that nigga put in a body bag if you want to. I didn't tell you I was coming because you didn't ask."

"You're such a smart ass. Ask for what when you made it clear the day before that you were going to Miss Penny's funeral."

"Well, I was, but then I felt bad that you said you needed me. Letting you down didn't sit well with me. It had me fucked up. So, I did exactly what you said. I sent an ass of flowers, my mother, and the murder mafia so that I could be here. What time do you need to be at this will reading?"

"Well, sugar lips. Now I don't need you."

"You always need me. Don't forget that."

"I don't need you to go to the will reading with me. When you said you couldn't come, I asked my papi to attend it with me. So yeah, I don't need you," chuckled Tavares.

"That's fine. I got business to handle anyway."

With a skeptical face, Tavares questioned, "Business like what?"

"See, now you in my business, lady."

"Boy, all your business is my business. What business do you have to tend to in Boston?"

"I hate to disappoint you, but my affairs are bigger than the tri-state area."

"Blah, blah, blah," joked Tavares.

"Nah, I have a meeting with Donnie O and Holton this afternoon. I'm going to introduce them so they can deal directly. I was gonna go with you and then shoot to the meeting. Now, I'm gonna relax like a motherfucker until it's time to chop it up with them."

"Oh, and you didn't ask me to attend?" Tavares asked, like she'd forgotten she wasn't a part of their business dealings.

"This is business, not pleasure. So, no, you aren't attending."

"You suck. Where's the meeting?"

"It's at the Ocean Prime. Yes, I do know how you love Ocean Prime. If you want to swing through after the meeting, we can have a late lunch, early dinner."

"Sounds like a plan," snickered Tavares.

Tavares had a few hours to kill before it was time to meet Holton. She spent it in bed cuddling, laughing, joking, and for once, not having sex with her other half.

"I know you want all this sexiness, but you have to learn to contain yourself and not always want to have sex with me."

Tavares had to crack up laughing.

"Boy, please. Sell that bullshit somewhere else. It's you always acting like the pussy monster wanting to have sex everywhere."

"At least you know I ain't looking for it elsewhere," Dora said, leaning in and playfully biting Tavares's nose.

While the lovey-dovey couple was planning their future together, the sabotage of their lives was happening sixteen hundred miles away.

"Good morning, welcome to New Life Recovery Center. How may I help you?" asked the Hispanic receptionist.

"Good morning. My name is Agent Carmen Vega. I'm here to see Lilly Montiago."

"Oh okay. Just sign in here," she said, passing the not-smiling Carmen a clipboard. "Let me copy your ID, and someone will lead you in."

Lilly was lying in her luxury suite reflecting after her therapy session and yoga class. After years of fighting demons, being a closet addict, and feeling partially dead inside, she felt alive for the first time since she started smoking crack. She hadn't felt so beautiful, full of life, and vibrant in over two decades. It felt good not to be chasing her next high while trying to keep her addiction a secret from her husband. Her therapy sessions helped her accept her past, finally face losing her son, and accept her finalized divorce. She didn't know what her next move would be when she left this paradise rehab, but what she did know was that she was done smoking crack. Her thoughts were interrupted by a light rap at the door.

"Come in."

"Lilly, you have a visitor."

"A visitor? Carlos, you must be mistaken. I haven't had a visitor since I arrived."

"Reception called up to the floor and said someone is here to see you."

Lilly got up to get dressed. She wondered if it was Holton or Tavares. Other than them, no one else would be getting on an airplane to visit her way in Puerto Rico. Lilly slid into a simple floor-length sundress and sandals and went to see if it was her ex-husband or stepdaughter there to visit her. Making her way to the courtyard where her visitor was waiting, she was surprised that it wasn't either of the people she suspected. It was a woman who reminded her of the one person she hated more than anyone in the world.

***

At 11:55 a.m. sharp, Tavares and Holton were strolling into James Dylan's office on Marina Bay in Quincy, MA.

"Damn, Papi, from the looks of this building and the location, I guess you weren't lying when you said he's all about the paper."

"Yeah, James gets the real paper. That's why I'm very curious to see what kind of dealings Damien had to be able to do business with him."

"Well, we're about to find out," Tavares said, taking her Chanel shades off and slipping them in her purse as the elevator doors opened.

Greetings were exchanged between Tavares and her father and Damien's mother, grandmother, and little brother.

"Good morning. I'm Dylan James, and I will be facilitating the will reading. Everything is laid out in writing, but Damien did a video as well. If you'll follow me to the conference room, we can get down to business. If you have any questions when everything is over, please feel free to ask."

Everyone made their way to the conference room that overlooked the water. They got comfortable as the video started. They were all anxious to see just what Damien had left them.

"What's up, y'all? If y'all are viewing all this chocolate handsomeness, then that means that I'm gone. I'm somewhere in the high heavens blowing a blunt with my main man God," Damien laughed.

Doll immediately started crying seeing her son's face. With her mother and son on each side of her rubbing her back, she tried to pull it together.

Like clockwork, as if he knew his mother would be crying, Damien stated, "Ma, wipe your eyes. I'm good. You have no reason to cry. I lived a full life in my short time on earth. Rollo, tell your mother to stop crying so we can get on with this.

"Are y'all wondering why I brought y'all here? I told myself that I wasn't in these streets for nothing. As the man of our family, if anything ever happened to me, I wanted y'all and my kids to be alright. Even though I never mentioned this will to any of you, I did my job. But, I didn't just want y'all to receive the things that I'm leaving you. I wanted you to smile one last time at all this sexiness," Damien smirked while rubbing his head.

Tavares had to chuckle. Even in his absence and in the grave, he was still stuck on himself and being his true self.

"Mommy, I paid your house off. You'll also receive a million dollars. I'm no longer here to fund your hair and nails. So, old lady, you better make it work. Either flip that money on starting your catering business, or spend it wisely. Ma, I know you think you're a hot ticket, but a million dollars can and should last you. Nana, I'm in the process of building you a dream house in Ridgeland, South Carolina. You always said your dream was to go back south and live right next to your sisters, Dalila and Dottie. I bought the land, and your house is being built. I hope that by the time you see this video, you'll be living in your dream house. You've dedicated your life to your family. Seeing them break ground on your new house was a feeling I can't even explain. You also have a million dollars waiting for you. Put your feet up, Nana, and live carefree.

"Little brother, Rollo. You're now the man of our family. Make sure you take good care of Mommy, Nana, and my kids. Hopefully, now mommy will break your pockets how she did mine," laughed Damien. "Don't worry. I'm leaving you a money flow to be able to do so. I'm also leaving you all my cars— the Benz, the Range Rover, and my Infiniti. I'm even leaving you my three businesses. There's five hundred thousand for each business for you to revamp them or build them any way you see fit. Little Damien will be co-owner of all of them. Hopefully, when he's of age, he'll get in line with you.

"Little Damien and my Baby Girl each have trust funds set up for them. They each have ten million. The money is to get them through college and start some form of business. If they choose not to attend college, they can't get the money until they're twenty-five. Tavares is the executor of their trusts as well as an additional account to take care of them until they're of age. She's the only one who can touch this money."

All eyes were now on her.

"I left Tavares in charge of their money because she's not going to take Shaunda's shit. She won't let her get the money or let the kids just blow through it. No offense, Mommy, but you're a softie. Tavares, are you sitting wondering what I left you?" laughed Damien. "Or, are you sitting talking shit because that's what you're best at?"

His laughter increased.

"Don't worry, chump. I saved the best for last. I left you the brownstone. Oh, and a key."

"A key," Tavares accidentally said out loud.

"Dylan James will give you the key and instructions. In addition, he'll give you a full copy of my will and trust with full details of everything in case there are any issues, which I don't foresee because I was very clear and concise."

Damien wrapped his fun video up by telling his loved ones that he loved them and not to be sad because he had a good life. When it was all said and done, everyone was in shock. They couldn't believe that Damien had really made sure that they were going to be okay.

"Thank you, Jesus," Nana Dancy said out loud.

When she received the details on her house, she would be packing and going down south to live modestly. She would enjoy her retirement years with her sisters that she missed so much. Doll felt even more like trash because she'd accused Tavares of having Damien's money and keeping it for herself. Rollo was done with the street game. He was going legit and building a legacy off the businesses that his brother had gifted him. Tavares was the only one who wasn't looking pleased, but she kept her thoughts and feelings to herself. She hugged everyone and told them she would be in touch about everything. After everyone left, she followed Dylan James back to his office.

"Miss Del Gada, I just need your signature on the paperwork, and we're all set. In addition to a copy of the will and trust, I had my secretary print you a simple breakdown of his instructions for everyone. Nothing is etched in stone until you sign off."

"No problem," Tavares said, giving all the documents her John Hancock. She was going to sit and thoroughly read everything before she dispersed anything.

"And this key that he left me?"

Dylan took an envelope from his desk drawer and passed it to Tavares.

"It's to a safe deposit box. The information on its location is in the envelope as well."

"A safe deposit box?" Tavares asked rhetorically.

"Yes. I don't have a clue as to what the contents of the safe deposit box are, but that's what the key is for."

"Okay," she said, rubbing her head.

She wasn't sure if she was frustrated that he left her in charge of everything or that he left her in charge and left everyone else the good stuff. Damien knew after the episode of catching him having sex at their brownstone that she wasn't going to want it.

"He thinks he's so slick," Tavares said to herself.

She was going to see about this safe deposit box before she cussed him out and hoped that he could hear her. As they rode down on the elevator, Holton could sense Tavares wasn't happy. She was back in her shades with her face tight and quiet.

"You okay?"

"Hell to the no. I can't believe this asshole dies, leaves me in charge of all this money that I still can't figure out where it came from, and had the nerve to leave me a Goddamn house he knew I would never step foot in. I wish I could bring him back to life and kill him again."

"Why don't you want the brownstone?"

"I caught Damien fucking someone in that house. I haven't been back there since that night when I beat the breaks off the bitch, packed my shit, and left."

"Do you want me to go with you to the safe deposit box?"

"No, I know you have the meeting with Dora and Donnie O. I can go alone. It's no big deal. It's not like he's left me anything spectacular in a safe deposit box."

"Are you sure, Baby Girl? I have a little bit more time until the meeting. Instead of going home to change, I can come with you."

"Nope, I'm good, Papi. After I go check the box out, I'm gonna go home and chill before I meet you guys at Ocean Prime."

"Have you talked to Lilly?"

"Uhhhh, not since I went back to Jersey. She calls me like once every few weeks. She's doing good, though. Why, you missing her?" teased Tavares.

"Don't play with me, girl. Your mammy is the only woman I'm worried about. Our divorce is finalized, and I just hope it's not going to make her relapse."

"Sorry to burst your bubble, Papi, but Lilly ain't worried about you or that divorce. It sounds like she's in good space and getting herself together. I've never heard her sound better."

"Good for her. I just want her to be happy and to enjoy this new chapter of her life."

"I know you and I never discussed it after that day, but thank you for sending Lilly to that rehab. I have a special place in my heart for Lilly. So even though Mami was dead set against it, thank you for me, not Lilly, for doing the right thing. If I was a betting woman, as you know I am, I would bet Lilly is going to walk the straight and narrow."

"Hell, she better with all the shit I gave her in the divorce," joked Holton. "And, you're welcome— not just for you, but Lilly also. She was my wife, and I love her. I just fell out of love with her a very long time ago. Even though it's your mother that I plan to spend my life with, I still want Lilly to not only be good, but happy. Now, give me a hug, and I'll see you in a little while."

***

Lilly was sitting across from Agent Vega with a blank stare. As she listened attentively, she was trying to figure out if this woman thought she was silly, stupid, or born last night. Due to Lilly's strong poker face, Carmen wasn't able to determine if Lilly was going for what she was selling.

"Again, Mrs. Montiago, you aren't a target of the federal investigation. However, your cooperation with any information would be greatly appreciated. It would also grant you immunity from any legal action that could come during the course of the investigation. Do you have any questions?"

Lilly let silence flow between them for a moment before she replied, "Bitch, are you fucking crazy?"

Carmen's eyes jumped. She was flabbergasted because that wasn't the response she'd seen coming.

"Seriously, bitch, are you fucking crazy? Do you think I don't know who you are, Carmen Vega? You came in here talking your proper talk. Talking about some fucking federal investigation about Holton, and you thought that you could get me to be the key witness in your case?"

Lilly had to laugh at the irony.

"You got me twisted with some young bitch who's new to this and not true to this. You were my husband's connect and mistress. Now, you want my help with throwing him in jail? You have a lot of fucking nerve coming in here trying to play me. As a wife, it's your job to know who your husband's sneaking around with. So, after damn near a decade, you think that I'm going to be the rat to glue your case together? I think fucking not."

"Mrs. Montiago, you must have me mistaken. I've never had an affair with your husband," Carmen lied through her teeth. "I'm here on official government business. I'm trying to help you before you find yourself in prison with Holton. What you will not do is sit here and call me names and make such ridiculous accusations."

"Lady, you're delusional," responded Lilly. "I don't have you mistaken. Holton was fucking you and playing your man for so long that he might as well have left me a long time ago for you. I've read messages, seen your pretty little pussy pics, seen pictures of you guys on trips, and everything in between. I have the right mistress. I don't know what game you're playing, but I'll be telling you nothing about Holton. Not that you need me to, because as far as I know, you were supplying him with his drugs, per the special cell phone he had just for you. So, how about you be the star witness in your OWN case, you snake ass bitch."

Carmen was in disbelief that Holton's wife knew everything—every single detail of their affair. She didn't know whether to keep playing poker or to fold. She decided on the latter of the two.

"Okay, listen, Lilly. I'm going to level with you. I *am* here on official business. Yes, I was fucking Holton, but not anymore. He fucked me over, and now I'm going to fuck him over. But, I need your help. Really, I can't see why you wouldn't help me, seeing that he left you, too. He even left you for that bitch Dolonda Del Gada. We both hate her with every fiber in our bodies, so why wouldn't you help me fuck them over?"

Lilly listened. She treaded lightly with her response because it was clear Holton's mistress was a woman scorned and was going to stoop to the lowest form of scum to do what she had to do to get him back for leaving her.

"Carmen, I want to help you. I really do. Yes, I do dislike Dolonda, but I love her daughter and Holton more. My hatred for Dolonda could never allow me to betray the people I love most. Therefore, I can't be a part of whatever revenge you're plotting against Holton."

"Lilly, you can and you will help me," Carmen said, now resorting to getting nasty. "If you don't help me, when all the chips fall into place, you'll wish that you had. So, you have two choices and only two choices. Either you help me and you come out on top, or you help Holton and find yourself a part of this investigation and more than likely going to jail with him. Do I make myself clear?"

Lilly looked left and then right before looking Carmen straight in the eye.

"Bitch, fuck you. Your scare tactics don't fucking scare me. I been with Holton since I was a teenage girl, and together or not, the last thing I AM going to do is help his scorned mistress throw him in jail. So, do whatever investigation you want. I'll take my chances in court. If I end up in jail, which I highly doubt seeing that this government employee traffics cocaine from the Dominican Republic, then I'll do my time. I'm not a fucking rat, and you best believe you'll be right in there with me."

Lilly got up from the table and left Carmen sitting to marinate in her rejection. Carmen left the rehabilitation center fuming mad. She hadn't given a second thought to what she'd do if Lilly told her to go fuck herself. She needed Lilly and not even a scare tactic worked. She cussed all the way back to the hotel.

"Fuck, fuck, fuck! What the fuck am I gonna do? I don't give a fuck. I'm going to take Holton Montiago down."

She didn't have an airtight plan, but she knew that her next move was going to be successful in taking Holton, Abdora, and Tavares down.

***

Tavares drove to the bank and told herself that if nothing was in this safe deposit box, she was going to fuck Damien up when she made it to heaven.

She'd just found safe deposit box 12082 when her phone started vibrating. She decided to ignore the call until she was done with the business at hand. Whoever was calling was determined that they were going to talk to her, though, because she felt her phone vibrate another four times.

Lilly gave up after the fifth try. She knew Tavares would see the amount of times she'd called and know it was important to call her back.

Tavares inserted the key and retrieved the box. She took a seat in the private room right behind her. The long black metal box only contained a letter. Tavares looked from the box to the letter. After doing it three times, she shook her head and looked to the sky.

"Damien, I'm going to kick your ass. You got me in charge of shit, but left me a fucking letter. Nigga, fuck you."

Since she was already there, she decided to read the letter to see just what this asshole had to say.

Dear Tavares,

If you're reading this letter, either something has happened to me, or you've outlived me. I know you well enough to know that you're dumb tight right now, chump. LOL. You're probably cussing me out for leaving you once again to make sure my shit is in order. But, if you don't do it, who will? You've been the glue that has kept my life together for so long that I couldn't think of anyone else I would trust to do it in my absence.

Are you fuming that you got to the will reading and all I left you was the brownstone and that key? Don't worry. By the time you get to the end of this letter, it will all make sense. So, just shut up.

First and foremost, I want to tell you that I love you. I love you more than you can ever imagine. You aren't just beautiful on the outside. Your heart is as pure as gold. I realized that too late. When I lost you, I really did lose the best thing that had ever happened to me. I had the best woman walking. You were brains, beauty, book smart, and gangster at the same time, and I fucked up. I have no one else to blame but myself for losing you. All you wanted to do was love me, and I took your love for granted.

I did you so wrong. No matter how many times I say I'm sorry, it will never erase the fact that I took your love and kindness for a weakness. The late nights, cheating, not coming home, the drama, sleeping with your slimeball friend... You deserved none of it. I owed you more because you gave me all of you. I never expected you to leave me. But, as I've sat and reflected a million times, I now understand why you left me. You loved me more than you loved yourself. If you stayed, I was gonna break you, your spirit, and your belief in love.

I've grown in the time that we've been apart. What I now know is that one solid, loyal woman will always top having a hundred bitches that I can't trust with my life. I think about you often. I wonder if you'll find your way back to me. However, in reality, I know the answer. You aren't coming back. Although you know I hate your bitch ass boyfriend, I appreciate that he treats you how you deserve. But, enough of this mushy shit.

I left you the brownstone because it was our home. It wasn't just a two-million-dollar property or a house. It was the place that you made a home. You treated me like a king there. You also allowed me to know that when those doors closed, I was at peace from the rest of the world. Nothing mattered because you were always there to take care of me and our home. I know I did the unforgivable by having sex there, but don't let that stop you from keeping it. It's yours. I pray that you'll keep it for you and the kids. If not, sell it, and I assure you that you'll get double what I paid for it. Oh, and it's paid off.

The real reason I left you this letter is because I didn't want anyone but you to know what I REALLY left you. If I'd said it in the will reading, my mother and grandmother would have silently felt some type of way. So, I figured the best thing to do was write you a letter telling you how much I love you and what I really left you at the same time. I don't suggest you share it with anyone. However, it's up to you what you do. Just remember that the love of money is the root of all evil. I want this money to bring you joy, not problems.

When you had you the baby shower and graduation party in Miami last year, I won the lottery. I hit BIG. I won the triple billion Powerball and was the only winner. I didn't tell anyone because the more money, the more problems. When I realized I was the winner, I contacted and retained James Dylan. I took the money and did what I thought was right. I walked away with $2.5 billion. I opened up the car wash, the Laundromat, and the liquor store. I not only own the buildings each business is in, but the land as well. I used a portion of the winnings to pay off the brownstone, all my cars, and set up everything for everyone in the will reading.

No amount of money can correct the wrongs that I've done, but it better damn sure come close. Hahahaha. I've left you everything that was left, which is over two billion. Why? Because you deserve it more than anyone in my life. You were the backbone to me surviving in the streets. You were cooking, cutting, and bagging up coke like a real G. While I was a good father and a stand-up man, chasing the money in the streets was what I was good at. But, you held everything else together. I love my mother, grandmother, brother, and kids, but I feel like this money should be yours. Why else would I have hit off numbers that related to you on your big weekend?

Tavares, take this money and live your dreams. You've always wanted to help underprivileged kids. Well, open a hundred group homes. You love to write.

Start a magazine or a publishing company. You still want to be a lawyer. Then, pay for law school and open your own firm. Whatever you do, just live your life and dreams to the fullest no matter what, because you deserve it. Below you'll find all the account numbers that I've put the money in.

Tavares, I love you, Baby Girl. This isn't goodbye, but more like see you later. I'll be waiting for you on the other side.

Love, Damien.

Tavares thought she was truly about to pass out. This was surreal and unbelievable. Her chest was tight, she could barely breathe, and her mind was racing a million miles an hour. The only thing she could do was cry like a newborn baby. She read the letter over and over. Each time she read it, she sobbed a little harder. Tavares felt like time had stopped in her spell of staining the letter with her tears. This felt so unreal to her. She just had to keep telling herself, "Damien left you over two billion dollars."

In a matter of minutes, he'd changed her life. She was absolutely about to level up, do some good, and live her dreams. It took her no time to let the wheels spin on the businesses that she was going to start. She already lived a good life, so she was going to invest wisely to ensure that neither her kids nor her grandkids ever had to work unless they wanted to. Tavares wasn't only going to do some good, she was going to do some bad. She had some people who were long overdue for her to make their world crumble. Now, it was going to happen. Becoming a rich bitch came right on time.

She wrote the account numbers down, pushed the letter back in the box that held her secret of being a billionaire, and got ready to make some moves. That fast life had changed, and she had a few stops to make. Leaving the bank, she couldn't decide who to trust with this information. Not that she didn't trust the people around her, but this kind of information could bring greed and ugly out of them. Tavares decided that she would keep the information to herself for now and share it only with her father and Abdora when she got with them.

She hopped in her Acura truck, still trying to come down from the information she'd just learned. She retrieved her cell phone from her bag to call an old friend who was going to help her put her plan in motion to ruin the lives of a few people who'd attempted to come for hers. But then seeing that New Life Recovery Center had called five times stopped her from calling out.

"Why do I have so many missed calls from them?" Tavares panicked. "Please, God, don't let something be wrong with Lilly or worse, she's gone AWOL."

Tavares prepared for the worst and called the number back.

"Good afternoon, New Life Recovery Center. How may I direct your call?" the switchboard operator cheerfully asked.

"Hi, my name is Tavares Del Gada, and I have several missed calls from you. I'm not sure if it was my stepmother, Lilly Montiago, or a staff member who called."

"Miss Del Gada, if there was no message left, I can assure you that it was your stepmother. It's our written policy that if a staff member calls, they have to leave a message at least once to let you know the nature of their call. So, let me put you through to Lilly. But, first, I have to ask you your password. As you know, no calls are transferred to a patient without the password you were given when you were added to her phone list."

"The password is Roxbury."

"Let me just verify that. One moment. Alrighty, you're all set. Let me transfer you."

Lilly snatched her phone off the cradle before it rang halfway through.

"Hello," she answered with urgency in her voice.

"Hey, Lilly. It's Tavares. I saw all your missed calls. Is everything okay?"

"Absolutely not. I had a visitor today."

"Really?" Tavares asked skeptically.

To her knowledge, Lilly had no one on her visiting list except her and Holton.

"Who came to visit you, because me and Papi are in Boston?"

"Carmen Vega."

"WHAT did you just say?" Tavares screamed with a racing heart, even though she'd heard Lilly loud and clear.

"From the tone in your voice, I take it you know who she is."

"Unfortunately, I do, Lill."

Tavares had a flashback to the airport.

"Oh, my God, Lilly. Me and Papi just saw her in the airport a few days ago. She must have been flying out there to see you. What the fuck did that cunt bag, cum-guzzling bitch want?"

"Tavares, listen to me carefully. That bitch is playing a dangerous game. She's upset that your father cut her off, left her alone, and wants nothing to do with her. She's trying to build a federal case against him. She really wants revenge for him ending things to be with your mother."

Tavares was blazing like a nine-alarm inside.

"WHAT?" she screamed for about twenty seconds. "Lilly, I swear to God. This lady, this lady."

Tavares was so infuriated that she was shaking.

"In the words of my boo, Pac, I ain't no killer, but don't push me."

She didn't know if the phones were recorded or tapped messing with that devil ass scorned federal agent, so she had to watch her words wisely.

"First, she tried to come for Dora last year and thought I was some sucker bitch and going to fold. Ooops, she blew that. Then, last week she stopped me and said she was going to come for Papi and Abdora. After I checked her, she told me I didn't want war with her. I'm sick of this bitch. She wanted war, so we're going to war."

"Are you serious? She tried to play me into being her key witness like it was all business at first. But, where she fucked up at is, I been a boss's wife too long. Furthermore, bitch, you been fucking my husband for years. She really thought I didn't know who she was until I pulled her card. Even if I was a rat, why would I help her? A main bitch and a side bitch don't ever team up for the greater good. I don't know what her personal is with your mother, but her trump card was we both hate your mother so help her.

"Tavares, it's no secret that me and your mother have never liked each other. But, realistically, I have no problem with Dolonda. My problem with her all these years was that I was living in a crack-induced delusion that she wanted your father and was trying to ruin what we had. Now that my mind is clear and I'm living in reality, I know your father has always loved and been in love with her. So, I have nothing against her. I told that bitch no matter what I feel for Dolonda, it would never make me betray the people I love."

"She doesn't even fucking know my mother. She just knows that my father is with her. She's one sick miserable bitch. But, what I do know is she fucked with the wrong bitch. She wanted a war, so it's a diplomatic war that I'm going to give her. It took me more than a decade to get my mother back and two decades to have a father. If she thinks she's about to come and fuck up my world, she has life fucked up. She has a better chance of seeing Jesus than throwing my father or fiancé in jail. Oh yeah, me and Dora got engaged."

"Wow! Congratulations. I'm so happy for you two. I knew he loved you from the night of my party."

"Thanks, Lilly. Listen, don't worry about the bitch Carmen Vega. Leave that to me. You just stay on the path that you're on and leave this to me. Trust me when I tell you, I got this. I have to run. I love you and will call you and check in sometime next week."

Returning the sentiment, the ladies both hung up in disbelief at Carmen Vega.

CHAPTER 21

As she sat in her car in the parking garage, Tavares kept replaying all the events with Carmen Vega over in her head. She couldn't do anything but have a conversation with the man up above.

"Lord, why is this lady trying me? Why God, why? Does she truly think this is a battle she's going to win? All she's doing is fueling me to destroy her life in the most unimaginable way. Even if I wanted to turn the other cheek, she's gone too far talking about throwing my father and Abdora in federal prison. I'm sorry in advance, God. All I can do is ask for your forgiveness, because my mind is made up. Even if I don't send her on a permanent visit to see you, it's a wrap for Carmen Vega."

Tavares called her attorney.

"Law Office of Katrina Raymond. How may I direct your call?"

"Hi, I'm looking for Katrina."

"May I please tell her who's speaking?"

"Yes, tell her it's Tavares Del Gada."

"One moment, ma'am. Let me see if she's available."

After a brief hold, the receptionist returned to the line and said, "I will transfer you now."

"Well, well, well... Look who knows me," Katrina joked.

"Shut your mouth," Tavares laughed at her long-time loyal friend.

Kat and Tavares had met in group home and bonded from day one. Something about them clicked, and they'd been tight to the present day. Even if they didn't talk often, they always stayed in touch and were always there for one another. Kat was so straight and narrow that Tavares never wanted her street dealings to bring any heat to her lawyer and friend. Katrina had always told Tavares when she grew up she was going to be a lawyer because

Tavares was going to need someone to defend her for always whooping someone's ass. She was true to her word and became not only a young but a prominent African-American lawyer in Boston. Now, Tavares was going to need her to make good on the second part when she choked the life out of federal agent Carmen Vega.

"Kat, I need to get with you like ASAP. This is like life or death."

"Okay, come to my office. I had two meetings, but from the sound of your voice, I can reschedule them."

"I would prefer to meet you for lunch."

"That's cool, because I love for a balling bitch to treat me to lunch," laughed Kat.

"Balling my ass, but meet me at Big Mama's in thirty minutes."

"See you there," Kat said, already getting up from her chair to go meet one of her closest friends.

Big Mama's was the one and only soul food restaurant in the city that made you feel like you were in the deep south because the southern cuisine was so good. Katrina arrived shortly after Tavares, who was nestled away in the back corner booth. She was accompanied by two tall drinks.

"If it ain't my blue-eyed devil," she greeted her friend, who didn't see her approach.

"Hey, you Haitian sensation," Tavares said, getting up and giving Kat a big hug.

"Goodness... Drinks before five. Is it really that deep?"

"Yes, girl, and it's never too early for a Patrón margarita."

Wresting her plump butt into the seat across from Tavares, Katrina asked, "So what's up, girl?"

"Same shit a different day. Before we get down to business, why weren't you at my engagement party?" Tavares inquired, giving her true-blue friend the side eye.

"Girlll, all the way here I said this heffa is gonna give me the blues."

"Uhhh huh," joked Tavares.

"I wanted to come. I really had every intention of being there, but Big Dana's stepfather had a heart attack the day we were supposed to leave. So, that just put everything in an uproar."

"Oh, my God. I'm so sorry to hear that. Well, I guess since it was a life-and-death emergency, I'll give you a pass," Tavares said playfully, rolling her eyes.

Tavares pulled a crisp one-dollar bill from her purse and slid it across the table to Kat.

"What the hell am I going to do that?" Kat eyed the money like it was poison.

"I'm here socially because I haven't seen you, but I'm also here on legal business," Tavares informed her. "That dollar is your retainer because if ever anything comes back or things hit the fan, I need this conversation to be protected with attorney-client privilege."

Kat cracked up laughing.

"Bitch, well, you're $199 short because I charge by the hour," clowned Kat.

She took the dollar and slipped it in her bag.

"Okay. What's up?"

"I need some things from you. Don't ask me no questions, and I won't tell you no lies. When I'm done, you'll know what subjects not to ask me any questions on. If I take a fall for my shit, I'll do it with my head high. But, I'll never drag you down with me."

Tavares's pitch said this was some real heavy shit. Now Kat was nervous. She wasn't nervous to help her friend. However, she never wanted to put herself in any kind of harm's way. Telling Tavares that was going to be a waste because she knew her homegirl was headstrong and did what she wanted when her mind was made up.

"Tavares, after what you did for me, I owe you my life. You know I'll do anything for you—no matter what consequences I have to face later."

Kat was referencing the unspoken secret between them. She was in an abusive relationship with her live-in boyfriend during their last year of high school. One night, she took his gun with the intention to wave it at him to tell him not to charge at her and whoop her ass. She accidentally pulled the trigger and killed him. The only person she knew to call was Tavares. Together they combined street beast with book savage. When it was all said and done, Kat walked away as the witness and Tavares the shooter. Tavares said she walked in on Vinny with his gun out threatening Kat. She said after all the times he'd beat Kat bloody, she feared he was going to shoot them. So, she took her chances and charged him to wrestle the gun from him. In the struggle, she shot him in self-defense. Due to a massive paper trail of hospital visits with bruises and broken bones and police reports filed on Vinny, Tavares was never charged.

Damien had gotten her one of the best lawyers in criminal defense without even knowing the truth. When Tavares's lawyer was done, Tavares was a hero. She took the fall because she knew Kat's natural-born schoolgirl square nature didn't have a chance of surviving a concocted lie to the judicial system. To this day, that secret was unspoken and the reason Kat always felt like she owed Tavares.

"Kat, cut the shit. You don't owe me anything. Nothing. Me and you are me and you. I did nothing for you that you wouldn't have done for me. Any time I've ever called you for legal stuff, you stop and drop everything for me. So, please knock it off. But, what I need from you is a background check on a federal agent named Carmen Vega and a wack bitch named Priscilla Hamilton. When I say background check, I need the real deal Holyfield. Every piece of information you can find. I mean I want to know when they get their periods."

"Damn bitch, it's that serious."

"Yes, they're fucking with my life, my man, and my family. Before I take the next course of action, I need to know all that I can about them."

"Okay, no problem. That Carmen Vega sounds so familiar, but give me a few days and I'll get you the info."

"Next order of business," Tavares said, with a long, deep sigh. "I need trust fund papers. I need them in the amount of five million dollars for Damien's soon-to-be baby. I'll call you later this afternoon once I go see Jazz to get the baby's name."

Kat gasped.

"What the fuck? How in the hell do you have five million dollars? And, you're accepting what that shady bitch did to you enough to give her that kind of money? Have you fell and bumped your Goddamn head?"

Tavares was silent for a moment.

"The next thing I need is legal, airtight adoption papers. I mean unquestionable. I need it to be so solid that if ever the papers have to resurface, there isn't anything that anyone can do."

Kat was trying to piece all this together as she continued to listen.

"I don't know the technical legal jargon of adoptions, but I would like this to be closed adoption. More specifically, I don't want either party to be able to know anything about the other. If you can get around the name of the adopting parent, please do. If not, their names are Charlene and Robert Clarke. Here's where it gets tricky, Kat. A lawyer is going to have to file the papers in family court to make this legally binding. Then, we're going to need another lawyer to appear in court on behalf of the mother. Because of the risk, I'm willing to pay each lawyer a million dollars."

Kat almost fell out of her seat. Gaining her balance and regaining her composure, she waved her hand in the air.

"STOP. Where are you getting all this money from? Did you rob a bank?"

"No, but we'll get there," chuckled Tavares.

"Do you want to tell me what all this is about?" Kat questioned. Even though she had a small idea, something wasn't adding up.

"Katrina Raymond, what did I tell you? Ask me no questions, and I will tell you no lies. The less you know, the less you incriminate yourself."

Tavares needed this to work. She asked with stern eyes and a strong tone, "Do you think you can pull this off?"

Kat just rolled her eyes.

"Absofuckinglutely. I'm great at what I do. But, I'm going to be the lawyer who appears on behalf of the birth mother."

"No, you're not. I can't let you do that."

"Tavares, it's the only way we can do this. The more people pulled in, the greater the risk. I can get the adopting parents a lawyer. It's a good friend of mine, and she'll only know that I'm turning her on to a high-paying client."

Tavares was skeptical, but she agreed.

"If all goes as I've planned, the papers and adoption won't ever come back to bite anyone. I just need this adoption to be the insurance policy that the Clarkes need to keep their baby. Now, last but not least. I inherited some money."

She went to explain but didn't like the look on Kat's face. It appeared that she got it all but didn't really get it, and she was beating her brain trying to piece all this together.

"Kat, will you stop overthinking? I'm not paying you to try to figure out what I'm up to."

Kat had to laugh because her friend had hit the nail on the head. She couldn't get the pieces of the puzzle to fit for the life of her.

"Tavares, I just can't figure out if that girl is putting her baby up for adoption, or why you're setting a trust up for the baby."

Silence filled the space between them.

"Kat, I'm going to tell you this part as a friend, not my lawyer. Mind your business."

Together they laughed.

"Fine, bitch. Just hurry the fuck up because my head is spinning, and I'm ready to order."

"Okay, brace yourself for the finale."

"Brace myself? It can't be no damn crazier than what you've already said."

"Damien left me two billion dollars in his will."

Kat yelled, "Oh, my Goddd!" so loudly that every last person in the restaurant turned around.

Tavares just grasped her forehead and shook her head in response to the volume her friend had yelled.

"I'm sorry, everyone," she said with a phony smile to all the onlookers. "My friend is a little dramatic. Really? Like fucking really?" Tavares said, still looking at Kat's face in utter shock. "As of right now, you're the only person who knows. I just learned this right before I called you. Here are the account numbers," she said, sliding a paper across the table. "Please check everything out."

"Where did Damien get all that money?"

"He won the lottery and told not a single soul except his lawyer."

"What are you going to do with all that money?"

"I don't know what I'm supposed to do with that kind of money."

"Bitch, just give me half since you're so discombobulated about becoming a dirty stinking filthy rich bitch."

"No, I'm going to ruin some people, help some people, and then I'm going to figure out how to invest it. And, can you close your mouth, because you're looking exactly how I did when I found out."

"Girl, I don't know what I'm going to with you."

"Just love me... Just love me," she replied, batting her big blue eyes.

"Now that you've stressed me out and snatched my soul with all this information, can we please eat?" Kat said, flagging the waitress down.

"Absolutely, and everything is on me," winked the blue-eyed devil.

"Goddamn right it is. And, I'm gonna need the rest of my hourly fee, you rich bitch."

"Be easy, Boo. I got you. All jokes aside, when everything is drawn up and delivered, I have a healthy, healthy fee. Let's put it this way. You can retire and buy you an island," Tavares blushed.

Business was done, so the ladies got down to enjoying each other's company. They spent the next hour laughing, joking, trash-talking, reminiscing, and catching up over food and drinks. After enjoying the social portion of their lunch date, Tavares paid the bill. Then, they headed out. When they got to the parking lot, Tavares gave Kat a big hug.

"I love you, Baby Girl. Please call me as soon as the information I need hits your desk."

The ladies departed to finish the rest of their business for the day. Tavares's next stop was Tufts New England Medical Center. She went directly to the floor where she spent her recovery time and where she visited Damien after her release. She approached the front desk.

"Hi, is Charlene working?"

"Yes," the amazon woman with a nose too big for her face responded. "She actually is on break. Let me call her on her cell. Who should I tell her is looking for her?"

"Tavares Del Gada."

"Okay, honey. Just one moment."

Within moments, the station coordinator returned.

"She's down in the cafeteria. Do you know how to get there?"

"Unfortunately, I do. Thanks," Tavares said and turned around to go find the nurse who'd taken such great care of her and Damien.

Charlene's face lit up seeing Tavares coming through the cafeteria doors. By the time Tavares made her way over, Charlene was standing with open arms and a huge smile.

"Oh, my gosh! It's so good to see you. You've really bounced back with your pretty self," the middle-aged, physically fit nurse complimented her.

"Let's sit," the beautiful chocolate nurse said, ushering for Tavares to take a seat in the chair across from her.

"Yes, I'm doing great, Char. I have no complaints. None at all. Is there a place we can go talk that's a little more private?"

"Sure, follow me. Is everything okay?"

"Yes, I just need a little more privacy to discuss something with you."

Charlene led them to an empty room on her floor and closed the door behind her.

"I'm going to need you to take a seat," Tavares said, not knowing how the conversation was going to go.

"Okay, sweetie."

"Charlene, I'm not great with beating around the bush, so I'm just going to be blunt about the reason that I'm here. You and I had an intimate conversation while I was under your care. You let me in about miscarrying not once but twice very late in each pregnancy. I could hear your pain. I saw your sorrow and the emptiness in your eyes. That weighed on my heart. You told me that it was the only wedge between you and your husband and it sounded like things would be great if only you could carry a baby full-term. Have you ever thought about adoption?"

"Yes, we have, but we don't have that kind of money," Charlene said with her eyes dropping as she tried to fight back the tears that were trying to run out.

"I have a baby for you."

"WHAT? What do you mean you have a baby for me? You don't just find babies."

"Here's the short version. I can't tell you the details of the closed adoption, but if you want this baby, it's yours. I want the baby to go to a loving family and give him or her the life they so deserve. I don't know your husband, but I got to know you while I was here. You're going to make a great mother. When I learned that this baby was going to be put up for adoption, you were the first person who came to my mind."

Charlene started crying like the newborn baby that she so badly yearned for. Tavares knelt down to wipe her tears.

"Don't cry. You don't have to cry."

"Having a baby is the only thing that my husband and I dream of. I don't know if I can handle getting excited and it doesn't happen."

"Char, listen to me. First, I need you to wipe your face and look me in my eyes so you can see that this is real. I have a baby for you. Tell me you want the baby, and the process will begin."

Charlene started crying again while nodding her head yes.

"Okay, there's one thing that you'll have to do to get this baby."

"I'll do anything except leave my husband to be with you," she joked as she wiped her face dry.

"This is the biggest and most important part of this. You can't tell anyone where you're getting this baby."

Charlene was confused.

"I don't understand. Are we doing something wrong?"

"We're doing nothing wrong. It's kinda like doing something out of charity, and then telling people you did it. Once you do that, the goodness behind the act is gone. This is something private and intimate that I'm doing for you as a thank you for how good you were to me and Damien, and I just don't want anyone to know. So, it's the only thing that is required for you to walk away with YOUR baby in less than four months.

"It's going to be a closed adoption. Everything will be legal and on the up and up. I'll pay all the adoption fees and for your lawyer to represent you through this. However, I stress that you can't tell *anyone* that I'm the person who helped you."

"Okay, I can do that. I won't tell a single soul."

Charlene threw her arms around Tavares and gave her the biggest hug she'd ever received. The tighter she hugged, the harder she cried.

"How will I ever repay you?"

"All you have to do is love that baby and be the best mother you can be."

"Tavares, I swear you're heaven-sent. God bless you."

"Thank you, Charlene. I appreciate that. I just wanted to help everyone involved. I have to go but I'll be in touch. In the meantime, I'm going to get the ball rolling on the adoption process. I have a wedding coming up, so I'm going back to Jersey. However, in the next few weeks, I'll be back with your lawyer's information and more information on when the baby is expected. Until the papers are signed, I don't think you should share this with anyone except your husband."

"Agreed," Charlene said, smiling from ear to ear.

Tavares gave her one last hug and was on her way. She braced herself for her final stop before going to see her two main men. As she pulled up in front of Jazz's house, she prepared herself for her acting debut. She'd never been good at fronting and faking, but she was about to win an Emmy for the role she was about to play. It was killing her with everything inside her to have to deal with her slimeball ex-best friend, but she had to do what she had to do.

As she climbed out of her truck, she let out a grim smile because Jazz was going to get everything she so deserved when things were all said and done. She rang the doorbell and patiently waited for the face that disgusted her to appear.

"Who is it?"

"It's Tavares."

Jazz snatched the door open with the speed of lightning. She was in shock to see the person who hated her standing at her front door.

"Tavares, come in."

"Hi. Sorry to pop up, but I was in town and wanted to know if we could talk."

"Sure, have a seat. This is a pleasant surprise after our conversation a few days ago."

"Yeah, I know. After you called, I did some long hard reflecting. I owe you an apology. I also want to clear the air. I'm really sorry for how I spoke to you the other day. More importantly, I'm sorry for abandoning you as a friend after things hit the fan. Things happen. Even though you made a mistake, I should have never opted to cut you off. We were better than that. I was just heartbroken, embarrassed, and unsure of how to move forward. But, I love you."

"Tavares, I'm so sorry. I know you were my best friend and that you loved Damien, but we couldn't help falling in love with each other. It was like we connected in a way that made it impossible not to fall in love. I thought that after you left him that it would be okay. You had finally found the love of your life. I didn't think that you would be upset for us finding the same kind of love. Although Damien and I fell for each other, Tavares, we never intended to hurt you."

Jazz was clearly delirious because the love she had with Damien was one-sided. He treated her no different or more special than any other chick he fucked around with after Tavares walked out on him and shattered his heart. The only way she differed was that she got a baby, and the others walked away with hard dick and bubble gum. It took everything in Tavares to not hop up and choke-slam the pregnant bitch who really thought what she was saying was okay. Instead, she just kept reminding herself that she would get the last laugh in the end.

"Jazz, we can't help who we love. Love is a blessing. If you and Damien found love together, who am I to judge or to be mad? Damien is gone, and I'm engaged to the love of my life. So as far as I'm concerned, it is what it is. There's no need to keep a wedge between us over a man. You were my best friend, and not even Damien should have come between us. I was wrong, and I want to right how I treated you."

Tavares almost choked on her words, but she was proud of the straight face and performance she was putting on.

"I just love you. I'm so glad that we can get past this. Having you back in my life will be a heavy weight lifted off me. I've prayed so many days and nights that we could rekindle our friendship. Now that you're back, I hope that you'll go through this pregnancy with me. With Damien gone, I feel so alone going through all this by myself. Since we shared the same kind of love with Damien, I hope that you can find it in your heart to share the same kind of love for his child."

Jazz's pregnancy hormones caused her to burst into tears. She was crying happy and sad tears. She shed sad tears because the reality set in that Damien was gone and she was on her own with the baby. The happy tears poured out because she had Tavares here understanding that she never meant to hurt or betray her, and now they were going to repair their friendship. While Jazz was crying, Tavares wanted to get up and console her as part of her act, but her heart wouldn't let her go that far.

"Look, you don't have to cry. It's going to be all right. Raising a baby isn't easy—especially not with the father deceased. I'm going to be here for you as a *friend*. Whatever you need. I'm even willing to fly here and go to your appointments with you. I'll get with the girls and give you a baby shower. You're not alone, which brings me to the other big reason I came by. I'm about to share something with you that no one knows. So, if you could please keep it between us, I would appreciate it."

"Of course, I will, Tavares. You know how we do."

Boy, don't I know how you do, Tavares said in her head.

"Well, even though you and Damien were in love," Tavares said, not being able to resist busting that clear shot, "for some reason, he never changed his will. He left me a great deal of money."

"What?" Jazz said, almost getting distressed but more jealous than anything. Even dead and gone he was still showing how much he loved Tavares.

"What do you mean a great deal?"

"It was a few million."

Jazz's eyes dropped to the white carpet on her floor, and she held her chest in disbelief.

"A few million?" she repeated like her ears heard wrong. "Tavares, I mean... No offense, but we were in love. How could he leave you everything and leave me to raise a baby on my own? He knew I was pregnant and could have at least left the baby something."

"I agree. That's no way to do the woman that you love—especially the mother of your child. However, you don't have to worry. I told you that I'm going to be here for you. As a friend, I couldn't imagine taking that money and leaving you with nothing to raise his child. Abdora and I are more than well off, so I don't need that money. My good conscience wouldn't let me sleep at night if I took that inheritance and then stood by and watched you be a struggling single mother. So, I went to see a lawyer today. I'm going to have her set up a trust fund for the baby for the full amount that he left me. It was five million dollars."

Jazz instantly became light-headed and dizzy.

"Five... million... dollars?" she asked slowly as she fought to keep it together. "Oh, my God. Tavares, you really do love me, and you really are a good friend."

Jazz started to whimper.

"Listen, bitch. Cut all that crying shit out. I can't take it," Tavares joked, but she was really serious. "The papers are being drawn up as we speak. All you have to do is sign a few places. Once everything is finalized, you'll get a copy of the trust, and the money will be set up in an account. The only thing I need from you is to keep this between us. There's a gag order clause in the trust. If you ever reveal where you got the money from, you'll forfeit the five million. I just want to do what's right without people knowing I had that kind of money and chose to give it to you."

"You don't have to worry. I'll never say a word."

"Alright, so once the papers are set up, I'll call you. The only thing I need from you is the baby's name. You'll be the executor of the trust until the baby is eighteen."

"Her name is going to be Aiko Damina."

"Oh, that's very pretty," Tavares spoke, while her acting skills slipped for a moment with her eyes saying *what the fuck.*

"I know a Japanese name is different, but I wanted a name that had meaning. It means 'the little loved one.' Since she was the product of my and Damien's undying love, I thought it was very fitting."

"I know that's right," Tavares said, cracking up at the foolishness burning her ears. "Well, Little Miss Loved One is going to be very well off. Listen, I have to run because I have a date with my father and soon-to-be husband, but I'll be back in a few weeks with the trust papers. When things slow down with my girl's wedding, the girls and I will get together to plan you a blowout baby shower."

"Tavares, I can't thank you enough. Not just for what you're doing for my daughter and to help me in Damien's absence... It means the world to me that you aren't upset that I was the love of Damien's life. He loved you... he loved you very much, but as you said, the heart can't help who it loves. Something between us just connected. It wasn't perfect, but I loved him and he loved me. I can never thank you enough for understanding that."

"Oh Jazz. Baby, I'm just sorry Damien is gone and you guys won't get to live your happily ever after. I'm just happy we could get past the ugly, and you're allowing me to be here for you as a *friend.*"

Jazz walked Tavares out happy as a pig in a blanket that she could maintain her fantasy love and have her friend back in her life. *So she thought.*

Tavares was in her car and not feeling bad about anything that she was about to do. In her book, you live by the sword, you die by the sword. She wasn't going to physically kill Jazz for breaking her heart as a friend, though she was going to shatter her heart just the same. Jazz had been her sister from another mister. That conversation showed her she was just as delusional about their friendship as Jazz was about this undying love between she and Damien had. Feeling victory coming, Tavares started her car and was off to silently celebrate with her two favorite men.

CHAPTER 22

Donnie O, Holton, and Abdora were drinking Remy 1738 and chopping it up like old friends. They'd sealed their new business venture with a drink and hadn't stopped drinking yet.

"Abdora, what time is Tavares joining us?" Holton questioned as he looked at his platinum Rolex thinking she should have arrived by now.

"I'm surprised the skinny fat girl isn't here by now. Your daughter is never late for a meal, especially when she isn't paying and pulling her wallet out," teased Abdora.

"Tavares... That your lady, right, Abdora?"

"Yes, with her gorgeous, larger than life personality. I'm hoping that you get to meet her if she ever shows up."

"My TT Nina was overwhelmed with her candid resemblance to my cousin DD."

"Donnie, your aunt looked like she saw a ghost," Abdora said, shaking his head. "The look on her face had us shaken up because *she* was so shaken up."

"Yeah, even when she called me, I could hear in her voice that she was rattled. She had me curious to see just how much this young lady could really resemble DD."

"Well, you know what they say. Everyone has a twin," Holton chimed in.

Catching the tail end of the conversation as she entered the private room, Tavares asked, "Who has a twin?"

"Hey, Baby Girl. You do," Holton said as he got up to kiss his daughter on the cheek.

"What's up, money?" Dora winked.

Sitting with his back to Tavares, Donnie stood to greet her. When he saw her face, his mouth hit the floor with the glass in his hand. His heart stopped. He was stuck and speechless.

"Yo, you good?" Holton asked, seeing all the color flooding from the pale face standing next to him.

"Mr. Donnie, are you okay?" Tavares asked, not understanding what had just transpired when he looked at her.

"Tavares, you don't resemble DD. You're the spitting image of her."

Donnie's chest was racing looking at his cousin, reincarnated twenty years younger.

Laughing him off, Tavares responded, "You look how Miss Nina looked. I guess I must have a twin."

As she took a seat next to her fiancé, Tavares could still see the look on Donnie's face.

"Mr. Ortega, stop looking like that, please," chuckled Tavares.

"Sweetie, you just don't know. I wish I had a picture."

"And, here I thought you got your good looks from me," Holton sarcastically rolled his eyes.

"Papi, you aighhht," laughed Tavares. "I get my hustle and my gangster from you and my slap a bitch quick and good looks from Dolonda."

Hearing that name, Donnie jumped up from the table.

"What the fuck did you just say?"

Everyone was looking at him like he was crazy, because he'd just gone from friendly to icy Dominican Gangster. They were trying to figure where the vibe had just gone wrong.

"I said I get my looks from Dolonda, my crazy ass mother."

Donnie took a deep breath and then looked at the two men before looking Tavares straight in the eye.

"Tavares, Dolonda is my cousin's name who me and Nina say you're a spitting image of. DD is her nickname, for Dolonda Del Gada."

Tavares screamed from the top of her lungs. She grabbed her mouth with one hand and chest with the other hand. Holton's mouth opened to speak, but no words would come out. The shock had him baffled and flabbergasted. Abdora looked around the room at everyone and felt like he was in the matrix. Seeing the reactions around him, Donnie's head started pouring sweat. His chest was tightening, and his legs felt like they were about to give out on him. He took a seat back at the table and tried to take deep breaths to slow his breathing down.

As he passed him some water, Abdora said, "Donnie, you gotta calm down. We're gonna get to the bottom of this."

After a few minutes, Donnie regulated his breathing. Holton and Tavares were back at the table with a million questions. Seeing that Donnie could breathe again and appeared alright, Tavares went in.

"Dolonda Del Gada is my mother, so now it makes perfect sense why I look so much like your cousin. But, why do you and Nina think that she's dead? My mother is very much alive and well. She has my twins right now. Yes, I want to kill her sometimes because she drives me insane, but she's alive. So, Donnie, can you please tell us why you've thought she was dead all these years?"

Donnie could hear Tavares, but his head was racing and spinning. His heart was pounding. This didn't make any sense. He'd buried his cousin, had a death certificate, and helped his aunt through her death. How was he sitting across from DD's daughter when Dolonda never had children? IF Dolonda was dead, who was in the casket that he'd paid for? Whose grave was he visiting when he came and saw DD? Donnie's face told the three people at the table that he was a million miles away.

Tavares began to cry. Not for the news she was hearing, but because it just seemed like it was always something crazier and crazier going on her life. This topped everything. Her tears snapped Donnie out of his trance. Abdora was wiping his baby's tears while her father grabbed her hand in comfort.

He whispered in her ear, "We play chess, not checkers. Boss up and wipe your face."

Following his instructions, she said, "Donnie, please say something. Please."

He regained his composure to try to explain his reasoning.

"I thought Dolonda was deceased because that's what my no-good, lowdown, trifling ex, Carmen Vega, told me. She's my daughter's mother."

Tavares, Holton, and Abdora's eyes met.

"That fed bitch is your baby's mother?" Tavares screamed.

She was so infuriated that no one ever saw what was about to happen next. Springing to her feet, she took her hand and knocked everything off the table.

"I'm going to murder that bitch with my bare fucking hands. This is the nail in the coffin for that sick twisted cunt!"

The level of anger and the volume of her voice had the three gentlemen looking like they'd just watched a beauty turn into a beast.

"Carmen is going six feet under!" Tavares yelled while clapping her hands and crying tears the size of raindrops. "There are no fucks given at this point. Fuck y'all daughter. Fuck her mother. Fuck her job. Fuck her. That bitch is a dirty, lowdown, evil bitch. I don't know why you two motherfuckers haven't offed her a long time ago," Tavares said, looking at her father and fiancé. "No fucking worries, though. I'm going to do everyone this table a favor and get rid of her ass. Papi, do you know she went to

Puerto Rico and visited Lilly today? Donnie, Lilly is my father's ex-wife."

Holton's neck snapped.

"What? See Lilly for what?"

"Oh, she's forming a federal case against you and tried to get Lilly to be her key witness. But, her days are numbered. Papi, you told me don't fuck with her. Well, she's fucking with me and what she doesn't know is she's fucking with the right one. I'm a savage when you're fucking with my man, my father, and now this shit with faking my mother's death. So you know what... Her days are numbered," Tavares repeated to everyone at the table to make sure they understood the words coming out of her mouth.

Donnie felt compelled to explain.

"Dolonda stopped speaking to my family and me for various reasons. She left Nina's home and became estranged from us. When my uncle, Dolonda's father, passed away, he left her five hundred acres of land back home. It was property in a remote area that was ideal to turn into cocoa fields. Nothing could be done without Dolonda. Carmen was working for the agency, and I asked her to find my cousin. She'd been searching for months and months, so she says. One day she calls and says she had bad news—Dolonda had been found dead. She overdosed, and her body had gone so long that she was unrecognizable and decomposed. She said that she identified the body as her sister and that me and Nina would have to just make arrangements for Dolonda."

Holton cut Donnie off. "Did you just say as her sister? Whoa, whoa, whoa... Donnie, my man, I'm gonna need you to play that back."

"Carmen and Dolonda are half-sisters. We were like ten when Nina found out that my uncle had a brief affair with her best friend."

"How did she find out?" Tavares inquired, still in shock that the agent trying to ruin her life was her aunt.

"Carmen's father, so we thought, tried to give her blood when she got sick. When neither he nor her mother had the same blood type as her, they went to TT Nina and Uncle Julio. Unc was a perfect match, and from there things hit the fan. When TT Nina found out, she wasn't mad. She was broken that her childhood love crossed her. She packed her and DD's things and moved here."

Tavares, Holton, and Dora's eyes were all exchanging stunned looks.

"This is so unreal that I don't even know what to say," Holton responded.

"Unreal... Y'all's family history has just topped anything I've ever heard," Dora said playfully, trying to lighten the mood. "But, why would Carmen make that lie up about her own sister?" Dora said, missing the biggest piece of the puzzle. "What was her motive?"

"Good question. Good, good question," Donnie said, wishing that he himself knew the answer.

"Because she's a sick, twisted, demented bitch. That's why," Tavares answered them.

Then, it hit Tavares.

"She did it to be able to bust the move with the cocoa fields. With grandpapi dead and my mother allegedly dead, she could get the fields and go into business with you."

"Ohhh shit," Donnie said, realizing that Tavares made perfect sense because that was exactly what had happened.

"That bitch is so lowdown!" Dora exclaimed.

Holton asked, "Donnie, do you think that all this time Carmen has known Tavares and I are related to Dolonda?"

"With that no-good, dick-sucking bitch, who knows, Holton? When she started fucking you, I was happy. Not only was it great money, but she became less of a headache in my life."

Tavares was trying to think straight, but her mind wasn't having it. Her mind was running a marathon with all the information she'd just learned.

"Do y'all know that Mami thinks Nina is dead as well?"

"Why does Dolonda think that?" Donnie questioned, not understanding all this madness that Carmen had created.

"She only told me that when she hit rock bottom and I went to foster care, she went looking for her mother for help. It was then that she learned that she'd passed away. But now, here's the bigger issue. Someone is gonna have to tell Nina that Dolonda isn't dead and tell Dolonda her mother is alive. And, guess who it's not gonna be. I've decided that after ingesting all this information after an extremely long day, I'm going on a vacation."

"Is that right?" Dora asked, being sarcastic.

"Yes, shut up. And, you're not going. I'm going to get on a plane with my girlfriends and run to Jamaica for a few days. When I get back, I look forward to hearing how you, Papi, and you, Donnie, are going to break the news to the important women in your lives that their mother and daughter are alive. I can only pray that as far as Mami has come, this won't be enough to break her sobriety and send her back into the arms of a glass pipe."

Holton was offended at the thought.

"That ain't about to happen," he snapped. "You ain't gotta worry about that shit."

"Papi, I'm rooting for Mami. But, this is some heavy shit that's about to be laid on her. So I just want us to be prepared that it may not be peaches and cream when we tell her."

"I love her, and we'll get through this, Tavares."

Hearing her father's sappy response, Tavares just rolled her eyes.

"Donnie, I don't know you, but if your reputation precedes you, then you're like my father and fiancé when it comes to not taking any shit. Although, I'm asking, begging, and pleading with all three of you men to not react with Carmen. She's mine to fix and handle. She might have lied to you, Donnie. Papi, she may be doing some snake shit to you, but I need you guys to please, please, please just let *ME* handle this. No one owes it to her more than I do."

Hearing the conviction in her voice, they agreed. Tavares was lucky she claimed it because after all Dora heard, he was sitting so quietly planning Carmen's disappearance. He was gonna let Tavares have this because it meant so much to her.

Curious, Donnie asked, "Tavares, exactly what is it that you have in mind? Because my men can just put a bullet in her head, and we can go on with our lives."

Giving nodding eyes, Dora and Holton thought it sounded good, too.

"That would be painless. Carmen doesn't deserve the easy way out. Do you know what it's going to do to my mom and Nina when they find out the other is still alive? It's going to crush them before they can smile. I'm going to inflict a greater deal of pain on Carmen. I don't have a plan yet, but I'm going to crush her. So when y'all hear it, just know it was me."

"Donnie, I know this is hasty for a first meeting, but I want to know if I can buy into the family business. I like the set-up at Nina's—or my grandmother's, if I should be technical. I want to buy in."

Holton and Dora were giving each other *what the fuck* eyes. Holton spoke up.

"Mija, you're not doing this."

"Why not?" Tavares asked, confused. "All three of y'all are kingpins, and now you and Dora don't want me to get a piece of the pie."

Neither Holton nor Dora were going for it. Dora checked Tavares for both of them.

"Yo, boo. You ain't buying into the coke game. I don't give a fuck what you did with that other nigga, but my woman, fiancée, soon-to-be wife doesn't have to trap no coke. I would never let you take these kinds of risks. We have kids. If anything ever happens to me, they need you. You want to start a legit business? Fine, do you. But, this shit here... You're not doing it. Conversation over."

Adding fuel to the fire, Holton stated, "You can't even afford to buy into a cartel, keep shopping at the mall, you shopping addict," he laughed.

Rolling her eyes, Tavares gave a grim smirk.

"Now, is that right? I forgot to tell y'all when I got here... I'm now a billionaire, thanks to Damien."

"What?" Dora asked with his eyes squinted, not believing his ears.

After informing her father, fiancé, and Donnie about the money, Dora said, "Boo, get the fuck outta here. You telling me that nigga hit big and left it all to you?"

"Okay, don't believe me if you want," laughed Tavares. "So yeah, I'm rich and about to buy all y'all out," she joked.

Tavares so badly wanted to fly her and her friends to Jamaica the following day for Bella's bachelorette party. Before that could happen, she had to deal with Dolonda and Nina. Her head was spinning for an easy way to inform the mother and daughter that the other was alive. Realistically, she knew there was no easy way, but it had to be done.

"Donnie, do you think you can get Nina here? Maybe tell her it's important that she fly to Boston and meet you."

"I can do that," he said.

"Papi, we aren't going to tell Mami what we know. We're just going to let Nina come and take it from there."

Agreeing to meet at Tavares's house the following day, everyone left Ocean Prime to get ready for what was going to be a very emotional meeting.

The following day Dolonda was making breakfast with Holton while Tavares and Dora were in bed playing with their twins.

"Baby Girl, you ready to do this?"

"Nope. Not at all, but this isn't the kind of thing that you can sit on. They both deserve to know the truth after almost twelve years. So let's get up out of this bed and get ready. Donnie will be here with Nina in about an hour."

Dora went to bathe and dress the boys while Tavares attempted to clear her mind and get ready. The doorbell rang while they were having breakfast. Tavares took a deep breath.

"I'll go get it."

"Who the hell is that this early?" Dolonda questioned.

"We'll find out soon enough," Tavares said, excusing herself from the table.

She opened the door and greeted Donnie and Nina with a bright smile.

"Good morning. Thanks for coming, Nina."

Nina was confused about what they were doing at Tavares's house. Donnie had told her nothing. He simply told her to get on a flight the next morning because they had an important meeting to attend. Nina gave Tavares a big hug as she crossed her doorway.

"What a surprise, pretty girl. I had no idea we were coming to see you. This crazy nephew of mine gave me no info. He just told an old lady to get on a plane."

"Oh, we have a big surprise for you, Nina," Tavares said, ready to give Nina the surprise of her life.

"Do you?" Nina gave her a big smile.

"Yes, I have someone I want you to see. Follow me."

Tavares's stomach was doing somersaults on the short walk to her kitchen.

"Mami, I have someone I want you to see."

When Tavares stepped aside, Dolonda saw Donnie. Her jaw dropped, and she gasped and jumped up from the island in excitement. Donnie stepped slightly to the right. Nina and Dolonda locked eyes. Nina cupped her face and began screaming as puddle-sized tears fell from her eyes. Dolonda started hyperventilating and saying, "Oh, my God. Mami, you're alive?"

Emotions and tears were flying around the kitchen like fireworks. Dora scooped his sons from their high chairs because they were looking scared from all the yelling.

"Boo, I'm gonna take them upstairs, but come get me if you need me."

Tavares nodded, but she hadn't taken her eyes off her mother and grandmother, who were wrapped in each other's arms, crying, and sobbing uncontrollably. Tavares, Donnie, and Holton watched the women. None of them had ever seen such a heartbreaking, emotional sight. The two ladies hugged, cried, and sobbed for well over an hour. The longer Tavares watched her mother and grandmother, her heart hurt more and more. No one deserved to believe that his or her mother or child was dead. The more her heart ached, the more she knew that she was going to destroy Carmen beyond repair. When she was done, Carmen was going to feel and know every inch of pain that she'd inflicted on her family.

Still with no plan, Tavares wiped her watery eyes and said to herself, "Carmen, I'm coming for everything you took from us."

When Dolonda and Nina took a seat at the table, hand in hand, they looked at the three sitting across from them.

"How did you guys figure this out?" Dolonda asked, so confused.

"Dora and I went to Nina's restaurant, and she looked like she'd seen a ghost when looking at me. She kept saying I looked like her daughter who had passed away. Me and Dora just thought it was a coincidence. Then, when Papi, Dora, and I met with Donnie yesterday, he said the same thing. When I said your name, it all came together."

Dolonda turned to her mother, who was an older and just as pretty but more refined version of her.

"Mami, why did you think I was dead?"

"Because that's what your no-good, lowdown ass sister Carmen told us. She told us you had overdosed, she identified the body, and all Donnie and I needed to do was plan your funeral."

Dolonda's face turned beet red.

"WHATTT," she screamed so long that the neighbors could have heard her. "Mami, Carmen is a snake in the grass if I ever met one. She's worse than scum. Only a heartless bitch could do what she did. I tracked her down when my drug habit spun out of control and I'd lost Tavares. I asked her if she had numbers for you and Donnie because you weren't at your address where I grew up. She told me that you had passed away and she had no contact with Donnie. I asked her to get my daughter and raise her until I was okay. She said okay. Then, she told me about all this land Papi had left me when he passed away. I told her to sell my land and use the money to care for Tavares. I even gave her Holton's name. I told her

Holton had no idea about Tavares, but if she found him, that he would step up."

"Oh, she found Papi, alright," Tavares said, sucking her teeth and rolling her eyes.

"What does that mean?" Dolonda asked, giving skeptical eyes to Holton.

"Dolonda, listen. I had no idea she was your sister."

"What the fuck does that mean?" Dolonda yelled.

Holton felt so awful and guilty even though it wasn't his fault.

"When I told you I had to cut my plug and side chick off, it was Carmen."

Dolonda got up and started rubbing her head and pacing the floor.

"What the fuck?" she yelled. "So you mean to tell me she's been fucking you all these years and never mentioned me or Tavares?"

"Never," Holton said in a low voice.

Tavares jumped to her father's defense.

"Mami, you can't be mad at Papi. Hell, Carmen has been harassing me and Dora for the last year, and I had no idea the fed bitch was my aunt. I believe Carmen concocted this whole grand scheme because she took your property to use for cocoa fields in the Dominican Republic. It was her goal to get into business with her baby daddy over here. But, she never thought that you and Papi would reconnect or that I would find out about my papi."

Dolonda was shaking her head, trying to wrap her brain around everything she was taking in.

"How can one person be so evil? For years, she's been looking all of you in the face and just carrying on with her lie that I was dead."

Looking at Donnie, she asked, "And, what the fuck made you have a baby with that bitch? When we were kids, I told you to stay away from her. I knew she always wanted to have your babies."

"Don't remind me. It was the biggest mistake of my life. I hate everything about that spineless bitch. I love Jade, but I hate that bitch."

Tavares cut the conversation off.

"Whoa, whoa, whoa... Donnie, did you just say Jade? What in the fuck is really going on?"

Everything made sense now. Everyone was looking at her oddly, trying to figure out why Jade's name had set her off.

"Jade is the reason Carmen has been coming for me and Dora. She was dating Dora when I met him. He cut her off when he and I got serious. Next thing I know, that cunt bitch was coming for us. I always told Dora her beef is more than his street affairs, it's personal. Everything is coming full circle."

After a day of playing catch-up, everyone was crying happy tears to have found each other. Dolonda hated to see her mother leave, but agreed to meet her back in Jersey in a few days. Everyone left having decided that they were going to let Carmen continue to think her lie was still buried. Donnie wasn't going to cut her out of business just yet or put a bullet in her head like he wanted to. Nina was going to continue dealing with her. They both had to play it cool for a few months more in order for Tavares to sufficiently take her down.

***

Tavares was busy over the next few months. She wasn't just planning Carmen's demise. She was also spending time with her mother and Nina. The mother and daughter duo wouldn't let up on helping her plan her wedding. She didn't complain because there was a time when she thought she wouldn't even have her mother at her wedding, never mind her grandmother. Even though the older Dominican women were overly opinionated, Tavares was appreciating the blessing of having them to share this experience with.

While they were in Nordstrom's trying on dresses, Dolonda started to cry. Hearing the light tears, Tavares came out of the dressing room.

"Mami, what in the world are you crying for now? I swear, Nanny Nina, since you've come back into her life, she's nothing but a big ole emotional crybaby. I can't take it."

Tavares rolled her eyes at her mother.

"I'm just so happy. My baby is getting married, and my mother and I are here to share in the experience. I can cry if I want to," Dolonda chuckled.

She had to laugh at herself because she had definitely turned overly emotional over the last few months. As Tavares twirled around in the most recent dress, in unison Nina and Dolonda said, "That's it."

Tavares hated to agree with them and their bossy selves, but they were right. The moment Dolonda zipped her up in it, she knew it was the dress she wanted. As they made their way to the register to pay for the dress, Nina beat Tavares to the punch, pulling out her wallet.

"Nina, put your wallet away. I have it and can afford it," Tavares said, not wanting or needing her grandmother to spend the small fortune on her dress.

Nina had to show Tavares where her smart mouth and sass originated.

"I don't care what you want. And, I don't give a damn if you can afford it. I can, too. So back your little ass up, and let me pay for this dress."

Tavares took a long, deep sigh and did as she was told.

She whispered in Dolonda's ear, "I don't know who gets on my nerves more, you or Nina."

Nina heard her granddaughter and looked her in the eye.

"I've missed your whole life. I can't get that time back. Ten thousand for a dress is a small price to pay in comparison to the lifetime of sentimental value for me."

Heading home, Nina couldn't stop thinking about all she'd missed because of Carmen.

"I want to kill Carmen with my bare hands," she stated to no one in particular.

"Nanny, don't worry. I promise you, her days are numbered. I don't want to implicate any more people than I have to. Just trust me when I tell you, I got this."

Everything Tavares needed to know about Carmen had been in the files from Katrina. Now, she was going to punish Carmen in the worst way.

"Tavares, you aren't going to do anything illegal, right?" Dolonda nervously questioned.

"Mami, is water wet?"

"Of course it us," Dolonda naïvely answered.

"Okay then. Just don't ask me no questions, and I won't tell y'all no lies."

While Tavares, her mother, and her grandmother were discussing the snake herself, Carmen was plotting and scheming a few miles across town. Getting so desperate to ruin Abdora, Holton, and Tavares, she pulled her daughter and her friends into her chaos.

"Now, y'all are ready, right?" Carmen drilled them. "All you have to do is party with them, hang with them, and make it your business to keep any of them from leaving the club."

"That's it?" Jamie asked.

"That's it," Carmen smiled.

"And, you're paying us three thousand dollars apiece to do this?" Kamari said, wondering why this was too easy.

"That's right," Carmen responded. "Party hard and leave the rest to me."

Doing as Carmen told them, that night the women went to King's on a mission. They were all in Abdora, Mid, Nas, Hawk, Bryce, and Mason's faces. The fellas were playing with fire, drinking, smoking, and popping bottles with their exes. Even though they knew better, they pretended they saw no harm since their wifeys were at home. They continued partying with the setup chicks. Dora didn't know what had gotten into Jade and her girls by trying to rock with him and his mans so hard, but he wasn't interested. In less than thirty days, he would be getting married to Tavares. He surely wasn't trying to invite any drama into his life.

By 3:30 a.m. Tavares was rolling over to her phone ringing nonstop.

"What the fuck?" she yelled, as she tried to fish for the mobile device with her eyes closed. Finding it, she answered half asleep and eyes still closed. Hearing, "You have a collect call," Tavares bounced up like she'd never been asleep.

Pressing one to accept the call, she said, "What the fuck are you doing in jail?" Hearing her raging tone, Dora said, "Boo, before you ill, just listen. We got set up. We left the club heading to grab some grub and got pulled over. They said we had improper lane change or some dumb shit. We were in my car and Bryce's. They searched both cars and found bricks of dope in each truck."

"WHATTTTTTT?" Tavares screeched. "I know you didn't have drugs in your trunk."

"Boo, come on. If I had bricks, why would they be in my trunk while I'm out partying and bullshitting?"

"Dora, I don't know what to say except I'll be in court in the morning."

Walking into court at 8:30 a.m., Tavares wasn't even mad. She was now aggravated. In a month, she would be becoming Mrs. Abdora Santacosa. Starting their new life with a trafficking case wasn't what she had in mind. On the back pew with Bella, Ebony, Rocky, and Dhara, Tavares impatiently waited for Dora and his co-defendants' case to be called. For two hours they'd heard drunk driving, domestic, drug, and larceny cases. Finally, it was time for the five fools to be led into the courtroom.

After the prosecutor was done painting the defendants as notorious drug dealers and murdering thugs who were flight risks, he asked the court for a million dollars bail on each. Tavares stood up.

"I have it."

The prosecutor, along with everyone else in the courtroom and the hefty four-eyed judge, looked at Tavares.

"Ma'am," the judge asked, "you have five million dollars?"

"Yes," Tavares answered her dryly.

"You do know you have to account for the origin of the money?"

Something told Tavares to turn around. Carmen Vega was standing in the doorway of the courtroom. She had a funny feeling that this had Carmen's name all over it. Tavares didn't look upset. Instead, she blew the snake a kiss.

"Ma'am, do you hear me?" the judge repeated.

"I'm sorry. Yes, your honor, I do know that."

"One million apiece and back here August tenth," the judge said as she slammed her gavel.

Tavares just smiled because by then, she would have dealt with Carmen and the bogus charges would be vacated. Forking over five million for the man she loved and his friends, Tavares and the ladies waited for them all to come outside. Tavares didn't give them a chance to say anything.

"Listen, assholes, either you lay your asses low or you owe me a million dollars right now."

"Yo, we hear you with your rich ass," Bryce said, being his usual sarcastic self.

"But, you know that wasn't our shit, right?" Mason asked.

"I know that y'all was set up, but I need my five million back. So, until we prove it was a setup, lay low. I promise when y'all go back to court, these charges won't even exist."

Tavares was now counting down the days until Carmen was sorry she'd fucked with her.

CHAPTER 23

The overly loud alarm buzzed in Tavares's ear after an epic night of celebrating with what felt like all of Newark for her and Dora's upcoming union. Only Dora could bring the city out to turn up on a Tuesday. His city showed up and showed out for them. It was the turn up for sure, because Tavares was still feeling it. Her body told her to hit the snooze button for ten more minutes as she half-opened one of her blue eyes and looked at the clock that read 7:05 a.m. However, her mind, still half-drunk from all the Patrón she drank, told her *don't play yourself*. So she wiggled and wormed slightly free of Abdora's body that was keeping her warm and turned the alarm off.

"Damn, I feel like we just went to sleep," she said to herself, feeling like the three hours of sleep she just borrowed were a pure tease. She was up, but she had to convince her head to move her feet to the floor. They weren't on the same page, as she lay naked snuggled under Abdora.

Patrón, epic nights, and wild sex didn't make good for early mornings. Tavares knew the moment that she stepped out of the bed she would be moving nonstop. The next few days would determine the fate of the rest of her life. She'd spent the last months researching and carefully formulating an airtight plan. One mistake, mishap, or miscalculated action would possibly cost her her children and Abdora as well as her freedom. She was convinced that her lethal weapon of being book smart and street smart was going to allow everything to go just as she planned. With a grim smirk, she wiggled herself completely free from Abdora and headed to the shower. The first part of plan entailed getting Abdora to the airport for his Vegas trip.

A month earlier while cruising down 24 South to Easton, MA to their wedding venue, Tavares jumpstarted her plan.

"What are the fellas doing for your bachelor party?"

"Here you go," Dora chuckled with his right dimple popping out. "Man, my niggaz keep saying we have to turn it all the way up since I'm officially going off the market, but I don't want that shit. I don't want no sweaty funky pussy on me as a way to celebrate that I'm getting married."

Tavares cracked up laughing.

"You would say that. Who doesn't have a bachelor party and trashy strippers before they surrender to the married world?"

"Me, that's who. It's pointless. You know as well as I do that as much as we frequent strip clubs just for the atmosphere, that ain't my thing, Boobie. We be in the club, and you're giving me lap dances," Dora shook his head.

"If your friends want to give you a bachelor party, just let them. Babe, whether you have sweaty pussy on you or not, you gotta have a bachelor party."

Tavares argued him down. Abdora didn't want it and didn't see the big deal, but to shut Tavares up, he agreed. Immediately, she was ready to put things in motion to get him out of town, because nothing would come together if he weren't long gone. Dora had to be miles away so that nothing would come back on him.

By the time they made it home from a long day of running around, Tavares went to the kitchen to cook while Dora sat in the living room. He kicked off his wheat construction Timbs and opened the chocolate brown coffee table drawer. He removed his backwoods and sour to roll him a long overdue blunt.

"Babe, when you go pick the boys up from my dad's, can you please stop and grab some food? I just don't feel like cooking."

"No problem, but I'm smoking this blunt before I do anything."

"That's fine, you pothead. Just make sure you smoke it downstairs in your man cave. You know that weed smoke in the common areas is a no-no. You'll have our damn kids getting high off contact and shit."

"Goddamn, I remember a time when you cussed me out to roll up so you could smoke. Now, you want to dictate where I smoke because you barely smoke," joked Dora.

"Whatever, just roll it and smoke it in the man cave," Tavares sang with sarcasm as she walked past him to go upstairs.

Tavares got upstairs and plopped down on her bed. She was beyond exhausted from all the back and forth between Boston and Jersey, the wedding planning, and her scheme that was planned with concise precision.

"I can't wait for all this to be over," she said out loud.

She stripped out of her PINK sweat suit, wrapped herself in a towel, and prepared for a long hot shower before her babies came home and her evening was consumed with playing with them.

Dora came upstairs smelling like that good, good weed and kissed Tavares.

"You stink," she said jokingly as she screwed her face up.

"You do too, and you just got out of the shower," laughed Abdora.

"Nigga please, I don't stink on my worst day. I'm hungry, so can you please hurry up?"

"What do you want to eat?"

"It doesn't matter."

"Easy enough," Dora said, giving his fiancée the peace sign and leaving to pick up his little men.

Tavares used the time to call Bryce and get him onboard for her plans for Dora's out-of-town bachelor party.

"Hey, Brother," she said when Bryce answered his phone.

"What it do, sissy poo?"

"I wanted to call you and talk about Dora's bachelor party."

Bryce bellowed in laughter, "The fuck you mean you want to talk about the bachelor party. Don't tell me you calling me to tell me you don't want us to give my nigga a bachelor party because I don't take you for that type, sis. He's all yours. Don't no one want that water head ass thug but you."

"Are you done, smart ass?" Bryce couldn't help but laugh again.

"I'm calling for the total opposite. I want to help plan something epic before my soon-to-be husband chunks his deuces to the single world."

"Let me find out," yelled Bryce.

"Let you find out what?"

"That you're the real motherfucking MVP!"

"Duh! What, you didn't know?"

"I don't know a woman alive that wants to help plan the bachelor party. That's why you're my girl!"

"Whatever, Bryce. So, I was thinking of going all out. Don't do it in Newark or locally. The whole crew, my pops, and Uncle Donnie should go someplace and do it up way big."

"That's what the fuck I'm talking about," Bryce said, unable to contain his excitement, loving the woman Abdora chose to make his partner in life more and more.

"I'm thinking Vegas."

"Man, listen, Sis, you don't want to send us to Vegas as we prepare to turn our brother over to you. Vegas ain't ready for all of us at one time. I love my girl, and you're trying to get a nigga left."

"As long as you don't come back with no diseases and babies you didn't leave with, you'll be good, so knock it off."

"What do you need from me?" questioned Bryce.

"Your credit card for starters, chump. I'm planning, but I'm sure as hell not paying for this. I'm cool, but not that damn cool," Tavares said, letting it be known she wasn't that much of an MVP. "Then, I need you to get a solid count of who's all going so I can book all the reservations for y'all as a group. Bro, collect their money up front so you don't get stuck with the bill, and then we're good to go."

"I ain't worried about getting my money back. Niggaz know I don't play when it comes to my bread. Give me two days, and I'll hit you back with a solid number count."

"Sounds good."

Tavares hung up and was happy everything was coming together. With only a week's notice, she told Abdora when he climbed in bed, "You're going to Vegas for your bachelor party."

He squinted his eyes, scrunched his face up, and looked her straight in the eye.

"Get your fucking money back. I'm not going way to Vegas to do some shit I don't want to do in the fucking first place."

"Why do you have to be such a party pooper?"

"Call it what you want, but get your money back because there ain't no way in fucking hell I'm going to Vegas days before our wedding. If I want to get lit and let some nasty, sweaty pussy dance on me, I can stay here in this bedroom with you," he said and burst into laughter.

"Abdora, how about this… You're fucking going. Your friends have an epic time planned for you, so you're getting on that plane and going to turn up. You're going to let some sweaty pussy dance on you, and you're going to enjoy it. Then, when you come home, I'll be waiting."

"Who the fuck…" was as far as Abdora got because Elijah woke up crying.

"Saved by the baby," laughed Tavares.

Scooting out of bed to go tend to her son, she knew she'd won the battle. Now, the day had finally arrived. Tavares stood in the marble and glass stand-up shower under the powerful showerhead for almost ten minutes in deep thought. She played back all the events that had led up to her revenge and decided she had no remorse or regret. Payback was a bitch, and they'd fucked with the wrong one.

Tavares showered, dressed, fed, and fucked Abdora before taking another shower and dressing again. She sat at the airport long enough to see his plane take off. With Dora in the high skies, Tavares was all smiles with the taste of revenge in her mouth.

At 3:00 p.m., as requested, her gate buzzed. Three cars pulled into the driveway. Bella, Rocky, and Cali were in one car. Randee, Leslie, and Mona-Lisa were in the second car. In the third car was the production team for the evening that Tavares had flown in from California. When the ten women entered the foyer of the house, Tavares got straight down to business.

"Okay, ladies. We're on the clock."

After passing towels, face cloths, and toiletries to her friends, she said, "Find a bathroom. When y'all are done, meet us downstairs in the salon." Then, she looked at the production team and said, "You ladies follow me."

While the production team got prepared, Tavares spoke to them.

"Sugar, Queenie, Cyndi, and Lisa, thank you so much for taking this job. I'm sure you don't get many clients who ask you to fly across the country and do all that I asked, but I hope the compensation made it worth your while. When I flew out to Cali, I couldn't and still can't go into great detail about why we need this transformation. I just want to stress to you the importance of us looking like each woman in the passport photos that I left with you."

Tavares needed everyone's identity to be disguised if she wanted to protect their freedom, which was why she paid a hefty fee to retain these women's services.

Sugar, the owner of the special effects makeup company, said, "You overpaid us. We're very clear that we're transforming you and your three friends. Then, we're transforming ourselves to look like them. But, I must tell you that you're one lucky lady, because we even fit the physical measurements. This transformation is going to be 100% smooth."

While they had no clue what Tavares had going on, they knew she'd flown out to meet them in person, paid them double what they asked, and covered all their expenses for the next three days. In all honesty, they didn't care why she'd retained them. They signed her nondisclosure agreement, took her payment, prepared thoroughly, and were here to get the job done.

By 7:00 p.m., Tavares felt like the molding, sculpting, and application of the clay faces, ears, teeth, and then the hair and makeup had taken a lifetime. Although, looking at her friends and their replicas, she couldn't have been more pleased. Sugar and her team had earned every bit of the one hundred thousand dollars Tavares had paid them.

"Ladies, we all need to get out of here. Y'all have a flight to catch, and we have to get to our event as well. Before y'all go, I want to say just a few things... I want y'all to have a blast in Atlanta. Sugar, I'm the life of the party. Okay, not really," laughed Tavares. "However, this weekend, I need you to be. If that's not you, you better get into character."

"Girl, that's me all day," the white girl who was going to be Tavares for the next three days stated.

"I need you to have an overly great time because, remember, you're the soon-to-be bride. I post a million selfies, so don't let me down. Mona-

Lisa, as my maid of honor, you can't let Sugar pay for anything. Matter of fact, you pick up the tab for everyone wherever y'all go. I want y'all to ball until y'all fall."

Tavares passed Mona-Lisa an envelope containing $30,000 in cash.

"Spend, splurge, and turn up. Everywhere y'all go, check in on World Playground and Picture Palace. Post so many pictures that y'all make people want to throw up."

Bella, Rocky, Randee, and Tavares passed their passports and cell phones to their duplicates.

"Why do we have to give our phones? Oh, my God," whined Rocky.

"Bitch, because we need our phones to hit off cell towers where we are!" Tavares rolled her eyes and said, "Everyone, it's time to go."

Mona-Lisa, Cali, and Leslie were airport-bound with the replicas while Tavares and her girls loaded in Sugar's rental. In the driver's seat, the mastermind was in deep thought. One wrong move and everyone in the car would be gambling with their freedom. Tavares didn't know how she'd lucked up and gotten friends who would put their lives on the line for her, but she knew she was blessed.

They were all laughing and smoking a blunt when Bella asked, "You okay?"

"I just want to say thank y'all. Not many bitches have loyal, literal ride-or-die friends. I owe y'all my life after this. No words can express my gratitude."

Randee rolled her eyes because she wasn't in the mood for sappy and mushy when mayhem was the mood for the evening.

"Tavares, you're killling our vibe," joked Rocky.

Bella, who was sitting across from Tavares, got serious.

"T, we aren't doing nothing you wouldn't do for us. You would give us your last breath, walk through fire, or kill for one of us. All we're doing is the same for you. After tonight, you're going to get everything that you're overdue for. No more chaos, drama, or bitches trying to come for your life. You're going to walk down that aisle and spend your life with the man who loves you more than life. So boss up, because them bitches don't know the murder mafia name extends past our boyfriends, husbands, and fiancés."

Arriving in the hood of Newark on Twelfth Street, the ladies parked and stared at what looked like a crack shack from the outside.

"Only silly bitches move to the worst street in the hood by choice. I swear, bitches are dumb," Rocky said, shaking her head.

Looking around, Tavares asked, "Y'all ready, heffas? We all got clean guns. Hold your bags tight and let's do this."

"As ready as we're going to be," Randee said, being the first to open her door.

The ladies approached the door with their presents in hand. This was going to be a housewarming to remember. Rocky rang the bell, hoping it even worked as ass run-down as the house was. Priscilla opened the door in moments. Her face tightened when she saw the four chicks. She thought her crew were the only females invited for the evening. Tavares wanted to drop-kick her, but she held back.

Instead, she gave her phoniest smile and said, "Hi, we're Nino's cousins."

Everyone waved, smiled, and said, "Hello."

"We're here for the housewarming."

Prissy's face softened hearing they were Nino's family. "They had new hardwood floors, so leave your shoes there and just head up the stairs."

Entering the living room where Nino and all his boys were chilling with Jade and her girls, the ladies did what they did best. They were themselves and let their strong personalities shine.

Tavares came in saying, "Yooooooo. What's cracking, you chump ass niggaz?"

Randee didn't even look in the ladies' directions as she said, "Waddup fools?" to the fellas.

Bella yelled, "The party can start now. We in the building."

And, Rocky said, "Hey, hey, hey, ladies," to the women who weren't looking friendly or welcoming.

Jade and her girls were already rubbed wrong, just as Tavares wanted. Tavares and her girls could feel the air in the room change. Jade and her squad were feeling some way. Their eyes said it, *who the fuck are these bitches just rolling up in here like they own the place?*

"Baby, these are my crazy ass cousins, Nikki, Diamond, Ashley, and Toya."

Jade gave a fake smile.

"Nice to meet you ladies. These are my girls, Jamie, Kamari, and Priscilla."

Counterfeit hellos and smiles were exchanged between the two groups of women. Before their arrival, Jade's girls were sizing up Nino's boys. Now they were eying what they saw as the competition.

"Cuzzin, please tell me who the fuck has a housewarming on a Wednesday?" Rocky aka Toya asked with her face screwed up, thinking that whoever scripted the occasion could have done a little better.

"Me, monkey face. That's who. You know I don't follow trends. I set them. I do what I want, how I want, and when I want," slick-talked Nino. "Nah, seriously, these niggaz was coming down and you savages said y'all was stopping through on the way to Atlantic City. So the timing just worked out. Now, come let me show you wenches the rest of the spot.

Big Ez, Molly G, Pooh, and Killa K, y'all keep these pretty ladies company. We'll be back," Tavares said, winking at her homies.

Making it to the second floor of the duplex apartment, Tavares, her girls, and Nino stepped in the master bedroom.

"You got everything, big head?"

"I sure the fuck do," Tavares laughed, ready to watch everything unfold.

She removed some pills and what looked like cocaine from her purse.

"Remember, the blue pills are the real ecstasy pills. So, those are for them. The red ones are placebo pills for everyone else. By the time they pop E-pills, throw back a few shots, smoke a blunt or two, and sniff this shit, it's going to be a wrap," Tavares laughed. "But, remember, we aren't doing it all at once. We gonna chill, hang, and rock out as normal and let it unfold slowly."

"I got this, nigga. You ain't schooling me."

Tavares just rolled her eyes at Nino.

"Why this don't look like the coke I get from Dora?"

"Because it's not, crazy. It's Fentanyl."

"What the fuck is this? Them bitches sniff coke a mile a minute. They ain't gonna want this."

"Of course, they are," laughed Randee. "Once you become a cokehead, you're just addicted to being high and putting something up your nose."

"They're bobble-brain bitches," Rocky chimed in. "I promise if you tell them it's better because it's heroin's cousin, synthetic dope but not going to get them hooked, they silly asses is going to believe it."

"Y'all know I'm gonna beat the fuck out that bitch Jamie, right?"

Everyone turned around to see where that random ass comment had just come from.

"Bitch, what the fuck are you talking about?" laughed Randee.

"Oh, I was just thinking out loud."

Jade realized that Nino and his cousins had been gone too long. She was cooling with their friends, smoking sour, and drinking Remy, but her clingy ass was missing Nino in less than twenty minutes.

She called, "Babyyy!"

Hearing the call, Nino and his homies made it back to the living room.

"Hey, pretty lady. What's wrong?"

"Oh, nothing, baby. I was just missing you."

"My bad, we were upstairs talking and then started smoking a blunt. But, you ready to have some fun?" Nino said, waving the ounce of Fentanyl and the pills around.

"Oh yeahh," Jade said, getting excited.

She gave Nino a kiss, grabbed some plates and a credit card to sort the lines, turned the music up, and was ready to rock star party. Jade, Jamie, Prissy, and Kamari were the only ones sniffing the lines. They'd formed such a habit in the last six months that they didn't even notice that it wasn't cocaine.

"Damn, this is some good ass shit," Kamari said from the instant euphoria.

"Now, girl, you know my man only gives me the best," Jade said, trying to brag.

The coke whores weren't even curious why the other people in the room didn't want any. They were just thinking, *more for us*. Tavares, Bella, Randee, and Rocky had popped their fake E-pills with the fellas. They were smoking blunts, talking shit, drinking, and playing spades while they waited for the drugs to kick in. Once Jade and her friends started talking a mile a minute, Tavares knew they were high. She winked at Nino.

"Oh shit. You wenches will never guess who's getting married."

"Who?" Tavares asked, as if she was really curious.

"Ole girl, Tavares, who used to fuck with the nigga Damien."

"Oh, is she?" asked Randee.

"Yeah, last night me and these niggaz went to the club. It was a celebration for them at King's, her man's club. That shit was rocking!" Nino said, giving credit where it was due

Hearing Tavares's name, Jade fell right into the trap.

"Fuck that wack ass, punk bitch and that fuck boy who's marrying her. I hate that bitch," she said in slow motion from being high.

She was instantly getting mad, so she snorted another line. Tavares snapped her neck around.

"Damn, Jade, you sounding real hostile over there. You alright?"

"I'm okay. I just hate that bitch."

"You ain't the only one," Priscilla co-signed as she snorted a line and passed it to Jamie.

"Damn, y'all got real smoke with Tavares, huh?" Big Ez instigated.

"Y'all know I love my baby because he's the best," Jade beamed with pride. "But, before I met Nino, I was engaged to the nigga she's marrying. He started fucking her, and then she got pregnant and trapped him. He wanted to be there for his kids, so he walked out on me to be with her."

Bella, Rocky, Tavares, and Randee's eyes locked, and they fought hard not to crack up at the fairytale they were listening to.

"Boo, I hate to tell you, but I fucked that bitch, too."

Everyone who was hip burst out laughing.

"Nigggga, when?" Tavares asked, enjoying the joke.

"Man, I had shorty calling me Daddy, but she was too clingy so I had to let her go."

"Bullshit, nigga," Randee said. "If I can remember correctly, you was chasing and sweating her and she dissed you."

"Nikki, you're a motherfucking lie. Jade, my cousins are hating. They know I had that bad bitch. Baby, don't worry. You got me now," smiled Nino. "So what she took that nigga? It's his loss. That bitch ain't as cute or smart as my baby."

Nino leaned in for a kiss and Big Ez, Molly G, Pooh, and Killa K were in tears laughing at all the comedy. As the night went on everyone was just having a good ole time. The music was bumping, Nino had got down in the kitchen, sour blunts were going around the room left and right, the drinks were endless, and the vibe was good. Jade, Jamie, Priscilla and Kamari continued to snort what they believed was cocaine and got higher and higher. The combo of the two drugs had the women acting up. They were laughing too much, feeling free, and kissing each other. They were touching each other in a sexual way and trying to give the fellas lap dances. Sitting in the far corner, Bella was recording with her phone while everyone else spectated the trashy behavior. The higher they went, the more they bashed Tavares, Cali, Bella, and Rocky. Priscilla kicked it off.

"I hate that bitch Tavares. Punk ass bitch made me drag her ass all up and down King's because her man was checking for me. Then, he made her call me and apologize for making me come out of character. And, I can't see for the life of me what Mason sees in her ghetto ass friend, Bella. Bitch tried to kill me just because me and Mason had something way realer than them. I can't believe he fucked around and married that overly ghetto bitch."

"But not before I got him drunk and fucked him," laughed Jamie.

Bella went to hop up and snatch her cap and Rocky had to snatch her all the way back.

"Fuck Bella, Tavares, and Cali. Them whack ass bitches ain't nothing but punk ass gold-digging whores. Remember them bitches tried to run down on me when they saw me with Javan? I had to toss a drink on Bella, slap the shit out of Tavares, and tell them bitches if they want these hands then let's do it. They both was begging Javan to save them."

The more lies the ladies spit, the less they noticed that everyone was looking at them like they had eight heads. They were gassing themselves so hard that it was a struggle for everyone else in the room not to laugh.

"Y'all the illest bitches I ever met," Pooh said with sarcasm.

"I love a gangster bout-it bout-it bitch," Killa K said.

"That's why Jade's my baby," smiled Nino.

Bella was looking at Jamie with scolding eyes.

"Jamie, you gotta be a special kind of whore bitch to fuck a nigga right before he's getting married. And, I do mean a special kinda whore."

"No, Nikki, I'm not a whore. He loved me. She forced him to be with her. I know she did."

"Bitch, a woman can't make no one stay nowhere they don't fucking want to be. What did your parents teach your ole stupid ass?" Bella purposely said, knowing her parents were murdered in front of her.

"I can dig it, J. Fuck them bitches," Priscilla said. "I just can't believe that nigga is marrying that whack ass bitch, knowing he don't love her like he loves me."

"Pausssse," yelled Rocky before she keeled over in laughter.

"You was engaged to him, Jade, but he loves you, Priscilla? What kinda crazy shit y'all got going on?" Rocky instigated.

"I know it sounds crazy," chuckled Jade. "Priscilla was his first love. I didn't even know her when she was with Dora. We met when I was her mom's nurse. It's pure coincidence."

"Well, if I was you, Priscilla," Tavares said, throwing propane on the fire, "I would call that nigga and say you need to see him one last time before you get married so he can make sure he's choosing wisely."

Everyone's eyes were plastered on Tavares like she'd lost her rabbit ass mind.

"Girl, if that nigga love you more than he loves that whack ass bitch, I bet he's going to come. If he comes, profess your love and let him say fuck that bitch."

Tavares gave a devilish grin.

"Diamond's right, Priscilla," Jamie co-signed.

"Priscilla, don't listen to my crazy ass cousin. That nigga was loving his bitch hard body last night."

"Nah, fuck that, Nino. Your cousin's right. I was that nigga's first love. He wanted to marry me, and I fucked it up. But, I love that nigga."

"Call that nigga and take your man back," Kamari said.

Jade didn't like this. If he took Priscilla back and had dissed her so bad, she was gonna for sure be tight.

"I'm about to call that nigga right now. I'm gonna put him on speaker."

Everyone shut up in a hurry to hear what was about to go down. Someone was gonna get their feelings hurt and not a soul in the room thought it was going to be their disguised friend. These chicks were high and about to let their girl make herself look like a fool.

"Jade, give me your phone."

"Give you my phone for what?" snapped Jade.

"Because I don't want to call him from mine," Prissy rolled her eyes, not wanting to admit that Dora had blocked her. As Prissy called Dora, the room was so quiet you could hear a pin drop. The coke whores were looking at her while everyone else had their eyes glued on Tavares.

"Yooo," Dora answered with the noise in the background so loud that it was clear he was some place partying.

"It's Prissy."

"Hold on for a moment. Let me step outside. What's up, Prissy?"

"I was calling because I want to see you."

"See me? See me for what?" Dora asked snidely.

"I want to see you before you go down the aisle. I want to see you one last time and talk to you face to face so you can decide if you're making the right decision marrying HER." Dora looked at the phone.

"Prissy, I'm outta town at my bachelor party. The bachelor party that my wifey planned, might I add. But, even if I wasn't, I wouldn't come check on you. I'm not bringing that kind of baggage into my marriage. And, I sure the fuck don't need to come see you to decide if I'm making the right decision. Fuck is wrong with you?" Dora asked in a tone that said *are you fucking crazy.* "I'm marrying the realest nigga on my team, yo. My broad would walk through fire for me, give me her last breath, and put her life on the line for me. So yeah, I'm making the right decision. I gotta go, but you be cool how you be cool. And, I would appreciate if you wouldn't call me anymore."

Dora didn't even give Prissy a chance to say a single word before he hung up on her.

Prissy was holding the phone, staring at it with her mouth wide open. She looked like her heart had just hit the ground. She wanted to so badly burst in tears but fought it, knowing everyone was looking at her. She thought Dora would always have a soft spot for her and that no one would ever replace her, but she learned otherwise today.

"Yoooooo," Bella screeched.

"That nigga just shut you dowwwn," Rocky shrieked.

Randee and the fellas were in stitches rolling.

"See, Priscilla, I told you don't listen to my cousin. That nigga love that bitch."

Tavares was silent with the same devilish grin she had when she amped Prissy up to call.

"Fuck that nigga," yelled Kamari, feeling super bad for her friend who not only got her feelings hurt, but in front of her girls and a room full of strangers.

"That's why that fuck nigga going to jail," she evilly laughed.

Tavares gave a quick wink to Bella, giving her the cue to start recording on the prepaid phone they'd bought for the occasion.

"Oh no, who's going to jail?" Randee asked like she wanted in on the gossip.

"That bitch ass nigga and his mans. They shitted on the wrong bitches."

"Would you shut the fuck up?" Priscilla roared, not liking that Kamari was running her mouth as always. She was running it in front of strangers about something that was top-secret.

"Prissy, relax. That nigga and his boys got bagged after the club with some bricks in their car, so now them niggaz is going down."

"How the fuck that happen?" Nino said, knowing this was what they needed.

"No real nigga goes to the club with the work in the trunk," Molly G added.

"Wellll, maybe it fell in the trunk when they was there," Kamari said.

Her high caused her to let the cat out of the bag. That was all Tavares needed to hear.

Moments later, she yelled, "I'm just about over this shit! Party over!"

Those were the code words. In unison, she and her girls whipped out their guns.

"All you bitches, get the fuck up and get in the corner," Randee yelled.

With fright and terror in their eyes, in slow motion, the women did as they were told. Nino and his boy grabbed the rope and the tape from the closet and started tying the women up.

"Jade, baby, if you weren't a slimy bitch and the daughter of a fed who sets niggaz up, we could have had something real," laughed Nino.

"You lying ass, dick-sucking, cum-guzzling, pussy-licking ass whores disgust me," Tavares said with murder in her eyes and her gun pointed at them with her gloved hand ready to pull the trigger. "Y'all bitches just sat here and told them war stories about me and Bella, but bitches, it's us."

Everyone started laughing because the joke was on them. All four of the women's eyes and mouths hit the floor. They were scared, high as a kite, and their hearts were racing. Kamari started convulsing and foaming at the mouth. She died within seconds. Emotionless, Tavares looked at her and then at her friends, who were crying and sobbing.

"So y'all thought y'all was gonna get away with setting Abdora and his mans up? Stalker ass bitches went to the club trying to entice them with y'all skanky ass pussies long enough for Carmen Vega to plant bricks of cocaine in their cars, huh! Well, every last one of you is going to sign these affidavits that Carmen paid you to do it. The first bitch who doesn't sign is getting a bullet to the head."

Randee, Bella, and Rocky pulled the affidavits from their purses, and each approached one of the tied-up women. With taped hands, Priscilla and Jamie signed. Jamie got pistol-whipped by Bella.

"That's for fucking my man, you trick ass bitch."

Jade wouldn't sign. She was crying and shaking her head no. Tavares was becoming irritated.

"Listen, bitch. You and your snake ass mother tried to come for me all because Dora didn't want you. Then, your side bitch ass mother was mad when my father kicked her ass to the curb. That made your lying, devil-in-disguise mother try to ruin me and the people I love. So sign, and I let you live. Or, you don't sign, and I kill you."

Jade didn't think she was playing. She signed as she cried. With no remorse, Tavares turned and shot her two friends in the head. Jade was crying even more and literally shitted on herself seeing her friends' brains explode. Tavares gave Nino, Big Ez, Pooh, Molly G, and Killa K the head nod. They promptly removed the tape and rope from all the dead women. Next, Big Ez held Jade's small frame down with no hard work involved. Molly G and Killa K each took a needle from Bella and Rocky and injected her with Fentanyl.

In less than five minutes, she was on the moon. She was slumped, not looking like she was going to make it. Nino put the murder weapon in her hands, making sure her finger print was specifically on the trigger. After untying everyone, the group collected all the evidence except the murder weapon that was still in Jade's lap. If by chance the fire department made it in time to save the soon-to-be blazing house fire, it was still going to look like Jade had bugged out from a bad batch of drugs and murdered two of her friends while her third friend had overdosed. It all worked as Tavares had planned.

When they were all done, Tavares said, "I have to do one last thing. Everyone stand behind me and be quiet."

She pulled out Jade's phone and Face-Timed Carmen. With the camera facing in the direction of the bloodbath, Carmen was screaming. She was yelling, crying, and gasping.

"Jadeee!!" Carmen was hollering on deaf ears.

Jade was some place between death and a one-way flight to hell. Tavares enjoyed her cries, sobs, and hurt for a few moments before ending the call. Tavares laughed with zero remorse. Carmen was owed everything she was about to get. Tavares didn't know if Jade was going to die, nor did she give a fuck. Either she was going to overdose on the lethal amount of synthetic heroine, die in the fire they were going to start on the way out, or worst-case scenario, she was going to jail for double homicide. It was a win anyway it happened, as far as Tavares was concerned. She just knew Carmen was going to be in the same pain she'd caused her and her family with all her chaos and lies.

The assailants did a triple look-over for anything that could place them there. They'd cleaned up everything. With trash bags on their feet and gloves on their hands, they wiped down the one room any of them had sat in or touched anything. Thanks to her criminal justice degree, Tavares was convinced they were home-free when she shined a flashlight on the ground at an oblique angle. There were no marks, stains, or footprints anywhere. The only things left in the room were the dead bodies of the worthless whores and their blood. Tavares was pleased.

Before they walked out of the door, Tavares went in her bag and handed Nino a thick envelope that contained $40,000 dollars.

"Split that with these crazy ass fools."

"We can't take that," Nino said, eyeing the envelope.

"Bro, y'all put your life on the line for me, infiltrating that bitch, playing her man, and helping me pull this off."

"Nah, you been through hell and back. I just wanted to see you come out on top."

Jamal, AKA Molly G, spoke. "Tavares, you been our nigga since forever. You called, and we came through. Keep that shit. We want something else," he said with a grim smile.

"And, what would that be, asshole?" joked Tavares.

"We want them low numbers on the bricks since you're the inside plug on the work."

Tavares had to laugh because she was definitely that since they learned her father was the plug and her uncle brought the rawest cocaine in the country.

They sealed the deal with a hug. Then, Big Ez, Molly G, and Killa K dropped the gasoline on the back porch. Rocky dropped a match and down the block to their cars they went to hit the highway back to Boston.

CHAPTER 24

Carmen was at her house bugging. She didn't know what she'd just witnessed, but it wasn't good. She was crying and pacing, pacing and crying. With every call that she made to Jade and got no answer, she cried a little harder. Where was Jade? What was Jade into? Had she been so caught up into destroying Holton, Abdora, and Tavares that she missed all the warning signs that her daughter was getting high, so wild, and out of control? Carmen called Donnie and got no answer. She called her daughter's friends, and they weren't answering either. She couldn't figure out who had done this, but she was going to find out.

She got dressed and raced to Tavares and Abdora's estate. No one was there.

"Oh, my God! Where is my daughter?" she sobbed. "Please, God, please let my daughter be okay. I promise I'll change."

Carmen didn't know she'd run all out of favors from God. Like thieves in the night, the accomplices and Tavares were on the highway heading back to Boston. Everything had gone as planned. Now they just had to lie low in Tavares's house until Friday when they were actually supposed to be back from Atlanta. Tavares wasn't feeling an ounce of shame. She was feeling something more like triumph. Carmen Vega had gone above and beyond to hurt her and her family, and now she was going to feel the same kind of pain. Tavares wasn't sure when she would be coming, but she knew Carmen would be out for blood after seeing those videos. It didn't matter, though. She was prepared.

After smoking three blunts of sour, Bella, Randee, and Rocky were fast asleep. Tavares didn't mind, though. She used the time to reflect. The last few years had been a roller coaster ride. It was a ride that Tavares was glad was almost over. It had been a journey of love, loyalty, lust, betrayal, ups, downs, highs, lows, chaos, and drama. She had found strength to leave Damien, who broke her to what she thought was beyond repair. Then, she'd fallen in love with Dora, the man of her universe. She learned that love didn't hurt; it healed. She even became a mother and a college graduate, months apart. After that, she faced the reality that betrayal always comes from the people you least expect. As a result, she lost a friend that she loved so much and would have given her life for. However, Jazz was going to be the last person she paid back before she went down the aisle and stepped into the newest chapter of her life.

The ladies touched down in Dorchester at Randee's house at 5:30 a.m. Following all the procedures, they removed their disguises. They were lying low at Randee's house, so they made the best of it. The ladies rotated throwing down in the kitchen. Rocky played bartender by concocting drinks she found online. Bella rolled blunt after blunt, making sure there were blunts constantly rotating. Randee played DJ. Tavares just maxed and relaxed with her feet up. She didn't think that she'd ever eaten, smoked, drank, or laughed so much in the course of one day. While everyone was good and tore up, Randee did something she never engaged in: she got sentimental.

"Tavares, I'm sorry you missed your own bachelorette party. I hope we did a good job entertaining you, considering we're stuck here until tomorrow. I just want to tell you that I love, respect, and admire you. You're a hell of a woman. You've been through hell and back, and you're still standing. You're going to be the most beautiful bride."

Randee went on for a few moments and just when Tavares went to cry, she said, "Bitch, don't you fucking dare."

Everyone laughed because that was the Randee they knew.

"Tavares, can you believe it? In less than forty-eight hours, we'll be prepping for you to go down the aisle to become Mrs. Abdora Santacosa," Bella said, truly happy for her friend and brother from another mother.

"Girl, I'm ready. I just want to thank all of you ladies for putting up with me, helping me, and making sure that tomorrow is everything that I dreamed it would be."

"Shit, if we didn't, who the fuck else would?" Rocky's shit-talking self added to the conversation.

"Who else deserves it more than you?" asked Randee. "You've been through so much, and now you're getting your happy ending."

"No lie, that's what it feels like," Tavares said, blushing.

When the sun started to peek in, Tavares was up quietly sliding in clothes while everyone else was passed out. She had one last takedown before she could truly fall into wedding mode. She left her friends a note that read: *Ladies, I love y'all long time. We're bonded by loyalty and unbreakable by trust. I have one more thing to do. I need to do it alone. Meet y'all at my house at 2:00 p.m.* Then, she called a cab and headed home to Natick to get her car.

As she sat on her bed applying lotion to her body, Tavares watched the sun come up into her room. She listened to the birds chirping and silently prayed to God and asked for His forgiveness. She'd done what she had to do, but she still had to repent her sins.

"Father God, I own what I did. But, I hope you know and understand that I did what I had to do for my family. I hope that you will forgive me, as I'm not sorry for what I did, but I am sorry for breaking one of your commandments."

Tavares finished her prayer and threw on a black maxi dress, some flat sandals, and black Chanel shades. As she looked in the mirror, she realized that she really had no remorse. She was going to go on with her day and life and sleep just fine at night. The caterer would be there in a few hours to set up for the brunch for her wedding party: her mother, Doll, Me-Ma, Nana Dancy, and Dhara. So she needed to get a jump on things. Before she headed out, she placed a call.

"Hey, me baby," her grandmother answered the phone.

"Hey Glam-Ma. I was just calling to check on you and the boys."

"We fine. I'm just over here loving all over dem. They're actually still sleep. We had a fun week. Me and Pa-Pa take dem to de zoo, de aquarium, de park, and de beach. Dem just such happy babies. We love having dem here. I think the more dey come, the more you Pa-Pa hates to send them back. Are you ready for your big day tomorrow?"

"I am, Glams. Of course, I have a million things to do, but everything for the wedding is all set. Since you kept the boys while all the other women went away, I want to do something special for you when I get back from my honeymoon."

"You no have to do dat. I was more den happy to keep dem sweet precious babies. That was a gift in itself. So you go do what you need to do, and we'll see you tonight at the rehearsal dinner."

Hearing that her boys were safe and sound, Tavares made her way downstairs to her car and was off and running. She was jamming to K. Michelle, feeling like she was on top of the world. She pulled up to Beth Israel hospital, valeted her red Porsche truck, and was on her way. She was walking like she owned the world, smiling from ear to ear. She stopped at the gift shop to get balloons and then remembered she didn't need them. On the quick ride to the second floor, Tavares reminded herself that no matter what, she wasn't going to feel ashamed since the delivering mom had no shame for her actions.

As she walked into Room 233, the air didn't feel as vibrant as Tavares felt. Jazz was lying in bed. She wasn't glowing with pride, joy, or excitement. Instead, she was looking like death. She was so zoned out that she hadn't heard the door open or Tavares come in.

"Hey, Mama," Tavares sang. "You don't look like the new mother of a beautiful baby girl. What's going on?"

Instantly, Jazz started to cry. She wasn't just crying. She was sobbing and shaking. Tavares approached her and began to stroke her messy hair.

"What's the matter? Why are you crying when you just gave birth twenty-four hours ago?"

"Tavares, they took my baby girl. They took her!"

Jazz could barely muster through her raindrop-sized tears and bawling. With a convincingly authentic confused look, Tavares spoke in a faux-shocked tone.

"What're you talking about? Slow down, breathe, get yourself together, and tell me what the hell you're talking about."

Jazz wept hysterically for about three minutes. Tavares stood looking at her blankly with no emotions and no sympathy. She just patiently waited to hear what Jazz had to say.

"I asked the nurse to bring me my baby from the nursery. She gave me a very odd look. Then, she informed me that the adopting parents had already taken her. I told the nurse she must have been confused and that I hadn't put my daughter up for adoption. I didn't think anything of it. I just thought she made a simple mistake. I thought when she came back, she would have Aiko, but she didn't. She came back with someone from the hospital's legal team. The gentleman told me that he had the adoption papers. I argued him down that they had me mistaken. He showed me the paperwork and my signature was on it."

Jazz began to weep again.

"I never signed adoption papers. I would have never put Aiko up for adoption."

"Well, Jazz, you did put Aiko for adoption."

"Tavares, no I didn't. I wouldn't do that to Damien and my love child."

Tavares cracked up laughing.

"You really are delirious. Jazzlyn, Damien didn't love you."

Jazz looked like Tavares had just driven a knife straight through her heart.

"I hate to be the bearer of bad news, but I read every last text between you guys when I received his property from the hospital. He didn't want you, and he sure didn't want that baby. So, putting the baby up for adoption was the best thing that you could've done."

"I didn't put my baby up for adoption," Jazz squawked from the top of her lungs.

Tavares chuckled.

"Remember the trust fund papers that you signed? Well, you kind of shoulda read them. Didn't anyone ever tell you, don't put your John Hancock on anything without reading it?"

Jazz was lost.

"Honey baby, don't look so disoriented. You weren't signing trust fund papers. I mean, you were, but not really," Tavares laughed like the Joker. "You legally signed away all your parental rights and put Aiko up for adoption with a clause that says no matter what, you can't ever get your daughter back. You legally gave your daughter away. It was legalized in court and everything. Your trust lawyer was so great when you met with her, right?" winked Tavares. "You didn't even need to present in court. Once again, you signed papers without reading them when you gave her permission to represent you without you being present." Tavares shrugged her shoulders in a nonchalant manner that said, "Oh well."

"OH, MY GOD! Tavares, you took my baby!" Jazz shouted. "You stole my fucking baby from me. How could you be so evil, lowdown, and conniving?"

"Tisk, Tisk, Jazz," Tavares taunted. "Now, you sound like the pot calling the kettle black."

Jazz tried to get up but the C-section method that she'd given birth by had her unable to move. She cried, screamed, and made threats.

"You're a dirty bitch! A lowdown, stinking, dirty bitch. I swear on my baby I'm going to kill you."

"Jazzlyn, that's not very nice. I didn't kill you when you betrayed our friendship for a piece of hard dick and bubble gum."

Tavares was laughing uncontrollably.

"I'm getting my daughter back. I'm getting my and Damien's daughter back!" Jazz exclaimed. "Then, I'm pressing charges against you. You're going to rot in the pits of hell in a cell. Your kids are going to be motherless, and Dora is going to be a single father. You just mark my words."

Tavares laughed so hard that she literally felt herself about to pee on herself. Her laughter turned to rage.

"Bitch, you might wish. I'm going to watch my babies grow up, unlike you. I'm going to love on the man who actually loves me back, unlike you. And, I'm going to live a happy life, unlike you. I don't care what story you tell people. Say she died at birth for all I care, but you aren't going to say a word. Because if you do, I promise you on YOUR baby's life, you're going to die a slow, painful death."

Tavares pulled her gun out. Knowing it wasn't loaded, she put it to Jazz's head and pulled the trigger. The terror on Jazz's face was priceless.

"This was just rehearsal. If you even attempt to call the police, mention this to anyone, or try to get Aiko back, I'm going to shoot you in multiple non-life-threatening places and let you slowly bleed to death," Tavares smiled. "But, to even the score, this is what I'm going to do for you. Not only am I going to cover your medical expenses, but I'm also going to leave you with this. Your daughter is going to be very well taken care of because that money in the trust is really going to her. And, she's going to be loved beyond your wildest imagination. So if I were you, I would kill myself and meet Damien in hell so y'all can be together forever. If not, that's your choice. But, I'm dead to you and you're definitely dead to me."

Tavares was laughing and Jazz was choking on her tears. Tavares had no sympathy or shame over the lifetime of pain she'd just caused Jazz. With the biggest, brightest smile on her face, Tavares blew her ex-best friend a kiss. She told her to have a good life and was on her way. She made her way to Nia's Exquisite Basket Boutique to pick up the custom baskets for all the attendees of the brunch. She was blown away by the breathtaking baskets.

"Nia, you did the damn thing. I knew that they'd be beautiful based on how highly recommended you came from Chanae. However, you exceeded my expectations."

All fifteen pink and black baskets were filled to the max with a variety of things. They had MAC makeup, Victoria's Secret shower gels and lotions, top-of-the-line perfumes, candles, picture frames, a Pandora bracelet with charms that represented the different things Tavares told Nia about each woman, a robe, and matching slippers. "Bridesmaid," "Mom" and "Grandmother of the Bride," and "Mom" and "Grandmother of the Groom" were all monogramed on the robes and slippers.

"Thank you. I really tried. You paid me an arm and a leg, so I wanted to give you your money's worth."

"You definitely did that," Tavares said, in awe at the baskets that she paid five hundred dollars apiece for. "I'm sure everyone is going to be extremely pleased."

'Tomorrow, I'll be at the wedding venue to set up the favor baskets by 5:00 p.m. sharp."

"Nice, I know they'll be beautiful."

Tavares was just about finished with all her errands. She headed out of Office Max tickled pink at the contents of the envelopes she was carrying. Enclosed was the video of Kamari damn near confessing, the signed affidavits, and a few pages from Carmen's background check that showed her illegal shady ways. She made three copies to send to the prosecutor on Dora's case, the Attorney General, and Carmen's boss. Dora's case would be tossed out long before they went back to court. If not, she would send everything to the media and cause an FBI scandal. Tavares was feeling orgasmic thinking about the revenge she'd returned to Carmen and Jazz. As she was laughing out loud, Abdora called.

"Hello there, Mr. Hella Handsome."

"What's up, money? Why you ain't answering your phone? I been blowing you up."

"Oh, nothing. I just finished up my errands. Now, I'm heading home to get ready for brunch with all the ladies."

Tavares forgot that she still didn't have her phone, so she thought quick. "My phone is in my luggage, so I just grabbed the bat phone when I was running out."

"Oh, okay. I thought you was cheating on me."

"Nigga please," Tavares said as she laughed.

"I missed you," Abdora confessed in his sexy sleepy voice. "How was Atlanta?"

"It was quite eventful," Abdora's fiancée answered, playing the chain of events over in her mind.

"I know you had a hard time sleeping without my dick poking you in the butt."

Tavares bellowed in laughter for the statement that she didn't see coming.

"Boy, please. I slept just fine, thanks."

"Well, tonight after our rehearsal dinner, you owe me a few days' worth of sex. So don't pull no stunts talking about not until we're married."

"Just because you said that, now you won't get any of this sweet, wet loving until we're husband and wife."

"Knock it the fuck off, girl. I been tearing that pussy up and gave you two fly ass little boys, so we ain't gonna get brand new now."

Tavares had to laugh because she knew as well as Abdora that he would be getting the business when they got home that evening. The happy couple chatted about the details of his fun-filled Vegas bachelor party.

"I'm glad I did come out here. Your pops and Bryce did the damn thing."

"Excuse me? You mean your soon-to-be wife did the damn thing. I planned all of that. They just footed the bill."

"Get the fuck outta here," Abdora said, in shock.

"Yes, from the penthouse suite to renting the club out to the ten baddest strippers in Vegas at the actual bachelor party."

"You're the shit, babe."

"I know," laughed Tavares.

"Them bitches was baddd, too! I even let the black-Asian one, who looked like Kimora Lee, give me a lap dance."

"Ohhhh shit," Tavares said, taken aback by the words she'd just heard. "So after all that shit you talked, you let some nasty sweaty pussy dance on you, huh?"

"She wasn't nasty or sweaty. She smelt like roses, could squirt, and was so bad I almost decided to marry her tomorrow instead of you. Don't ask me how but she was squirting cherries out her pussy. I was in awe and told her if you can't get that trick down-pat, she's for sure taking your place."

Tavares laughed so hard she almost peed on herself.

"You know what... This conversation is over now. I just got home and got shit to do. I love your punk ass, and I'll see you in a few hours. Before the fellas go to the hotel, y'all come by the house. There will be plenty of food and drinks from brunch."

"Okay, lady. I love you too, and don't be jealous because my could-have-been wife can do magic tricks with her pussy that you can't."

Tavares didn't even respond. She simply hung up on her jerk of a soon-to-be husband. By 2:00 p.m. the ladies had arrived and the brunch was in full swing. They caterers had a carving station, a fondue station with different kinds of sweets to dip in the chocolate fountain, and a breakfast bar where they were making omelets, eggs, pancakes, and waffles to order. Tavares couldn't have been more pleased with the food and how beautiful her backyard had been transformed with a tall black party tent that occupied the whole space. Chanae and Chelsee had come and decked everything out in pink and black décor.

Tavares and her brunch guests were having a great time. Laughter, smiles, and great vibes were flowing through the air. She was watching the women dance, eat, and drink and couldn't help but thank God that she'd made it to see this day. As she looked around, she could hear a noise.

"Someone turn that music down. Do y'all hear that?"

"It sounded like the door," someone said.

"OMG, who's banging like that?" Dolonda asked.

"Mommy, who knows. Y'all keep partying. I'll be right back." When Tavares got up, she whispered in Randee's ear, "If I'm gone more than five minutes, bust the love move."

Randee knew that meant to leave Carmen her parting gift in the trunk. The overpowering bang at Tavares's front door made her smile.

"Hello?" the soon-to-be bride answered.

The guest on the other side of the door didn't answer. Instead, they continued to loudly rap on the door. Opening the door with a huge smile plastered on her face, Tavares found the person she'd been expecting. Carmen Vega pushed past her and invited herself in.

"Geesh, come in, why don't you?"

"I don't have time for your fucking shit. Where the fuck is my daughter?"

Not speaking above a whisper, with a straight face Tavares answered, "Your daughter? You have a daughter? Where is your daughter? Did you lose her some place?"

"Don't play with me, you little bitch. I got the video, and I want to know where the fuck my daughter is."

"You seem very upset. If you can't find your daughter, maybe you should call your co-workers," Tavares taunted as she spoke calmly in a condescending tone.

"Do you think I'm fucking playing with you? Do you?!" yelled Carmen, trying to hold it together but really on the verge of tears.

"Listen, I don't know where your daughter is, nor do I give a fuck. Go find that cunt, coke-sniffing, pussy-licking ass gold-digger," Tavares responded now with sarcasm and disrespect in her voice.

"Do you know who you're fucking with? Do you?" an enraged Carmen yelled. "You must not know who Jade's father is. You can't possibly know who he is to be playing this dangerous game. He'll bury you alive if we don't get Jade back without a hair on her head touched."

Tavares had to laugh.

"I don't know who Jade's father is, but I know who he isn't. He ain't Donnie Ortega."

"I beg your fucking pardon. So you know Donnie's her father and still want to play with your life? You're a bold little bitch."

"Nah. Actually I'm a smart little bitch because Donnie isn't Jade's father."

Carmen's face said she didn't know if Tavares was bluffing or pulling her card.

"You're wondering how I know that, right?" Tavares was glowing.

"Well, your daughter has mommy issues. She told her pretend boyfriend all about you never having time for her. You're always busy with work or fucking a married man. Then, she said that she loved her father but they didn't have a connection. And, you're such a snake that I said maybe they don't have a connection for a reason. So, after her fake boyfriend fucked her, we got a hair sample. And, lo and behold, Donnie is not the father," Tavares said in her best Maury voice.

She was holding her stomach, she was laughing so hard.

"You don't know what the fuck you're talking about, you little bitch."

"Maybe you'll believe Donnie once he gets the DNA test and comes to kill you."

Carmen pulled her gun out and put it straight to Tavares's forehead.

"If you don't tell me where my daughter is in two minutes, I'm going to kill you. You'll be going in the grave. Fuck getting married. I've been looking high and low for my daughter since I got that video. This is the last place I'm coming to find out her whereabouts."

Carmen looked at her Rolex.

"You have one minute."

Tavares didn't flinch, move, or look worried.

"Carmen, Carmen, Carmen... instead of being here, you should be trying to find your coke whore daughter. Lord knows how you would feel for the rest of your life not knowing where she is or if she's alive."

Carmen pulled the trigger.

"What the fuck?" she screeched when Tavares's head didn't come off her shoulders.

"Oh, the bullets... yeah, about those. That fine married motherfucker you've been fucking, he kinda works for me," laughed Tavares. "Funny how you thought he was into you, right? Nah, he was getting paid to do that, sweet pea. After he fucked you the other night and you went to the bathroom to shower, he took your bullets. I kinda figured you would show up here. Too bad you trusted the wrong person and weren't smart enough to check your gun coming all the way here. Oh, and he got me all the notes you've been keeping. You've been obsessed with me and Dora for a while."

Tavares was laughing so hard she was crying.

"You think this is funny?"

Tavares got serious. Real serious.

"I do, Carmen. I don't know who's more gullible—you or Jade. All it took was two men to give y'all some hard dick and attention, and y'all fell right into my trap. Guess the apple doesn't fall too far from the tree. Side bitches run in your family."

Carmen had no other choice. She was going to have to use her trump card. What other choice did she have to find her daughter, who was either dead or someplace fighting for her life?

"You have to tell me where Jade is."

"Hold that thought, Carmen."

Tavares sent a text to Bella, *Bring everyone in the house.* Looking totally unbothered, she asked, "Now what were you saying?"

"You have to tell me where Jade is. She's your family. She could be hurt or dead. You can't do this, she's your cousin."

Tavares gave Carmen a bitch-please look before she spoke.

"Auntie Carmen... I can call you Auntie, right?" Tavares mocked. "You ain't no family of mine, and that cokehead bitch of a daughter ain't no family of mine either. Blood makes you related, not family. You don't give a fuck about family, so why should I? So miss me with that shit."

When everyone walked in from outside, Tavares went full throttle.

"If you gave a fuck about family, you wouldn't have stolen your sister's land, faked her death to her mother, fucked her cousin, pinned a baby on him, left her daughter in foster care, and then found her baby daddy to try to have a whole relationship with him, now would you, Auntie Carmen?"

Everyone was looking at Carmen while she was looking at Tavares like *how did she figure all this out?* Dolonda went charging toward her sister. It took Bella, Rocky, Mona-Lisa, and Dhara to hold her back, but not before she hawked a loogie on Carmen.

"You're a conniving, piece of shit bitch. You're my sister, and you looked my mother in the face and told her I'm dead. There's a special place in hell for you. I hope you die a slow, painful, miserable death, you deceitful, spawn of the devil cunt bitch!"

Carmen was speechless. She'd wished and prayed that this wouldn't happen when she found out the person who stole her daughter's man was the niece she left in foster care.

"You side bitch baby. I gave you my land, and in exchange, you said you would find Holton because my mother was dead. You also said that you'd get my daughter from foster care in the meantime and raise her. All these years, my daughter was fucked up, lost in the world, and thought I left her. Bitch, not even at my worst would I have just abandoned her to fend for herself."

Carmen tried to say something, but she couldn't. She burst into tears. Her tears became sobs. Her sobs became wailing. No one had any sympathy for her.

"I'm sorry. I'm so sorry, Dolonda. I know I was wrong. I was young, dumb, and jealous. But, pleassse, please tell Tavares to tell me where Jade is. She's in trouble, please."

"I ain't telling my daughter shit. Find that little bitch on your own."

Just having buried a child not too long ago, Doll felt for Carmen. Carmen was a piece of shit and deserved to deteriorate in hell, but Doll's heart still hurt for her as a mother. She looked at Tavares.

"Baby Girl, let God deal with her. You're a mother. Just tell her where she can find her daughter."

Straight-laced with no chaser, Tavares looked at Doll with icy eyes.

"I ain't telling that devious ass evil bitch shit. I don't give a fuck if she ever finds her daughter. When she finds her, I hope she's a corpse."

Carmen's phone rang, startling her.

"Hello," she sobbed, paying all the cold eyes plastered on her no attention.

"Carmen, it's Greg. I have some not so good news."

"Please, Greg, please tell me you found Jade." Silence.

"Carmen, there's no easy way for me to say this."

"Greg, I don't care what state she's in or what trouble I have to help her out of. Please just tell me you found her."

"We found her."

"Thank you, Jesus."

Tavares felt her heart drop.

"Where is she?"

"Carmen, Jade is gone. We found her body in a fire the other night. It wasn't until we ran the prints this morning that we found out it was Jade." Carmen screamed.

"NOOO! Oh, my God, Nooooo."

Tavares smiled while everyone else just stared at the hysterical woman.

"What happened?"

Carmen's heart was racing and her tears wouldn't stop.

"The coroner says it was an overdose. She died before the fire burnt her."

Carmen fell to the floor screaming and crying, "My baby. Oh, my God, my baby is gone."

Nina finally spoke after being paralyzed since stepping in the room and laying eyes on Carmen.

"Carmen, come," she said. "You poor baby. Just come. No one deserves to lose a child," Nina said as she extended her arms for a hug.

"Nannie Nina, don't hug that bitch," Tavares screamed.

Foolishly believing that fast that Nina pushed a decade of heartache aside, Carmen got up and walked to her. The moment she got close enough, Nina wrapped her hands around Carmen's throat and proceeded to choke what little life out of her that was left.

"Ohhh shit! Nannie Nina is gangsta!" screamed Tavares, not expecting what had just happened.

"Mami, let her go! Let her go, Mami!" Dolonda screamed.

The color was draining from Carmen's face. Her oxygen was slowing down. Nina wouldn't let go no matter how hard Dolonda tried to pry her hands free. Her anger, hurt, and agony had given her the strength of a bull.

"Bitch, I hope you feel the pain I've felt every day for the last ten years."

Doll and Dhara saved Carmen's life by helping Dolonda pull her free. Hitting the floor, Carmen was choking from her loss of breath and tears. No one moved to help her. They say you don't kick a person while they're down, so Tavares didn't. Instead, she grabbed her purse. Pulling out her pretty hot pink Glock that she was licensed to carry, she put it to Carmen's temple.

"The difference between you and me is that I have bullets. You played Russian roulette with my life, and you ruined my mother and my Nina's lives. You deserve for me to shoot you right here. But, since you like to plan fake funerals, I want to take joy in knowing you're planning a real one. I want to smile knowing you're in the same pain you caused my grandmother and mother by telling them each other was dead. You have two minutes to get the fuck up and out of my house.'"

With a limp body, Carmen crawled to the door and to her car. She felt like she was living in a bad nightmare.

"How did this happen, God? My baby girl is gone. She's all that I had. Why would you take the only person in the world that I love? Why?" Carmen cried as she started up her rental car.

The pained woman never thought her sister would get clean, that her niece would find out about Holton, or that any of the acid connections would come back to her. With a heavy heart and uncontrollable tears, Carmen had just learned karma had no expiration date. She was a crying mess, driving on the Mass Pike until she saw two state police behind her with lights on.

As she pulled over, she tried to pull herself together. She rolled her window down with her badge in hand.

"Hi, I'm agent Carmen Vega. How can I help you, officer?"

"Well, Agent Vega, you were swerving," the State Trooper said, omitting that they'd received an anonymous tip of drugs being trafficked in the vehicle.

Trying to wipe her bloodshot red eyes, Carmen stated, "I just found out my daughter died in a fire."

"My condolences, ma'am. I'm really sorry for your loss, but I'm going to need you to step out of the vehicle."

Shocked, Carmen yelled, "For what? I've done nothing wrong."

"Ma'am, you have drugs visible. So I'm going to need to search this car."

"DRUGS!? This is a rental car. I just flew in town, and I'm heading back to Logan Airport. I don't have any drugs."

Flashing his light in the back, the officer asked, "What is that?"

Turning around, Carmen got the shock of her life. There was a perfectly positioned brick of cocaine on the floor of the passenger seat.

"Officer, I have no idea where that came from. I'm a federal government employee. I'm being set up."

"Ma'am, that's for a court to determine. Right now, I'm just doing my job. "

While Carmen continued to rant about her job that she would soon be fired from and how much she didn't appreciate the treatment from one of her own, the officer gave her a bitch-please look.

"Ma'am, please just step out of the vehicle."

"That little bitch!" Carmen screamed as she punched the steering wheel.

When she got out of the car, she stood to the side with the trooper from the second car. When he popped the trunk, the trooper had to look from the trunk to the agent and then from the agent back to the trunk.

"Agent Vega, please step over here for a moment."

Pointing to the contents in the trunk, State Trooper Ray Green looked at Carmen, disgusted.

"You took an oath. I detest nothing more than dirty cops. In the commonwealth, we take trafficking drugs very seriously."

Carmen almost shit her pants looking at the ten bricks of cocaine and maybe five thousand ecstasy pills. She began yelling and screaming belligerently.

"Those aren't my drugs. I'm being set up. I'm being set up by a Dominican drug cartel. I have to get back to Jersey."

Everything Carmen had done was coming back ten-fold. She was cuffed and off to jail to stew in her karma.

***

After Carmen was gone from the house, Tavares looked around the room at the women.

"What happened here doesn't change the vibe. We're here to celebrate what's going to be one of the best days of my life. Don't look so sad. Y'all are killing me," Tavares laughed. "That miserable bitch got what she deserved. I'm sorry that I'm not sorry. I want everyone to go back outside and finish eating, drinking, and partying. Dora, Papi, Uncle Donnie, and all Dora's groomsmen will be here shortly. I need y'all to fix them sad faces because I don't want Dora asking me a million questions. I want us to enjoy our evening, and I'll talk to him tonight."

With a hurt heart and soul, but grateful to learn the truth, Nina asked her strong granddaughter, "Tavares, are you sincerely okay?"

"Gangsta Nana, I'm just fine. I went from no family to a whole damn family, two babies, friends that are like family, and a man that loves me to the

428 | Acid Connections 3

end of the earth. This is the start of a new chapter, not just for me, but for all of us. So, yes, I'm fine. Carmen is the one whose gonna need you to ask her if she's fine when she gets everything I owed her."

Everyone was looking at Tavares trying to figure out how she did it. She always smiled, even though the hardest times and situations. They didn't get that Tavares had mastered weathering hard times and making the best out of life since she'd lost her mother as a child. All of the ladies were heading back outside when the phone call Tavares had anxiously been waiting on came through.

"What's up, Unc?"

"That slimy bitch is heading to jail. She won't be ruining your wedding or anyone else's life. The drug charges are gonna stick."

Tavares smiled from ear to ear.

"Thanks, Unc. I appreciate you."

"No thanks needed, sweetheart. Family sticks together. At least you Montiagos do," laughed Vanny-Bell's husband.

Hanging up, Tavares cried happy tears. When everyone was partied out and gone, Tavares sat Dora down.

"We need to talk, my soon-to-be husband."

"Damn Boo, why you looking so serious?"

"I just need to talk, and I need you to listen without saying a word."

"Alright, I'm all ears," Dora said, leaning in and kissing the woman he was ready to make his wife. Tavares started from the beginning, not skipping one single detail, and told Dora everything she'd done while he was gone. When Tavares was done speaking, Dora didn't say a word. His face was flushed, and for the first time in his life, he was speechless.

"Dora, please say something."

"I love you, Tavares. I knew the first time I saw you that you'd be my wife. God created you for me. I'm ready to make this next chapter of our life the best chapter or our lives. We're going to spend the rest of our lives together, with NO ACID CONNECTIONS, and show people that black love exists. I mean, you're a mix-breed mutt, but you're still my baby," laughed Dora. "Now let's get to this hotel to get some rest and get ready for your dream wedding."

CHAPTER 25

As Tavares and Dora lay in bed together, Tavares said, "You know we're breaking the rules. You aren't supposed to see the bride on the day of the wedding. You're bringing us bad luck already," she joked, looking up at Dora as she was tightly nested in her safe place, wrapped in his arms.

"Boo, listen. We aren't people that play by the rules. We make our own rules. It's just who we are and what we do."

"Clearly," Tavares rolled her eyes. "Can you believe that at the end of the day, I'll be Mrs. Tavares Santacosa?"

"Yep, and I'm ready to be a house husband," Abdora joked.

"Oh fuck you. You got the roles reversed."

"I done got me an educated, rich bitch. I'm getting out the game. I'm gonna put my feet up, relax, and help you jump off all these companies. Your club is gonna be dope. FYI, Mrs. Santacosa, I'm not cutting you no slack as my competition just because you're my wife."

"Please don't, because I'm about to put you out of business."

They laughed together.

"Seriously, Dora, I want you to do whatever it is you want to do. Open ten legit companies, do nothing, enjoy life with the boys, or whatever your heart desires. You've had us from the door, so now we're gonna build an even bigger empire together."

Dora loved this woman. He responded with a passionate kiss that awakened his lower head. After another hour of rolling in the sheets, together they showered and were off to prepare for their day.

By 4:00 p.m., Tavares was almost ready for her 7:00 p.m. wedding. She'd received a manicure, a pedicure, and her hair was slayed thanks to Bree. She and the wedding party were just waiting for the makeup artists to finish up the mothers and grandmothers and make it to them. Everyone was sipping champagne, talking shit, smiling, snapping pictures, and enjoying the prep for their friend's well-deserved day.

"Pass me my phone," Randee said to Tavares, who was glowing.

"Bitch, today is my day. Make this the first and last thing any of you heffas ask me to do."

Randee looked down at her phone and screamed so loud everyone jumped. She began to tremble. Mona-Lisa rushed over.

"What's the matter?"

Randee was frozen and just passed her phone.

Mona-Lisa read out loud what had just wiped all the color out of Randee's face.

"Randee, Mona-Lisa, and Leslie, I just want to say goodbye. I love you ladies forever. My family has disowned me for having a baby out of wedlock. I've lost the only man I ever loved, and my baby is gone, too. I have nothing else to live for. Tell Tavares I said, thank you. I'll meet y'all on the other side."

Jazz had prepared her group suicide text before popping thirty oxycodone pills. As she started to fade, she hit send. Moments later, she was heading to the afterlife.

With gasps from the Jersey bridesmaids, Randee, Leslie, and Mona-Lisa were shaking. Randee tried to call Jazz almost twenty times before she realized that she'd really committed suicide. Mona-Lisa looked at Tavares, who didn't look moved.

"What the fuck, Tavares? Aren't you going to say anything? And, what does she mean tell Tavares thank you?" Leslie asked, knowing Tavares knew what it meant.

Tavares responded, "If y'all are going to cry, can you please finish before the makeup artists get here? I don't want y'all's makeup running. It will have y'all looking like raccoons."

Each of their jaws dropped.

"Are you that fucking cold?" Mona-Lisa screamed.

Tavares was ever so calm. Nonchalantly, she said, "What do you want me to say? I don't give a fuck if that bitch killed herself. She wasn't my friend."

"She was your friend," sobbed Leslie.

Tavares took a deep breath.

"No, I was *her* friend. When her hypocrite pastor daddy was molesting her, I helped her through it by going to every therapy session with her. When Winston was busting her ass, I sent Damien to check that bitch ass nigga. When she had no place to go because her man was a bitch and her daddy was a pedophile, I took my money and paid first, last, and security for her apartment. I furnished that bitch and everything because I THOUGHT she was my friend. What did she do? Help herself to my old nigga. Then, she thought a fuck meant they were in love. She got pregnant and said she was having his love child. So I DON'T GIVE A FUCK that she killed herself. So y'all want to cry and be brokenhearted for your friend, be my guest. But, yeah, I'll pass. Today is all about me. I'm getting my happily ever after."

Tavares's anger and rage stopped everyone in the room from expressing how foul they thought she was. They knew Jazz had broken her heart, not by fucking Damien but by betraying the genuine love Tavares had for her. However, they still thought Tavares could have shown a little more sympathy. As they left to console each other, Mona-Lisa, Leslie, and Randee went back to Leslie's hotel room. They had to cry it out before they could put on a face of makeup and smile for Tavares. With her three best friends gone, Tavares told Rocky to roll a blunt. She thanked God for the surprise wedding present and was ready to go down the aisle.

At 8:00 p.m., the sun had set, and two hundred candles were lit. The wedding began under an elegant, fully draped white tent. The aisles were stylishly draped with white and black fabric. Massive chandeliers were suspended between the draping. Four-foot-tall square cylinders stood at the ends of every other aisle, each filled to the top with black roses and one white candle on top. Perfectly recreating John Legend's video, there was an organist at a white piano with black rose petals scattered on it. Next to him was a violinist; together they were playing "All of Me."

The parents and grandparents of the bride and groom began to walk down the aisle of the waterfront venue. Mona-Lisa and Mid, Bryce and Randee, Hawk and Leslie, Mason and Bella, Rocky and Nas, and Rollo and Cali were intertwined. The groomsmen were adorned in perfectly tailored Ralph Lauren black suits, not tuxedos. They were tieless to give them a modern, fly guy look. The women were beautiful in three differently styled snug floor-length black dresses. Their faces were beat to the gods, and they were blinging in their simple yet elegant faux diamond accessories. Dora stood looking like new money in the same suit, only in white.

Just as it was time for Tavares to come down the aisle, Holton leaned in and kissed her on the cheek.

"You're the most beautiful girl in the world. You're everything and more that I could ever want in a daughter. Abdora is a great man, and I know, because I raised him after Dorian passed. You're going to live a rich, full life of joy, happiness, and prosperity. Enjoy it, because you're long overdue for it."

Fighting back her tears, she said, "Thank you, Papi." The processional music started, and Tavares and Holton set on their way to Jennifer Hudson's "Giving Myself."

Everyone stood and cupped their mouths in awe at Tavares's beauty. Her makeup was natural, but it made her blue eyes pop underneath the lace birdcage veil. The slim-cut gown with a flaunting sweetheart neckline was exquisitely embellished with beading and had a sheer illusion. The curvy mermaid silhouette of the dress wowed the guests as Tavares walked with grace. As the lyrics played, there wasn't a dry eye in the room by the time Tavares got halfway to her soon-to-be husband.

Even Dora had to wipe the tears that were beginning to fall as he looked at the woman who was ready to give herself to him fully. She was his rib—the woman that God knew he needed and created solely for him. She wasn't just his lady, but his best friend and his partner in crime. On his darkest days, she was his guiding light. When the world went left, she went right. Never did he have to question her love and loyalty. Now, he was going to repay her for the rest of his life by loving her to the best of his ability.

Seeing Dora cry made Tavares begin to tear up. Looking at him and listening to the song she'd chosen for her processional reminded her that this man had come into her life and changed her world. He showed her love didn't hurt and that you loved with your actions, not your words. She felt like she was flying, high off life, and she didn't want to come down. Tavares had found freedom, joy, and happiness with Abdora. His love brought her completion. Now, hand in hand at the altar, she and Dora were ready to say "I do" and start the next chapter of their lives with no more **ACID CONNECTIONS**.

47618945R00242

Made in the USA
Middletown, DE
30 August 2017